Antonio and Alessia

TARA CONRAD

HIS ONE HER ONLY PUBLISHING

Dear Reader

Content Warning

This story dives into some intense and emotional themes that might be triggering for some. To see a full list of potential triggers, just scan the QR code—it's quick and easy.

Remember, your mental health always comes first, so please take care of yourself while reading.

Check Content Warnings Here

*For those who know that even the darkest nights hold stars, and that
hope is never truly lost.
This book is for you.*

Contents

Prologue

ANTONIO

The flickering glow of candlelight casts dancing shadows upon the walls of the underground room beneath my restaurant. I stand inside what looks like a crude dungeon, a stone alcove, off our main room, my face illuminated by the wavering gas-powered flames.

"It's said that blood is thicker than water," I begin, my voice echoing through the room. "But loyalty is a currency more valuable than gold. And yet, for all the years I've dedicated to this family, all the sacrifices made in the name of honor and duty, I've been repaid with betrayal and humiliation."

I pause, my hand tracing the rough edges of what appears to be ancient stones, my mind consumed by memories of past slights and injustices.

Above me, the Procession of the Saints, with all its pomp and circumstance, is about to start. My restaurant is filling with people unaware of what's about to occur beneath them.

"Valentino Comiso, my own flesh and blood," I continue, my voice tinged with bitterness. "He may wear the mantle of leadership, but his heart is black as coal. He's squandered the trust of our family. Tarnished the honor of our name, and for what? Power? Prestige? It no longer matters. His sins cry out for retribution, and I am the instrument of justice."

With each word, my resolve hardens, my gaze unyielding as I stare into the darkness ahead.

"And so, I intend to see Valentino pay for his crimes. No stone will go unturned, and no deed will be left unpunished. The time for reckoning has come, and I will be the architect of his downfall."

And with that solemn oath, I set in motion a chain of events that will forever alter the course of my family's legacy, plunging us into a darkness from which there will be no return.

Antonio

T he afternoon sun filters weakly through the curtains, casting a warm glow on the table where I'm having lunch with my mother. She's finished her lunch, but I'm still pushing mine around on my plate, my appetite lacking from my earlier conversation with Alessia.

I came here to talk to my father about a shipment we're expecting this week, one that needs to be funneled through *Casa delle Ombre*, the restaurant my father runs to launder money for *La Famiglia*. With everything moving so fast, and this being our most important front, we need to make sure the paperwork is airtight.

But my father left early with Cecilia. He's letting her get more involved with the business than I think she should be.

I glance at my mother, trying to keep my frustration in check. "I don't get why he's doing this. Why let her in?"

She sets her cup down carefully, eyes calm. "Your sister's smart, Anton. She wants to prove she can handle the hotel."

"She shouldn't be handling any of it," I snap, my voice sharper than intended. "This world isn't for her."

"Cecilia's not a little girl anymore," my mother replies evenly.

"She's nearly finished with her degree, and more importantly, your father trusts her."

I sigh, leaning back in my chair. "He's letting her get too close. I don't think she understands what she's getting into."

"She's stronger than you give her credit for," my mother says quietly, though I can sense her patience thinning. "You can't protect her forever."

"I can't believe you're okay with this." I shake my head and push my plate away. "Cecilia shouldn't be involved at all."

A pause lingers between us before she speaks again. "Your father wants to give her a chance, Antonio. She's capable. You have to let her grow."

I don't want to argue with her, so I say nothing. Cecilia's strong, sure, but this isn't about strength. It's about the danger, the target she's putting on her back when she doesn't need to.

The doorbell rings, breaking the tension. "I'll get it," Mom says as she stands, leaving me alone with my thoughts.

As though my patience wasn't already wearing thin. Earlier this morning, Valentino saw me talking to Alessia. It was a brief encounter, nothing more than a few tense words, but I knew it would rub him the wrong way. And here he is. As soon as I hear the front door creak open, his voice oozing false charm as he greets my mother, I know my cousin's not here for a friendly visit.

"Valentino, it's so nice to see you," Mom greets him, her voice warm as always.

"It's good to see you, too, Aunt Nicki," Vigo replies smoothly. "Is Antonio still around?"

"He's in the kitchen having a late lunch," she answers.

"Thank you," he says, his tone light but insincere. The second I hear his voice, my appetite disappears and I throw the rest of my lunch in the trash.

Unlike Vigo, I respect my mother and refuse to have this conversation with her in the other room. I push open the French doors to the backyard, stepping out just as I hear him enter the kitchen. The door clicks shut behind me, and I can feel him there, right at my back.

"How are you this afternoon, cousin?" Valentino asks, his voice laced with thinly veiled contempt.

"I'm fine," I say as I turn slowly, keeping my expression neutral. "What brings you here? I thought you'd be busy with your company."

"Alessia is the reason for my visit," he snaps, crossing his arms and staring me down. "I saw you talking to her this morning."

I meet his gaze, refusing to rise to the bait. "I dropped you off and decided to visit my parents. I can't control who walks down the street. We exchanged a few polite words. It was nothing more than that."

But I knew it wasn't just *nothing*. It was Alessia. And it was the first time I'd spoken to her in years. The moment our eyes met, it hit me harder than I expected. I tried to keep my walls up, tried to stay detached, but seeing her again stirred up everything I'd worked to bury. I told myself it was just small talk, meaningless, but deep down, I knew it wasn't that simple.

He takes a step closer, his eyes narrowing to slits. "You'd do well to remember Alessia's my fiancé now."

Alessia is only twenty-two. Their marriage wasn't supposed to happen until she was twenty-five, but it's no surprise her father agreed to move it up. To Draco Moretti, this union is nothing more than a business transaction. The sooner the two families are tied, the more secure he thinks his position will be.

The thought twists a knot of bitterness in my chest. Alessia deserves more than to be used as a pawn in her father's game, more than to be tied to a man like Valentino. The idea of her with him, trapped in a marriage for power and convenience, makes my stomach turn. But I can't let my true feelings show.

"It sounds as though congratulations are in order," I say, a smile curling on my lips.

"Yes, they are," Vigo replies, his tone dripping with self-satisfaction.

I nod, maintaining my neutral mask. "I do understand your concern. Alessia's a special woman," I say, forcing a placating smile. "But you have nothing to worry about. I respect your engagement, and I'll be sure our men do as well." I drop my voice, lowering my tone.

Valentino's always been paranoid, constantly looking for betrayal even when there's none to be found. He studies my face for any sign of deceit. "Good," he says coldly. "Because if I catch any one near her again, you included, they won't live long enough to regret it."

His arrogance is insufferable, always acting like he's above everyone, untouchable. The idea that he would threaten me over a few unimportant words makes my blood boil. Swallowing my anger, I manage, "Of course, cousin. I wouldn't dream of over-stepping."

"And let's be honest, Anton," he says, his sneer deepening, his arrogance seeping through. "You gave it your best shot, but I outsmarted you and secured a future with her. Alessia needs more than you could ever give her. She needs a real man—a leader."

The sting of his words ignites a dark fire inside me, but I don't let it show. "You're absolutely right, Vigo. I tried and failed," I say, my voice calm, though the thought of Alessia being trapped with him twists something deep in my gut.

I take a step closer, clasping a hand on his shoulder. "You, though," I add, my tone low and controlled, "are exactly the kind of man any woman would be lucky to marry."

Lucky? I scoff, holding back a bitter laugh. Alessia's anything but lucky being forced to marry this arrogant bastard.

"Exactly," he agrees.

"You were born to lead," I add the compliment bolstering his already oversized ego. "Alessia doesn't know how lucky she is."

"No, she fucking doesn't," he snaps, and I realize I hit a nerve. "She dared to leave my house without permission, using her father as her excuse." Valentino's rage spills out as he begins pacing across the patio. "Then, she refused to start planning our wedding."

"When's the big day?" I ask casually.

"Two weeks," he says, stopping briefly before resuming his relentless pacing.

The timing blindsides me, but I quickly steady myself.

"Our wedding will be a statement to the other *Famiglias,* showing them who truly holds the wealth and power."

"A wedding fitting for our future Capo and his wife," I reply.

"Yes," he agrees, puffing out his chest.

"How do you plan on making her cooperate?"

Valentino laughs, a harsh, grating sound. "Alessia will learn her place. She'll realize her resistance is futile and that her only option is to submit to my demands," he says, his eyes gleaming with something sinister.

I force a smile, masking the disgust churning in my gut. "And if she doesn't?"

"Then I'll have the pleasure of teaching her." He shrugs, his casual indifference chilling. "There are many ways to break a person's spirit."

I can only imagine the brutal things he has planned for her. He'll start with something subtle, like isolating her to break her spirit. When that doesn't work, it'll turn physical. He'll pull out his whip or his knife, anything to scar her body, all while masking his abuse as discipline. Valentino will savor every scream and tear as he shatters her will, leaving her too broken to fight back.

The thought of Alessia being forced to endure his twisted methods sickens me. But I can't let my emotions betray me. "Yes, you could go that route," I say thoughtfully, lowering myself onto the outdoor sofa. "Or you might want to try something different." I dangle the thought in front of him, hoping it's enough to shift his focus and that I can spare Alessia some pain.

Valentino stops pacing and turns to face me. "Incentives?" he repeats, clearly confused.

I gesture to the chair across from me. "Come sit," I say calmly.

Once he's settled, I continue, "To make someone like Alessia comply, it's not just about lessons and discipline. You need to balance it with kindness and affection."

"Why would I do that?" he asks, still puzzled.

"To confuse her," I reply, my voice steady. "You need to make her question her defiance by showing her what a good life she'll have *if* she does things your way. Make it seem like it's her choice to be compliant."

A slow grin spreads across his face. "All I have to do is promise her the moon and the stars."

"You've got it," I agree, continuing to bolster his ego. "She'll be the perfect *donna*, and she'll reinforce your image as our future leader."

"And it'll prove to my father that I'm ready to take my rightful place," he says, his eyes widening in excitement.

"Exactly," I say, sitting back and crossing one leg over another, hoping I did enough to spare Alessia some pain.

Vigo stands abruptly. "I hope you don't mind if I rush out. I've got some things I need to take care of," he says, already moving toward the door. "I know I can always count on you to be there for me."

I rise to my feet, offering him a slight nod. "I'll always have your back." The words rolling off my tongue effortlessly.

As he hurries away, I call after him. "Enjoy the rest of your day, cousin."

Valentino's putty in my hands. He's so easy to manipulate. A smile, a subtle suggestion, and he's convinced it's his idea—that he's the one calling the shots. He trusts me completely, oblivious to the fact that it's his biggest mistake.

Alessia

My head's still spinning from the shock of the engagement and from Val's even crazier announcement that the wedding is only two weeks away. It's no secret I was *promessa* to Valentino, but I was supposed to have a few more years. The agreement was clear—the wedding wouldn't take place before my twenty-fifth birthday, which is three years away.

Yesterday, after leaving the Comiso's house, I went straight to my father, demanding to know why the plan had changed. I begged him to make Valentino wait. I shouldn't have done it. I know better than to provoke his temper. My father not only refused, he grabbed my arm so tightly it left bruises. Then he hit me.

The sting of the slap, the ache of the bruises, still lingers. It's a reminder of how little control I have over my own life. There's no escaping it. My time's up. In two weeks, I'll be married to a man I despise.

I'm trying to put it aside for right now. I'm due at the wedding planner's office for a little over an hour, which should give me enough time to swing by Starlight Studios to drop off a new batch of photographs. They're selling faster than I can take them.

"I think these are your best yet," Ophelia says, pointing to a picture of the sunset from the Race St. Pier, her eyes lighting up with admiration.

"Thank you," I reply with a modest smile. "I just happened to be in the right place at the right time."

"It's more than that, Allie," she insists as she continues looking through the digital images. "Each one tells a story, captures a moment in time."

"That's what I love about photography," I say, my voice softening. "I'm able to freeze moments in time, capturing their beauty forever."

As I reach for another photograph, I catch Ophelia's gaze shifting to my hand. Instinctively, I curl my fingers, trying to hide the glint of my ring.

"Did you get engaged?" she asks, a hint of surprise in her voice.

A warm flush spreads across my cheeks. "I did."

"Oh, let me see the ring," she says, her excitement genuine.

I hesitate briefly before slowly uncurling my fingers to reveal the ring.

"It's beautiful," she says, her eyes lighting up. "He has great taste."

"Thank you," I murmur, touched by her sincerity.

Then, she lights up with an idea. "Why don't we have a gallery show? I'm sure your fiancé is thrilled about your success and would love the chance to celebrate not only your success here but also your engagement."

The mention of Valentino sends an unwelcome shiver through me. The thought of him in a space that's entirely mine is unsettling. "I'll mention it to him," I say and pull out my phone, hoping to dodge any more questions about my personal life. "Unfortunately, I have to run. I have an appointment with the wedding planner."

"These will be on the website by the end of the week," Ophelia assures me.

"Thank you." I wave as I leave the gallery.

Somehow, I have to keep this part of my life hidden from Val for as long as I can, because if he finds out, I'm terrified of what he might do.

With fifteen minutes to spare, I arrive at the wedding planner's office. A beep sounds as I pull the door open and step inside.

"Ms. Moretti," Shannon gushes, her voice dripping with enthusiasm as she practically floats toward me. 'I'm absolutely thrilled to be planning your special day!' Her tone is just a little too sugary, her excitement clearly rehearsed.

"Thank you, Shannon. I appreciate you fitting me in at the last minute," I reply, forcing myself to sound gracious.

"Your wedding is going to be *the* event of the year," she gushes, her tone dripping with exaggerated enthusiasm. "There was no way I'd pass up the opportunity. I cleared my schedule right away."

Two weeks to plan the *event of the year*, and I can't even bring myself to care. Why should I? It's not like I want this marriage to happen. Valentino texted me, telling me to choose whatever I wanted, reminding me that money was no object. I'll make it look special, if nothing else, because that's all this is. An illusion.

I plaster on my practiced smile, "Where do we start?"

"Your fiancé asked me to wait until he arrived to begin," she informs me, glancing at her notes.

"Pardon me?" I ask, certain I misheard.

"Mr. Comiso called this morning," she continues. "He asked that we wait for him before we get started."

Right on cue, the door swings open. Valentino strolls in, dressed in his usual Alexander Amosu suit, his cellphone pressed to his ear.

"Just get it done, Angelo," he barks an order into the phone. "I'll be unavailable the rest of the day."

He disconnects the call. His black eyes lock with mine, instantly filling the space with his presence.

"If you have to work, I can handle this on my own," I say, maintaining an air of politeness.

"There's nothing more important than planning our wedding," Val replies, leaning in to kiss me.

At the last second, I turn my head, and his lips land on my cheek instead.

"We're not alone," I murmur, casting a glance at Shannon. "Please forgive him. He's very eager to be married," I add with a light, forced laugh.

"Men," Shannon says, a blush creeping up her cheeks. Her gaze shifts to Val, and in that brief moment, something passes between them. It's subtle, but enough to send a wave of unease through me. "Let's get started, shall we?"

Shannon settles in beside Val on the plush leather couch, sliding closer than necessary even though there's a perfectly good chair just a few feet away. Her knee presses against his leg, and neither of them bothers to pull away—or maybe they just don't care. Leaning into him, she arches her back slightly, pushing her chest forward as she flips open a large binder.

The whirlwind of wedding planning starts—colors, flowers, music, place settings. I'd thought maybe I could bring myself to care but watching them together makes it impossible.

Shannon's hand rests on Val's arm as they discuss the linens, her fingers lingering far too long, tracing small circles as if it's the most natural thing in the world. It's painfully obvious they're comfortable with each other. He doesn't even bother to glance in my direction. Why would he? To him, I'm nothing more than a business arrangement, just another deal to seal.

We're strangers bound by a ring, nothing more.

Instead of fighting it, I let them take over. The choices, the plans—they mean nothing to me. I'm just waiting for this charade to end.

"Have you chosen your dress?" Shannon asks as if she suddenly remembered I was here.

"Not yet."

Her hand flies up to her chest, her expression theatrical. "What are you waiting for? There'll barely be enough time to get your fittings done and have any alterations made."

"I have an appointment tomorrow."

"Excellent," Val says and takes my hand. "I'll go with you."

"No," I say firmly. "You can't see the dress until the ceremony."

Val raises an eyebrow, clearly unimpressed. "I didn't realize you believed in old wives' tales."

"It's tradition," Shannon chimes in, placing her hand on his thigh.

"Well," Val says. "I'm not much for traditions. Are you, *sweetheart?*"

"Whatever makes you happy," I reply, knowing there's no point in arguing.

"Let's move on," Shannon says, pulling out fabric swatches.

Without hesitation, Valentino picks up the most expensive one. "This," he declares with certainty, "is perfect."

I glance at the swatch, feigning interest. "It's lovely."

"Lovely? It's magnificent," Shannon exclaims. "Shantung silk is the finest linen you can get."

"All eyes will be on this event. I'll accept nothing less than the best," Valentino adds.

Shannon nods, clearly impressed. "Of course, Mr. Comiso. Let's move on to the floral arrangements."

"I want roses, lilies, orchids." Valentino's eyes gleam as he starts rattling off flowers.

Shannon taps furiously on her tablet, her focus entirely on the details, while my mind drifts. For so long, I held onto a fragile hope—that somehow, I wouldn't be forced into this. That I'd find a way out, or maybe Val would change his mind. That hope, faint as it was, was the only thing that kept me going.

Part of me even held onto the impossible idea that Antonio might somehow come back for me, that he'd rescue me from this nightmare. My mind drifts back to high school—to those stolen moments when it felt like we had all the time in the world. To the last day he ever spoke to me.

"We can't keep doing this," Antonio says as the smile disappears from his face. "Hiding. Sneaking around. It's been six months, Alessia. I want to take you out on a real date."

I want the same things, too, but I don't see any way for that to happen. "Antonio," I say softly, his name carrying all the uncertainty I can't fully express.

"I'm serious," he says, using his finger to lift my head. "I want to go to your father. I'll tell him straight up that I want to date his daughter."

"No. It won't work." I shake my head, hoping he doesn't press the issue.

"Why not?" he asks. "I'm not scared of him. I'll tell him how I feel about you. I'll make him understand."

I'm afraid of what my father will do to him if he tells him about us. I couldn't live with myself if anything happened to him. "You don't understand, Antonio. He won't listen. He won't approve."

"How do you know that if we don't try?"

"Because I know him," I whisper. "He's controlling. He'll never let me be with anyone he doesn't choose."

"I don't care," he replies, his voice soft but firm. "I'll do whatever it takes to make this work. You deserve more than hiding and sneaking around."

His beautiful brown eyes draw me in. They make me want to believe in the future he sees for us, but reality is too strong and pulls me back. "I don't know if it's possible."

"We'll make it possible," he says.

But now, I see how blind I've been. Antonio was the one person I thought truly cared—the only one I couldn't let go of. But when I needed him most, he walked away, proving he was no different from anyone else. That truth cuts deeper than anything. To him, I was just a fling, someone to forget. And the void he left behind gave Val the perfect opportunity to convince my father I belonged with him.

"Alessia, what do you think of this centerpiece?" Shannon asks, holding up a design that I actually like.

Before I can answer, Valentino interrupts. "It's too simple. We need something more extravagant, something that reflects our status."

I clench my jaw, swallowing my frustration. "Of course, Val. Whatever you think is best."

He grins, satisfied with my answer. "See? It's not that hard doing things my way."

As the meeting drags on, my patience wears thin. Valentino's arrogance is suffocating. The way they openly flirt and brush against each other only adds to the pressure. Inside, I'm seething, but on the outside, I keep up the façade of a happy bride-to-be.

Finally, Shannon gathers her things, still beaming. "I think we've made great progress today. I'll send over the finalized plans for your approval."

"You have my number," Valentino says, standing. Instead of shaking her hand, he kisses her cheek. "Call me, and I'll stop over and pick them up personally," he says, his voice low.

"That sounds perfect," she giggles, blushing again.

I struggle to not roll my eyes.

As soon as we get outside, I turn to Val. "You should've taken her in the back room and fucked her."

He raises an eyebrow, clearly unfazed. "And what makes you think I haven't?"

"I figured as much," I mutter, looking away, my stomach twisting.

"She's convenient." Val shrugs, completely indifferent. "It's nothing you need to concern yourself with. You're the one who'll be in my bed every night."

I clench my jaw, trying to hold back the bile from rising in the back of my throat. "Right," I say, my voice hollow. "Lucky me."

Antonio

Valentino didn't bother to give her more than two weeks. Two weeks to plan a wedding that's more a spectacle than a celebration. But that's who he is—always desperate to claim what he believes is his, even if it was never meant to be. Control, wealth, Alessia—they're nothing but conquests, pieces to be owned, not cherished.

While Val's busy building his perceived empire, the rest of us are left scrambling, working around the clock to keep the business running while making sure this damn wedding goes off without a hitch.

Carinwood Estate is a stunning place, sprawling and elegant, set just outside the city. I've heard the whispers. Aunt Domenica wasn't exactly happy about the choice of venue. She would've preferred the ceremony to take place at the family church. But it's the one thing Alessia insisted on.

My mind drifts back to that early fall day, when Alessia and I sat under the bleachers in our usual spot. The air was cool, carrying the first hints of autumn. A light breeze kept blowing her dark hair across her face. I can still see her tucking it behind her ear as she smiled at me. In that moment if felt like nothing else mattered—it was only me, her, and the way she made everything feel right.

"Do you ever think about what your wedding would be like?" she asks, catching me off guard.

"Not really," I shrug. "Never figured I'd have a say in it."

Alessia was always quiet and thoughtful. She rarely talked about the future, but for some reason, that day, she was different. Lighter. Peaceful.

"I want to get married in Italy. By the sea," she says, a dreamy quality in her voice. "The sun would be setting just as we said our vows.

She looks up at me, her dark eyes full of hope, as though she could see the scene unfolding before her. I swallow, trying to keep my voice steady.

"Who's standing there with you?" I ask, the words slipping out.

But then we were interrupted. The coach's whistle cut through the air, signaling the end of football practice. A group of guys jogged past, shouting and laughing, and the moment shattered, disappearing as if it had never happened. Just like that, our conversation was left unfinished.

I never got to hear who the groom in her daydream was. I always hoped she would've said my name, but then again, I never deserved to be anyone's choice. Not then, and certainly not now.

The sound of a loud crash snaps me back to the present. My head jerks toward the noise, and I hurry around the corner. A young woman is kneeling on the ground, frantically picking up the pieces of a shattered centerpiece. Her hands tremble as she tries to clean up the mess, clearly upset. Without thinking, I rush over to help her.

"Let me get that for you." I crouch down to pick up the larger pieces.

"You don't have to do that, sir," she replies, her voice trembling. "I can't believe I was so careless." A tear trickles down her cheek, but she quickly swipes it away.

"It was an accident," I offer, trying to soothe her.

"My boss won't see it that way. He's going to take this out of my pay." Her hands shake as she continues gathering the broken pieces.

"You ruined one of our centerpieces?" Valentino's voice booms, causing heads to turn.

"I'm sorry, sir," the girl stammers, shrinking under his glare.

"Sorry won't replace this," he growls, stepping closer, glass crunching under his shoes. "Do you know how much this costs?"

I rise to my feet, putting myself protectively between the girl and Valentino. "It was an accident. Back off."

"Look at Antonio playing the saint again," Valentino sneers, crossing his arms with a mocking grin.

"I'm just trying to be a decent person. She's upset enough without you making it worse."

"In our business, kind saints don't last long," he retorts, stepping closer as if to challenge me.

"Maybe," I say evenly, refusing to rise to his bait. "But even in our world, respect goes a long way."

"Caring too much is a quick path to an early grave, cousin," Valentino says, his voice lowering. His words more pointed as his frustration begins to show through. "True strength is gained through fear. One day, you'll learn."

"Everyone chooses their own path," I say with a slight shrug. "I choose respect."

"That's why I'm a leader, and you aren't." He punctuates each word with a jab of his finger at my chest. Then, his attention shifts back to the girl. "Get this mess cleaned up," he snaps before turning on his heel and walking away.

For a moment, no one moves. It's as if even breathing too loudly might draw his wrath back. The staff exchange wary glances, fear clear in their eyes.

I take a deep breath, exhaling slowly to dispel the lingering unease. "It's alright," I assure her. "He's gone."

Little by little, the staff members return to their tasks, though their movements are noticeably more cautious. The girl looks up, her eyes filled with a mix of gratitude and disbelief.

"I'll speak with your boss," I assure her. "If he insists on being reimbursed, I'll take care of it."

Her eyes widen. "You don't have to do that."

I offer a reassuring smile. "I want to. It's the right thing to do."

She exhales softly, her relief visible in the way her shoulders drop. "Thank you."

I nod, meeting her gaze. "No need to thank me. Let's just get this cleaned up."

As we work, I feel the eyes of the staff on us, their silent appreciation evident. It's a small victory, but in this world where fear often reigns supreme, a little kindness goes a long way.

Out of the corner of my eye, I spot Alessia watching from a distance. Her expression is a complex mix of relief, sadness, and something else I can't quite place. Our eyes meet briefly, and she mouths, *thank you*. Before I can react, she turns and disappears.

As I stand in the middle of this extravagant venue, watching the staff fall back into perfect synchronization, I can't help but be reminded that although this venue is beautiful, it's not the wedding Alessia dreamt of.

It's not Italy and there's no sea.

Valentino

"Gentleman," I address the men who've gathered, my voice cutting through the din of conversation. "Thank you for coming this evening. I've ordered some entertainment for us."

I catch Rico's eye from across the room and motion for him to open the door. Moments later, several scantily dressed women saunter in, immediately drawing the attention of the men, whose eyes light up with anticipation.

"Eat, drink, and indulge yourselves." I raise my glass of whiskey. "Especially you, cousin. Grab that blonde over there and get yourself laid. It'll do you a world of good." My comment earns a chuckle from several of the men.

The blonde sashays over to Antonio, her hips swaying seductively. He shakes his head, but she isn't deterred. She begins unbuttoning his shirt. His hands fly out, grabbing her wrists, stopping her before she can go any further.

I cross the room in several long strides. "Is there a problem here?" I ask as he drops her arm.

"Not at all," Antonio replies smoothly. "As much as I appreciate your gift, my sole focus is your safety."

I smirk, turning my attention to the blonde. "I think that's code for he's not man enough to handle you." My voice drips with mockery. "Perhaps my cousin didn't take his little blue pill."

The blonde giggles as I pull her against my side. "I, however, don't have such problems," I announce proudly, my dick already tenting my pants. "Come with me, and I'll show you how a *real* man fucks."

The room erupts in laughter, my guests thoroughly enjoying the spectacle. Antonio stands back, his expression unreadable.

"Anton," I say, clasping his shoulder as I pass. "Always so serious. That's why I trust you with my life."

"I've always got your back," he replies, his voice steady, his gaze unwavering.

The lights dim, and the bass pounds in sync with the growing energy. Two women begin sensual dances at the poles, while others are already giving lap dances to men seated throughout the space.

There are never any rules except the ones I make. And tonight, there's only one—indulge. This night is about pleasure, decadence, and debauchery in its purest form. The women I've brought in know exactly what they're here for, and they waste no time getting to work, offering themselves to my friends like offerings on an altar.

Every desire is to be satisfied, every boundary pushed. This is my world, where I dictate how far we go, how much we take, and how much we enjoy. Tonight, anything goes as long as it feeds our appetites.

Settling into the overstuffed leather chair, the blonde straddles my lap, her fingers weaving through my hair as she grinds her pussy against me. I sip my whisky, savoring the burn as it slides down my throat. I sink deeper into the chair as she trails her lips down my neck, her touch sending a shiver of need straight to my cock.

Glancing around the room, I take in the scene as my friends indulge in the pleasures laid out before them. Across from me, Rico's already shirtless, a brunette working between his legs.

Another lounges on the couch, two women at his side, his hands on them while their mouths explore each other.

The air buzzes with hedonistic energy, and I revel in it, knowing this is just a glimpse of the power that will soon be mine. The blonde keeps up her teasing, but I've had enough.

Gripping her neck, I pull her in for a rough kiss. She moans into my mouth, her fingers swiftly unfastening my pants. Lifting my hips, she slides my boxers down, freeing my hard cock.

"You're so big," she purrs, lowering to her knees and taking me into her mouth.

Without warning, the door flies open, and one of Moretti's men steps in, his suit crisp, his expression serious. Before he can move further, Antonio and Dante intercept him.

I watch them exchange tense words. Antonio glances at me, and I nod, signaling for him to let the man through. "What do you want?" I ask, impatience lacing my voice.

The man steps forward, handing me an envelope. "It's from your father."

Annoyed, I tear it open and quickly skim the note—a reminder about the wedding rehearsal tonight. Predictable.

Antonio steps closer. "Everything okay?"

I crumple the paper and toss it aside. "Tell my father I won't be there. I'm a little busy," I say with a smirk, glancing at the blonde between my legs. "He'll get over it."

Antonio nods. "I'll pass the message along."

Before they turn to leave, I look directly at Moretti's man, a grin tugging at my lips. "Why don't you stay? You can fuck her while she's blowing me. She won't mind," I say casually.

As if on cue, the woman arches her back, sticking her ass up in the air, presenting herself.

The man tenses, eyes widening briefly before he gives a stiff nod and quickly exits with Antonio.

With a laugh, I turn my attention back to the blonde, her lips still working my cock.

Tonight's about me. I'm not leaving my own bachelor party

for some pointless rehearsal. What's there to rehearse anyway? I show up, say a few words—any idiot could do it.

I pull the blonde off my cock and drag her back onto my lap. Her lips crash against mine as the music pulses around us. Lifting her just enough, I position myself at her entrance and pull her down onto my hard length. She gasps, her nails digging into my shoulders as her body clenches tightly around me.

My thoughts drift deeper and darker. What I could do if we were alone, with no eyes watching.

Gripping her wrists hard enough to bruise, I'd pin her down and tie her up, leaving her naked, vulnerable, completely at my mercy. The fear in her eyes would fuel me as I take out my knife, dragging the cold metal over her exposed skin. Her gasps would only push me further as I pierce her delicate flesh, watching the blood pool before I lap it up, savoring each drop. Again and again, I'd cut her, until she couldn't tell where the pleasure ended and the pain began.

Power isn't just about taking—it's about owning, possessing, and breaking someone down until they're completely under your spell, willing to do whatever you desire. The thought courses through me as my hips drive up, fucking her roughly, each thrust feeding the dark satisfaction growing inside me. Unable to stop, I grab a fistful of her hair and yank her head back, exposing her neck. My teeth sink into her smooth skin until the metallic taste of blood fills my mouth.

She gasps, her body tensing around me, and it's all I need to push me over the edge. My release hits like a brutal wave, my grip tightening as a guttural growl escapes me. I don't care that she hasn't come—that her pleasure is meaningless. She's nothing more than a body to use, a hole to fuck, and she's served her purpose.

In this moment, I'm untouchable. The king of this world.

Alessia

We've been gathered in the small chapel that's housed in the estate for what feels like an eternity, and Valentino still hasn't shown up. Giovanni sent a message to him almost half an hour ago, but there's been no sign of him. I've been standing at the end of the aisle, watching the doors with growing frustration, hoping that with each passing minute, he won't come at all. Praying he changed his mind and called off this charade.

My father sits in the front pew, his foot tapping in annoyance. "I don't see why we need to be here," he mutters under his breath, loud enough for anyone nearby to hear. "There are other matters that need my attention." He's been complaining all day, frustrated that the priest insisted the rehearsal was necessary.

Our mothers sit in the last row, their voices low as they go over last-minute details for tomorrow. I hear the occasional murmur of flowers and seating arrangements, but I can't focus on any of it.

The heavy walnut doors creak, and I hold my breath, expecting to see Valentino saunter in with that smug grin of his. But when the doors swing open, it's not him. It's Antonio.

For a moment, I'm frozen, memories of our past rushing back —the stolen glances, the fleeting touches, the quiet moments only we shared. He steps in, his eyes scanning the room for a brief second. Our eyes meet, and it's as if the years fall away.

"Where is he?" Giovanni's voice slices through the moment as he walks over to his nephew, pulling Antonio's attention away.

Antonio hesitates, his gaze briefly looking over his uncle's shoulder to the priest, who seems to understand the silent message and leaves the room without a word. Leaning in close to Giovanni, Antonio whispers something I'm unable to hear.

"On the night before his wedding?" he asked, a mix of shock and disappointment on his face.

"Yes, sir."

Giovanni exhales sharply, running a hand through his hair. "I have half a mind to call this whole thing off," he mutters.

My head snaps up at his words, a spark of hope igniting in my chest.

"Don't be so dramatic," my father interjects, rising to his feet with an air of finality. "Alessia knows her place," he says coldly. He walks toward the door, his voice dismissive as he calls, "Let's go. I have more important things to do as well."

"Where are you going?" My mother asks, her voice soft as both she and Domenica look at my father expectantly.

"Valentino isn't coming," he replies, not bothering to hide his irritation.

"Is he okay?" Domenica asks concerned.

My father chuckles. "He's more than fine—he's buried in some pussy right now."

Domenica gasps at my father's crude language, her eyes darting to her husband, who stands frozen in the middle of the chapel. My mother remains silent, lips pressed into a thin line, her stance tense.

"Come along, Alessia," my father orders. "We're going to dinner."

"I'm not hungry," I say quietly, having lost my appetite.

"Suit yourself," he says with a shrug and turns to my mother. "Let's go, Sophia. I've wasted enough time here."

Giovanni lingers for a moment, turning back to me with a weary, almost apologetic look. Refusing to let Val's disgusting behavior affect me in front of everyone, I offer him a reassuring smile. With his wife's hand in his, they walk out together, leaving me alone with Antonio.

His gaze meets mine. "I'll walk you to the dining room."

"I'm not going to my wedding rehearsal dinner while my fiancé is screwing another woman," I laugh bitterly. It's not a secret we don't love each other. Most men would've at least pretended the night before their wedding, but not Valentino.

Antonio sighs. "I'll escort you back to your room."

I shake my head slightly and step toward the door. "I didn't say I was hiding in my room. I'm going for a walk." Without waiting for a response, I push the door open and step outside.

"Alessia, wait," Antonio calls as he hurries to catch up to me, his footsteps heavy on the tiled floor. "What the hell are you up to?"

I stop abruptly, spinning around to face him. "Take me to Val," I demand.

He blinks in surprise. "You can't be serious."

"I'm dead serious," I reply crossing my arms defiantly. "If you won't bring me to him, then tell me where he is, and I'll go myself."

Antonio sighs, rubbing the back of his neck—a gesture so familiar it stirs something inside me. He always did that when he was trying to stay calm but couldn't. "You can't wander the grounds alone," he says, even though I already know that.

I smirk, tilting my head. "Then I guess you'll have to escort me, won't you?"

He shakes his head, muttering, "This is a terrible idea."

"I think it's a brilliant idea," I shoot back.

Antonio holds my gaze for a moment, then lets out another sigh, clearly giving in. "Fine," he grumbles. "Let's go."

Antonio leads me down so many hallways that I'm completely disoriented. "Are you sure you know where you're going?" I ask as we move deeper into the castle.

He gives me a confident nod as we stop in front of an old wooden door. "I'm positive," he says, pushing it open and revealing a staircase descending into a lower floor. "Do you trust me?"

I hesitate, my gaze shifting between Antonio and the shadowy stairwell. If it were anyone else, my answer would be a hard no. But this is Antonio, the boy I once loved. My heart and mind battle each other for control as I weigh the risks. Finally, I whisper, "Yes, I trust you," my voice barely steady, my eyes lingering on his deep blue ones longer than I should.

For a moment, his confident demeanor falters. I see it—the way his body relaxes, as if he's just become painfully aware of how close we are. But then he catches himself, and his body tenses. "They're a bit steep," he says, his voice a little rougher than before as he holds out his hand.

I take his outstretched hand, hoping that maybe, just maybe, the spark we once had would reignite. But there's nothing. His hand is warm, steady, but distant. And in that moment, I realize the truth I've avoided for so long—Antonio left me of his own free will. All the excuses I made for him, all the reasons I convinced myself must have forced him away... none of them mattered. He never cared enough to stay.

The wood creaks beneath our feet. "What's all this down here?" I ask as I look down the narrow passage.

"Mainly rooms for staff. Break rooms and storage," he explains. "But there's also a few party rooms."

"Why would anyone want to party down here? It's creepy."

Antonio chuckles, but his face turns serious as we come to a stop outside a door that's flanked by two guards I don't recognize. The muffled sounds of music come from the other side.

"You don't have to do this," Antonio says, turning to face me, a look of concern on his face.

"I want to," I reply, standing my ground.

"What good's it going to do?" Antonio pleads, lowering his voice. "It won't change who he is, and you have nothing to prove."

"I have *everything* to prove," I snap. "I'm the one being forced to marry him. It's me who's going to be expected to wait in his bed until he's ready to take his turn with me." My voice trembles, but I stand my ground. "You'll either open the door, or I'll call my father's men and have them do it for me."

Antonio's jaw tightens as he considers my words. Finally, he turns to the guards. "Let her in."

They pull the door open, and I'm hit with the full force of the music. As I step inside, the dim lighting reveals a scene worse than I thought. A naked woman dances on a pole, her legs spread as she holds herself upside down. Several men are pleasuring themselves while they watch her performance.

My stomach churns as I look around. Women in various stages of undress are draped over men. Some are on their knees, their heads between spread legs. Others straddling laps, their breasts bounce as they ride the man under them. Off to my left, a woman is bent over the pool table, a man's cock shoved in her ass as he thrusts from behind. Moans of pleasure and the smell of sex fill the air.

I lean closer to Antonio so he can hear me above the music and ask, "Where is he?"

Antonio motions toward the far corner of the room. My eyes

follow until I spot him. My fiancé has his dick buried in the ass of a brunette, his hand fisted in her hair. She's straddling another man who's thrusting between her legs, her underwear shoved into her mouth like a gag.

For a moment, I'm stunned. I expected to find him with a woman, but not like this.

Antonio's hand rests on my arm, his voice gentle but urgent. "Alessia, let me get you out of here. This isn't worth it."

I shrug off his touch, quickly forming a plan in my head. Looking around, I catch the eye of a handsome stranger sitting at the bar. His gaze locks on mine as I straighten my shoulder. "Game on," I whisper as I walk toward him, swaying my hips.

"Alessia," Antonio calls, but I ignore him as I stride past Valentino toward the handsome stranger.

Without breaking eye contact, he sets his drink down.

"What's the sexiest man in the room doing by himself?" I ask, leaning into him.

Placing his hands on my hips, he pulls me between his spread thighs. "I was waiting for you."

"Well, I'm here now." I purr, biting my bottom lip. "What are you going to do with me?"

Before he can answer, a sharp voice cuts through the air. "What the fuck is going on here?" Valentino's grip on my arm is tight as he yanks me away from the man.

"I'm just taking advantage of the entertainment," he replies with a smug grin.

"She isn't part of the *entertainment,*" Valentino snarls, his grip tightening painfully. "This is my fiancé."

The man's face pales. "Oh fuck," He raises his hands, backing off quickly. "I had no idea."

Valentino motions to someone, and the music suddenly cuts off. The whole room falls silent as he sneers, "Dante, take this piece of shit and get rid of him."

"No," I protest, pulling against his hold. "It's not his fault. I approached him. He had no idea who I was."

Valentino's eyes darken. "Then, let this be a lesson for you. Don't fuck around or people get hurt."

"I heard you were having a party," I snap, finally breaking free of his hold. "I figured I'd come and have some fun, too."

"It doesn't work that way, sweetheart," he says coldly, gesturing toward Dante. "Get him out of my sight."

"Antonio," I plead, my voice desperate. "Do something to stop this, please."

Valentino laughs. "Antonio's a lowly soldier. He takes orders from *me*." He watches as Dante drags him away. "Make sure his death is slow and painful."

The man's terrified eyes stay locked on mine as tears spill down my face. My stomach drops, knowing it's my fault he's about to die.

"Val, please don't do this," I beg, but he shrugs utterly indifferently.

"He touched what didn't belong to him," Val says flatly as he takes a long, slow drink of the whiskey the bartender just handed him.

I stand there trembling with fear and fury. "What do I have to do to stop this?" I ask desperation in my voice.

The corner of Val's mouth turns up in a sneer. "That's not the way this life works, Alessia. You should know better than that." He motions to Antonio. "Get her out of here so I can get back to enjoying my party."

"I hate you," I whisper, but he just laughs.

Antonio leads me to the door. Before we're even out of the room, the music turns on, and the party resumes as though nothing happened. I glance back to see Valentino already inside a woman while he fondles another.

"Alessia," Antonio says, drawing my attention.

"He's a monster," I murmur as I let him lead me out of the room.

We walk in silence, the tension heavy between us, until we round a corner. Without a word, Antonio suddenly steers me into one of the side rooms, closing the door quickly behind us.

"What are you doing?" I ask, panicked.

He doesn't answer. Instead, he pulls his cell from his pocket and taps the screen, putting it on speaker.

"Where are you?" a male voice answers.

"I'm with Alessia. I need a favor," he replies, his eyes locked with mine.

"What's wrong?"

"Val ordered a hit on Vincent Romano."

"He did what?" the man asks, raising his voice.

"I need it stopped," he says, his tone calm and steady. "I'll explain later."

There's a long pause before he responds. "I'll talk to Giovanni. Give me a minute."

We wait in tense silence, my heart in my throat. After a few agonizing minutes, the man comes back on the line. "It's done. Your uncle took care of it. Vince has been let go with our apologies."

Relief washes over me, and I let out a breath.

"Your mother's asking if you're bringing Alessia over to the rehearsal dinner?"

I shake my head.

"She's not feeling well," Antonio replies without missing a beat. "I'm taking her back to her room."

"Okay. Goodnight, son."

Antonio disconnects the call and pockets his phone.

"Thank you," I say, feeling the tightness in my shoulders ease.

"You can thank me by not being so reckless next time," he replies.

Antonio walks me to my room in silence, his posture rigid, arms crossed tightly over his chest. He doesn't look at me, his eyes fixed ahead. As we approach the door, my personal guards step forward, taking their positions.

"Thank you again," I say.

Antonio gives a slight nod before turning and walking away.

The moment the door to my room closes, I lock it and lean against the wood. Reality crashes over me and my legs give way. Sinking to the floor, I pull my knees to my chest. The man I'm supposed to marry, the man who owns my future, is a monster. Tears sting my eyes, but I force them back.

Crying won't save me from this nightmare. Nothing will.

Valentino

T he alarm on my cell fills the room with a high-pitched beeping. I reach out, silencing it with the swipe of my thumb. Looking to my side, I find the blonde from the party.

"Good morning, handsome," she purrs, her hand trailing down her chest, her eyes lowering to my erection beneath the sheets.

She was the perfect little plaything last night, letting me tie her up and use every hole. I made her scream into the sheets as I took everything I wanted. Her tears only fueled my satisfaction as I shoved myself deeper, watching her struggle.

"Time to go," I say, sitting up and swinging my legs over the side of the bed.

She slinks up behind me, wrapping her arms around my waist. "I'd rather take care of this," she murmurs, wrapping her hand around my dick as if she has some claim to it.

I grab her wrist tight enough to make her flinch. "I said get your clothes and leave." My voice comes out cold, causing her to jerk away. I stand, not bothering to hide my irritation and walk toward the en suite. "You better be gone before I'm done."

I don't look back because her feelings don't matter to me. She was nothing more than a quick fuck. All that matters is that she's gone before I'm done showering.

Usually, I wouldn't let a willing body, or even an unwilling one, go to waste, but this is my wedding day. Tonight, I'll be claiming my wife. Alessia's virginity is something I've made sure to preserve.

Knowing I'll be the first to bury myself inside her cunt, to tear her open and make her scream, fills me with anticipation. I'll fuck her until she's raw, until every thrust leaves her aching, a constant reminder of the pain I can, and will, inflict. It's a promise of what's to come, a reminder that she belongs to me and no one else.

An hour later, I'm standing in front of the full-length mirror, adjusting my bowtie. Anticipation thrums through my veins, a mixture of excitement and raw determination. This is the day I've been waiting for. Today, I prove to my father that I'm prepared to rule *La Famiglia*.

"Are you ready?" Antonio asks, leaning against the doorway with his arms crossed. His expression is carefully neutral, but I sense a hint of something lurking just below the surface.

"This is the moment I've been waiting for," I respond, my voice thick with triumph.

He raises an eyebrow, his tone edged with skepticism. "I never realized you were so interested in marriage."

"Marriage?" I scoff, turning to face him. "I don't give a damn about the marriage. Today's about proving to my father that I'm ready to become Capo."

Antonio straightens. "Maybe you can put your career goals aside for today. For Alessia's sake."

"Put it aside?" I step toward him with deliberate slowness.

"This is the start of a new era, Anton. I'll be in control, and you'll be by my side. Think of the things we're going to accomplish."

He watches me cautiously. "My father will be by your side for the foreseeable future."

"For now," I reply, lowering my voice conspiratorially. "But once I'm in charge, I'll have the power to shape this family into something far more powerful than it is now."

The thrill of the future takes root inside me, knowing that soon enough, the old guard's days will be over. I can practically taste the power and control I'll have. I won't be taking orders from my father or his lackeys much longer. No, I'll surround myself with men of my choosing—loyal, ambitious, and willing to do whatever it takes to bring my vision to life.

Antonio continues to watch me, but as usual, he doesn't let his emotions show. "If we don't leave now, we'll be late," he says, breaking the silence.

I grin, adjusting my jacket one last time. "Let's get this over with," I say, my voice cool and steady. I step out of the room, Antonio falling in behind me as we make our way toward the chapel.

A new era is dawning, and I'll be the one holding all the cards.

Alessia

Outside the window of my bridal suite, the sun beams brightly. There's not a cloud in the sky. By all accounts, it's the perfect day for a wedding.

This morning, I was greeted by hair and makeup artists. My long black hair has been pinned in a simple yet elegant low bun. I opted for a more natural look with a hint of shimmer on my eyes and soft nude lipstick.

The bridal party, assembled more for appearances than for any real connection, was already waiting. Laura, a girl from high school, one I was never particularly close to but who my father insisted be here, stands among them. Alongside her are a cousin I rarely speak to and the daughters of my father's associates, girls I barely know. None of them really matter to me, but today, they're part of the spectacle.

"Alessia," Mom says, coming up to stand beside me. There's an unmistakable distance between us, a reminder that we've never been close. I wish it were different, that she could offer comfort instead of this cold formality. "It's time to get dressed."

"Of course." Untying the knot of my silk robe, I let it glide down my arms, and set it on the nearby chaise. Standing in nothing but a strapless ivory balconette bra and panties, with a matching garter holding up my silk stockings, I feel exposed in more ways than one.

"Wait until Val undresses you tonight," my cousin says. "He's going to have quite the treat."

"I can't wait," I say, injecting false enthusiasm into my voice, hoping it sounds convincing enough.

"I wish he was going to be undressing me." One of the other bridesmaids says, her voice dripping with envy. A few of the others giggle, and I have to fight the urge to roll my eyes. Instead, I wonder how many of them Val has already slept with, how many have had their turn in his bed while pretending to envy me now.

My mother, wine in hand, awkwardly tries to remove the gown from the hanger, her focus more on her drink than the task. Laura steps in to help, steadying the dress as I step into it. I keep my gaze fixed on the mirror as she pulls it up and fastens it in place.

The gown is lovely. Off the shoulder with an A-line cut and a court train that drapes elegantly behind me. The lace-up corset hugs my waist, highlighting every curve. It's the kind of dress girls dream about wearing on their wedding day.

Once I'm dressed, I lower myself carefully onto a chair, and my mother positions the antique Belgian lace veil over my head. The cathedral-length veil, sparkling with Swarovski crystals, adds the perfect amount of brilliance to the traditional gown. The photographer clicks away, capturing every moment as if this is truly the happiest day of my life.

A tear slips down my cheek, and to my surprise, Mom gently wipes it away. Her touch is unexpectedly soft, almost tender—something I'm not used to. "You make the most stunning bride," she says, her voice filled with emotion. "Valentino's a lucky man. He'll realize that. You'll see."

For a moment, it almost feels like she's the mother I've always needed her to be.

"I'm sure he will," I reply softly.

"Are you ready, Alessia?" My father's voice cuts through the room, his presence commanding as always.

Taking a deep breath, I gather every ounce of strength I have left, then rise to my feet. I walk toward him with slow, measured steps. "I'm ready," I say, praying my voice sounds confident, even if I feel anything but.

THANKFULLY, THE CEREMONY IS SHORT AND TO THE point. There are no heartfelt vows, no declarations of undying love—just the mechanical repetition of standard lines spoken without emotion. It feels more like a business transaction than a marriage. When we're pronounced husband and wife, I force myself not to stiffen in Val's hold.

I glance toward Antonio, catching his eyes as he watches us, his expression unreadable. He doesn't blink, doesn't look away, and the intensity of his gaze makes something twist painfully inside me. I always wanted this to be him. Instead, it's Valentino's lips pressing against mine and everything about it feels wrong.

As soon as the ceremony ends, we make our way through the glass doors that lead to an expansive terrace. White roses and twinkling fairy lights frame the space, the setting sun casting a golden glow over the polished tables adorned with pristine linen and crystal glassware. The guests mingle, champagne flutes in hand, while servers glide between them, offering canapés on silver trays. To anyone else, it looks like the perfect wedding—the *event of the year*.

"You barely touched your food," Valentino observes.

"I'm not hungry," I reply quietly, pushing my food around on my plate.

His voice drops low and commanding. "You look ungrateful. Put some food in your mouth and eat."

I pause, the fork clattering lightly when I set it down. Leaning in, I whisper fiercely, "I may have been forced to marry you, but that doesn't mean you get to dictate my every move."

His expression hardens as he leans in close, his lips brushing against my ear. "How wrong you are," he hisses. "Now that we're married, you'll obey my every command."

Before I can respond, our guests begin tapping their silverware against their glasses, chanting, "*Bacio, bacio.*"

Valentino flashes them a charming smile, turning to the crowd like an actor to his audience. His hand grips the back of my neck, firm and possessive, as he pulls me toward him. His tongue forces its way between my lips, a dominating kiss that I endure only because I know better than to resist while everyone's watching. But what I really want to do is sink my teeth into his tongue so he thinks twice before kissing me again.

After the meal, Valentino and I are called to the dance floor for our first dance as husband and wife. The soft strains of *Con Te Partiro* play as he pulls me against him. his grip on my waist bruising and possessive. He twirls me around, his movements polished for the camera.

Val leans in, his breath warm against my ear. "I can't wait until we get to the honeymoon suite," he murmurs, his voice thick with desire. "Can you feel what you do to me?"

I stiffen as his erection presses insistently against my stomach, a reminder of what Valentino expects tonight. My mind races, desperate for a way to stall the inevitable. "That's going to have to wait," I say, forcing calm into my voice.

"Wait?" His tone is laced with confusion and irritation.

"I have my period," I say quietly, my gaze averting his, hoping it will make him uncomfortable.

Valentino's jaw clenches for a split second before he schools his features into indifference. "I see."

We continue our dance in strained silence. My lie has only bought me a few precious days of reprieve. Eventually, I'll have to face him. The thought sends a shiver of dread through me, the future feeling more like a noose tightening around my neck.

The applause from the guests snaps me back to the present as the music fades. Val releases me and walks off the dance floor, his departure seamlessly replaced by my father as *Lauretta* by Enrico Musiani begins to play. It's a sentimental song, a father's tribute to his daughter on her wedding day.

I wish today was the kind of day the song celebrates—a day shared with someone I truly loved.

As we dance, my father's hand grips mine with no warmth, his voice low and calculating. "Alessia, my beautiful girl," he says, though the words sound hollow. "You've done well. This marriage secures our future. The Comiso family is a powerful ally."

I nod, my throat tightening. "Yes, Papa."

His grip on my hand tightens, and I wince inwardly. "Remember, this is about more than just you. The Comisos are powerful allies. This marriage solidifies our position and will expand our influence."

"I won't, Papa," I reply, forcing myself to meet his gaze, though resentment burns just below the surface.

This dance, meant to be a tender moment between father and daughter, feels hollow, stripped of any warmth or affection. My father speaks of alliances, power, and doors opening, as if love has no place here.

I nod along, even as my heart sinks deeper. Every instinct screams at me to shout, to tell him how much I hate this, how much I despise the man I've been forced to marry. But I can't. I know all too well what happens when I anger him. I've been raised to sacrifice, to endure, all for the sake of the family.

As the song ends, my father releases me, his grip lingering just a moment too long. "You've done your duty today. Val owns you now—don't forget it," he says, his voice cold and final, as if sealing my fate with those words.

With the formalities over, Valentino disappears, leaving me

alone in the sea of guests. Seizing the opportunity, I slip away from the music and laughter, finding a quiet bench at the edge of the estate. The night sky is breathtaking, stars glittering like diamonds—a stark contrast to the chaos that fills my life. I wish I had my camera to capture the serenity of this moment.

"What are you doing out here?" Antonio's voice startles me, pulling me from my thoughts.

"I needed a few minutes to myself."

"You shouldn't be out here alone," he says, his tone gentle but firm.

"I'm hardly alone. There are guards everywhere," I snap, though my frustration fades quickly.

Antonio sits beside me, his presence oddly comforting. "I know tonight wasn't easy for you," he says after a moment of silence.

"You have no idea," I say, bitterness slipping into my voice.

He sighs and grips the back of his neck. "You're strong, Alessia. You'll get through this."

A bitter laugh escapes me. "Strength has nothing to do with it. It's about survival."

He meets my gaze, his eyes filled with an intensity that catches me off guard. "Then survive. And don't let him break you."

We sit in silence under the night sky, scattered with stars, a witness to our conversation. His words linger in the air between us. "Why do you care?" I ask, searching his face for answers.

He hesitates, his expression conflicted. "Because you deserve better than this. Better than him."

A lump forms in my throat, and I struggle to keep my emotions in check. "I don't need your pity," I whisper.

"It's not pity. It's respect." He stands, his eyes lingering on mine for a moment before he turns to leave. "You should go back inside. People will notice you're missing."

As I watch him leave, a familiar emptiness creeps in, reminding me of the last day I watched him walk away—just like this. I want to reach out and ask him to stay. But I don't. I can't. Instead, I bite my lip, forcing myself to remain still, watching him disappear like a shadow slipping back into the night, leaving me alone with the stars and the memory of what we used to be.

Antonio

"There you are, cousin," Valentino slurs, his breath reeking of alcohol as he claps a hand on my shoulder. I catch him just as I'm passing the bar. His weight nearly knocks me off balance. "Have you tried the whiskey?"

"No, I haven't," I reply, masking my irritation with a polite smile. "Why aren't you with your bride?"

"I have the rest of my life with her," he says with a lazy wave. He turns to the bartender without missing a beat. "Pour my cousin a glass of Macallan."

"How do you like it, sir?" the bartender asks.

"Neat, please," I say, and watch as he pours the rich bronze liquor into a crystal tumbler.

"Thank you." I lift the glass from the bar and take a sip, letting the complex flavors unfold on my tongue—tropical fruit, coffee, dark chocolate, with a subtle hint of orange.

"What do you think?" Valentino asks, his eyes gleaming with pride.

"It's very good," I respond, allowing a smile to play on my lips. The whiskey is excellent, but it doesn't distract me from my growing frustration with him.

Valentino leans in, lowering his voice as if sharing a well-guarded secret. "I have my sights set on one of the elusive bottles from 1926," he says, his tone dripping with ambition. "There were twelve bottles with labels painted by Valerio Adami, an Italian artist. One was reportedly destroyed in an earthquake, and another is rumored to have been opened. That leaves ten."

"And you want one?"

"Of course, I do," Valentino continues. "It's a rare piece of history and will be a symbol of my reach—of my power."

"I see," I say, leaning my elbow on the bar. Movement from the back of the tent catches my attention. Alessia has returned. Her eyes catch mine for the briefest of moments before she looks away, her expression carefully neutral.

I nod slowly, suppressing the disgust rising in my chest. "Just like your wife?" I murmur, unable to resist the bitter jab.

Valentino laughs loudly, an obnoxious sound that cuts through the air. "Alessia? She's nothing more than a pretty face. The Macallan, now that's true value."

Watching Val marry Alessia has stirred something darker than I expected, setting my nerves on edge. My hand tightens around the glass as anger builds inside me. If this were my wedding, the last place I'd be is at the bar, getting drunk. I'd be at Alessia's side, making it clear to every man here that if they did so much as look at her, they'd all die. Not because she's a shiny new possession, but because she'd be my wife—my partner.

"You're a lucky man, Vigo," I say, my voice tight.

"Luck has nothing to do with it," he boasts, downing the rest of his drink in one long gulp. "It's all about knowing how to play the game." Raising his glass he offers a toast. "To power and control, cousin."

"To power and control," I echo, clinking my glass against his, though the words leave a bitter taste in my mouth.

I watch him, disdain building with every passing moment. He's obsessed with material wealth and status, as if owning a rare bottle of whiskey will somehow prove he's worthy of leading our family. Meanwhile, he's too blind to see the true value of what he already possesses—Alessia.

"If you'll excuse me, Vigo," I say, setting the glass on the bar. "There's someone I need to speak to."

I don't wait for his response before turning and striding across the terrace, my eyes locked on the petite brunette I plan to spend the night with. I need a distraction, something to numb my feelings. And for tonight, she'll do.

Valentino

The reception is winding down. Alessia managed to avoid me all evening, but now she's stuck by my side, my arm draped around her waist—a display of affection meant only for the eyes of our guests as we bid them farewell.

We'll be staying at Carinwood tonight. In the morning, we'll fly out to the Amalfi Coast for our month-long honeymoon. She'll have no choice but to get used to being alone. Isolation without effort.

While in Italy, I plan on making a short trip to Sicily to meet with Giancarlo De Guido. Although he spends the majority of his time at his residence in Cianciana, he conducts the majority of his business in Pittsburgh.

Rumor has it he's looking to expand into Philadelphia. My father wants nothing to do with him. Says his methods are too violent. But I see an opportunity—an opening to expand our business, to make my own mark, so I'm taking it.

Rico appears in the doorway, and I make my way over. "Have the arrangements been made?" I murmur, keeping my voice low so only he can hear.

"Yes, sir," he replies quietly, handing me a silver key attached to a black keychain. I slide it into my front pocket. "Is there anything else you need?"

"No. That's all." I dismiss him with a wave. He exits the room, leaving Alessia and me alone.

Her gaze lingers on him until he's out of sight. Then, she turns to me. "What was that about?"

"Business," I say with a shrug.

"Business?" She raises and eyebrow, her tone sharper now.

"Since I can't spend tonight with my wife. I've made alternate plans," I say smoothly.

"You're despicable," she spits out, her voice cold and hard. "I can't believe I'm married to someone like you."

Pulling her closer, I savor the way she tenses against me. "You'll get used to it, Alessia. This is your life now."

Her jaw clenches. "I'll never get used to it." She tries to pull away, but I tighten my grip.

"You don't have a choice," I reply, my voice dropping to a dangerous whisper. "You're mine now, and you'll do as I say."

Her eyes glisten with unshed tears. "I hate you."

"Good," I smirk, brushing my thumb across her cheek. "Hate is better than indifference. It means you care."

Her gaze burns with defiance. "You disgust me."

"Get used to that feeling," I say coldly and push her away from me. "Let's go. I want to get on with my night."

She doesn't move immediately, her eyes filled with a mixture of anger and pain. But finally, she turns and walks away, her back stiff with resolve. I watch her go, satisfaction coursing through me. She can resist all she wants, but in the end, she's mine.

We make our way through the grand hall of the estate, meeting several guests who offer their congratulations and farewells. Alessia maintains her composure, a tight smile plastered on her face as she exchanges pleasantries. I keep my arm around her, a possessive grip that doesn't loosen until we're out of the public eye.

As we reach the main staircase, I pause, leaning in close to whisper in her ear. "Go straight to our room. Rico will accompany you to ensure you don't get lost."

Her eyes flash with fury, but she bites her tongue, wisely refraining from arguing with me in front of one of my men. I watch until her slender figure disappears around the corner. As soon as she's out of sight, my mind shifts to the night ahead.

Valentino

After I stole Alessia from Antonio, he changed. He became dark and cold. He started fucking anything with a pussy just to feel in control again. That's when I met Lena. She was the latest girl he was banging against the wall in the supply closet at *Casa della Ombre*.

I wanted a piece of Lena, too.

One night, after a party, I invited them both back to my hotel room. That was the first night Antonio and I shared her. Lena had no complaints. From that point on, it continued—sometimes with Lena, sometimes with other women. We did that for years, fucking our way through Philadelphia like we owned the whole damn city.

I don't know why Antonio stopped. Maybe he got bored. But I didn't. Lena has always been one of my favorites. She likes it rough, and she knows how to obey.

The scent of her amber and vanilla perfume greets me as I push the room's door open and step inside. Lena's waiting for me on her knees, just as I requested. My cock stirs at the sight of her perky tits and her dusky rose-colored nipples already stiff and begging for attention. I catch a glimpse of her bare pussy between her spread thighs.

I glance toward the bed and spot the black bag with every-thing I need. "Go to the bed," I command, removing my tux jacket and sliding the bowtie from around my neck.

She obeys, crawling across the floor with slow, deliberate movements. When she reaches the bed, she glances over her shoul-der, biting her bottom lip. I say nothing, unbuttoning my white dress shirt and tossing it onto a nearby chair. Walking over to the bed, I unzip the bag and begin pulling out the toys.

Lena's brow furrows as she sees the collection—a ball gag, riding crop, nipple clamps, butt plug, and a blindfold. She's used to me being rougher with her, so these seem almost laughable in comparison. This bag was meant for Alessia. I'd planned to go easy on my bride for her first time. But with Lena? I'll have to find ways to get creative.

"Get up." She gracefully rises to her feet. "Open your mouth," I command, holding up the ball gag. She parts her lips without hesitation, letting me slip it in. I hold it in place with one hand while fastening the strap around her head. "We don't want my new wife hearing you scream while I fuck you, do we now?" I murmur. She shakes her head, eyes wide with understanding.

"On the bed. Head down, ass in the air."

My cock strains against my zipper watching as she positions herself, reaching back and spreading her ass cheeks, offering herself to me. Grabbing the lube, I squeeze some onto the glass plug before working it into her tight hole. Lena moans as the cool toy slides in. She loves this. Once the plug is fully inserted, I spear a finger inside her pussy.

"You're wet for me already," I murmur, pulling my hand away.

Unzipping my pants, I let them drop to the floor and kick them aside. Wrapping my hand around my cock, I stroke myself, watching as Lena wriggles her ass, silently begging for more.

I'm hard and ready to go. Before entering her, I grab a fistful of her hair and yank her up onto all fours. My hand closes around her throat, cutting off her air.

"Do you like being my dirty little whore?" I growl, my voice dripping with satisfaction. "Knowing that's all you'll ever be to me now?" When she doesn't shake her head in response, I squeeze her throat tighter, demanding the answer I already know.

She nods quickly.

"Good girl. Now take my cock."

With one hard thrust, I slam into her, not giving her time to adjust. I start fucking her relentlessly, her pussy gripping my cock and pulling me deeper with each stroke. Releasing her throat, I grab her hips, driving into her harder. Her legs tremble, fists gripping the sheets. Her muffled moans grow louder, even with the gag silencing her.

Fucking her isn't enough—I need to hurt her, to make her feel every bit of pain I can give. I pull out abruptly, her body tensing in confusion, and grab the crop from next to me on the bed. Without warning, I bring it down hard on her bare ass, the sound of leather against flesh echoing through the room.

She gasps, her back arching involuntarily, but I don't stop. I bring it down again and again, each strike harder than the last. Her skin blooms under the crop, turning a deep, vibrant shade of red as I cover every inch of her ass. The welts rise almost immediately, her body trembling with every stinging blow.

The crop won't do any permanent damage, but I can make it cause her pain—extreme pain. Each strike makes her body jolt, her breath coming in ragged gasps, but it isn't enough. It's too controlled, too restrained for the darkness that stirs inside me.

The craving to hear her scream takes over, a dark hunger twisting inside me. It has to be loud—loud enough for everyone to know, for Alessia to understand what kind of monster I really am. That thought alone sends a sick thrill through me, unraveling the last bit of control I had. My hands are shaking as I rip the ball gag from her mouth, but I don't give her time to catch her breath. I want her gasping, begging, screaming. I want to see her shatter beneath me.

Flipping the crop in my hand, I grip the thin leather shaft and turn the solid wooden handle toward her exposed skin. The next strike lands with a dull, brutal thud. She cries out, the sound ripping from her throat. The handle hits harder, deeper, and I feel the satisfying give of flesh beneath it. I don't stop. I drive the handle down again, and this time, it breaks the skin—her blood pooling in thin lines where I've split her open.

Her screams rise, raw and desperate, exactly what I wanted. The sight of blood on her reddened skin makes my pulse quicken, my need growing more vicious. I strike her again harder, watching the fresh blood mix with the bruises, knowing I'm pushing her to the edge.

"Please stop." Tears stream from her eyes, soaking the sheets beneath her. "I can't take it."

"Stop?" I chuckle darkly, the sound low and mocking. "I've barely gotten started."

She tries to get away, weakly struggling, but I grab her hips, holding her in place.

"No," she cries out, panic threading her voice.

I yank her head back by her hair, pulling her closer. "What did you say?"

"N-no," she stammers, trembling beneath me.

My fist connects with her face. "You don't tell me no." Grabbing the riding crop again, I continue to rain hell down on her, each strike more ruthless than the last.

It isn't until my arms burn from effort and my cock aches, desperate to be inside her that I stop. My eyes fall on the plug in her ass, and I smirk. Slowly, I begin to move it in and out, her body shivering with the sensation. Her moans mix with tears, helpless and broken.

I smack her ass. "You're still crying," I sneer. Reaching down, I run my finger through her soaked pussy. "You're dripping for me," I mumble, rubbing her clit. "Do you want to come?"

"Yes," she whispers, her voice choked with tears.

"Stop crying and beg." Her body quakes beneath my touch as she fights to hold back her sobs. I press harder against her clit, forcing a stifled whimper from her. "Beg," I growl, my voice harsh and unrelenting, leaving no room for defiance.

"Please. Please let me come," she pleads, her words barely holding together.

Yanking the plug out, I toss it aside and drive into her without warning. "You always take my cock in your ass so well," I groan, pulling out only to thrust back in harder, making her scream again. The last remnants of control fade, and the pace becomes ruthless, each thrust harder and more brutal than the one before.

Tension coils tight in my balls, fueled by the sight of her blood and the sound of her desperate sobs. My cock throbs with the need to finish. I shove two fingers into her pussy, feeling her walls clench around them, but this was never about her pleasure—only mine.

I grip her hips, digging my fingertips into her flesh. She'll wear the marks from my fingers and my crop for days. It's that thought that pushes me over the edge. My cock throbs inside her, filling her ass. My breathing is heavy as I pull out and drag my finger through the cum leaking from her hole, swirling it around in her blood and dragging it up her back.

Sitting back, I admire my work.

"You will not wash this off tonight," I say, my tone sharp and demanding. "Do you understand me?"

"Yes," she whimpers, barely able to speak.

Rising to my feet, I make my way toward the bathroom.

"Val?" she calls. I stop but don't turn around. "I didn't—" she starts, but I cut her off.

"You can finish yourself off while I shower," I snap, my tone cold, as I disappear into the bathroom without a second glance.

Alessia

Valentino put his guards outside the honeymoon suite, locking me in as if I were a prisoner instead of his bride. The door might as well be iron bars, trapping me inside this gilded cage. I pace the room, fingers clenching and unclenching as anger and humiliation churn inside me. Each step reminds me of how little control I have, how I'm nothing more than his possession.

Then I hear it—the unmistakable sound of a woman's scream, muffled but clear enough to reach me from down the hall. I grip the edge of the dresser, struggling to keep steady as fury courses through me. He's flaunting his infidelity, making sure I hear every moment of it.

I catch my reflection in the mirror and pause, questioning why I'm still in this dress, hours after the ceremony. My makeup is flawless, my hair perfectly styled, but I barely even recognize the person looking back at me. As the tears finally fall, I begin to pull the pins from my hair and remove the makeup, trying to strip away everything that ties me to this day.

Sinking onto the edge of the bed, I bury my face in my hands. Every fiber of my being screams to run, to escape, but I know there's no way out. Valentino's grip on my life is ironclad. I think back to all the times I dreamed of a different future, one filled with love and happiness. How naïve I was to believe that was possible.

A knock at the door startles me. I quickly wipe the tears from my face and take a deep breath, forcing myself to regain some composure. When I open the door, a young woman from the estate staff stands there with a tray, her expression polite and professional.

"Mrs. Comiso, I've brought you some tea and a plate of fruit and cheese," she says, her voice calm but gentle.

"Thank you," I reply quietly, stepping aside as she places the tray on the small table.

"If you need anything else, please don't hesitate to ring," she adds, offering me a sympathetic look, likely noticing the tear stains on my face, before quietly leaving the room.

The door clicks shut behind her, and the silence settles around me, leaving me feeling even more alone. I sit down and pour myself a cup of hot water, letting the chamomile tea bag steep. Picking at the fruit, I'm grateful for the small gesture of kindness on what feels like the cruelest night of my life.

With the warm cup in my hands, I step out onto the balcony. The soft night air brushes against my skin as I gaze over the estate grounds stretching out before me, bathed in moonlight. Everything appears peaceful and calm, a sharp contrast to the turmoil I feel inside.

Leaning against the railing, my thoughts wander to the life I'll never have. What would it be like to marry for love, to live freely, without the chains of this world? What if I had been born far away from the mafia's reach, where power and control didn't shape every decision, every breath?

The thought lingers, bittersweet, but I know it's only a fantasy. There's no escaping this life.

Walking back inside, I slowly untie the ribbon at the back of my wedding dress, loosening the tight corset. The dress slips off my shoulders and falls to the floor in a pile of satin and lace. Stepping out of it feels like shedding the last pieces of the day, a small, fleeting relief. I pull on an ivory silk nightgown and climb into bed, the exhaustion of it all finally taking over.

Sleep pulls me under, and for a few brief hours, I escape the nightmare of my new life.

A ROUGH SHAKE JOLTS ME AWAKE. BLINKING, I LOOK UP and find Valentino standing over me, fully dressed, with an arrogant smirk plastered on his face. "Rise and shine, *princess*. If we don't leave soon, we'll miss our flight."

I sit up, my head still foggy from sleep. "You made me spend my wedding night listening to you fuck another woman, and now you think you can waltz in here and make demands," I say, rubbing my eyes, my voice filled with barely restrained anger.

"That's exactly what I think," he replies, his voice dripping with condescension. "You'll have to get used to how things work around here, princess. I'm the one in control of everything. The sooner you accept that, the easier this will be for you."

"You're disgusting."

He chuckles, dismissing my words with a shrug. "I've been called worse. Now get up and get dressed. We have a flight to catch, and I won't tolerate being late."

Slipping out of bed, I pad to the bathroom to take a hot shower. The warmth soothes my tense muscles, allowing me to feel a momentary sense of peace.

As I step out of the shower and reach for a towel, I realize in my rush to get away from Valentino, I forgot to grab my clothes. I hesitate, not ready to face him like this. My nightgown is still in the bathroom, but it doesn't offer much coverage. I stall for time by blow-drying my hair, knowing I'll eventually have to go out there.

Ensuring the towel is tightly secured, I crack the bathroom door, hoping he's left the room. I'm disappointed when I spot him lounging on the bed, scrolling through his phone. When he notices me, he lowers it, his gaze locking onto mine.

"Did you forget something?" he asks, his tone mocking while his eyes rake over my body.

Ignoring him, I walk to the closet with my head held high, determined not to let him see how much his gaze unnerves me. I can feel his eyes on me, scrutinizing every move, but I refuse to give him the satisfaction. Grabbing a simple dress from the closet, I slip it on quickly, making sure to keep my back to him the entire time.

When we're ready to leave, he steps toward me, placing a hand on my lower back and guiding me out of the room. "Remember, Alessia, you're mine now," he says, his voice low. "When we're in public, you'll act the part. Smile. Be the perfect wife. Understood?"

Silence. It's the only act of rebellion I can manage right now. Valentino won this battle, but the war is far from over. Each day, I'll be plotting, planning, waiting for the right moment.

I will survive. I will escape. And one day, I will be free.

Alessia

The plane touches down in Naples, and we're among the first to disembark. After we collect our bags, Val leads me to a private car waiting out front. The driver opens the back door, and I slide in, the buttery soft leather cool against my skin.

"You will be on your best behavior for my men," Valentino says, leaning into the open door, his tone firm.

I glare at him. "Where are you going?"

"I have business to attend to," he replies as if I should've known better than to ask.

"Business?" I repeat, my disbelief giving way to frustration. "On our honeymoon? Aren't we supposed to at least keep up appearances?"

His expression hardens, eyes narrowing with disdain. "Appearances are all that matter, Alessia. But don't mistake this trip for something it's not. You should be grateful I'm even letting you go without me. That's more freedom than you deserve."

My hands ball into fists in my lap. "Grateful? For what? Being dragged around like a prisoner while you play at being a mafia king?" My words come out sharp, but I don't care.

Valentino leans in close, his face mere inches from mine. "Watch your tone. I will not tolerate your disrespect."

I meet his gaze, refusing to back down. "I'll never be the obedient little wife you want, Valentino. Never."

His lips curl into a slow, calculating smile. "We'll see about that."

The cold edge in his voice sends a chill through me. I've heard the stories, the whispered rumors of his cruelty. If I push him too far, I know he won't hesitate to show me just how brutal he can be.

When I don't respond, he steps back and signals his men. Rico climbs into the passenger seat while Dante slides in beside me in the back. The door shuts with a heavy thud.

I remember Dante from when we were teenagers—he was always by Antonio's side. I wonder now if his allegiances have shifted, if he's more loyal to Valentino than Antonio these days.

The driver glances at me in the rearview mirror. "Three hours. Maybe more. The road is," he hesitates as he searches for the word. "*Piccola.*"

"*Grazie.*"

He nods politely, and the car pulls away, gliding smoothly into motion. Through the tinted windows, Valentino's figure grows smaller until he's out of sight. Settling in for the drive, the view outside shifts as the sprawling city of Naples gradually fades into the backdrop.

For a while, the passing scenery goes unnoticed, until something in the distance catches my attention—the unmistakable silhouette of Mt. Vesuvius. A surge of excitement stirs within me, cutting through the heaviness in my chest. Sitting up straighter, my breath catches.

"Please stop the car," I say quickly, my voice a little too eager.

"*Scusami?*" the driver asks, confused.

I fumble through my rusty Italian. "*Ferma la macchina, per favore.*"

He slows to a stop, and before anyone can react, I grab my

camera, fling the door open, and jump out. The cool air rushes against my face as I begin snapping pictures, drawn to the volcano's raw beauty, eager to capture every detail.

"*La strada è pericolosa. Devi tornare in macchina,*" the driver calls, but I barely register the words.

Behind me, Dante exchanges words with the driver, their voices low. He doesn't force me back into the car, though. It seems he's allowing me this moment, whether out of patience or reluctance, I'm not sure. Either way, I continue snapping until I have all the photographs I want.

Once I'm back in the car, I murmur, "*Grazie,*" as a small smile tugs at the corners of my mouth. It's the first time I've felt anything close to joy in days.

The driver shakes his head as he pulls back onto the busy road. This time, instead of wallowing in self-pity, I roll my window down and focus on the breathtaking views. The narrow road twists and turns along the cliffsides overlooking the sea.

I'm in awe as we drive through arched tunnels that look as though they were hand-carved through the mountain. Much to the annoyance of my driver, I ask him to stop the car several times so I can take photos of the panoramic views.

By the time we arrive at the luxurious villa perched on the hillside, I almost forget why I'm here. The view is stunning, and the villa itself is a masterpiece of Mediterranean architecture. For a moment, I ignore everything and allow myself to appreciate the beauty surrounding me.

"Mrs. Comiso," a voice says, interrupting my daydream. I turn to see a man in a crisp suit standing by the entrance. "I'm Paolo, your concierge. Please allow me to show you to your suite."

THREE WEEKS HAVE PASSED SINCE I LAST SAW OR HEARD from Valentino. The staff and Valentino's men are the only company I've had. It's a strange, almost surreal existence—living in such luxury, yet knowing that any sense of freedom is nothing more than an illusion.

As the days blur together, I try to find moments of escape. Each morning, I explore the villa grounds, strolling along the cliff-side paths with the cerulean water stretching out endlessly below. The beauty of the Amalfi Coast is undeniable. In those moments, I almost forget the circumstances that brought me here.

Photography has always been my escape. My camera is a constant companion, rarely leaving my side. I lose myself for hours, capturing the stunning vistas and vibrant colors of Italy. With each click of the shutter, I claim a small victory—a way to hold onto something that's truly mine, a quiet act of defiance.

The staff are kind and courteous. Paolo, in particular, has been attentive, bringing me books from local shops and treating me with a consideration that makes me wonder if he pities me, though he never lets it show. Despite the grandeur, it's the simple pleasures that bring me the most joy—reading a book on the terrace, sipping espresso in the garden, or feeling the warmth of the sun on my face.

Dante and Rico have been extremely accommodating. On several occasions, they allowed me to venture into the nearby town, staying just far enough away that I easily blend in with the tourists and locals. It's in these moments, wandering the markets, tasting fresh produce, and indulging in gelato by the sea, that I feel a semblance of normalcy. As if I'm just another visitor enjoying the charm of Italy.

The evenings are quiet, spent watching the sunset paint the sky in hues of pink and gold. I dine on exquisite food at a table set for one. Afterward, I retreat to my suite, enjoying the quiet and solitude the villa provides.

Just as I start to settle into this rhythm, my peace is abruptly shattered.

I'm on the balcony, lost in the view, when the distant thrum of a helicopter reaches my ears. My stomach tightens. I glance up, watching as it descends onto the helipad at the far end of the estate. A figure steps out, and even from this distance, the way he walks is unmistakable.

Valentino.

He's back.

I steady myself as he enters the villa, his presence immediately suffocating. He strides toward the balcony, his eyes finding mine, and the weight of his gaze is like a tightening grip, making it hard to breathe. "Enjoying yourself, Alessia?" he asks, a hint of amusement playing on his lips.

Swallowing hard, I meet his gaze. "I was, until now."

His smile widens, a predatory gleam in his eyes. "Good. I wouldn't want you to get too comfortable. Don't ever forget who holds the power here, princess."

"How could I forget?"

His eyes narrow slightly. "My men told me you've behaved very well." He pauses, gesturing toward the bed. "As a reward, I brought you something. You'll wear it tonight."

I say nothing, refusing to acknowledge his so-called gift.

He steps closer, his voice dropping to a low whisper. "It's been three weeks since I've touched a woman. After dinner, I plan to make up for lost time."

Valentino's return means the game resumes, and this time, he's going to take something I've held onto for years—something I always thought would be Antonio's. Instead, tonight, my virginity will be stolen by a man who will never appreciate its significance. To him, I'm just another object, something he can own and control.

Valentino

lessia took the bag and disappeared into the en suite. That was over an hour ago, and my patience is wearing thin. Ten more minutes—that's all I'll give her before I insist she opens the door.

My phone buzzes with an email notification. Opening my inbox, I find the message I've been waiting for. While in Sicily, Giancarlo tipped me off about a rare 1969 Duncan Taylor Macallan single malt scotch whiskey. It's not the elusive 1926 bottle I truly desire, but it'll be a fine addition to my collection.

The current owner is asking for one hundred thousand dollars—a modest sum to secure such a prized bottle. I reply promptly, arranging the wire transfer. By the time we're back in the States, it'll be resting in my cellarette.

Sliding the phone back into my pocket, I stand up. Alessia has taken long enough. Irritated, I pound on the door. "What's taking you so long?".

"I'm finishing my makeup," she replies.

"You've had more than enough time," I snap, impatience marring my tone.

There's a long pause before she speaks again. This time, her voice trembles slightly. "I don't want to do this."

"Stop this nonsense, Alessia. Open the door or I'll break it down."

The bathroom door creaks open, and she steps out slowly, her face flushed and eyes cast downward. The sheer white lingerie clings to her body, leaving nothing to the imagination. She wraps her arms around herself, trying to cover up.

"This is ridiculous, " she mumbles.

"You're being dramatic," I remark, my eyes darkening with desire. Hooking my arm around Alessia's waist, I pull her against me. "Do you feel what you're doing to me?" I grind my erection against her.

"I feel," she says, struggling to get out of my hold. "Let me go."

"Stop," I say, my grip tightening. "Drop your arms. I want to see what's mine."

My eyes rake over her exposed form, scrutinizing every detail. The sheer lingerie leaves nothing to the imagination—her curves and the way her breasts rise and fall with each breath.

Satisfied, I release her wrist. "That's better," I state plainly. She'll learn not to hide herself from me. If she doesn't comply willingly, there will be consequences. "Sit down, dinner's getting cold."

I take my seat across from her and uncover the dishes. The aroma of roasted lamb and truffle risotto fills the space.

"Eat," I command, lifting my fork.

She picks at her food, barely lifting her eyes. "While I was in Sicily, I made significant progress with the DeLuca *Famiglia*," I say, watching her closely. "We struck a deal that will allow them to move their product through Philadelphia."

"Their product?" she asks.

"Humans," I respond casually and take a bite of the roasted lamb, savoring the rich flavor.

Her fork clatters against her plate as she looks up at me, horrified. "You're letting them move trafficked people through our city? Are you insane?"

I raise an eyebrow, unimpressed by her outburst. "It's a growing business. The profits are skyrocketing. This deal will secure our position, bring in wealth beyond measure, and solidify my power."

She shakes her head, her anger rising. "You're going to ruin lives. How can you be so heartless?"

I sigh, barely containing my annoyance. "Don't be naïve. I'm not the one rounding them up. People want this, and I'm just making sure it happens."

"You have the power to make things better, but you're choosing to make it worse," she argues.

"Enough," I snap, my patience thinning. "This is happening, whether you like it or not. Now, be quiet and eat your dinner."

She shoots me a glare but keeps her mouth shut. I finish my meal in silence, watching as Alessia absently pushes the food around on her plate. Once I'm done, I set my glass down and make my way to her side of the table.

"It's time," I say, holding out my hand.

Her eyes widen, fear flashing in them. "Can't we just talk?"

"No," I reply coldly. "I've given you three weeks to prepare for tonight. I'm not waiting any longer."

She takes a step back, shaking her head. "I don't want this, Valentino. Please."

Grabbing her wrist, I pull her toward the bedroom. "You'll do as I say."

She tries to pull away, but my grip only tightens. "You're hurting me."

"Good," I say ignoring her protests and pushing her onto the mattress. She scrambles backward, but I grab her ankle and pulling her toward me. "Fighting turns me on, princess."

"Please," she begs, tears streaming down her face. "Valentino, don't do this."

"Enough," I hiss, climbing on top of her and pinning her beneath me. "This is happening. You don't have a choice."

Her fists beat against my chest, her body rigid with resistance, but it only fuels my determination. Not wasting time undressing her, I tear the lingerie exposing her fully to me. My hand travels down her toned abdomen. Alessia clenches her thighs together, trying to keep me out.

I've waited long enough. It's time to take what's mine. "Open," I command. I wedge my knee between her legs, catching my first glimpse of her smooth pussy. My cock throbs as I slowly work my finger deeper. "So damn tight."

"You're a monster," she yells, sinking her teeth into my arm.

"Dammit," I hiss. "That hurt."

"Good," she snarls, clawing at my chest. "Get your filthy hands off of me."

Grabbing her arms, I pin them above her head. "Fuck, I like it when you fight me." With my free hand, I open my pants, releasing my thick cock. Her eyes widen in terror as I stroke myself.

"Please, just let me go," she pleads.

"Not until I have this," I say as I rub the tip against her entrance. "I knew you wanted me. You're fucking soaked."

"That's only my body protecting itself," she says through her tears.

Slowly, I force my way in.

"Please, stop," she pleads.

"Begging only makes me harder," I laugh, pushing in some more but hitting resistance.

"I hate you."

"You can hate me all you want," I say as I thrust in hard, causing her to scream. "But now I own you." Her body grips me like a vice. The sensation is so overwhelming it nearly pushes me over the edge. I've never fucked a virgin before. Maybe I should do this more often.

Her screams and muffled sobs are music to my ears. I thrust deeper, harder, the pleasure almost too much to handle. "You're going to look so beautiful gagged and bound to my bed," I groan, bending down biting her nipple. She hisses in pain as she thrashes beneath me, driving me closer to the edge.

I'm not going to last much longer. My hand moves between us, finding her clit, circling it with my thumb. I usually don't care if the woman I'm with feels any pleasure, but this time, I'm going to make sure she does. Alessia needs to learn that her body belongs to me—that I control everything. "You're going to come for me like a good girl."

"No," she gasps, shaking her head.

"Oh yes, you will," I growl, my fingers flicking her clit as I thrust deeper. "Come all over my cock."

Her body shudders as her orgasm overtakes her. With a final thrust, I explode inside her, groaning as my release takes over. When the last wave subsides, I pull out and roll over. "You should thank me for letting you come," I say, breathing heavily.

"Fuck you," she spits, tears still falling.

"You ungrateful little bitch." I grab her by the hair and force her to look at me. "That's the last time I'll tolerate your mouth," I warn, my voice low and dangerous. "Coming on my cock is a privilege that you will thank me for." Her eyes blaze with fury. "Now."

"Thank you," she whispers through her tears.

"Better." I release her with a slight shove.

Alessia turns away from me, curling up into a ball.

"Goodnight, princess."

I've been waiting to claim her virginity since the day I told Antonio that Alessia was mine. I can't wait until we return home so I can see the look on his face, knowing I possess something he can never have.

As her quiet sobs fill the room, I drift off to sleep.

Alessia

He raped me, and I orgasmed for him. How could my body betray me like that? The thought churns in my mind, a sickening mix of shame and confusion. Sitting up in bed, I clutch the sheets around me, trying to shake off the memory of his touch on my skin—inside me.

Valentino lies beside me, sound asleep. I can't bear to look at him—the man who stole everything from me. We're isolated in a luxurious villa, miles away from anyone who could help me. Even if we were surrounded by people, no one would dare stand up to him.

Careful not to wake him, I slip out of bed and tiptoe to the en suite. Shutting the door behind me, I catch my reflection in the mirror. The face staring back at me is a haunting reminder of my humiliation.

The shower comes on, water running as hot as I can stand it. Stepping in, I scrub my skin until it's red and raw, as if I can somehow erase the memory of his touch. Steam fills the room, matching the fog clouding my thoughts. With my forehead pressed against the cool tile, tears mix with the water cascading down my face.

How did it come to this? How could my body betray me in the most intimate way.

The water eventually runs cold, but I stay under the stream, shivering, until the chill becomes unbearable. Wrapping a towel around myself, I return to the bedroom, praying Valentino's still asleep.

He stirs as I enter, his eyes blinking open. "Couldn't sleep?" he asks, his voice relaxed.

I freeze, hoping not to fully wake him.

With a small sigh, he turns away, his eyes drifting shut once more. I crawl back into bed, lying as far from him as possible. The early morning light filters through the curtains. A cruel reminder that another day is beginning.

IN THE DAYS THAT FOLLOW, I TRY TO PUT ON A BRAVE face, playing the role of the dutiful wife, while inside, I'm screaming. Valentino makes the most out of our last week in Italy, dragging me to lavish restaurants where he can flaunt me like a shiny new toy.

He continually boasts about his plans, his eyes gleaming with ambition. "I can see it now," he says, a dangerous hunger in his tone. "I'll be unstoppable. The money, the power—it's all within my grasp."

I nod absently, trying not to upset him. I've quickly learned that disagreeing with him is a painful mistake.

Valentino leans in, his hand resting possessively on my knee. "You're a part of this too, Alessia. Together, we can have everything."

I force another smile. "Of course, Valentino. Together."

Our honeymoon eventually comes to an end, and we board a crowded flight back to Philadelphia. I pretend to sleep, hoping to steal a moment of peace.

"I know you're awake," Val whispers, his lips brushing against my neck while his hand trails up the inside of my thigh.

Opening my eyes, I'm met with his dark stare, I gently push his hand away. "We're surrounded by people."

Valentino sits up slightly, his hand still resting possessively on my leg. "We're newlyweds, Alessia. It's important that we maintain appearances," he says. "We'll be landing soon. When we do, I expect you on my arm, like the eye candy you're meant to be."

Ignoring his comments, I ask, "Where will we be living?"

He leans back, a smug grin spreading across his face. "As you know, we own most of the block. My father prepared one of his houses for us."

"I see."

"I expect you'll find it to your liking," Valentino continues. "It's a spacious property with all the amenities you could desire."

"I'm sure it's lovely," I reply evenly.

I shift in my seat to look out the window, watching the clouds pass by.

"This will be a new chapter for me," he murmurs. "A chance for me to build my empire."

I bite back a sigh. It's always about him—his power, his ambitions. I wonder where I fit into his plans and how much it'll cost me.

"Is he downstairs?" I ask Guido, one of our newer soldiers who's guarding the entrance.

"He is. Dante brought him in through the back entrance about twenty minutes ago."

Salvatore, the man waiting downstairs, owes a substantial gambling debt—a debt that, like his arrogance and disregard for our warnings, has become quite an annoyance. The hum of voices inside blends with the clink of glasses, a stark contrast to the tension simmering below.

Adjusting the collar of my jacket, I feel the weight of the night settling over us. This issue with Salvatore should've been dealt with weeks ago, but Vigo insisted Dante accompany him and Alessia on their honeymoon, delaying everything. Now that Dante's back, it's time to get to work.

"Let's move," I say as I lead the way down a narrow staircase. Each step echoes in the confined space, a harbinger of the confrontation awaiting us below. We pass through our meeting room into an unfinished section of the basement where harsh, flickering overhead bulbs cast a sickly, uneven glow across the space.

At a battered table in the corner sits Salvatore, his posture tense as he nervously taps ashes from a cigarette that burns low between his fingers. He looks up as we approach, his eyes widening with a mix of fear and defiance.

"Antonio," he starts, his voice shaky but attempting to muster some semblance of bravado. "I've been trying to explain to Dante that I just need a little more time, and I'll have your money. This is all overkill."

I stop a few feet away, my gaze fixed on him, cold and unwavering. This is where I'm in my element. There's a strange satisfaction in the rhythm of it all. The way things unfold, the certainty of consequence. It's not about power but the process and precision. The understanding that in our world, everything has a price.

"You've had more than enough time," I reply evenly.

"My little girl was sick," he blurts out too fast, giving away his lie. "I needed the extra cash to take care of her." He stabs out his cigarette on the table.

I tilt my head and lower my voice with fake sympathy. "Why didn't you come to me? I'd never deny a child medical treatment."

He shifts in his seat, uneasy. "Yeah, I should've called you. I'll know for next time," he says, moving to stand. Dante shoves him back into the chair, holding him down by the shoulders.

"But you didn't call me? Did you? No. You disappeared." Leaning forward, I plant my hands on the table. "Do you take me for a fool?"

"No, Antonio," he stammers, his eyes darting nervously between Dante and me. "You know I don't."

"Then why lie to me about a child you don't have?" I ask, my voice lethally quiet.

"I made a mistake. I can get the money, I swear," he insists, desperation seeping into his voice. "Just give me a few days—"

"Enough," I cut him off sharply. "I've given you more chances than you deserve. Now you come into my house and lie to my face. It's time to settle up."

Salvatore's shoulders slump in defeat, the weight of his situation pressing down on him like a vice. "You don't have to do this," he pleads. "I just need a little more money for a game tonight. Then, I'll be able to pay you everything I owe. Please, Antonio—"

I meet his gaze with unwavering determination. "It's too late for second chances," I say firmly, my voice echoing in the basement's stagnant air. "Let's get this over with, Dante. I have other things to do tonight."

The room falls silent, except for the shuffle of footsteps and the quiet rasp of Salvatore's uneven breaths. Dante drags him from his chair, forcing him to his knees. I remain poised, watching with a mix of resolve and regret. This is the price of defiance in our world—a world where debts are settled with finality and loyalty is forged through actions, not words.

Salvatore begs and pleads for his life while I pull my Glock 19 from its holster, screwing the silencer in place. The click of the magazine snapping into place echoes in the small room.

My father's always on my case to use one of our unmarked guns to make sure nothing's ever traced back to me. I understand his concern, but I have complete faith in our men. They make sure there's a thorough clean-up and that the bodies are never found. Their meticulous work is why I feel entirely at ease using my own gun.

Turning, I lift my arm, aim at the man who now has a wet spot down his leg, and pull the trigger. His body slumps to the floor as blood pools around him. Calmly, I click the safety into place and remove the silencer, passing it to Dante before holstering my gun.

Without a word, I turn and leave the room. The night outside feels still, a stark contrast to the cold finality inside, but to me, it's just another debt settled. Another reminder of what it means to cross the Comiso *Famiglia*.

Alessia

y eyes open, and for a moment I'm disoriented. Pushing up on my elbows, I glance around the still unfamiliar room. Even though Val and I have been back for several weeks, it still doesn't feel like my home. The decor is extravagant, every room meticulously arranged, but it all feels cold and impersonal—like I'm a guest in someone else's life rather than living my own.

Valentino told me to do what I wanted with the house, so I am. I met with a designer last week. We settled on a muted, neutral pallet that'll go perfectly with the antiques my grandparents left for me and the modern pieces I purchased.

When I reach my arm over to Val's side of the bed, I find it cold. He must've gotten up early. The less I have to see of him, the better. I never thought I'd actually *prefer* him to stay out with one of the women he sleeps with. But since we've returned from Italy, he's come home every night demanding sex. There's no tenderness, no affection—just his relentless need to dominate.

With a groan, I push myself out of bed, ignoring the ache in my limbs. I need to get out of this house, even if it's just for a little while. My camera, full of photos from Italy, sits on the dresser—a reminder of the freedom I felt there. A trip to the gallery might be just the slice of normalcy I need.

I pull on a pair of jeans and a loose sweater—something practical for an afternoon out. The last thing I want is to draw any unnecessary attention, especially with Valentino's men everywhere. I know there's no slipping out alone, but maybe he'll allow one of the friendlier guards to go with me. Grabbing my camera bag, I sling it over my shoulder and head downstairs, bracing myself for whatever comes next.

Antonio stands in the hallway, deep in conversation with a man I don't recognize. I'm caught off guard seeing him here. A part of me hopes that the small kindness he showed me the night of my wedding might still be there. But as I approach and his eyes shift to me, any trace of warmth is gone, replaced by cold detachment. He's just as callous as the rest. And yet, he still feels more familiar than anyone else. Cold or not, he seems like the safest choice.

"May I speak with you for a moment?"

He dismisses the man and turns to me. "What can I do for you, Mrs. Comiso?"

I roll my eyes. "Really? What's with the formalities?"

"You're married to Valentino now," he replies, his tone carefully measured.

"That's not my fault," I mumble under my breath, causing Antonio to raise an eyebrow. "There's no reason you can't call me Alessia. If Val has a problem, I'll handle it."

He seems to ignore my request. "What do you need?"

"I want to go out. Can you take me?"

His eyes narrow slightly. "Where do you want to go?"

"I need to go to the store to pick up a few things."

"What kind of things?"

"Personal things," I reply vaguely, hoping he won't push for details. "It's important."

He studies me for a long moment, his expression unreadable. "As long as your husband approves, I'll take you."

Relief washes over me. "Thank you."

Reluctantly, I go to Val's office to ask permission. He barely glances up from whatever he's doing, his tone curt. "Do whatever you want. I'm going out anyway," he mutters, dismissing me before I can even get the words out.

Antonio and I walk to the garage in silence. As I follow him, a twinge of guilt nags at me for not being completely honest but selling my pictures is something Valentino can never know about.

"Where are we headed?" Antonio asks as we get into one of the sleek black cars.

I input the address for Starlight Studios in the GPS, and he pulls out of the driveway. Staring out the window, my thoughts race as I think about the photos I've taken and the potential buyers for them.

Antonio slows to a stop outside the gallery. I know better than to step out before he comes around, so I wait until he opens the door for me.

"Do you mind waiting outside?" I ask, my voice steady but imploring. "I want to get our honeymoon photos developed. Some of them are personal."

His eyes scan the street, vigilant as ever. "Go. I'll be right here."

Inside, Ophelia greets me with a bright smile. "Allie, it's good to see you. How was your honeymoon?"

"It was lovely. Thank you for asking," I respond, forcing a smile.

"Do you have some more photos for me?" she asks eagerly.

"I do." I pass her the memory card.

She slides it into her computer, tapping a few keys before the images of the Amalfi Coast fill the screen. Her eyes light up as she clicks through them.

"This is some of your best work yet," she says, admiration in her voice.

"Thank you," I reply, feeling a surge of pride despite everything.

"Have you spoken to your husband about having a show?" she inquires.

I swallow the lie before it comes out. "I have, but he'd rather I not do it. He's worried about too much public attention."

She frowns. "That's a shame. You're so talented."

"I know," I say, hating the resignation in my voice. "But I understand his concerns."

Ophelia clicks to one of my favorite shots, a panoramic view of the coast at sunset. The sky was full of pinks and reds. "Would you mind printing this on a canvas? I'd like it for my new house."

"Of course," she says, jotting down the details for the matte and frame.

After I pay for my purchase, I return to where Antonio's waiting patiently, his gaze distant but alert.

"All set?" he asks as he opens the car door.

Hesitating for a moment, I glance at him. "Can you not mention this to Val? He doesn't need to know where I went."

For a moment, there's silence between us. Antonio starts the car, his expression unreadable. Finally, he nods, his tone steady but relaxed. "I won't say anything."

"Thank you, Antonio," I say softly. "It really means a lot to me."

"No problem."

The drive back to the estate is silent, each of us lost in our own thoughts. I steal a glance at Antonio, wondering, just for a moment, what would happen if I told him the truth—that Val is hurting me. Would he help? Deep down, I know the answer. His loyalty lies with his family, and any kindness I thought existed between us is buried beneath that duty.

As the house comes into view, a sense of dread sinks in. Valentino might not be home now, but when he returns, it all starts again—his demands, the unspoken rules I have to follow, the nights I'm forced to endure him. There's no escape, just the endless waiting for him to take what he thinks is his, again and again.

The sudden ring of Antonio's phone jolts me, and I flinch. He glances at me, curiosity in his eyes, before answering the call. "Where are you?" A man's voice fills the space.

"I'm with Alessia. What's up?"

"You need to get to the restaurant. Now."

"I'm on my way," he responds curtly. Disconnecting the phone, he turns to me. "You need to go inside."

"What's wrong?" I ask, anxiety creeping in.

"I don't know," he says, his voice firm. "That's what I'm going to find out."

Valentino

My father called earlier this morning, requesting I join him for lunch. I've been expecting this.

"Today's the day," I say aloud.

I knew once I married Alessia, he'd have no more excuses. He has no choice but to step down, finally allowing me to take my place as the head of the family. Everything I've been planning is about to fall into place.

I quickly send an email to Giancarlo, letting him know I'll be able to move our timeline forward and that I'll be in touch soon. With that handled, I leave for the restaurant.

As soon as I walk in, Lena spots me and makes her way over, swaying her hips.

"Is my father here yet?" I ask when she stops in front of me, her gaze lingering a bit longer than necessary.

"I haven't seen him," she says, stepping closer, her voice sultry. "I haven't seen you in a while either." Her finger trails along my arm.

Glancing around, I notice the restaurant's nearly empty. The few patrons around are too engrossed in their conversations to pay attention. "I've been busy," I reply, keeping my tone casual, even though I'm already getting hard.

"It sounds like you're working too much." She drops her hand, cupping my erection. "Maybe you need a break?"

My eyes dart between the clock on the wall and Lena. "Maybe I do."

Taking her by the wrist, I lead her to the back office. As soon as the door closes, the tension between us snaps. Unbuttoning her silky shirt, I pull the cups of her bra down, exposing her breasts. I capture a nipple between my teeth and tug.

"Valentino," she breathes. "I've missed you."

"Prove it," I growl, pushing her to her knees. She looks up at me, her eyes hungry, and eagerly takes me into her mouth. A groan escapes as my fingers tangle in her hair.

"Don't stop," I command, my voice rough. It's been too long since I've had an experienced mouth wrapped around my dick. My grip tightens as I thrust deeper into her throat.

"Valentino," she gasps, pulling back for a moment. "I want you."

"You want me?" I pull her up roughly and bend her over the desk. My hands slide up her thighs, hiking up her skirt as she arches her back.

"Is this what you wanted?" I growl, my voice thick with lust. Gripping her hips, I drive into her with hard, relentless strokes.

"Yes," she pants, her fingers digging into the edge of the desk. "Harder."

I give her what she asks for, pounding into her, the room filled with the sounds of our bodies colliding. There's nothing tender or gentle about this—it's raw, primal, and exactly what I need.

"Valentino," she cries out. "I'm close."

Her body shutters as an orgasm ripples through her. The sight and feel of her climax push me over the edge, and I spill into her with a guttural groan.

Pulling out, I quickly adjust my clothes as she smooths down her skirt. There's no need for sweet talk or empty promises of romance. This was never about anything more than satisfying an urge.

Just as my hand reaches for the door, it swings open, and I almost collide with my father. His gaze sweeps over me, then lands on Lena standing behind me, her face still flushed.

"What's going on here?" he demands.

"I was having a word with Lena," I reply casually, without bothering to look at her.

His eyes narrow, suspicion clearly evident. "You have tables waiting, Lena. Get back to work."

"Yes, Mr. Comiso," she says quietly as she slips out of the room.

Once she's gone, my father's expression hardens, "You're a married man, Valentino."

"I'm aware," I respond, meeting his gaze without flinching

"Have you no desire to be faithful to your wife?" he presses.

I shrug dismissively. "My wife doesn't care what I do in my free time. Actually, I think she'd be pleased to know I'm satisfying my needs elsewhere."

"You must give her time. Alessia needs to know she can trust you before—"

"I don't need you telling me how to conduct my marriage."

He sighs, his shoulders slumping in defeat. "We'll have lunch downstairs."

"Fine. Let's go."

The walk down is quiet, tension simmering between us. My father doesn't have to like how I live my life, but I refuse to let him force his outdated views on me.

When we walk into the meeting room, I notice the table is set for three.

"Who else is joining us?" I ask, a hint of annoyance creeping into my voice.

"I invited your Uncle Marco. He's running a bit late and said to start without him."

A server arrives, taking my father's drink order. "What can I get for you, sir?" she asks.

"I'll have my usual."

"Whiskey on the rocks?" she confirms, casually brushing against my arm as she does. My father's gaze moves between us, clearly catching the interaction.

"I called ahead for our food order," he says, his tone a bit tighter as he turns his attention to her. "How long until it's ready?"

"The chef was waiting for your drink order before plating."

"Tell him we're ready."

"Yes, Mr. Comiso," she responds, giving a slight nod.

After she leaves, I don't bother to wait. "I assume we're here to discuss your retirement."

My father looks up. "I'd prefer to eat before we discuss business."

"There's no reason to wait," I argue, barely masking my impatience. "I do have a wife to get home to."

He sighs, looking weary. "Very well, Vigo. Let's get to it." He takes a deep breath, his tone more serious. "The Comiso family has been in control of this city for generations."

"I know all that

"It's crucial that we continue this legacy with strength and wisdom."

"I understand the importance of our family's legacy."

My father's gaze sharpens. "There's more to being a leader than ambition. It's about earning respect and trust."

"I have respect," I snap, irritated. "And trust. You can ask anyone."

"Respect is not demanded, Valentino. It's earned." A knock on the door interrupts us. "Come in," he calls.

The server returns with our drinks and food. I glare at my father but remain silent until we're alone.

"You think I haven't earned it?"

He hesitates, looking me in the eye. "Valentino, I've been considering my next steps very carefully. To ensure the family's continued success and stability, I've decided that Marco will take over as Capo," he states, his voice firm.

I freeze, momentarily stunned. "What?"

"You need more time to prove yourself," he says, standing his ground. "That's why I'm promoting you to underboss. It will give you the experience you need to eventually become Capo."

Fury burns through me. "After everything I've done—after marrying that frigid bitch, you're still giving it to Marco?"

"Calm down."

"Calm down?" I shout.

"Son, this isn't about punishing you. You'll have your chance," he says, his expression softening slightly. "But you need more time in a leadership role before taking the top spot."

"More time?" I ask, my temper flaring. "What more do I need to do?"

"It's crucial that you gain more experience as underboss and earn the trust of our men. You need to demonstrate wisdom and restraint—qualities I'm afraid you still lack. Marco has the experience and respect of the family," he continues, but I barely register his words.

"You're holding me back. I'm ready now."

"Your actions say otherwise," he snaps back, his voice rising. "This isn't about what *you* want. It's about what's best for the family."

"This is my rightful place," I hiss through clenched teeth. "I won't let you take it away from me."

My father's face pales, but he remains resolute. "You will respect my decision."

"Respect?" I laugh bitterly. "You've never respected me."

"Valentino, calm down," my father says, his voice strained.

"Calm down? This is bullshit," I shout, slamming my fists onto the table. Plates and glasses rattle with the impact. I shove my chair back violently, the legs scraping against the floor. "I'm tired of being treated like a child," I roar, grabbing a glass and hurling it against the wall. It shatters, fragments scattering across the floor.

"Enough," my father commands, but there's a tremor in his

voice. "This is exactly what I'm talking about. You must control your temper in challenging situations. You're reckless."

"I'll show you reckless," I sneer, grabbing him by the collar and dragging him from his chair. "You've never believed in me." I shake him violently.

My father's eyes widen, a mix of shock and fear flashing across his face. "You're ruining everything," I yell, stepping closer until I'm right in his face. "Every sacrifice I made, every plan I put into place. All for you to throw it away on some ridiculous notion that Marco's better suited. You think I can't handle this? You think I'm weak?"

He gasps for air, his hand trembling as it clutches my arm. "Valentino, stop."

"Stop?" I laugh maniacally. "You've underestimated me for the last time. I am Valentino Comiso, and I will take what's rightfully mine," I growl and release him with a shove, sending him sprawling to the floor.

He clutches his chest, his breathing growing ragged. Pain and betrayal fill his eyes before he slumps forward, his body giving out.

"What's wrong with you? Get up," I demand coldly, but he doesn't respond.

The door bursts open. "I'm sorry I'm late," Uncle Marco says, slightly out of breath. "Nicky needed..." He stops mid-sentence, his gaze shifting from me to my father. "What happened?"

"I don't know. He just collapsed," I reply, my voice devoid of concern.

Uncle Marco rushes across the room, dropping to his knees beside my father. "Call an ambulance," he barks his orders at me. "Now."

The world shifts around me. Even as my father lies unconscious at my feet, I feel nothing. All I can focus on is the power within my reach—the power that's about to be mine.

Antonio

Once I'm alone in the car, I call Dante to get more information about what's going on.

"Are you alone?" he asks.

"I am."

"Guido called. Bossman and Valentino were having lunch. Your uncle collapsed. I don't have all the details. All I know is that your father's there and an ambulance was called."

"I'm on my way," I reply and hang up.

My heart hammers in my chest, adrenaline surging as I blow through every red light in the city. I'll deal with any traffic violations later. Getting to the restaurant as fast as possible is my only concern.

The car screeches to a stop behind an ambulance that's parked outside the restaurant. I burst through the front door, hurrying across the dining room. Taking the steps two at a time, I rush downstairs. EMTs are crowded around Uncle Gio, performing chest compressions.

I spot Valentino standing in the far corner. "What happened?"

"We had just got our food and were discussing the future of the family," Valentino explains. "Dad was telling me it was time for me to take over as Capo."

Studying him, I try to read between the lines of his carefully constructed facade. "And then what?" The suspicion in my voice is unmistakable as I press for more.

"He just collapsed," Valentino replies, his voice strained but composed.

"Collapsed out of nowhere?" Suspicion creeps into my voice, the feeling that there's more to the story lingering in my mind.

His gaze falters briefly, a hint of defensiveness crossing his expression. "Yes. It happened so suddenly. I was still in shock when your father arrived."

"Stay here," I say, turning toward my father, who stands nearby, watching everything unfold.

"What happened?" I ask quietly, my eyes fixed on Uncle Gio's motionless body on the floor.

Dad's face is etched with worry. "I got here late," he admits. "I found him like this and called for help immediately."

"We need to let them work," I say, fighting to keep my voice steady while panic claws at me from within. The thought of losing him feels unbearable.

A glance at Valentino reveals a crack in his mask. But he quickly regains his composure, surveying the room with an air of cool detachment.

The minutes crawl by painfully slow as we watch the EMTs work with urgency, hooking him up to machines and preparing to transport him to the hospital. "I'll go with him," Dad says, already moving to follow the stretcher.

Valentino nods. "I'll handle things here," he states calmly, despite the gravity of the situation.

Pushing past him, I rush to catch up with the EMTs. "Which hospital are you taking him to?" I ask as they load the stretcher into the ambulance.

"Thomas Jefferson," one of them answers.

"I'll go home and get Aunt Domenica and Mom," I add quickly, already turning to go back to my car.

My hands shake as I race back across the city. I hit the phone button on my steering wheel, calling Enzo, our Consigliere.

"How is he?" he asks, his voice tense.

"It doesn't look good," I admit, my voice tight. "I'm heading to get my family."

"Do you know what happened?"

I tread carefully, avoiding my suspicions for now. "Uncle Gio and Valentino were having lunch. Vigo said he clutched his chest and collapsed. By the time I got there, he was unconscious," I say, clearing my throat and pushing my emotions aside. "My father's with them. They're heading to Thomas Jefferson. We need to send guards."

"I'll take care of it," Enzo replies firmly. "Is Val with them?"

"No. He stayed at the restaurant."

"He didn't go with his father?" Enzo's question is laced with accusation.

"I think he was in shock," I say, covering for him, though doubt lingers.

We end the call just as I'm pulling up in front of my parents' house. Across the street, I spot Alessia on her porch.

"Antonio." She hurries across the street. "Val called and told me what happened.

"Where's Rico?"

"He's in the house. I told him I'd stay on the porch."

"That's where you should be," I correct her, my tone firm. "Now's not the time to be taking off alone."

"I'm not alone. I'm with you," she counters, crossing her arms.

"Go back home, Alessia." I gesture across the street.

"I'm going to the hospital with you," she says defiantly.

"No. You're not."

"Yes, I am."

I grab the back of my neck, feeling the strain. "I don't have time for this right now."

"You're right," she says, her tone softening. "Go get your mom. I'll get Domenica."

Alessia's dark brown eyes, full of determination, meet mine. "Fine," I agree reluctantly. "But don't leave her house until I get there."

She lowers her arms before turning and hurrying toward Uncle Gio's house.

Dealing with Rico will have to wait—right now, getting to the hospital is all that matters. Once Alessia is safely inside, I head into my parents' house to get my mother.

Antonio

The ride to the hospital is tense. Aunt Domenica sits in the back seat, dabbing at her eyes with a handkerchief, while my mother holds her, whispering soft reassurances. Alessia, in the front passenger seat, casts worried glances my way every few minutes. It's clear she has a hundred questions, but she stays silent.

Cecilia's still in class, unaware of what's happening. Dante's on his way to inform her and bring her to the hospital.

When we arrive at Thomas Jefferson Hospital, the sterile smell of antiseptic greets us as soon as we step inside. The harsh fluorescent lights and stark white walls do nothing to calm our frayed nerves. At the check-in desk, I give my uncle's name. The receptionist nods somberly and makes a quick phone call.

Within minutes, a nurse arrives and leads us through the corridors to a private waiting room, away from the chaos of the emergency department. Inside, I find my father pacing restlessly.

"Marco," my mom cries, hurrying over to him. He wraps his arms around her as she breaks down.

"Shh," he murmurs, pressing a kiss to her forehead. "Gio's strong. He'll pull through."

Even as he says the words, I see the doubt clouding his eyes.

"I need to be with him," Aunt Domenica whispers, her voice trembling with desperation.

"The doctor said he'll be out when they've stabilized him," Dad explains. "Until then, all we can do is wait."

Alessia gently takes Domenica's arm, guiding her to an empty seat. My mother joins them, offering quiet comfort. Moving to the doorway, I watch as medical staff move briskly through the halls.

A gurney rolls past, the patient groaning in pain beneath an oxygen mask. Across the hall, an elderly couple sits together in another waiting room, the woman gently stroking the man's hand. Their silent companionship, filled with decades of shared history, is both touching and heart-wrenching.

The intercom crackles, announcing a code blue from another part of the emergency department. A team of doctors and nurses rush by, their focus determined, ready to face the crisis head-on.

People pass by, each face reflecting a different story—hope, fear, or exhaustion. A young mother cradles her child, whispering soothing words as a nurse checks the little one's vitals. Nearby, a middle-aged man paces, speaking in hushed tones over the phone. Every moment reminds me of the fragile balance between life and death.

I'm about to move when my father steps up beside me.

"Are you holding up okay?" he asks, his voice laced with concern.

"I think Valentino had more to do with this than he's letting on," I say, keeping my voice low.

His eyes narrow slightly and he leans in closer. "I've been thinking the same thing. He seemed too calm, too unaffected. Even for him."

"Vigo said Uncle Gio told him he wanted him to take over as Capo just before he collapsed," I whisper.

Dad shakes his head. "It doesn't make sense. Gio and I talked earlier today. He called the meeting to tell Vigo I was stepping in for now."

"What do you think we should do?"

"We'll figure it out, Anton. But for now, we focus on your uncle."

Every minute feels like an eternity. I'm just taking a seat when the doctor walks in, his expression grave. "Are you the family of Mr. Comiso?" he asks.

"Yes, we are." My father steps forward. "This is his wife," he adds, motioning to Aunt Domenica.

The doctor closes the door and sits next to her. He takes a moment to gather his thoughts before speaking. "I'm Dr. Langley, the cardiologist on call. Your husband suffered a major heart attack."

A collective gasp ripples through the room. Aunt Domenica clutches my mother's hand tighter, her face pales. Mom's eyes widen, filling with fresh tears.

"The heart attack affected a large portion of his heart, causing extensive damage to the tissue. Right now, his heart is very weak," Dr. Langley explains.

"What can be done for him?" I ask.

"WE'VE ADMINISTERED MEDICATIONS TO HELP HIS heart pump more effectively and to prevent further clots," he replies. "If he stabilizes, we may consider more advanced interventions—angioplasty, or possibly bypass surgery."

"What are his chances of survival?" Aunt Domenica asks, her voice barely a whisper.

The doctor's expression is grave. "It's hard to say for certain. The next 24 to 48 hours are critical. We'll do everything we can, but I need you to be prepared—there's a possibility he won't recover."

Aunt Domenica stifles a sob and my mother wraps an arm

around her. "Can we see him?" she asks, her voice choked with emotion.

"Yes, but only two at a time," Dr. Langley instructs.

My father steps forward. "I'm sure you know who Mr. Comiso is." The doctor nods. "We have security on the way. Until they arrive, my family stays together."

Dr. Langley hesitates. "All right, but please, keep it brief and quiet. He's still in critical condition, and we can't risk any unnecessary stress."

Uncle Gio lies in the hospital bed, tubes and wires connecting him to the equipment, each breath assisted by the mechanical hiss of a ventilator.

Aunt Domenica rushes to his side, clutching his hand. My mother follows, whispering a desperate prayer. I stand at the foot of the bed, struggling to reconcile the image of him now as he clings to life with the strong man I've always known.

Alessia places her hand on my arm. "He's going to be okay," she whispers and I want to believe her, but seeing Uncle Gio like this makes it hard to hold on to hope.

My father stands near the entrance to the room, arms crossed, body tense, and expression unreadable as he keeps watch, knowing our men haven't arrived yet.

Alessia stays close, her calming presence steadying me. The urge to pull her closer is almost overwhelming, and for a moment, my arm moves to wrap around her. But I stop myself because she's not mine to hold.

Suddenly, the machines start beeping erratically. The medical team springs into action, rushing into the room. My father quickly moves the women aside, guiding them to a corner as doctors and nurses surround Uncle Gio.

Aunt Domenica clutches her handkerchief to her mouth, her eyes wide and filled with terror, unable to look away as they work on her husband. Silent tears streak down her face as she grips my mother's arm, trembling.

A nurse begins compressions, pressing down rhythmically, trying to coax Uncle Gio's heart back into a steady rhythm. Each push forces blood through his body, keeping his organs alive while his heart struggles. Another presses a mask over his face, ensuring he's getting enough oxygen while his body fights to hold on.

Dr. Langley steps in taking charge, his voice steady but urgent as he issues commands. The team moves efficiently, placing defibrillator pads on Uncle Gio's chest while the doctor directs the timing of medications, his instructions cutting through the chaos.

Aunt Domenica lets out a soft whimper. "Please, Gio...please."

With the defibrillator charged, Dr. Langley calls for everyone to clear. A shock jolts Uncle Gio's body, causing it to convulse. We all hold our breath, watching the monitor. There's a spike—a small flicker of hope, but it fades as quickly as it came.

Undeterred, the team continues, cycling through compressions, medication, and shocks, each step crucial in their attempt to restart his heart.

My father grips my shoulder, his face pale. "This doesn't look good, Anton."

A lump forms in my throat, and my stomach knots as I watch everything unfold. I'm used to being the one who knows what to do—but right now, I feel completely helpless. The team works tirelessly, but it's clear that despite everything they're doing, Uncle Gio is slipping away.

The line on the monitor, once spiking with each attempt to revive him, now lies flat. A single, steady tone fills the room, signaling the end. I stand frozen as Dr. Langley reaches up and turns off the machine, cutting the sound. The silence that follows is even more unbearable, the finality settling over us.

"I'm sorry," the doctor says softly, his eyes filled with genuine sympathy. "He's gone."

Aunt Domenica lets out a wail of raw, agonizing grief. Mom clings to her, both of them sobbing uncontrollably. Dad holds them tightly against his chest. Alessia places a hand on my arm, reminding me I'm not alone even as numbness washes over me. Everything feels distant and unreal.

The door bursts open, and Valentino strides in, his face etched with shock. "What happened?" he demands, looking around, his voice laced with disbelief.

"He's dead," I say flatly, my gaze locking onto his.

Studying him closely, I search for cracks in his facade.

"That's not possible. We were just having lunch," he says, as if trying to convince everyone.

Aunt Domenica, her voice trembling, asks, "Did he say anything before... before he..."

Valentino's gaze drops to the floor for a moment before he looks back up, a steely resolve in his eyes. "He told me he was proud of me and that he was ready to introduce me as the new Capo," he replies as he steps toward his mother. "I'm sorry I didn't get here sooner."

"You're here now," she sobs as she clings to her son.

On the surface, Valentino's grief appears raw, even genuine, but something feels off. A lingering doubt hangs in the air, though the full picture remains unclear.

Valentino leads his mother to the bedside. Aunt Domenica reaches out to stroke her husband's cheek. Then, leaning down, she whispers something softly, words meant only for the man she spent her life with.

Seeing Uncle Gio's lifeless body becomes too much to bear, prompting me to turn away. As I do, my gaze falls on Alessia standing silently behind Valentino. Even with her husband beside her, her gaze lingers on me.

After we say our goodbyes to my uncle, we leave the hospital. My father holds my mother close, and Aunt Domenica stays near Valentino. Alessia walks by my side, but as we reach the parking lot, she hesitates, looking torn. The conflict in her eyes is clear— she wants to stay near me, but she knows her place is with her husband, even if she hates him.

"Antonio," she says softly. "I have to go with Val."

"I know."

Driving out of the parking lot, an ominous thought settles over me.

Something dark is on the horizon, something that will change everything.

Valentino

Uncle Marco and Antonio take their places, standing vigil beside the casket as I escort my mother into the viewing room, her arm linked with mine for support. She carries herself with remarkable poise until her eyes fall on my father's corpse, her composure crumbles. Tears slip silently down her cheeks as she places a single red rose beside his folded hands, a quiet, final tribute to the life they shared.

Once our immediate family finishes their private viewing, the room is opened to the public. Alessia joins me in the reception line as mourners begin to trickle in, their voices hushed with respect. Among them are representatives from other *Famiglias* who came to pay their respects. Their presence is a reminder of the intricate web of alliances my father held within the community.

Despite the complicated relationship with my father, I understand the importance of keeping up appearances. One by one, guests approach, offering their condolences. I meet each of them with a practiced expression as I accept their gesture of respect.

My father-in-law, Draco, is one of the last through the line. "Your husband was a good man," he says as he kisses my mother on the cheek. "He'll be greatly missed."

She dabs at her tear-filled eyes, unable to find her voice.

Draco turns to me, his eyes sharp. "I'm sorry for your loss," he offers, extending his hand.

"Thank you."

"I assume you'll be stepping into his shoes?" he asks, his tone probing as if testing the waters.

"I will," I say without hesitation.

"I'm looking forward to a strong alliance under your leadership," Draco continues.

"Father, discussing business at a viewing seems inappropriate," Alessia interjects quietly.

I grip her arm, my voice dropping low. "You'd do well to remember your place," I warn. "Or perhaps you need a lesson on how to behave?"

Alessia's gaze is steady and defiant, but she wisely bites back her response.

Draco's lips twitch into a faint smile. "My daughter was never good at minding her place. It's good to see you using a strong hand with her."

"I'll ensure she becomes the model Capo's wife," I say with pride.

He nods approvingly. "Once again, we're sorry for your loss."

"Thank you for your condolences," I reply, keeping my tone even. "I look forward to a prosperous future for our families."

THE FUNERAL ITSELF IS A GRAND AFFAIR, A FITTING tribute to the Capo of the most powerful family in Philadelphia. The church is packed with mourners, not just family and friends but also members of rival families who came to pay their respects. I sit at the front, the image of the grieving son, though my mind is far from sorrowful.

As the service begins, Uncle Marco steps up to the podium to deliver my father's eulogy. His voice carries through the church as he speaks of my father's unparalleled wisdom and unwavering strength. He paints a picture of a man who was a pillar of the community, someone who led with honor and compassion.

When he finishes, others step forward, close associates and family members, each recounting stories that present my father as a heroic figure, a man whose leadership brought years of peace and prosperity. They speak of him as a patriarch whose kindness touched everyone around him.

But as they talk, I sit there, my gaze fixed on the casket, my mind elsewhere. My thoughts swirl with the future that now lies before me. I can't help but feel a rising excitement—my father's reign is over. No one will ever know what was really said in that room before he collapsed. They will only know my version of events. How my father gave me his blessing to take over as Capo.

He ruled with tradition, with softness. That's not how I'll lead. My rule will be one of strength, of control, of absolute power. Today marks the beginning of a new era. One where I usher our *Famiglia* into an age of dominance, with me as the *Capo dei capi*—the boss of bosses, ruling with an iron will and unwavering authority.

Antonio

Valentino's been the acting head of the family for several weeks now since Uncle Gio's passing. Tonight, however, we're conducting his official induction. High-ranking members of our organization will be in attendance, including my father, who'll continue serving as Vigo's underboss, and Enzo, our Consigliere, who will conduct the ceremony.

I've never attended an induction ceremony, as Uncle Gio had been Capo long before I was born. Tonight should feel significant—exciting. Instead, it's shrouded by unanswered questions surrounding my uncle's death and the suspicion Valentino knows more than he's letting on.

The restaurant is bustling tonight, packed as usual for a Friday evening. I look around, hoping to spot my father making his rounds, talking to customers, and keeping an eye on things.

"Looking for someone?" Lena sidles up beside me placing her hand on my bicep.

"Is my father here?"

"I think he's in the office," she replies, her tone turning sultry. "Need help with anything? It's been a long time, Anton," she adds, her voice dripping with seduction.

I met Lena after everything went down with Alessia back in

high school. I needed a distraction, something to keep me from thinking about her. Lena was perfect for that—an easy fuck with no strings attached.

I wasn't attached to Lena—there were never any feelings involved. She was just a way to pass the time, so when Valentino wanted in, I didn't care. There was no jealousy, no reason to keep her to myself. We agreed to share her. Hell, the three of us have been together more times than I can count, and it didn't bother me at all.

But things changed when Valentino's desires started to spiral into something darker, more twisted. He pushed boundaries. Took things to extremes that made me uncomfortable. And Lena? She didn't just accept it. She seemed to thrive on it.

I remember one night vividly, up in the penthouse of one of our hotels. Valentino had arranged a private party, just the three of us. At first, it seemed like any other night, drinks and some kinky fun, but then he started bringing things out I'd never seen before —things that made my stomach churn.

Valentino placed a blindfold over Lena's eyes before he bound her with thick leather restraints that had steel chains threaded through them, securing her to a spreader bar at her ankles, forcing her legs apart. Her wrists were locked into steel cuffs that had sharp edges on the inside—dangerous enough that too much struggle would break her skin. Each cuff was attached to the bedposts with steel carabiners.

Once he was satisfied that Lena couldn't move, he clipped on nipple clamps, tightening them until she gasped. With a wicked grin, he added the clit clamp. I thought that was it, but he was far from done. He picked up a silver butt plug, covering it with lube before he slid it in her ass. Then, Valentino connected an electrostimulation device, running wires from the clamps to the control box he held in his hand. His thumb rested lightly on the dial, teasing her as the low hum of electricity filled the room.

The first jolt hit her hard, her back arching against the restraints, her body straining helplessly as the electricity surged through the clamps at her nipples and clit. Her breath caught in her throat. A sharp gasp followed by a moan as she tried to process the overwhelming sensations. Valentino seemed pleased with himself and increased the intensity with each flick of the dial, her body jerking uncontrollably with every pulse of electricity.

But he didn't stop there. Vigo picked up his bullwhip, dragging it lazily across her thighs before delivering a sudden, brutal lash. The crack of leather echoed through the room, her body convulsing under the combined force of the whip and the relentless shocks. He reveled in it—the sight of her writhing in agony and ecstasy. Her skin, flushed and marked from the whip, glistened with sweat, but she didn't beg for him to stop. She begged for more.

Lena's moans turned to desperate cries as Valentino turned the voltage up even higher, his eyes glinting with sadistic pleasure. Every jolt forced her body to twitch and spasm. The restraints dug into her skin, causing small rivulets of blood to drip down her arms. The chains rattled as she fought against them, but there was no escape.

Tonight was no longer about fucking around and having fun. Valentino was using her as a canvas for his darkest desires, pushing her to the edge and seeing if she'd break.

As I watched, a knot twisted in my stomach. This wasn't the kind of game I wanted to play anymore. I liked being dominant in the bedroom, but what Valentino was doing was something else entirely. It was dangerous, sadistic, and without limits. That night, I saw the true extent of his darkness. And I wanted no part of it.

"I'll pass," I mumble, pulling my arm back and walking toward the office.

The door's closed when I get there. I knock quick before opening it and stepping inside, finding my father buried in paperwork.

"You're early," he says without looking up.

"Is everything ready for tonight?" I ask, trying to shake off the lingering unease.

He looks up, his expression serious. "It is."

I sit across from him, leaning forward with my elbows on my knees. "Do you think Vigo knows more about what happened with Uncle Gio than he's saying?"

"I don't know." Dad sighs, rubbing his temples. "When I walked in, he was just standing there, watching his father on the ground. It didn't sit right with me. But maybe he was in shock."

His words hang between us. Tonight, Valentine will be inducted as our new Capo, and everything will change.

"I can see what you're thinking, but we have to keep our suspicions to ourselves," Dad warns. "If Valentino even senses doubt, it could mean our lives."

"I know," I reply, my voice tight. "But it's hard to sit by and do nothing when I know Uncle Gio didn't feel Vigo was ready. He told me himself just a few weeks ago."

My father's eyes narrow. "And that's exactly why we need to act like nothing's wrong. Like we're fully behind him."

"I just wish I could stop this before it's too late," I say, frustration bubbling inside me.

"We need proof," Dad says, his voice firm. "Without it, all we have are suspicions."

"I know you're right, but it doesn't make it any easier."

"Good," he says, his expression softening slightly. "Just remember, our priority is to protect our family. Even if that means protecting Valentino."

"I understand," I say, though the words feel bitter. "I won't let you down."

He offers me a small, strained smile. "I know you won't, son."

Before I can respond, the door swings open, and Valentino strides in. His eyes dart between us, picking up on the tension.

"Am I interrupting something?" he asks, trying to keep his tone casual but unable to hide his hint of suspicion.

I straighten and force a smile. "Just going over the details for tonight."

Valentino's gaze lingers on us a second longer than necessary, but he nods. "Good. Everything needs to be perfect."

Dad clears his throat. "Of course, Vigo. We're making sure everything's in order. It's an important night for not only *la famiglia* but also you."

Valentino's eyes narrow as he focuses on my father, "I expect you to be by my side tonight. We need to show a united front."

"Naturally," Dad replies, keeping his tone even. "I'll be there."

Satisfied, Valentino's expression eases, but there's still something lurking behind his eyes—doubt, perhaps. "Good. Tonight marks a new beginning. One where I'll grow even more powerful." He shifts his attention to me. "I can count on you to support me, right?"

"Of course," I say, forcing another smile. "I'll always have your back."

"Perfect," Valentino says and turns to leave. "I'll see you both soon."

The door closes behind him, and the tension in the room turns suffocating. I drop my head in my hands.

"We need to be more careful," my father says, his voice low. "From now on, we don't discuss this here."

"I know," I reply, taking a deep breath to steady myself. "I'll do what I've always done—protect our family. No matter what the cost."

Valentino

For too long, my father dangled the promise of leadership in front of Uncle Marco, making him believe he'd take over until I was *ready*—whatever that's supposed to mean. He's always been second in command, the one my father relied on when things got tough. I know he wanted the top spot. Now, I'm stepping into the role he thought was his, and I can't help but question his loyalty to me.

Antonio's always been my right hand, my protector. He follows my lead without question. But Marco's his father. If he starts whispering in Antonio's ear, planting seeds of doubt, he'll poison him against me. That's something I won't allow. I need to keep them apart—need to keep Antonio close to me.

I'm sitting at the bar nursing a whiskey when Antonio and Uncle Marco step out of the office. I don't hesitate. I need to assert my control. "Antonio, a word," I call out, my voice carrying an edge of authority that leaves no room for argument.

Antonio glances at his father. "I'll see you downstairs," he says before walking over to me, his expression a mix of curiosity and concern. "What's up?"

"I've been thinking," I say, swirling my whiskey and taking a sip. "With all the changes happening, I'm concerned rival organizations might see this as an opportunity." I set the glass down and lean in. "There's something important I need you to do. Something personal," I add, my tone more deliberate.

"Whatever you need," Antonio says, his loyalty evident in his eyes.

I nod, a slow smile creeping across my face. "I've been thinking," I say, my voice slick with false sincerity. "I'm giving you a promotion. From now on, you'll be in charge of Alessia's security." I pause for effect, letting my eyes linger on him. "She means a great deal to me, and with all the shifting pieces right now... well, I need to make sure she's safe. You know, from anyone who might get the wrong ideas." My voice drips with an undercurrent of manipulation as I watch for his reaction.

Antonio's eyes widen for just a moment before he schools his expression. "You want me to guard Alessia?" His voice carries a hint of disbelief as if he can't quite believe I'm letting him work that closely with her. "Is there a specific threat you're worried about?"

I shake my head, feigning concern as I play the part. "It's not about any one threat. It's about being proactive. Alessia's my wife, and as the new Capo, I can't afford to take any chances," I say, keeping my tone measured, watching him closely for any signs of hesitation.

Antonio's shoulders relax as he takes a seat beside me. "I understand, Vigo. I'll make sure she's safe. But if there's something else going on, tell me, and I'll handle it."

I glance away as if weighing my thoughts, then meet his eyes again. "It's just precautionary. I don't want anyone thinking they can hurt Alessia to get to me."

"You don't need to worry. I'll ensure she's safe."

"We're in this together," I say firmly, my gaze locking onto his. "Don't let anyone tell you otherwise."

Antonio's expression remains solid. "You have nothing to worry about. I'll always have your back."

"Thank you, Anton."

As Antonio heads off, I finish my whiskey, a sense of control settling over me. With Antonio focused on Alessia, I can keep him close and ensure his loyalty remains unwavering. I'll do whatever's necessary to solidify my power.

A HUSH FALLS OVER THE ROOM AS THE CEREMONY begins. The gas-powered candle flames dance, casting dark shadows over the alter where a large intricately carved wooden table bearing the symbols of our family's power sits. On it is an ancient dagger, a ledger bound in worn leather, a silver chalice filled with red wine, and a throne draped in crimson fabric—an unmistakable symbol of my new authority.

Marco stands on the altar beside me. My father's trusted underboss, who's supposed to be my anchor, but instead, his proximity fuels my paranoia. Around us, the highest-ranking members of our family form a semi-circle.

Enzo steps forward. His voice carries the weight of tradition as he addresses the room, each word dripping with authority and history.

"Tonight, we gather to honor the memory of our fallen Capo, Giovanni Comiso, and to anoint his successor," Enzo intones, his gaze sweeping over the assembly. "This ceremony, steeped in the traditions of our ancestors, marks the continuity of our family's strength and unity."

Enzo's eyes fall on me. "Valentino, as you stand before us, ready to take your place as Capo, know that this ceremony binds you to a new life—one dedicated to *La Famiglia* above all else." He lifts the ancient dagger, the blade gleaming in the candlelight. "This dagger symbolizes the power and responsibility bestowed upon you as our new leader."

I move to stand by the table, my heart pounding with a mix of excitement and a sliver of unease. Enzo holds the dagger before him.

With a swift motion, Enzo pricks my finger with the sharp blade until he draws blood. He holds up a small piece of paper bearing the image of a saint. "This blood symbolizes your birth into *La Famiglia*. As your blood stains the saint, so does your soul become one with us."

Enzo presses my bleeding finger to the paper. Crimson seeps into the image. "If you ever betray this family, may your flesh burn like this saint."

The paper is set alight, and Enzo holds it up for all to see the symbol of the vow being taken. The room falls into a deep silence, the crackle of burning paper the only sound.

"As this saint burns, so will your soul if you disobey or betray us," Enzo declares. "You enter alive, but you will only leave dead."

When the flames die out, he turns back to me. "Do you, Valentino, swear to uphold the honor, strength, and loyalty of this family above all else, even at the cost of your life?"

"I do," I reply.

Enzo lowers the dagger and continues, "Drink from the chalice, a symbol of your commitment to our family and its traditions."

I raise the chalice to my lips, the wine's bitterness lingering on my tongue. As I lower it, I glance at Marco, searching for any sign of betrayal. He remains expressionless, but the seed of doubt lingers.

Enzo turns to Marco. "As underboss, you will stand by Valentino's side, guiding him and ensuring the family's continued strength."

Marco steps forward, his gaze meeting mine, steady and unreadable. "I will," he replies, his voice calm but carrying the weight of unspoken tension.

"Now, you will receive the kiss of brotherhood, sealing your vow to this family," Enzo says.

Marco leans in, kissing me on both cheeks. The gesture is a

tradition, a symbolic act that signifies loyalty and unity within the family. As Marco steps back, Enzo concludes the ceremony.

"Valentino, you are now the *Capo dei capi* of *La Famiglia*. Lead with wisdom, strength, and loyalty."

I take my seat on the throne and grip the armrests as each member of the family offers their gesture of loyalty—some with a nod, others a hand over their heart, and a quiet murmur of affirmation.

I settle back into the throne. The feeling of power and control is intoxicating.

Everything is now mine, and I plan to lead with an iron fist. With me in control, *La Famiglia* will experience power and success like it never has known before.

After Valentino stepped into the role of Capo, he assigned Antonio to oversee my personal security—a move that shocked me. Valentino spouted some nonsense about being concerned rival families might try to hurt me to get to him. But I didn't buy it for a second. He never does anything without an ulterior motive. There's more to this than concern for my safety, but what exactly? I'm not sure.

Having Antonio around is both difficult and comforting. He's a reminder of what we once shared, of a past I can't quite escape, yet his presence still brings an odd sense of safety. Maybe it's because, despite everything, I trust him more than I should.

Antonio often makes excuses, saying he has other tasks to attend to, leaving Dante to babysit me more often than not. Even when he's here, Antonio's different—detached. He follows orders, but there's no warmth like he's deliberately avoiding being too close.

But today, Antonio has no choice but to be here. Valentino sent Dante out of town on some business, so Antonio is stuck with the job he's been avoiding. He's walking silently next to me as we cross the street to visit Domenica.

Since Giovanni's passing, Domenica has been drowning in

loneliness. Though their marriage was arranged, Giovanni was the great love of her life. I've made it a habit to spend a few hours with her each day, hoping my presence might offer some small comfort amidst her grief.

I knock gently on the door, hearing her familiar, faint *come in*, before stepping inside. It's been nearly a month since Giovanni's death, but sorrow still hangs thick in the air. Domenica sits by the window, where she always is, her gaze distant and unfocused, lost somewhere beyond the glass.

She turns slightly when I enter the room. "Alessia, dear, you didn't have to come," she says, her voice barely above a whisper, though a small glimmer of appreciation softens her tired eyes.

"I want to be here," I reply gently, crossing the room to sit beside her. "How are you feeling today?"

She sighs a sound that carries the weight of her heartache. "Every day without him feels like an eternity. I keep expecting him to walk through that door and to hear his voice, but..."

I reach out, taking her hand in mine. "Giovanni was a good man. I can't imagine how difficult this must be for you."

"He was," Domenica replies, her fingers tightening around mine. "And now, it's as though a part of me is missing. The house feels so empty without him."

We sit in silence for a while. The only sound is the soft rustle of the leaves outside. Her pain is palpable and tugs at something deep inside me.

"I brought some of your favorite tea," I say, trying to offer a small comfort. "Maybe we can sit outside for a bit. It's a beautiful afternoon."

A small smile tugs at her lips. "That sounds nice. Thank you."

As I prepare the tea, the routine feels almost soothing, a brief moment of normalcy in the midst of her grief. The kettle whistles, and when I glance back, I see Domenica holding a photograph of Giovanni, her fingers tracing the edges gently.

"When Giovanni and I first married," she begins softly, her voice distant with memory, "I was so scared. I didn't know if we'd ever truly love each other. But he was so patient and kind. Over time, I realized how much he meant to me."

I pour the tea and bring the cups outside to the patio. Domenica follows me, and we settle in the garden. "Anyone could see how deeply he loved you."

She nods, tears welling I her eyes. "He did. And I loved him. I don't know how to move on without him."

"Take your time," I reassure her, giving her hand a gentle squeeze. "You don't have to rush through this."

"You've been such a comfort," Domenica says, her voice filled with gratitude. "I know you and Valentino are still finding your way, but don't take a single day for granted." Her words catch me off guard. "I know you feel forced into this marriage, but my Gio and I are proof that love will come."

She has no idea who her son really is—the cruelty that lurks beneath his polished facade, the awful things he's already done to me. I can't bring myself to shatter her illusion, to tell her the truth about the man she raised. Instead, I smile and play along. "I'm sure you're right."

My phone vibrates on the table, breaking the moment. I glance down at the screen and sigh.

Valentino: Where are you?

Alessia: I'm with your mother.

Valentino: You didn't tell me you were going anywhere.

Alessia: You weren't home. Antonio brought me.

Alessia: I didn't think I needed your permission to visit my mother-in-law.

The texts show read, but there's no reply.

"Is everything alright, dear?" Domenica asks.

I force a smile. "It is. Nothing important."

"I'm sorry for interrupting," Antonio says, stepping onto the patio.

"You're never an interruption, Anton," Domenica replies warmly.

"Valentino's on his way," Antonio says, a slight hesitation in his voice. "He's not in the best mood."

I offer a nod of appreciation. "Excuse me for a moment," I say, standing and hoping to interrupt Valentino before he causes a scene and upsets his mother even more.

Just as I step inside, the front door slams. Heavy footsteps approach as Valentino storms down the hallway.

"What the hell are you doing here again?" he snaps, his eyes narrowing as they land on me.

"I told you in my text. I'm visiting Domenica," I reply evenly. "She needs support right now."

"She needs to move on," he growls, his tone harsh. "Sitting around feeling sorry for herself won't bring him back."

Anger flares inside me, but I keep my expression neutral. "Grief doesn't work on your timetable. Maybe you should try spending some time with her. She could use the support of her son."

He steps closer, his voice lowering dangerously. "There are more important matters to attend to."

"Like what?" I challenge.

"I've been busy working—making new deals," he sneers. "And I expected to come home to my wife, not to find her wasting time on things that no longer matter."

I lift my chin, refusing to back down. "Nothing's more important than family. Not even your precious business."

His eyes flash with fury. "You don't decide what's important, Alessia. I do. From now on, you won't be visiting my mother, or anyone for that matter. Do you understand?"

"I'm not one of your men, Valentino," I say, meeting his gaze with equal intensity. "You don't get to order me around."

His expression darkens as he steps even closer. "You may not be one of my men, but you *are* my wife. You will follow my rules."

I take a deep breath, keeping my voice steady. "I will continue to visit Domenica. She needs someone, and clearly, you can't be bothered with your own mother."

"You're treading on thin ice, Alessia," he hisses, his grip suddenly latching onto my arm with a bruising force. "You think you can defy me?"

Pain shoots through my arm, but I refuse to show any weakness. "This isn't about you. It's about doing what's right."

"You will do as I say, Alessia, or you will face the consequences."

"Let go of me, Valentino," I say through clenched teeth.

"Valentino," Antonio says from behind me.

Valentino's grip on my arm loosens as he looks over my shoulder. "What do you want?" he snaps.

Antonio steps forward. "Is everything alright?" he asks, his tone steady but filled with an undercurrent of concern.

Before Antonio can say more, I step in quickly, forcing a light laugh as I rub my arm. "It's nothing, really. Just a little misunderstanding—newlywed things, you know." I offer a playful smile, trying to ease the tension. "Nothing to worry about."

Antonio looks between Val and me. "Are you sure you're okay?"

"I'm perfectly fine," I say, my voice a little too cheerful as I meet Antonio's gaze, silently pleading with him to let it go.

Valentino narrows his eyes at me before turning his attention back to Antonio. "See? No problem. Just a private conversation between husband and wife."

Antonio's jaw tightens. "Your mother is in the other room. You don't want to upset her with your newlywed spat."

Valentino turns to me, his expression hard. "This isn't over," he warns before storming out of the house and slamming the door behind him.

I force a small, dismissive smile, turning to Antonio as if brushing off the tension. "Marriage can be overwhelming. We got a little heated over nothing, really." I give a small, awkward laugh. "He'll cool off."

Antonio doesn't seem convinced, his eyes studying me carefully. "Alessia..."

"It's fine," I cut in, keeping my voice light even though my heart is pounding. "He'll be fine. "I'm going to say goodbye to Domenica. Will you walk me home after?"

"Of course," he answers without hesitation. "I'll be waiting outside."

I return to the patio where Domenica is waiting, her expression curious. "What did Valentino want? He seemed upset."

I force another smile. "He came home and wanted to take me out on a date. He got worried when I wasn't there."

Her face brightens. "That's wonderful. He's been so preoccupied with taking over for his father. I'm glad to see him making time for your relationship."

I nod, playing along. "Yes, it's nice to see him making an effort."

Domenica pats my hand, her eyes filling with hope. "Enjoy your evening, dear."

"Thank you, Domenica," I say softly. "I'll see you tomorrow."

As I step outside, I find Antonio waiting on the porch. "Ready?" he asks, offering a small, comforting smile.

"Ready," I reply, although the last place I want to go is home.

We take a few steps in silence. The cooling air calms my nerves. I steal a glance at Antonio, my thoughts swirling. Without thinking, I finally break the silence. "Antonio," I hesitate, then push forward, my voice soft but laced with a question I've been carrying for too long. "What happened between us? Why didn't you go to my father?"

He doesn't answer right away, his jaw tightening as he stares straight ahead. The silence stretches between us. When he finally speaks, his voice is low and filled with something I can't quite place. "Things changed," he says, keeping his gaze forward. "You know that."

"But you didn't even try," I whisper. "You just let me go."

Antonio stops walking, turning to face me. For a moment, there's a hint of the boy I once loved in his eyes. Then, just as quickly, it fades, replaced by the cold distance that's become so familiar.

"I realized there wasn't anything worth fighting for," he says, his tone harsh and emotionless.

His words are unexpected and hit me like a slap across my face. My chest tightens as I search his face for some sign that he doesn't mean it—that it's a lie.

"That's not true. I don't believe you," I say, my voice trembling with hurt.

Antonio's expression hardens further, his blue eyes locked on mine. "I don't know what to tell you."

The pain in my chest twists, and I can't stop the words from spilling out. "And what about me? What about us? Wasn't I worth fighting for? Or did I mean so little to you?"

Antonio flinches, just barely, but I catch it before he stiffens, his mask of indifference slipping back into place. His voice hardens as he speaks, his words cruel and deliberate. "I was a stupid kid back then, saying things I didn't mean. This," he says, gesturing toward himself, "is the real me."

His eyes darken, filled with something dangerous. "You think Valentino's ruthless? He's nothing compared to me. I've done things, Alessia—things you couldn't even imagine. I kill and torture without a second thought. You see the monster your husband is, but I'm worse. I don't hesitate. I don't flinch. I do whatever needs to be done, no matter how dirty or brutal."

He takes a step closer, his voice low, cold. "You think there's still some part of me that's good? That's kind? There isn't. That boy you remember, he's dead."

His words crash over me like a tidal wave. I realize I don't know the man standing in front of me. He's painting himself as a monster, a killer—someone far removed from the Antonio I once loved. I search his face, desperate to see something, anything that says he's lying, that this is just another wall he's built around himself.

But all I see is a man who's lost himself to the darkness.

Antonio

I watch the pain ripple through her body. The hurt flashing in her eyes—the hurt I put there. Her shoulders sag, the life draining from her posture, and I realize just how much damage I've done. I should feel something, regret or guilt, but I don't allow myself to feel anything. This is how it has to be.

"Let's go," I mutter, breaking the silence that's suffocating us both. "Valentino's going to be looking for you."

She doesn't respond. Just follows me, her movements stiff, like the weight of my words is physically dragging her down.

I try not to think about the way she looked at me like I was a stranger—like she didn't recognize the person standing in front of her. But I can't shake the image of her face, the way her lips pressed together to stop whatever she wanted to say. The way her hands trembled, just slightly, as if she was holding back more than words.

We reach the house, and I stop, watching her as she hesitates on the doorstep. Her hand lingers on the handle for a moment before she finally turns to me, her eyes still filled with that same hurt, that same desperate need for answers. But I don't give her any. I can't.

"We need to go inside," I tell her, my voice cold. "Valentino's waiting."

She nods, her face blank now as if she's built her own wall, protecting herself from the truth I've just handed her. Without another word, she opens the door and steps inside. I follow behind and find Valentino waiting for us in the foyer, his usual arrogance replaced by something more dangerous.

"Alessia," he barks, his voice cutting through the quiet. "Go up to our room. Now."

Alessia turns to me as if she's looking for some kind of reassurance. I keep my face impassive, giving her nothing. Her shoulders slump as she turns toward the stairs. I watch her retreat, the knot in my stomach tightening. Valentino's temper is volatile, and that unpredictability unnerves me more than I care to admit.

Once Alessia's out of earshot, Valentino turns his piercing gaze on me. "Antonio," he begins in a low, commanding tone, "From now on, Alessia does not leave this house without my explicit permission. Understood?"

I meet his gaze evenly, though inwardly, I bristle at the command. "Has there been a threat against Alessia that I need to be aware of?" I ask, although I know his orders are less about danger and more about control.

He lets out a sigh, his frustration evident. "Alessia's reckless. Headstrong. She doesn't understand her place by my side yet. Her defiance makes me look weak, and I won't tolerate that."

I bite back the response I want to give, instead offering the one I know he expects. "Whatever you think is best."

"Good," he replies, satisfied. "I'm counting on you, Antonio. I can't afford distractions right now."

"You know I always have your back," I assure him, keeping my tone neutral despite the unease gnawing at me.

Valentino waves me off, already done with the conversation. "You're free to go. I won't be needing you tonight." His voice drops to a murmur as he strides purposefully toward the stairs. "I need to teach my wife a lesson about disrespecting me in public."

I stare after him, a chill creeping up my spine. The air is thick, charged with something dark and heavy. I glance up the staircase, fighting every instinct to intervene, to protect Alessia, but knowing there's not a damn thing I can do.

This is the life I've chosen—this world where loyalty outweighs conscience. Where crossing the wrong line means risking everything. For now, I have to follow Valentino's orders. But that doesn't stop the gnawing doubt, the slow realization that I've turned into someone I swore I'd never become.

Alessia

He sent me to my room like I was a child. But what really upsets me is that I listened to him. I should've stood my ground. Instead, I obeyed. Why? Because I didn't want to cause another scene in front of Antonio. He's Val's cousin—his most trusted associate. As much as I want out of this nightmare of a marriage, the last thing I want is to be the reason for tension or a fight between them.

Valentino's footsteps grow louder, each one sending a fresh wave of dread through me. I know what's coming—another one of his lessons. It's not the first, and I'm sure it won't be the last. The door creaks open, and Val steps inside, a wooden paddle gripped in his hand.

"Why are your clothes still on?" he asks, his tone demanding.

I meet his stare, refusing to flinch.

"Answer me, Alessia."

I force down the bile rising in my throat. I can do this. I refuse to let him see me cower. "You only told me to go to our room," I say, trying to sound sweet. "You didn't tell me to undress, and I didn't want to disobey you."

"Don't get fucking smart with me," he growls, his voice rising.

"You know what I expect," he says, his voice raising with each word. "Take off your clothes. Now."

My hands shake as I fumble with the buttons on my blouse. Valentino watches, his eyes gleaming with a predatory intensity. My fingers move to the zipper of my skirt, but my hands are trembling so badly that I can't get a grip on it.

"Move faster," Valentino snaps, stepping closer.

I'm finally able to unzip my skirt and let it drop to the floor.

"All of it," he commands.

I swallow hard, my mouth dry as I reach behind to unclasp my bra. It falls to the floor quickly, followed by my panties. I stand there, naked and vulnerable, forcing myself to keep my chin held high. I won't give him the satisfaction of seeing me break.

Valentino's eyes rake over me with a twisted satisfaction. "Bend over the bench."

I hesitate for just a second before moving across the room. The spanking bench stands like an ominous figure, always there, a reminder of his control. I fold my body over the center, gripping the handles on the other side, my legs splayed on the rests. My heart races in my chest as I wait for him to unleash whatever cruelty he has in mind.

The first strike of the paddle takes my breath away, the sting sharp and searing. Tears well in my eyes, but I blink them back. He wants to see me cry, but I won't give him that satisfaction. Another strike follows, then another, each blow harder than the last, each strike punctuated by his harsh breathing.

Finally, after what feels like an eternity, he stops. My body shakes uncontrollably, and my skin burns. Slowly, I push myself up from the bench, turning to face him. His eyes are cold, but there's a glint of satisfaction in them—like he's accomplished something.

"Remember this," he says, voice low and threatening. "Next time you think about defying me."

I don't respond. I simply stare back at him, my silence a small act of defiance.

"I'm going out," Valentino declares and turns, leaving the room. The door slamming shut behind him.

For a long moment, I stand there, my body throbbing with pain. Slowly, I gather my clothes, my mind racing. I can't keep living like this. I can't keep letting him control me, hurt me.

Somehow, I have to find a way to escape this hell I'm living.

Antonio

The blonde I brought from the club pushes up on her elbow, watching as I remove the condom and toss it into the wastebasket beside the bed. I never bring anyone to my apartment. That space is mine, untouched by the women I entertain for a night. Using our hotel helps keep them away from my real life—no strings attached.

"I'll have my driver take you home," I say, picking up her discarded clothes from the floor and handing them to her.

"I don't have anywhere else to be," she purrs, biting her bottom lip as her eyes rake over my naked body. "Wouldn't you rather I stay for a while?"

I shake my head, giving her a tight smile. "I prefer to be alone."

She sits up, the look in her eyes shifting from sultry to slightly wounded. "Is it something I did?" she asks, frowning as she pulls her top over her head.

"No," I say, keeping my tone neutral as I step into my boxers. "It's not you."

Her frown deepens, clearly not used to this kind of rejection. "You're really not going to let me stay?"

I suppress a sigh. This part is always tedious. "I'm not. But my driver will make sure you get home safely."

She narrows her eyes, her irritation flaring. "You know, most guys would kill to have someone like me in their bed."

"I'm not most guys."

She huffs but doesn't argue further, slipping on her clothes with sharp, irritated movements. Fully dressed, she grabs her purse and turns to me. "I had a good time last night," she says, her voice softer now, almost pleading.

"So did I," I offer, not wanting to be a complete asshole.

When I don't say anything more, she gets the hint and heads toward the door. I follow, making sure she has everything before she steps into the hallway. My driver's already waiting outside, as per my text. As soon as she's out the door, I gather my things to head home.

An email notification pops up on my phone. Hoping it's the message I've been waiting for, I click the icon, my heart racing as I read the subject line. I quickly open the email, my eyes scanning the text.

From: JBillings@qmail.com

To: Antonio.Luciano@Lucianoconsulting.com

Subject: 1926 Macallan Whiskey - Available for Purchase

Mr. Luciano,

I am pleased to inform you that we have acquired a rare 1926 bottle of Macallan whiskey. Given your interest in this particular vintage, we wanted to offer you the first opportunity to purchase it.

Distinguishing this offer further, this particular bottle has undergone reconditioning by The Macallan Distillery, with both the capsule and cork replaced. Additionally, a 1ml liquid sample was taken and compared with another 1926 bottle at the Edrington offices in Glasgow. The capsule was recreated by a producer in Austria, providing an identical match to the original.

The selling price is $1,200,000.00. We can arrange a discreet and secure transaction at your earliest convenience.

Best regards,

John Billings

A rare smile tugs at the corners of my mouth. This bottle is the perfect belated wedding gift for Valentino. He's obsessed with rare whiskeys, especially the 1926 Macallan. The price is steep, but this particular bottle will bolster his ego and reinforce the illusion of my loyalty. I quickly compose my reply.

From: Antonio.Luciano@Lucianoconsulting.com
To: JBillings@qmail.com
Subject: Re: 1926 Macallan Whiskey - Available for Purchase
Mr. Billings,
Thank you for your quick work. I'm impressed by your efficiency in locating this bottle. I'd like to move forward with the purchase immediately. Please send over the details for the transaction.
Best,
Antonio Luciano
I hit send, satisfaction washing over me. This gift is more than just a token of goodwill—it's a calculated move. Another piece of the puzzle to keep Valentino blind to what I'm really after. He won't suspect a thing. He'll only see my generosity and loyalty. Meanwhile, I'll keep digging for the truth about his involvement in Uncle Gio's death.

It's all part of the game.

Valentino

Although I made sure the marks were hidden beneath her clothes, Alessia will feel the bruises from her punishment for days. One way or another, she'll fall in line—become the well-behaved arm candy she was bred to be. It's only a matter of time before she stops resisting. And once she does, I'll get her pregnant with my heir, securing the Comiso legacy for another generation.

But tonight, I need someone who shares my desires and won't fight me at every turn.

Alessia may be mine, but she's not ready to accept the darker side of what I need. And right now, I'm craving someone who appreciates the pain I inflict. Someone who knows what I like and won't put up a fight.

I grab my phone.

Valentino: Are you working tonight?

Lena: I am.

Valentino: What time do you get off?

Lena: I'm working until close.

Valentino: Not anymore. I'm on my way.

Lena: We're packed tonight. Marco isn't going to let me leave early.

I don't give a shit what my Uncle Marco thinks. Lena's off the clock as soon as I get there. She's more valuable to me with her legs spread and my cock shoved in her cunt than she is waiting on tables.

Valentino: I'll deal with him when I get there.

Pocketing my phone, I bound down the steps to find Guido, one of our newer men. "I'm going out," I announce.

"Where do you need to go?" he asks, trailing behind.

"Doesn't matter," I order. "Where are the keys?"

His eyes dart around nervously. "Sir, you're not supposed to go out without a guard."

I step closer, my voice low and threatening. "I'm the one who makes the rules around here. Don't make me ask again."

He reaches into his pocket and passes me the keychain.

"Alessia's not to leave this house. Do you understand?"

"Yes, sir," he murmurs, keeping his gaze low.

I turn on my heel and head for the door to the garage.

"What time should I expect you back?" he calls after me, hesitant.

I stop, hand on the doorknob and glaring over my shoulder. "Do I have a curfew?"

"N-no, sir. It's just," he stammers but quickly corrects himself. "I made a mistake."

"That's what I thought."

It's a busy Friday night in Philadelphia, so the streets are crawling with cars. By the time I pull up to the valet outside the restaurant, I'm already in a foul mood.

"Good evening, Mr. Comiso," the valet greets, but I brush past him.

"Yeah, I'll be here for a while," I say curtly, not bothering with formalities.

Inside, the restaurant is packed. I spot Lena taking orders at a nearby table and make my way toward her, placing a firm hand on her lower back.

"Excuse me," I say to the diners, flashing a tight smile. "There's an emergency Lena needs to attend to. Your meal is on the house tonight."

One of the women at the table smiles back. "Thank you."

"Of course," I murmur, steering Lena away.

"What the hell, Val?" she whispers as soon as we're out of earshot. "I'm in the middle of my shift."

"I told you I was coming." I tighten my grip on her waist.

"An emergency?" She raises an eyebrow.

"Yes, a very big one," I smirk, leading her to the back hallway.

Just then, Uncle Marco steps in front of us, blocking our path. "I wasn't expecting you tonight," he says, his eyes narrowing as he looks between Lena and me.

"Change of plans," I reply smoothly. "If you'll excuse us. Lena and I have some business to discuss."

"May I speak to you? Alone?" Marco's voice is tight.

I glance at Lena. "Wait for me downstairs."

She steps aside, and I approach my uncle, lowering my voice. "What do you want?"

"You can't just pull my waitress off the floor mid-shift. We're swamped tonight," he says, his tone measured but firm.

"I suggest you have someone take her tables," I reply, my impatience rising.

"We're short-staffed as it is. If you want to wait at the bar until her shift is over, that's fine. But she's not leaving now."

I step closer, only inches from his face. "I didn't come here for your permission, Marco. I'm in charge now. If I say Lena's done, she's done."

"Might I remind you that this is my restaurant," he says, holding his ground. "And Lena is *my* employee."

"That can change," I reply cooly.

"Is that a threat?"

"Take it however you want," I say, brushing past him. "Now, make sure I'm not disturbed."

If I had any doubt about Marco's loyalties before, they're gone now. He still thinks he should be in charge—a mistake that'll cost him. Anyone who isn't with me is against me and will be dealt with accordingly.

But I'll deal with that later. Right now, I have other things in mind. Downstairs, Lena's already naked and kneeling as she waits for me like she knows what's expected. Tonight, my thoughts are more twisted and darker than usual, and I intend to explore every one of my desires.

"On your feet," I command. Before she's found her footing, I push her into the room we use for torture. Then, I pull out my knife, the handle familiar and cold in my grip. The blade glints under the fluorescent light.

"What are you going to do with that?"

"Did I give you permission to speak?" I ask as I trace the flat side of the blade against her cheek.

She shakes her head slowly.

Moving behind her, I slide the blade down her spine, eliciting a soft gasp. The knife's edge barely kisses her skin.

"Get on the table," I command, and she scrambles to obey.

I make quick work of restraining her arms and legs to the cuffs that are already attached to the table. Pressing the blade against her inner thigh, I apply just enough pressure to pierce her skin. Her legs quake, but she doesn't make a sound.

"Do you feel that?" I murmur, my lips brushing against her ear. "It's the power I have over you?"

"Yes," she breathes, her voice barely a whisper.

"Good," I growl, dragging the knife down her other leg. Blood wells up immediately, a dark contrast against her pale skin. "After tonight, anyone who looks at you will know you're mine."

Her eyes widen as the blade travels upwards, tracing the curve of her hip. I see the struggle in her eyes. The battle between submission and primal fear. It's intoxicating.

I press the blade deeper this time, carving a line across her ribcage. Lena's cries echo in the small space. Her tears. Her pain—I covet them. I don't stop cutting deeper into her skin, marking her with each stroke.

"Val," she whispers. "I don't want to do this."

"Did I ask what you want?"

She squirms against the restraints. "You're scaring me,"

I slam my hand on her waist, steadying her with a bruising grip. "Shut the fuck up," I snarl, the venom in my voice silencing her.

I stand over her as I continue to trace patterns along her ribcage. Each cut is deliberate—calculated. The blade sinks deeper into her flesh with every stroke. Lena's whimpers turn into frantic gasps, her body jerking against the restraints in a desperate attempt to escape the pain.

The sight of her blood only intensifies the twisted satisfaction pooling inside me. I soak in her sobs, savoring the music of her agony. Every shudder, every broken cry fuels me as I continue my work, cutting deep, jagged lines between her breasts.

When I've finished, I step back for a moment and admire my work. Blood pools on her skin, each line a reminder of the control I hold. A twisted smile tugs at my lips as I lean down, dragging a finger through the blood between her breasts. I hold her gaze as I bring it to my mouth, sucking the crimson stain off my finger and savoring the metallic taste.

Lena's breathing grows erratic. Her face blanches, and her chest heaves as though she's on the verge of losing control. A dry sob escapes her lips as she swallows back bile. She squeezes her eyes shut in a desperate attempt to distance herself from what's happening.

I bask in her fragile composure, the way she clings to the last remnants of her dignity while fear claws at her insides. The sight of her barely holding herself together only intensifies the rush coursing through me.

Satisfied with my work, I place the knife on the table and yank her to the edge, her arms straining against the restraints as her body tenses. Undoing my pants, I take my hard cock in my hand and line it up with her entrance. I thrust inside her without warning, forcing a sharp cry from her lips. I grip her hips tightly, keeping her pinned in place as I drive into her with ruthless force. Tears spill down her cheeks, each one stoking the fire of my arousal. Her sobs fuel my hunger, pushing me to take her harder.

Keeping myself buried deep inside her, I grab the knife and press its cold edge against her throat, just enough to break the skin. Lena tries to pull away. "Move again, and it'll go deeper," I growl.

Her eyes snap open wide with panic as I drag my finger through the fresh blood trickling from the wound. Leaning in, I trace my tongue along the cut. The surge of power, the feeling of complete control over her, floods through me—intoxicating and addictive.

With the knife still in one hand, I start thrusting again, hard and unrelenting, her gasps growing frantic beneath me. The sharp bite of the blade and the slick heat of her body push me closer to the edge. It only takes a few more punishing thrusts before I pull out, grabbing my cock and stroking myself until thick streams of cum splatter across her chest, mingling with the blood still dripping from her fresh wounds.

The sight is raw and brutal—erotic.

"I can't believe you did this to me," she sobs.

"Don't act like you didn't love every second of it," I sneer, tucking myself back into my pants and zipping them up. I unfasten the restraints, releasing her without a second glance.

Lena sits up and looks down at the marks I carved into her. "You had no right to do this to me."

"You wanted this as much as I did," I scoff. "Your cunt was dripping when I shoved my cock inside it."

"You're insane," she says as she gets off the table and starts grabbing her clothes. "This is the last time you'll ever touch me. I'm going to Marco."

Before she can take another step, I grab a fistful of her hair and yank her against me. "I'll fuck you whenever and however I want," I growl, my voice low and menacing. "And you won't say a word to Marco or anyone else if you want to keep breathing. Got it?"

She hesitates, her lips trembling, then finally mutters, "Yes."

Good," I say, releasing her. "Now get dressed. I'll drive you home."

"I don't want a ride," she says, her voice shaking.

"That wasn't a request," I snap, texting the valet to bring my car around. "What kind of man would I be if I didn't make sure my whore got home safely?"

Lena opens her mouth as if to argue but quickly shuts it, recognizing that it's pointless. Luckily for her, her shirt is black, hiding the bloodstains. I'm not in the mood for any questions about what I do behind closed doors.

As we emerge upstairs, I keep her close to me. The restaurant closed an hour ago and is empty, save for a few employees cleaning up for the night. They glance at Lena, taking in her tear-streaked face, but quickly avert their eyes, knowing better than to get involved.

When we step outside, I nearly collide with Marco. His eyes flick to Lena, then back to me, his face tightening. "What the hell did you do to her?"

I roll my eyes, tired of this. "What are you talking about?"

Marco motions toward Lena. "She's crying."

"He didn't do anything, Mr. L.," Lena says softly. "I'm just having a hard time because..." She pauses, pressing the heels of her palms to her eyes. "Because I've been in love with him for years, and even though I knew he'd never marry me, I still hoped. It's hard to accept."

"If my nephew had any decency," Marco says, pinning me

with his stare. "He'd let you go find someone who can love you the way you deserve. And he'd go home to his wife, where he belongs."

"Get in the car, Lena," I order.

With her arms crossed over her midsection, Lena heads to the car and gingerly slides into the passenger seat. The valet closes the door behind her.

Marco turns to me, his eyes cold. "Go home to your wife, Valentino."

I step closer to him, pointing a finger in his face. "That's the last fucking time you undermine me in front of anyone. Do you understand?"

Marco says nothing, but I can see it in his eyes—he thinks he's better than me. Thinks I'm not fit for this role. I need to come up with a plan to shut him down before he becomes a problem for me.

Antonio

T he room is empty, giving me a moment of quiet before the captains arrive. I came early, needing time to wrap my head around the mess we're in. Weapons and money laundering—that's always been our business. But now, thanks to Valentino's deal with *La Fortaleza Oculta*, we're running drugs. A line I never wanted to cross.

And to make things worse, he made an even riskier move with Giancarlo DeLuca, dragging us into human trafficking—a trade I never thought we'd touch. Even the thought of it makes me sick.

Everything Uncle Gio worked to build feels like it's hanging by a thread. I'm not sure how much longer we can keep on this track before it all unravels.

I look up from my phone when the door opens, and Dante walks in. "You're here early."

"I was hoping to talk to you alone," he confides, closing the door behind him. "Vigo's really going through with this?" he presses.

"It seems that way," I reply with a weary sigh.

Dante sinks into the chair next to me. "Have you tried talking to him?"

"All he can see is the money these deals will bring," I say, tension lacing my voice. "The fact that he's flooding our streets with drugs and selling human lives like they're commodities means nothing to him."

"Giovanni never would've allowed this," Dante mutters. He opens his mouth to say something but hesitates, shaking his head slightly.

"What is it?"

Dante shifts in his seat. "I know it's not my place, and I'm probably out of line, but are you sure your uncle gave his blessing for Valentino to take over?"

Dante and I have been friends since grade school. I always knew what this life was. I was born into it—it's in my blood. Dante didn't have that. He earned his way into this world by proving his loyalty time and time again. I've never had to question where he stands. If there's anyone I can trust with my suspicions, it's him. But I'm not ready to share them—not yet. The last thing I want is to put him in a position where he's forced to choose between me and Valentino.

Before I can answer him, the door opens again, and my father walks in. His face is tense.

"What are you doing here?" I ask, startled by his unexpected appearance.

"There's been a change of plans."

Alarm spikes through me, and I sit up straighter. "What do you mean a change of plans?"

"Valentino cancelled your meeting. He's texting the captains now," he informs us.

As if on cue, Dante's phone dings. He pulls it out and scans the message.

"What the hell's going on?" I demand.

"Valentino and I are meeting with Giancarlo DeLuca. Emilio

Salazar, *La Fortaleza Oculta's* kingpin, will be joining us," my father replies.

"That's the most fucked up idea he's had yet," I reply, annoyed.

"He promised them we'd personally welcome them to the city," my father explains, rubbing a hand over his face.

"Dante and I will go with you," I insist, already moving to stand. "You're going to need backup in case this goes south."

Dad raises a hand, stopping me. "He told them we'd be alone."

"What the ever-loving fuck?" Dante cuts in. "I hope you told him he's insane."

"I told him it wasn't a good idea, but he refused to change the plan," Dad says, exasperation lacing his tone. "Valentino made a deal—just him and I, unarmed," he adds.

"No fucking way," I bark, raising my voice. "He expects you to go in there unarmed and without backup. That's suicide. You'll be sitting ducks the second you walk through the door. There's no way I'm letting you go in blind. Dante and I are coming with you—"

"Like hell you are," Val declares from the doorway, his voice smooth as he steps inside.

I slam the table as I stand. "Do you have any idea what you're doing?"

"Of course I do," he replies, a smug grin on his face.

"Neither of these men are our allies, and you're sending yourself and my father—two of the most powerful men in our family—alone and unarmed? That's beyond reckless."

"It's a show of good faith," Vigo says, his voice dripping with false reassurance.

"It's insane." I turn to my father. "You didn't agree to this, did you?"

Dad pins me with his stare. "If Valentino says it's safe, I trust him."

Silence lingers between us, my shock still sinking in as I stare at him, waiting for some sense to surface. Valentino doesn't miss a beat and changes the subject. "I've arranged a party," he says, his tone so casual it's almost unsettling. "Giancarlo's offered some of his finest acquisitions for our pleasure tonight."

"Acquisitions?" I question.

"Women, Antonio," Valentino replies, rolling his eyes. "Even you can't be that naïve."

"Where did these *women* come from?" I press, ignoring his backhanded comment.

"Here and there," he says, waving his hands dismissively. "He's moving them through the city to their final destination. We get to sample them tonight as a thank you for our new arrangement."

"Trafficked women?" I ask, bile rising in my throat.

"Who cares where they came from," Valentino shrugs, brushing off my concerns. "They're already in the penthouse. I sent my men there to start the party. You and Dante should head over."

"I need to get back to my detail with Alessia," I mumble, unease gnawing at me.

"There's no need," he says, a sly smile creeping onto his face. "I've ensured she's unable to go anywhere."

I want to ask what he's done to her this time, but this isn't the time or place to get into that.

"Then let me follow your car. I'll stay out of sight," I suggest, trying to find a way to protect my father. "You need backup, just in case."

"We have an arrangement," he says, trying to placate me. "There's no need for weapons."

"Val—"

"I have everything handled," he cuts me off, his tone patronizing. "Go enjoy the party. You look like you need to get laid." He flashes me a smile that sends chills down my spine. "You trust me, right?"

"Of course, I trust you," I say, keeping my voice steady.

"I knew I could count on you," he says with a satisfied nod.

"I'll always have your back," I murmur, repeating the phrase I've said to him since we were kids—though now they feel like a bitter lie.

Valentino

I wait for Anton and Dante to head to the party before sitting down with Marco to finalize the details for tonight. Once I'm sure they're out of earshot, I invite my uncle to sit.

"Tonight's an important step for the future of our family," I begin. Uncle Marco nods, but I see the wariness in his eyes. "It'll pave the way for everything I do moving forward."

"You've made your stance clear on the direction you're taking *La Famiglia*, so I won't argue my objections again," he says. "That said, the idea of the two of us going together to this meeting alone is reckless."

"We won't be traveling together," I explain. "You need to give me more credit than that.

"It's not about credit," he says, leaning forward slightly. "You're a savvy young man, but you're also new to this level of leadership. There are lessons only time and experience can teach."

I raise my hand, cutting him off. "Enough. Your car's waiting. Leave your weapons here."

I watch as Marco hesitates, his gaze searching mine before he removes his gun from its holster and locks it in the safe. "My car will follow a few minutes after yours," I continue, standing. "For *security*, we travel separately."

Without waiting for a response, I turn and leave the room. Everything about tonight has been carefully planned, down to the last detail. Giancarlo needs to see that I'm a man of my word, someone who honors his agreements. Drugs and humans are where the real power lies now. Aligning with DeLuca and *La Fortaleza Oculta* will secure my position in both.

But every deal comes with a price.

I stand at the restaurant window, watching as Marco climbs into the back of his car. He doesn't realize the trap he's walking into. The route I've arranged for him will lead straight into an ambush. Once Marco's out of the way, there will be no one left to question my authority or undermine my decisions.

It's time to set my plan into motion.

As his car pulls away, I signal my men. They nod and slip into position, ready to execute the next phase. The importance of what I'm doing tonight isn't lost on me. It fuels my resolve. This is the moment I've been waiting for.

Several minutes later, my car arrives. I slide onto the smooth leather seat. Everything's falling into place. Giancarlo and Emilio will see me as decisive and ruthless, a leader who won't hesitate to do what needs to be done.

As I replay my conversation with Marco, I think of his warnings about security. If only he knew—he's the backup plan, the sacrifice pawn in a much larger game.

Giancarlo made it clear—Marco has to be removed. Though they never did business together, word travels fast in our world. Men like Marco and my father cling to their old-school principles, keeping the business "clean" by avoiding human trafficking and drugs. Giancarlo sees Marco for exactly what he is—a liability.

He refuses to move forward with the deal until Marco is out of the picture, and Emilio stands firmly with him on this. Both are presenting a united front—nothing happens until Marco is eliminated. They're watching tonight, waiting to see if I'll deliver.

It just so happens that Giancarlo's demands line up perfectly with my own suspicions about Marco's loyalty. Ever since he walked in and found my father dying on the floor, he's been questioning my authority, watching me like a hawk. I know it's only a matter of time before he turns Antonio and the rest of my men against me. He won't stop until he steals the position that's rightfully mine.

Marco and I were never going to coexist in this new order. His removal isn't just about pleasing Giancarlo—it's about securing my place. It's kill or be killed, and I won't stop until every threat, every hint of opposition, is buried beneath my feet.

The city lights blur past the windows, the glow of nightlife barely registering. My focus is razor-sharp, locked on what needs to happen tonight. There can be no mistakes. This is my moment to secure my place as the king of Philadelphia.

When I arrive at the meeting spot, a nondescript warehouse on the outskirts of the city, I step out of the car and adjust my jacket. Giancarlo's men meet me at the door, moving in to pat me down checking for weapons. I remain calm, fully aware that everything hinges on tonight.

Inside, the atmosphere is electric. Giancarlo and Emilio are already here, their expressions guarded but curious. They know how significant this meeting is. How it will shape the future of our alliance. I offer a confident smile, extending my hand. "I appreciate you taking the time to meet tonight," I say, my voice steady.

Emilio steps forward and shakes my hand. "We're here to ensure our partnership gets off on the right foot."

"Absolutely," I reply smoothly. "Our interests are aligned, and tonight's events will prove my commitment to our agreement."

As the meeting progresses, we sip our whiskey, discussing the next steps—the timing of shipments coming into the port and how everything will be coordinated. I nod along, keeping my responses sharp, but my focus is divided.

My phone sits on the table next to my glass, and every time it vibrates, I glance down, waiting for confirmation. The whiskey burns in my throat, but it's the waiting that's the real agony.

Finally, the message I've been waiting for arrives.

Unknown Number: It's done. There are no survivors.

I allow myself a fleeting moment of satisfaction before looking up. "Gentlemen," I say, my voice carrying authority, "I believe this marks the beginning of a prosperous future for all of us. To our new alliance."

We raise our glasses in a toast, sealing the deal. The words carry more meaning than the toast itself. Giancarlo and Emilio exchange a glance, and I know they understand what I've just confirmed. Marco's out of the picture. My commitment to them is solidified, and from this moment forward, there will be no one left to question my authority.

As the meeting concludes and we part ways, a grim satisfaction settles in. Marco's sacrifice was a necessary step. With the DeLuca *Famiglia* and *La Fortaleza Oculta* on my side, the possibilities are endless.

The night may be dark, but it's full of promise.

The future of La Famiglia is now mine to command, and I'll lead it with a newfound sense of authority and ruthless brutality, forging it into the empire it was always destined to be.

Antonio

Vigo's insistence that Dante and I attend his so-called party doesn't sit right. He's always thrown lavish gatherings packed with women, booze, and excess—but never anything like this. These women aren't here by choice. Trafficked women are a new filthy byproduct of his deal with the DeLuca *Famiglia*.

The thought makes me sick, but what bothers me more is how hard he's pushing for us to be there. That bastard's too savvy to demand something like this without a reason. He knows damn well that a Capo and his underboss don't go to a meeting unguarded. At the very least we should be in the area keeping eyes on the situation. So why the hell is he so desperate to get us to the hotel tonight?

Yet, here we are, walking into his trap—or at least what feels like one.

"I'm going to follow them," I say, my eyes scanning the road ahead as unease coils tighter in my chest.

"You can't," Dante snaps back. "Valentino was so damn insistent on us going to this party. If we don't show, someone's going to notice, and they'll report back. I'm sure he's covered all his bases."

A tight knot forms in my gut. "I don't like this."

Dante's expression mirrors my own tension. "I don't like it either, but whatever's happening, we have to play along. There's one thing Valentino missed," Dante says, holding his phone so I can see the screen. "The trackers on the cars. Once we've made our appearance, I'll slip away."

"I'm going with you."

"We both can't leave. It'll look too suspicious," he warns, glancing around the room before fixing his eyes on me.

My hands tighten on the steering wheel until my knuckles turn white.

"Anton," Dante says firmly, his voice drawing my focus back to him. "I won't let anything happen to them."

THE PARTY IS AS REVOLTING AS I THOUGHT IT WOULD be. The women are here, but they're not guests. They're prisoners, their eyes hollow, bodies moving as if they've lost the will to live. I sit off to the side, nursing a glass of whiskey, watching our men. Some of them are taking advantage of the women. I make a mental note of who they are. When the time comes, they'll regret this.

But the smarter ones see what's going on. Instead of indulging, they're making sure the women have food, water, and safety. At least for tonight.

My phone buzzes on the bar.

Dad: Something's wrong. The driver left the route.

Antonio: Did he say why?

Dad: He has the divider up and locked.

Fuck. I shoot to my feet, my heart hammering in my chest. Without a word, I slip out of the room and into the hallway. I hit Dante's number. Two rings, then it connects.

"Where are you?" I bark.

"We're ten minutes behind them, but the signal just went dead," Dante says, his voice tense.

"My father texted. The driver left the usual route to the warehouse district. They locked the divider. Something very fucking wrong."

"We've got two cars on them. They can't be that far," Dante replies, his voice low and resolute.

The phone buzzes again. My father's calling. I quickly answer and merge the call with Dante.

"Where are you?" I demand.

"East Oregon," Dad says, his voice tight. "The railyards are coming up ahead."

"We're on our way," Dante cuts in.

"The door locks engaged. I can't open them. I'm stuck in here."

He pounds on the glass. "Rico, open the fucking divider." His voice is muffled, thick with panic, but I hear it clearly through the phone. It's no use—the divider is soundproof. The driver either can't hear him or doesn't care.

"Dante, where the hell are you?" I shout.

"South Delaware. We're going to cut them off," Dante replies, urgency lining his words.

Dad's voice drops, cold and grim. "Vigo set me up. Promise me you'll take care of your mother and Cecilia, Anton."

"No," I say, grabbing the back of my neck, panic starting to rise. "You'll be fine. Dante's on his way. He'll get you out."

Tires screech in the background.

"Anton, promise me," Dad yells.

Before I can answer, gunshots ring out.

Glass shatters.

My heart stops.

"Dad! Dad!"

The line goes dead. The silence on the other end is suffocating.

I slam my fist into the wall. My mind races with fear and fury. This can't be happening. Not to my father.

"Dante, move faster," I shout into the phone, desperation clawing at me.

"We've got eyes on them," Dante's voice comes through strained.

More gunfire echoes through the phone, the sound of screeching tires filling the void. Dante's voice rises over the chaos, sharp and commanding.

"Return fire," he orders. "Don't let that bastard get away."

I pace the hallway, helpless, my heart racing. Every second feels like an eternity.

"What's happening, Dante?" I demand, my voice cracking.

"We got Rico before he could make a run for it," Dante says, gunfire still crackling in the background. "The others took off as soon as it went down, but Rocco and Brian are on their tail."

Minutes drag by, filled with the distant sounds of the firefight. My mind is a whirlwind, bouncing between rage and fear.

Suddenly, the gunfire stops. Dante's heavy breathing fills the silence. Gravel crunches under his boots as he steps out of the car.

Then, there's a long, agonizing pause.

"Fuck," Dante roars, his voice raw with fury.

"Dante, what's going on?" My voice shakes, and I struggle to catch my breath.

Dante's voice, barely a whisper, breaks through the phone. "Rico's still alive. But your father. Rico got to him first, Anton. He's dead."

"No, no, no," I murmur, sinking to my knees. The world blurs, my mind refusing to accept the reality. "He can't be dead. Dante, he can't be."

"I didn't get here in time," Dante says, his voice cracking with guilt. "This was too organized. It all happened so fast, and I was too late."

I bite back a sob, tears stinging my eyes. My knuckles turn white as I grip the phone. I already know who gave the order. I've known it in my gut since the moment Vigo told us his crazy plan. But hearing it out loud—that's what will make it real.

"Who ordered it?" I demand, my voice barely above a whisper.

There's a shuffle of movement, and I hear Dante ask, "Who gave the order, Rico?"

"Valentino," Rico coughs, his voice strained.

The name is like a dagger to my heart. "Kill him," I say coldly.

A single gunshot rings through the line.

Dante's breathing is ragged as he comes back on the phone. "It's done."

Tears stream down my face as I choke out, "He was set up. Valentino set us all up."

"I know," Dante's voice is rough with emotion. "We'll make him pay for this. But right now, you need to get out of there. Rico turned on your father, and we don't know who else might be involved. You're not safe."

"I don't give a damn about safe," I growl, my grief turning to rage. "I want blood."

"We will," Dante promises, his voice steady, though laced with pain. "But not like this. Marco wouldn't want you getting yourself killed in a fit of blind rage."

His words hit me hard. I take a breath and force myself to stay grounded. "Fine," I manage through clenched teeth. "But Dante, I swear—Valentino will pay for this. Every single one of them will."

"We'll make it happen," Dante replies, his voice unwavering. "I'm coming to get you."

The reality of my father's death crashes into me like a tidal wave, and I collapse to the floor in the hallway. Valentino—my cousin, the man I've spent my life protecting, betrayed me. Every time he asked for my loyalty, I gave it willingly. And this is how he repays me? He killed my father.

But this isn't over. Not even close.

I will avenge my father's death.

I will take down Valentino and anyone who stands with him.

They will all pay.

Valentino's phone rings, each tone stoking the anger simmering beneath my calm. When it finally connects, I don't give him a chance to speak. "My father called."

I keep my voice steady, gauging his reaction. I know he's behind this, but I need to hear it in his tone, feel the shift in his words. If he thinks I suspect him, he'll run or fortify his defenses. No, I need him to believe I'm still on his side. Let him feel secure in his lies.

When he least expects it, I'll make my move.

"Is there a problem?" he asks, his voice calm and controlled—too controlled.

"Rico left the planned route, so I sent Dante and a team to track them down and make sure nothing was wrong," I explain, keeping my tone even.

"What the hell are you talking about?"

"Rico shot my father. He's dead," I say flatly, letting the words land like a hammer.

"No," he roars, his tone shattering the pretense of calm. "And Rico?"

"I gave Dante the order to kill him," I respond, my voice colder than I intend.

Valentino falls silent for a beat, then growls, "Someone must've turned him. One of the other families. Don't worry. I'll find out who's behind this attack."

"This is war, Vigo," I say, the word war hanging in the air between us like a promise. "Whoever did this must pay."

"Of course, cousin," he replies, his voice smoothing out again. Too smooth. "I'll wrap up this meeting and meet you at the hotel."

"I'm not staying," I tell him. "Dante's on his way back to pick me up. I need to go home and tell my mother and Cecilia. I want extra guards on them until we find out who's responsible."

"I'll assign a few men," Valentino offers.

"If you don't mind, I'll choose the men," I say. "Cecilia needs to be comfortable with whoever's around." And I need to be certain of where their loyalties lie.

"You're right. I didn't consider that," Valentino concedes.

The elevator dings open. Dante steps out and I wrap up the call quickly. "He's here, now. I'll speak with you later."

Dante approaches me, his expression grim. "Anton," he says quietly. "I'm so sorry."

"Valentino will pay for what he did," I mutter, my voice barely above a whisper, venom dripping from every word. "But for now, I'll wait him out. He'll be expecting retaliation, so I need to play along, make him think I believe this was a hit from an opposing family." I pull my shoulders back and stand straighter. "I'll give him no reason to doubt my loyalty."

Dante nods. "I'm with you. Whatever it takes."

I glance at him, acknowledging his loyalty. "Thank you."

"What do you need from me?" he asks.

"Take me to my mother," I say, the weight of the impending conversation pressing down on me.

"Yeah. Let's go," Dante agrees.

The ride to my parents' house is torturous. The engine hums in the background, indifferent to the world collapsing around me. I stare out the window, but the familiar scenery is nothing more than a blur. My mind's consumed by loss and the sickening truth —Valentino orchestrated it all.

With each block we pass, the darkness pulls me deeper into its clutches. The grief of losing my father is a raw, festering wound. But it's the rage that fuels me. Valentino, that smug bastard, believes he's untouchable.

He's wrong.

I close my eyes, trying to shut out the world, but images of my father flood my mind. His body, cold and still, lying in a pool of blood. His face, once full of life and strength, now pale, empty. His eyes, always filled with love and pride, vacant. The hands that taught me everything, motionless.

I imagine the betrayal he must've felt in those final moments. The fear and pain knowing his nephew betrayed him. My grief hardens into hatred.

The car turns the corner, and the familiar streets of my childhood come into view. My mother's left the lamp on in the downstairs window, just like she always did when my father was out on business, waiting for him to return safely.

My mother's inside, unaware of the storm that's about to tear through her. My father was her rock and now he's gone. The thought breaks me, but I steel myself. She'll need me to be strong now.

As the car rolls to a stop, I take a deep breath, gathering my strength. "Let's do this," I say, stepping out into the cold night air.

I walk toward the house, each step heavier than the last. My resolve hardens with every movement. Valentino thinks he's won, but he has no idea that tonight, he's created his own executioner.

The front door creaks as I step inside. The house is silent, the steady ticking of the grandfather clock the only sound cutting through the stillness.

"You're finally home," my mother calls softly from the top of the stairs, her voice filled with relief as she peers down.

I pause, my heart heavy. "It's me, Mom."

Her face changes, concern creasing her brow. "Antonio? What's going on?"

I take a breath, knowing there's no easy way to break this. "Mom, we need to talk. Can you come downstairs?"

She nods slowly, descending the stairs as she ties the belt on her robe. Cecilia follows behind her, her eyes scanning my face.

"Antonio, what's going on?" Cecilia asks.

I motion for them to sit on the couch. Dante stands nearby, a silent presence. Cecilia's eyes flick toward him, but they quickly return to me.

I sit beside my mother, taking her hands in mine. "There's no easy way to say this," I begin, my voice thick with emotion. "Dad's gone."

For a moment, she stares at me as if trying to understand the words. "Gone? What do you mean, gone?"

Tears well up, but I push them down, forcing myself to stay composed. "Dad was killed tonight."

The color drains from her face, and she grips my hands tightly, as if I'm the anchor keeping her from being swept away by the torrent of her grief. "No, no. Not my Marco," she whispers, shaking her head in disbelief. "That can't be true."

Cecilia gasps, her had flies to her mouth, stifling a sob. She turns to Dante, who steps forward, wrapping his arms around her.

"Who did this?" my mother's voice is barely audible.

I swallow the bitterness in my throat. "An opposing family. They saw an opportunity and took it."

Her eyes widen with shock, and for a moment, I think she might collapse. "But why? Why would they do this?"

"Power," I say, my voice hardening. "They wanted to send a message."

Tears stream down her face, and she clings to me, sobs wracking her body. I hold her close, my own tears mingling with hers.

"I promise you," I whisper fiercely. "We'll make them pay."

Cecilia moves to sit beside us, her arm wrapping around our mother. "We'll get through this together," she says, though her voice trembles with uncertainty.

"I've made arrangements to have a guard stationed at the house," Dante says. "And I'll be here for anything you need," he says, glancing briefly at Cecilia before looking back at me.

"Thank you, Dante," my mother whispers through her tears.

Dante nods, his expression resolute. "I'll always be here for your family."

The room falls silent, save for the soft sound of my mother and sister's tears.

Beneath my sorrow, the fire inside me burns hotter.

Valentino awakened his worst nightmare—a monster forged from betrayal. He'll pay for every tear shed. Every ounce of pain. Slowly, carefully, I'll dismantle everything he holds dear, piece by piece, until he's trapped with no way out.

He won't see me coming until it's too late.

T he meeting stretched well into the night, but there was no urgency to leave. Too much was at stake, with plans unfolding, new alliances being forged, and the satisfaction of solidified control settling in.

When I pull into my driveway, I notice the lights still on at my aunt and uncle's house across the street. Antonio's car is parked out front, along with several others I recognize. I'm sure they've gathered after hearing about Marco's death.

I feel nothing. Why would I, when it was my order that sealed his fate? But I know the show must go on. I'll have to get Alessia and break the news to my mother, then make an appearance, playing the part of the grieving nephew.

As for my wife—I'm sure she's learned her lesson after spending the day locked in the basement.

"Get up," I order.

"Fuck you," Alessia retorts, still defiant.

"Don't tempt me." I grab her arm and pull her to her feet. "Unfortunately, I don't have time for that right now. We need to collect my mother and go to Aunt Nicki's."

She stiffens. "Why? What's wrong?"

"Marco was killed tonight," I say, my tone flat and rehearsed as if I'm reading a script I've prepared in my mind.

Her breath catches. "What? How?"

"He was shot on the way to our meeting."

"How did anyone get past his guards?" she asks, her disbelief palpable.

"He didn't have any with him."

"How could you let him go without guards?" she snaps, her voice rising with frustration.

I whirl on her, irritation flaring. "Stop fucking questioning me."

She presses her lips together, wisely dropping the subject, and we head for my mother's house.

When we arrive, I let myself in and find her asleep in my father's chair. She hasn't slept in their bed since he died, choosing his chair instead. I find the whole thing ridiculous.

"Domenica," Alessia says, gently shaking her shoulder.

My mother stirs, blinking up at us. "Alessia? Valentino? What are you both doing here?" she asks, glancing between us with confusion.

Her eyes widen. "What's wrong?"

"Uncle Marco was shot and killed tonight." I force my voice to break, just enough to sound sincere.

Her hand flies to her mouth, and her face crumples as tears begin to spill. "Not Marco, too."

"It's a tragedy," I murmur, offering false gravity. "We need to be with the family right now."

My mother nods, her shoulders trembling with silent sobs. "Let's go," she manages.

Alessia takes her by the hand, and together, we leave the house and walk next door. Dante's standing by the door when we arrive. The embodiment of loyalty in the face of tragedy.

Inside, the house is filled with hushed voices. My mother immediately seeks out Nicki, embracing her tightly, both of them overcome by their shared sorrow. I watch the scene unfold before

I approach my aunt. "I'm so sorry for your loss. Uncle Marco was a good man and will be greatly missed."

Tears flow freely down her face, her sorrow raw and unfiltered. "Thank you, Valentino." She dabs at her eyes with a tissue. "I can't believe he's gone."

"I know," I reply, my tone low and soothing. "I'll find out who did this. I promise."

Moving through the room, quiet words of comfort are offered where needed, reinforcing the image of a strong, compassionate leader.

Antonio steps out of the kitchen, a cup of coffee in his hand. "Vigo. I didn't expect you tonight."

"I know the pain you're feeling right now." I pause. "And knew I needed to be here."

A quiet nod follows. "It means a lot."

My hand settles firmly on his shoulder. "Uncle Marco was loyal to both my father and me. I'll do everything in my power to avenge him."

Antonio's expression shifts, his jaw tightening. "I'd like to be the one to handle the guilty party."

"Of course, cousin." I meet his gaze with practiced sincerity. "But for now, we need to focus on supporting the family and arranging the funeral."

"Yes, I do." His response is clipped. With that, he steps away, moving to sit beside his mother on the sofa.

I stay just long enough to offer a few more words of comfort, each one carefully calculated. Everyone needs to see me not only as the grieving nephew, but also the Capo ready to avenge his uncle's death. But I can't linger too long.

Turning to Alessia, who's sitting quietly near my mother, I say, "We're leaving."

She hesitates, "This is bringing up memories of losing your father. I want to be here for her."

"You're coming with me," I reply coldly, dismissing her concern.

"Valentino, she needs someone tonight," Alessia insists, her voice soft but pleading.

"My mother will be fine. We're leaving. Now."

Not wanting to cause a scene, Alessia swallows her protest.

As we step outside, my facade of grief fades, replaced by the cold, unshakable determination that's been driving me all along. My plan is in motion, and the pieces are already falling into place. Soon enough, everyone in this organization will be forced to choose where their loyalties lie.

And there will be only one option—me.

Even after his father's death, Antonio hasn't slowed down. It's as if his grief alone is fueling him, driving him to work around the clock, chasing down leads, and trying to piece together who was behind his father's murder. I doubt he's even slept. Val's office has become his war room. The relentless search for answers consuming him.

The problem is, I think he's looking in all the wrong places. I want to tell him as much, but this house has eyes and ears everywhere—and I don't know who I can trust.

"This is for Antonio," I say, holding up a plate to the guard stationed outside the closed office door. "Can I bring it to him?"

"He asked not to be disturbed," the guard responds curtly.

"The man has to eat," I fire back.

He narrows his eyes at me, clearly displeased at my insistence, but I don't back down. Finally, he knocks on the door.

"What is it?" Antonio calls from inside.

"Mrs. Comiso would like to speak with you," the guard announces flatly, as he opens the door.

"Let her in," Antonio replies.

"Thank you," I say, flashing a sweet, yet fake smile at the guard. He doesn't react, simply closing the door behind me.

"I made you some lunch," I say, placing the pasta on the desk next to him.

"Thanks," he mutters, barely glancing at the food.

"Have you made any progress?"

He leans back in Val's leather chair, letting out a deep sign. "Not really."

"Where's Valentino?" I ask curious why he's not helping.

"Meeting with his new associates."

"I thought his top priority was finding out who was behind this attack?" I ask, gauging his reaction.

Antonio stiffens slightly, then shrugs it off. "Was there something you needed?" he asks, changing the subject.

I hesitate, choosing my words carefully. "It's strange, isn't it? Valentino didn't come right home the night it happened and now he's barely involved in the investigation."

For a fraction of a second, Antonio's eyes narrow before he forces a smile. "Valentino has his methods."

Before I can push further, Val strides into the room, eyeing me suspiciously. "What are you doing in my office, Alessia?"

I stand up straight, keeping my expression neutral. "I brought Antonio some lunch. Have you eaten? I can make you a plate, too."

Antonio stands and steps between us. "Alessia was being the perfect hostess," he says. "You've done well with her lessons."

The Antonio I once knew would never have complimented Valentino, let alone admired his cruelty. His words make me uneasy, but I maintain my composure.

Valentino's gaze drifts to the plate of food before returning to me. "And discussing business, it seems."

"Alessia was expressing her concern about your safety given everything that happened," he says, his smile never wavering. "She only wanted to know if I've made any progress. There's been no harm done."

Valentino studies me for a moment longer before turning his

attention back to Antonio. "Make sure you're focusing on the task at hand, cousin. We need results."

"Of course," Antonio replies smoothly. "I'm on it."

"And you," Valentino says, turning his cold gaze back to me. "Need to stay out of our business. Do you understand?"

"I do," I reply, lowering my eyes. "I'm sorry for overstepping."

Valentino nods, his tone dismissive. "Go find something to do."

"Do I have your permission to go for a walk?"

Valentino sighs dramatically as he walks to the door. "Dante," he calls.

"Yes?" Dante appears almost immediately.

"Alessia wants to go for a walk. Escort her," Valentino orders.

"Not a problem, boss."

"Thank you," I say sweetly, stepping up on my tiptoes to kiss Valentino's cheek. The gesture makes my stomach churn.

Valentino turns to Antonio. "And you doubted my methods," he says as I walk out of the office. "You could learn a thing or two from me," he adds as he closes the door.

"Are we walking in the park, Mrs. Comiso?"

"That would be nice," I reply, keeping my tone light. "Mind if I get my camera first?"

"Whatever you'd like," he answers.

I hurry upstairs to get my camera. It's a beautiful day for photos, but I have something more important in mind—I need to stop by the gallery.

When I return, Dante holds the door open for me. "Ready?" he asks.

"Yes, thank you," I say as I step outside. "Do you have a preference for which way we go?"

"Not at all. Lead the way." He gestures for me to go ahead.

We walk toward the park, the warmth of the sun on my skin a brief comfort. I snap a few pictures of the flowers, the kids playing nearby, but my mind is on the gallery. After a while, I clear my throat and turn to Dante.

"Actually, Dante, would you mind if we made a quick stop? There's a gallery nearby. I'd like to drop off some photos to be developed."

Dante hesitates, glancing around. "A gallery? Valentino only said the park."

"I know. But it won't take long. I really need to get these photos developed. It's important," I plead.

He shifts on his feet looking torn. "I don't want to upset Val. I know how he gets."

I place a hand on his arm, meeting his gaze. "Please, Dante. It won't take long."

He sighs, still unsure. "Alright, Mrs. Comiso. But we need to be quick."

"Thank you," I say, relief flooding me. "And please, call me Alessia."

Dante shakes his head, a faint smile on his lips. "It's easier if I stick with Mrs. Comiso. Less chance of slipping up when we get home."

"I understand," I say with a slight nod.

He pulls out his cell, powering it off. "Do you have your phone with you?"

"I left it at home. I know Valentino tracks it."

Dante slides his phone into his pocket, glancing around nervously. "Let's hope he doesn't check mine."

"I'm sure he's distracted with Antonio," I say, trying to reassure him.

We continue walking, though Dante seems more on edge now, glancing over his shoulder more frequently. The streets are bustling with life, and I capture moments of everyday beauty—a street vendor selling flowers, a couple sharing an ice cream cone, a child chasing a butterfly. Each click of the shutter helps calm my nerves.

As we approach Starlight Studios, anticipation settles in. Dante holds the door for me, and I step inside.

"Allie, it's good to see you," Ophelia says with a warm smile.

"I have some new photos to drop off," I say, handing over the memory card.

"I can't wait to see them," she says, her eyes bright. "You always bring such unique perspectives."

I smile, trying to keep my nerves in check. "Thank you."

"Your last set sold out," she continues, her voice full of admiration. "I have your payment."

I press a finger to my lips, signaling her to keep her voice down. Ophelia slips an envelope into my hand, and I quickly glance over my shoulder to ensure Dante isn't watching, before tucking it into my pocket.

"Thank you," I whisper.

"Are there any you want prints of?" she asks.

"Not today," I reply. "I hope to have some more for you soon."

"I'll be looking forward to them."

After gathering my things, Dante leads me back outside. "Shall we head back to the park?" he asks.

"Yes," I reply, a hint of relief in my tone.

Valentino can't ever find out about the gallery. The money. This isn't only about doing something I love—it's my lifeline, my eventual way out. I can't endure the abuse or being raped much longer.

One wrong move, one slip up, and everything falls apart. What would Val do if he found out? I can't bear to think about the consequences.

No. I have to stay focused on the only thing that matters—my freedom.

Antonio

O nce Alessia's out of earshot, Vigo takes the seat I vacated behind his desk. "We need to talk," he says, gesturing for me to sit.

I drop into the chair across from him and watch as he casually spears a forkful of pasta—my lunch. He chews slowly, watching me for a reaction, but I give him nothing.

"She's come a long way these past few months," he remarks, wiping his mouth.

"Whatever you're doing, it's working," I reply, stroking his already oversized ego.

Vigo grins. "I'm glad you can see I was right about how to train her. Someday, you'll have a woman to do the same with. Fortunately, I've got all the tools you'll need." He takes another bite, savoring his self-satisfaction.

"You said we needed to talk," I remind him, steering the conversation back on track.

"Ah, yes." He sets the fork down, his expression sharpening. "With your father gone, God rest his soul," he pauses, savoring his dramatics. "I need a new underboss. Someone I can trust completely."

Suddenly, the room feels smaller. The air thicker. The audacity—acting like he didn't have a hand in my father's death. I keep my face blank, refusing to let him see the revulsion boiling within me.

"You'll be my new underboss, Anton," he says as though he's doing me a favor. "You're blood. And I know you'll be loyal."

"Of course," I say, my voice steady. "Whatever you need."

"I knew I could count on you." He pauses, a satisfied smile spreading across his face. "Along with overseeing Alessia's security, you'll take over running the restaurant. Keeping the money flowing through it is critical to our operations."

"I understand," I reply, voice-controlled. "I'll make sure everything continues to run smoothly."

"Alessia will be starting work this week," he says, leaning forward, his eyes gleaming with malice.

"Work?" I ask.

He lets out a snicker. "She's going to be *Casa della Ombre's* newest waitress. It'll make it easier for you to keep an eye on her—make sure she stays in line."

My disgust for him grows. The restaurant is the last place Alessia should be. He uses the downstairs as his personal whorehouse where he fucks Lena as often as possible. Forcing his wife into that environment is sickening.

But I can't show it.

"That makes sense," I manage to say, each word tasting bitter.

"Excellent," he says, leaning back. "I knew I could count on you."

"I'll always have your back."

Vigo launches into a ramble about responsibilities and expectations, but I barely hear him. My thoughts are consumed with his downfall. His arrogance will be his undoing.

"I want to throw a party," he says suddenly, clapping his hands.

"For what?" I ask, raising an eyebrow.

"To celebrate your promotion, of course," he says, oozing condescension.

"If that's what you want," I say, standing to leave. "I've got some leads I need to follow up on."

"Fine." He waves me off dismissively. "Plan something for Friday night at the restaurant."

I pause at the door, my hand on the knob. "You want me to plan my own party?"

He looks up from his phone, incredulous. "You don't think I'm doing it, do you?"

"Of course not," I say smoothly. "I'll take care of it."

"Good," he mutters, already returning to his texts.

It isn't until I get outside that I'm able take a deep breath. Looking up at the sky, I whisper, "I won't let your death go unpunished, Dad."

Dante appears at my side. "Going somewhere?"

"Yeah," I say, glancing between him and Alessia. "Did you get any good shots today?"

Alessia's face lights up. "I think so. The park was so full of life. I didn't want to come home."

"You were at the park the whole time?" I ask, raising an eyebrow.

She nods slowly. "I must've dragged Dante around a million times."

I turn my gaze to Dante, who just shrugs, unaware that I already know about Alessia's activities. "And how was the gallery?" I ask, gauging her reaction.

Panic flashes across her face. "Don't worry. Your secret's safe with me."

Relief washes over her. "Thank you, Anton."

Hearing her call me *Anton* again stirs something in me. She hasn't called me that since we were teenagers, before Valentino's influence tainted everything. For a moment, the memory lingers, dark and bitter, but I bury it quickly. The poison's still here, and I can't let it spread any further.

"You'd better go inside before he starts looking for you."

She's taken enough chances today. The last thing she needs is for Vigo to see her speaking to us and decide he needs to teach her another lesson.

"Thanks again, Dante," she says, shooting him a grateful smile before slipping into the house.

"How'd you know about the gallery?" Dante asks, his voice low.

"I've taken her a few times."

"And Val doesn't know?"

"No. He'd put a stop to it if he did."

Dante's face hardens. "The way he treats her—"

"It's about to get worse," I say, voice darkening.

"What are you talking about?"

"He promoted me to underboss."

"Congratulations," Dante says, though his tone is far from congratulatory.

"Thanks."

"How does that affect Alessia?" he asks, his curiosity piqued.

"I'll be running the restaurant. And Alessia will be working there."

"Are you fucking kidding me?" Dante's face twists in disbelief. "He's making his wife work alongside the women he regularly comes to fuck?"

"Yep," I say, my tone flat. "It's a dick move. But would you expect anything less?"

Dante scrubs a hand over his face in frustration. "Did you find out anything useful while you were here?"

We exchange a few words about the scraps of information I've gathered. Valentino's tracks are well-covered, his plans buried deep. But I can't shake the feeling there's more to it—more of our own men involved than we realize.

I glance back at the house, suspicion gnawing at the edges of my mind. "It's only a matter of time," I murmur, more to myself than Dante.

"Before what?"

"Before he slips up." My voice is steady, a promise woven into the words. "And when he does, I'll be ready."

Alessia

"Alessia," Val's voice booms from his office as soon as I step inside. Unease creeps up my spine as I make my way to his office. "Where have you been?"

"You gave me permission to go for a walk with Dante," I remind him.

"That was two hours ago," he snaps.

"I brought my camera," I say, holding it up. "Would you like to see some of the photos I took?"

"You and that ridiculous camera," he sneers, disdain dripping from his words. I school my features, refusing to show him how much his comment stings. "Come clear my plate. It'll be good practice for you."

"Practice?"

"Practice," he echoes, leaning back in his chair with a smirk. "You'll need it for your new job."

"What new job?"

"You're going to be waitressing at my restaurant."

"*At Casa della Ombre*?".

"Yes," he confirms, the grin on his face growing wider.

"Why would you make me do that?"

"Does the princess think she's too good to have a job?"

"It's not about having to work. It's about the fact that you expect me to work alongside your whores."

"Watch your mouth."

"Or what?" I shout, my patience finally shattering. "I'm sick and tired of watching my mouth. I refuse to let you humiliate me like this."

"Shut the fuck up," he growls, rising from his chair.

"Make me," I challenge, my eyes blazing with defiance.

In a flash, he's in front of me, his hand striking my face with such force that I stumble, catching myself on the edge of the desk. Pain radiates through my cheek, and I feel the hot sting of tears.

"You'll work at the restaurant," he hisses, grabbing my arm and spinning me around. "Or anywhere else I say," he continues, shoving me against the desk, lifting my skirt.

"The door's open," I say, struggling to pull away.

"You think I don't know that?" he asks, the metal clinking softly as he unbuckles his belt, followed by the whisper of leather sliding through the loops. "You earned this by arguing with me. You deserve to be humiliated."

He brings the leather down across my backside, the bite tearing a cry from me.

"Keep yelling," he warns. "And my men will come. They'll get to see you bent over like the dirty whore you are."

He strikes my upper thighs, and I bite down on my bottom lip to stop myself from screaming. My body shakes as he continues, strike after strike, until my knees wobble, threatening to give out. Then he kicks my legs apart, the sound of his zipper filling the room.

"Val, please," I beg, my voice breaking. "Don't do this."

"You should be grateful," he spits, his breath hot against my neck. "Do you know how many women would kill to be in your place? And yet, you keep acting like a spoiled bitch. Maybe I should just kill you and be done with it."

He thrusts into me and a sharp pain tears through my body. I can't stop the sound that escapes my lips.

Grabbing a fistful of my hair, he yanks my head back. "I said shut the fuck up," he snarls, his hips driving into me.

"Is everything—" I hear Dante's voice, but I can't see him.

"Everything's fine," Val snarls, halting his movements.

"I heard Alessia scream. I didn't realize—" Dante stammers, flustered. "I'll close the door."

"You'll leave it open," Val orders sharply.

"You have your wife bent over your desk with your cock inside her. I'm not the only man here."

Val's laugh is cold. "And you think I care?"

Mortification grips me, my face flushed with shame. I want to disappear, to escape this nightmare, but there's nothing I can say or do to stop it.

"No, but—"

"She's a hot piece of ass, I get it," Val says, his voice laced with cruelty. "Perhaps you'd like to join in? See what she's like for yourself?"

"No," Dante says, disgust evident in his voice. "At least allow her some dignity."

"If you aren't going to fuck her, then get the hell out," Val roars.

"Yes, sir," Dante mumbles. His heavy footsteps echo down the hallway as he retreats.

"See what you've done?" Val sneers, his grip on my hips tightening. "Now all my men will know you like to take it up your ass. You won't be able to walk through here without fearing one of them bending you over and fucking you like the slut you are."

Tears pour down my cheeks as I shut my eyes, wishing myself far away. Far from this room, from Val, from everything. His grunts are the only sound as he uses my body and empties himself inside me.

"From now on, you'll keep your mouth shut when you're told

to do something. Do you understand?" he growls, his voice dripping with vitriol.

I nod, too stunned and broken to speak.

"Good," he spits, shoving me away. "Now get out of my sight."

With trembling hands, I right my skirt and hurry out of the room. I need to get away from him.

A hand wraps over my mouth, and I'm pulled into an empty room. I struggle to get away.

"It's just me," Dante whispers urgently. "Stop fighting, and I'll let you go. Okay?"

I nod, and he slowly drops his hand.

"What do you want?" I ask, my voice cracking.

"I want to make sure you're okay," he says gently, his concern clear.

"I'm fine. Can I go now?" My voice shakes as I try to leave.

Dante grabs my arms, turning me to face him. I keep my gaze down, desperate for him to let me go.

"You're not fine. Your lip's bleeding," he says, scanning me for more injuries. "And your eye's already bruising. Did Val do this to you?"

"I tripped and fell."

"I heard him yelling at you from across the house," Dante presses, his eyes searching my face.

"We had a disagreement," I say hoping to sound convincing.

"It sounded like more than that."

"Val has a kink for being watched." The lie slips from my lips. "That's all you saw. Now, I really need to go."

Dante steps aside, allowing me to pass. Just as I reach the door, he calls, "Alessia."

I pause, my hand on the doorknob, but I don't turn around. "Please, don't say anything more," I whisper. The last thing I need is to hear him offer help I can't accept.

For a moment, there's only silence. I stand frozen, bracing

myself for what might come next, but Dante says nothing. He watches as I open the door and walk out. My body aches with every step, but the pain is nothing compared to the storm swirling inside me.

Val may think he's broken me, but one day, I'll be the one to break him.

Antonio

I'm sitting in my father's office, *my* office now, at *Casa della Ombre*. He ran this part of the business for as long as I can remember. Even though he's gone, his presence lingers in every corner, guiding me.

I remember coming here as a kid, sitting in this very chair while he worked. He'd ruffle my hair and tell me one day, this place would be mine. Back then, I didn't fully grasp what that meant—that one day, he'd no longer be here. But now, I do.

It's up to me to protect what he built and find a way to take Valentino out without turning *La Famiglia* against me. Thinking of him gives me the clarity I need to stay patient. To plan carefully.

As I'm lost in thought, there's a soft knock on the door.

"Come in," I call.

"I'm sorry to interrupt," Alessia says as she steps in. "Valentino wants me to start work today."

I turn to look at her, my heart nearly stopping at the sight of the bruises on her face. I jump up from my seat and rush over to her. "What the hell happened?"

"I tripped and fell," she says with a slight shrug, her eyes avoiding mine.

"Don't lie to me," I say, my voice rising with anger. "Did Valentino do this to you?"

She hesitates before answering, "Yes."

"I'm going to fucking kill him," I growl, clenching my fists at my sides.

"No," she pleads. "He can't know I told you."

I force myself to take a breath, even as rage bubbles under my skin. "I can't let this go, Alessia."

She looks at me, her eyes filled with both anger and pain. "You knew he was hurting me. Why do you care now?"

Guilt twists in my gut. She's right, and I can't deny it. I've known. Maybe not everything, but enough. "I should've stepped in sooner. I'm sorry."

She shakes her head, not convinced. I can't blame her.

"But this," I pause, searching for the right words, but not finding them. "I can't stand by and watch this get worse."

"Worse?" she repeats, frustrated. "If Val finds out I told you, it'll only get worse. You don't understand what he's capable of."

I'm torn between wanting to hurt Valentino like he's hurting Alessia and the terror in her eyes. It's not just fear of him—it's fear of what will happen if I go after him.

I take a deep breath, forcing myself to stay calm though every instinct is screaming at me to do something, anything. "Alright," I say, though it feels like I'm betraying everything I should do. "For now, I won't do anything."

She exhales softly, but all I see is the tension in her body.

"But if you come in wearing bruises again," I pause, my voice hardening. "There's nothing you can say that will stop me."

She nods, wiping a tear from her bruised cheek.

I guide her to a chair and sit her down gently. "You shouldn't be working today."

"I have to," she insists. "Valentino will suspect something if I don't."

I sigh, hating that even though he's not here, he's still running the show. "Fine," I relent, even though it feels wrong. "Let's do the paperwork to get you on the books, and then I'll have one of the girls start your training."

"Valentino told me I'm not to be paid."

I stop mid-movement, the pen I'm holding almost snapping in my grip. "What did you say?"

She avoids my gaze, her voice barely above a whisper. "Valentino gave clear instructions. I'm not to be paid for my work."

"Of course he did," I mutter, slamming the pen down on the desk. "He has to make sure you're reminded who's in control."

Alessia winces at the sharpness in my voice. "I'll figure something out," I say, my tone firm but quieter now. She doesn't deserve any of this.

For now, I put my anger aside and focus on what I can control. "Come on, I'll introduce you to Isabella," I add, leading her out of the office. Isabella's one of the few servers Valentino hasn't taken an interest in, which makes her the safest option.

When I return to my office, I slump back into my chair. I can't let this continue. Valentino may be family, but he's crossed a line that can never be forgiven. There's another knock at the door. I glance up, half-expecting more trouble. Instead, it's Dante.

"I already talked to her," I say before he has a chance to speak.

"I figured," he replies. "But that's not why I'm here. There's a contractor waiting for you. He says he has an appointment?"

"Perfect," I say as I stand. "Where is he?"

"I had him wait at the bar," Dante says, his brow lifting slightly. "Why do you need a contractor?"

"I'm having some work done downstairs," I explain, heading for the door. "I'm turning one of the old spaces into a soundproof dungeon."

This is just the first step in a much bigger plan. Even though I trust Dante with my life, I can't tell him everything. It's safer this way. If things go south, he can't be implicated if he doesn't know anything.

Dante raises an eyebrow. "A dungeon? I didn't think you were into that kind of thing."

"It's not for me," I say with a smirk. "I'm sick of Valentino using our meeting room for his shit. This will keep him, and anyone else who needs it, out of the way."

Dante chuckles, shaking his head. "Well, as long as it keeps Val's dick out of our work space, I'm all for it."

For now, he'll think this is about keeping Val out of the meeting room, and that's exactly how it needs to stay.

"That's the plan," I reply as we walk into the bar area.

The contractor, a burly man, is chatting with the bartender. He stands when we approach.

"Mr. Luciano?" he asks, extending a hand.

"Antonio is fine," I say, shaking his hand. "Thanks for coming on short notice."

"No problem," he replies.

"Let's take a look at the space," I offer.

We head downstairs, the noise from the restaurant above fading as we move deeper into the cool, dimly lit basement. The walls are lined with old bricks. We eventually reach the dug-out space, an unfinished room with potential.

"This is it," I say, gesturing around.

The contractor looks around, impressed. "I've heard rumors about Philadelphia's underground tunnels, but I thought they were nothing more than urban legend."

Philly's underground tunnels has been whispered for generations—secret passageways used for everything from hiding revolutionaries to sheltering runaway slaves.

"The tunnels are real, but we've made sure ours are no longer connected to the main system." I turn back to the task at hand. "I want this space fully soundproofed and outfitted with everything we talked about."

The contractor makes notes on his clipboard. "It'll take a few weeks, but we'll get it done."

"Good," I reply, crossing my arms. "And I don't need to remind you about the NDA."

"Of course not," he assures me. "I've got three trusted men working with me, and your attorney already had them sign."

"I know," I say, keeping my tone even.

He glances at the room. "Mind if I grab a few measurements?"

"Go ahead," I say, stepping aside.

As he starts working, Dante leans in, his voice low. "You really think this will keep Val out of trouble?"

"I don't know," I admit. "But it's a start."

Even in its unfinished state, I can already see the room for what it will become—something far darker than anyone else realizes. It's more than just a space for indulgence. I keep the thought buried deep, just like the secrets that will soon fill these walls. It's the first step, the foundation of something much bigger.

And when the moment arrives, these walls will bear silent witness to the fate that awaits Valentino.

<h1 style="text-align:center">Antonio</h1>

onight's supposed to be a celebration—a party in my honor. The restaurant is closed for the private event, filled with our long-time associates including Draco Moretti and his top men. But the real tension comes from the unfamiliar faces—Giovanni DeLuca and Emilio Salazar, dangerous men with deadly ambitions.

Valentino's confident that the evening will go off without a hitch. But in a room full of power, egos, and shifting alliances, control is only one misstep away from disaster.

Sitting at the bar, I swirl the whiskey in my glass, watching the amber liquid catch the light. The atmosphere is tense, thick with cologne and anticipation. Our guards search every guest as they arrive, but it does little to ease my nerves. I take a slow sip, letting the burn settle deep in my chest.

"Ready for your big debut tonight?" Valentino's voice cuts through the noise as he slides onto the stool beside me. The bartender doesn't even ask, immediately pouring him his usual— whiskey on the rocks.

I force a smile. "You know parties aren't my thing. I would've preferred to slip into the role quietly."

"Don't be ridiculous. This is an event worth celebrating," he says as he walks away.

Servers weave between the guests, offering drinks and hors d'oeuvres, while the low hum of conversation fills the room. Men in tailored suits gather in small clusters, talking business, veiling their threats with polite smiles.

With his drink in one hand and a cigar in the other, Valentino moves through the crowd, flashing that charismatic grin. As the night wears on, his laughter grows louder, each drink fueling his arrogance. He's the center of attention, and he knows it.

A knot forms in my chest when I spot Alessia, not on Valentino's arm where a queen should be. Instead, she's waiting tables. Her face is composed, but I see the strain in her movements. The bruises that had been glaringly obvious earlier are now masked beneath layers of makeup. They're still visible but far better concealed than before.

Isabella approaches, carrying another tray, and I catch her eye. "Did you help her with the makeup?" I ask quietly.

"I've been there," she admits. "I learned how to hide the worst of it when I needed to. Figured I could help."

I glance at Alessia again, then back to Isabella. "Thank you."

Isabella offers a slight, understanding nod before returning to her work.

A movement catches my eye—Draco Moretti. He's watching me, his gaze sharp and calculating. He follows my line of sight straight to Alessia. He looks at her with casual indifference before his expression darkens. Without a word, he makes his way toward Valentino.

"Ah, my favorite son-in-law," Draco calls out as he claps him on the back, loud enough to draw attention. "Looks like you've been keeping her in line."

Draco chuckles, glancing at me once more before turning his full attention back to Valentino, the jab unmistakable.

Vigo flashes a grin, his eyes glinting with cruel satisfaction.

"You know how it is. Sometimes, you have to remind them who's in charge."

Their laughter grates against my nerves, but I keep my expression neutral, watching the exchange from a distance.

The men around them chuckle. I grip my glass until my knuckles turn white. The urge to shatter it in my hand surges, but I force myself to stay calm. This is not the place to make a scene.

All I want to do is get the formalities over with and go home, but the night drags on.

Valentino's newest associates are deep in discussion, their tones low. I don't trust either of them, but they're here on Valentino's invitation.

Dante catches my eye from across the room, his expression focused and knowing. He senses the same undercurrent I do—tonight's balance could tip at any moment.

Lena moves cautiously through the crowd, trying to keep her distance from Valentino. Usually, she'd be all over him, but tonight, she's avoiding him like the plague.

Valentino's eyes follow her, a predatory gleam in them. He corners her near the kitchen, gripping her arm tightly. She tries to pull away, but he leans in, whispering something that makes her flinch. Then, with a rough tug, he drags her toward the stairs leading to the basement.

Disgust churns in my gut. I know exactly what he's about to do—fuck his mistress downstairs while his wife is forced to serve the very men who should be bowing at her feet.

What feels like an eternity passes before Valentino returns, his face flushed. He grabs a fresh drink from a passing server downing in one go and grabbing another.

Lena trails behind him, eyes downcast, mascara streaking her cheeks. There's a shift between them, subtle but unmistakable. From my seat at the bar, I watch as Lena blends into the crowd, hurrying toward the ladies' room.

Valentino stumbles toward the stage at the far end of the room, tapping the microphone. A few people wince from the feedback. The chatter begins to die down, and all eyes turn to him.

"Ladies and gentlemen," he begins, his voice booming through the speakers. "Thank you for joining us tonight to celebrate my dear cousin and his, let's say, unexpected promotion to underboss."

Polite applause ripples through the room, though I can see the skepticism in some of the men's eyes. Vigo gestures for me to join him. I down the last of my drink before making my way over, keeping my expression neutral.

"Come on, Antonio, don't be shy," he grins, slapping me on the back as I reach the stage.

The applause fades, and Valentino's voice drops. "Since we were kids, I've kept Antonio by my side because, as we all know, every leader needs a loyal side kick." He pauses as the room erupts in laughter, the humor hitting precisely as he intended.

Valentino raises his hand. "Alright, enough joking. Let's get serious for a moment." The applause fades, and his voice drops, taking on a darker edge. "Antonio's been my right-hand man for years, dependable as ever. But let's be honest—he's always been second to me. Just like his father was second to mine."

My body stiffens. I've endured a lot from Valentino, but dragging my father's name into this? That's a low blow.

His eyes gleam with cruel delight as he continues, "He's the kind of guy who'll never step up and try to steal the spotlight. That's why he's perfect for his new role." A wave of uneasy laughter sweeps through the crowd.

"Antonio's been loyal. Like a dog," he says, his laughter ringing out, mocking. "I never have to worry with him by my side."

"I'll always have your back, cousin." The lie slips from my lips.

Valentino swirls his whiskey. "That's what I like to hear— loyalty." He pauses, his smirk deepening. "It's funny, though. Where does it really stand when the stakes are high?"

The room falls into tense silence, every eye on me. I glance at

Dante, who gives a subtle nod, his gaze focused. He's not only observing, but he's also gauging the shifting power dynamics.

"And speaking of loyalty," Val's eyes shift to Alessia, standing off to the side. "Why don't you tell us what you really think of her, Antonio? What do you see when you look at my wife?"

The sudden shift catches me off guard. I know what he's doing—trying to humiliate me, maybe even provoke me. But I won't give him the satisfaction.

"Alessia's your wife and a respected member of our family," I reply calmly.

"Come on," Valentino taunts. "Tell the truth. Or are you too scared?"

My jaw tightens. "Alessia's a beautiful woman. Intelligent. Strong-willed."

"Beautiful, yes," Val sneers. "But have you ever wondered what it would be like to fuck her? To have what's mine?"

The air in the room shifts, thick with tension. Alessia's face flushes with a mix of anger and humiliation.

"Of course not," I reply, keeping my voice steady. "I would never—"

"Not even back when you two were together? Before she was promised to me?" Val leans in, his breath reeking of whiskey. "You never dreamed of it?"

The crowd shifts, nervous laughter filling the gaps. I keep my face impassive, determined not to give him the satisfaction of a reaction.

"I'll let you in on a little secret," he murmurs, his voice dripping with cruelty, half to me, half into the microphone. "Alessia's a terrible fuck. She's horribly boring. I'm hoping she can learn a little something about how to please a man while she's working alongside my favorite whores."

Valentino's gaze shifts to Lena, who's waiting tables, her movements nervous and uneasy. "Lena here," he continues, flicking his hand toward her with careless arrogance. begs for my cock. "Her cunt drips for it every time. You should give her a go," he slurs, his words dripping with mockery. "Almost forgot—she used to let you fuck her, too."

"Were you not able to satisfy her? Is that why she stopped letting you into her cunt?" Valentino spits the words, his sneer curling as flecks of saliva hit my face. I wipe it away with the back of my hand. He turns back to Alessia, a cruel smile twisting his lips, and continues his drunken tirade. "Maybe Alessia will spread her legs and let you try out all her holes—if you don't mind sloppy seconds." His eyes light up as though he's had a sick revelation. "Hell, the two of you can watch me fuck Lena. Maybe you'll pick up a few new tricks."

Lena's tray slips from her hands, the glasses shattering on the floor, the crash piercing through the uneasy quiet. Alessia's face crumples, and I see her fighting back tears. Valentino stumbles forward, still grinning like a fool.

"Enough, Vigo," I say, my voice low but firm.

"Enough? We're just getting started," he replies, raising his glass to take another sip of whiskey. His aim falters, and the drink spills down the front of his shirt, but he barely notices.

"The party's over, cousin," I say flatly.

I catch Dante's eye. He's already making his way toward us.

Grabbing the microphone, I force a calm, composed tone despite the turmoil inside. "Excuse me, everyone. I apologize for Valentino's behavior. He's had a little too much fun this evening, and I think it's best if we get him some fresh air."

Valentino, oblivious to the shift in the room, keeps rambling, his words slurring into incoherence. Dante and I guide him off the stage, his loud, unrestrained laughter echoing as we make our way down the back hallway. He stumbles, barely able to keep himself upright, still grinning like a fool.

"You know," Valentino mutters, slurring his words, "I've always been meant to be the one in charge. I'm the best there is."

"Yeah, Vigo. Something like that," I reply, keeping my tone carefully placating.

We reach my office, where Valentino's personal guards are already waiting. "I pulled the car out back," Guido informs me.

"Take him home. Get him sobered up," I instruct, my voice level though the fury boiling inside me threatens to spill over. "I'll make sure Alessia gets home safely."

Valentino stumbles into their arms, barely managing to stay on his feet, his words slurring together. "You can have her if you want," he spits, his last attempt at provocation before they begin to drag him away. "She's useless—barely worth the effort. Maybe I should've let you have her all along," he adds, his tone dripping with malicious satisfaction, a reminder of how he lied to his father to arrange the marriage, making sure my future would never include her.

I don't take the bait. My expression stays neutral as I hand him over to his guards, watching as they guide him toward the back exit.

"What the hell was that?" Dante asks once Valentino's out of sight.

"I have no idea," I mutter, grabbing the back of my neck. "We need to get back out there, do some damage control, and then get everyone the fuck out of my restaurant."

For the next hour, I work to clean up the disaster Valentino left behind. I smooth things over with our associates, both old and new, assuring them this isn't typical behavior. My face stays calm, my posture relaxed, while inside, I'm seething.

Valentino had no right to speak my father's name, to soil his legacy with his drunken lips. The sound of it made my blood turn cold, my pulse slowing to a steady, ominous thud. The rage it stirred was something deeper, darker—a quiet storm building, poised to unleash its fury and consume everything in its path.

His fatal mistake, though, was dragging Alessia into his drunken spectacle. With every vile word, every degrading comment, he signed his own death warrant. The way he spoke about his own wife, humiliating her in front of everyone, stripping away her dignity as if it were a mere trinket to be discarded. It was a cruelty that I cannot and will not overlook.

I can endure the insults, and the cheap shots aimed at me. But what he did to her? That sealed his fate in blood.

Every instinct screamed for me to wrap my hands around his throat, to feel the slow ebb of life slip from him as his breath faltered. But I didn't. I stood there, absorbing his insults, letting them roll off me as though they meant nothing. Not because they didn't matter but because something far darker began to stir inside me.

Reacting in anger would've been a mistake—a foolish, reckless misstep. Control is what matters. Every move must be exact, like the steady beat of a pendulum marking the slow, inevitable passage of time toward his ruin.

And now, the plan begins to creep into my mind, a quiet, sinister whisper.

The bottle of Macallan, still wrapped in its packaging at my apartment, is waiting. Soon, it will serve a purpose much darker than what it was meant for. When the moment comes, the whiskey will play its part—but what flows through him will be far more insidious.

Something undetectable, working its way through him like a creeping shadow.

The pain will come, slow and excruciating.

His fate was sealed long before he ever saw it coming.

Valentino

Tonight isn't just important—it's a bold demonstration of my power and control, leaving no doubt about who commands absolute authority. Antonio may think this night is about his promotion, but it's really about me. Every deal struck and every move made tonight will show them that nothing happens in this family without my hand guiding it.

I glance at the clock. It's almost time to head to the restaurant. Turning, I find Alessia at her vanity, carefully applying makeup, trying to hide the bruises. Stepping forward, I grab her wrist. "Leave them," I say, my voice firm.

She hesitates, lowering the brush as her eyes fall. Heat floods through me, my cock already hardening at the sight. The thought of her going to the party with my marks on her skin, and my cum dripping down her thighs, sends a surge of lust through me. Knowing that everyone will see what belongs to me and what I've done to her stirs something darker inside. Those bruises are mine, and so is Alessia.

"Get up," I snap, my voice edged with impatience.

She stands slowly, her eyes reflecting a mix of defiance and fear. That look annoys me—how she dares to think she has the right to challenge me.

I let my gaze sweep across her body. "Take off your clothes."

She hesitates, her hands trembling slightly. "Valentino, I'm going to be late for work."

"Did I stutter?" My tone darkens.

Her shoulders slump as she unbuttons her silk ivory blouse and unzips her black pencil skirt, letting it fall to the floor. She stands there in her lingerie, her eyes burning with humiliation.

"Turn around and bend over."

When she doesn't move fast enough, I shove her onto the bed, rough and unkind. She knows better than to resist. "You won't need these." I rip off her lace panties. "I want every man in the room to know you've been used."

"I can't work like that," Alessia protests.

"Why not?" I ask, already opening my pants. "You think you're better than any of the other bitches who work there? You're nothing more than a possession," I hiss as I thrust into her. Leaning in close to her ear, I whisper, "A body to be used at my whim."

She goes limp beneath me. The urge to whip her, to hear her cries and feel her fight me is strong, but we don't have time. Instead, my fingers dig into her waist, and I fuck her hard and fast, spilling inside her. Then, I pull out, leaving her used and motionless on the bed.

"Get dressed," I snap, adjusting my clothes. "We're leaving in ten minutes."

Alessia moves mechanically, picking up her discarded clothes and slipping them back on. I watch her in the mirror as I fix my hair. Satisfied with my appearance, I head downstairs and pour myself a glass of whiskey.

Tonight, the restaurant will be filled with the city's most influential figures, all gathered to witness Antonio's promotion. Little do they know this party isn't really about him. It's a display of my control and strategic brilliance. Everything that happens in that room will be a testament to my power.

Finally, I hear Alessia's footsteps behind me, but I don't turn.

With my drink in hand, we step outside. Guido holds the door open, and I slide into the backseat, my anticipation already building.

THE RESTAURANT IS CLOSED TO THE PUBLIC TONIGHT, reserved for my private event. Guards stand at the entrance, ensuring no unwanted guests slip in. As we step inside, the room hums with hushed conversation. Men in expensive suits gather in small groups, their expressions serious.

I move through the room, exchanging nods, shaking hands, and receiving murmurs of appreciation. I take a moment to savor it, each interaction reinforcing the control I hold over them all.

Finally, I spot Antonio at the bar, sipping his whiskey.

"You ready for your big debut?" I mock, my tone dripping with false encouragement.

"You know parties aren't my thing," he replies, forcing a smile. "I would've preferred to slip into the role quietly."

"Don't be ridiculous," I scoff. "This is an event worth celebrating."

I grab my own drink and return to working the crowd. This is where I thrive——surrounded by power, commanding respect without needing to say a word.

Out of the corner of my eye, I catch sight of Alessia balancing a tray, her hair falling slightly over her face as she tries to hide the bruises. A wave of satisfaction washes over me.

She may resist, but it changes nothing. Alessia's beneath me— just another possession to be used as I see fit. Until she fully accepts her place, she's no better than the shit I scrape off the bottom of my shoe.

Draco catches my eye from across the room and makes his way over, his voice booming as he approaches. "Ah, my favorite son-in-law," he calls out, clapping me on the back with a heavy hand, making sure everyone nearby takes notice.

"Looks like you've been keeping her in line," he adds, his chuckle low and deliberate, a hint of mockery lacing his words as he throws a glance at Antonio. The jab isn't lost on me.

I flash a slow, deliberate grin, letting the cruelty behind it sink in. "You know how it is," I say smoothly, my voice carrying just enough to be overheard. "Sometimes, you have to remind them who's in charge."

The night proceeds as planned. Laughter and the clinking of glasses fill the air. I make my way through the crowd, basking in the admiring glances. Antonio sits at the bar, brooding and serious, as always. He's lucky to have me elevating him. Without me, he'd be nothing.

I spot Lena serving drinks across the room, her tight skirt drawing appreciative glances from the men around her. The way her white blouse stretches over her chest sends a rush of arousal straight to my cock. It's not about her—it's about knowing I can take her whenever I want. Knowing she wears scars, she can never erase.

She tries to avoid my gaze. Unacceptable.

I stride toward her and grab her arm, pulling her close. "Do you think I can't see you pushing your tits into other men's faces?" I growl into her ear. "My dick's hard watching you."

"I'm just trying to do my job," she whispers, pulling away.

"Put the tray down," I order, my voice low and commanding. Lena hesitates for a moment too long, so I wrench it from her hand and set it on the nearest table. Grabbing her arm, I lean in close. "Don't make a scene," I mutter, my grip tightening. "Unless you want me to bend you over one of these tables and fuck you in front of everyone." She won't dare resist now.

I pull her along, quickening my pace as we head down the hall. Her heels click on the floor, and she stumbles, struggling to keep up. The promise of what will happen in the basement looms closer. Each step is heavy with anticipation.

The door slams shut behind us, echoing in the empty space. I turn to her, eyes narrowing. "Get on your knees."

She looks up, defiant. "You're doing this with your wife upstairs?"

"I don't give a fuck who's upstairs," I say, already unbuckling my pants. "Now open your mouth."

She obeys, her lips parting just enough. The moment I thrust into her mouth, satisfaction surges through me. "You take my cock like a good little slut," I growl, gripping her hair tighter, forcing her to take every inch. Her throat tightens around me, and I let out a low chuckle. "Can you taste Alessia on me?"

Lena gags, her eyes watering. She pushes at my thighs as she struggles to get a breath. Watching her fight drives me to fuck her face harder. Her choked gasps spurring me on.

I slam into her over and over, each thrust harder than the last. My pace is relentless. Tightening my grip on her hair, I force her to take me deep into her throat, using her like she's nothing. I don't stop until I've emptied myself inside her.

"Clean me."

Lena licks my cock until there's no trace of cum left. Without another word, I tuck myself back into my pants and start climbing up the steps.

When I return to the main floor, the lights blur slightly. Everything feels like it's swaying around me. A server passes by with a tray, and I snatch a whiskey, downing it in one go before grabbing another without a word. The burn of the alcohol barely registers as I glance around the room.

My eyes land on Alessia. Her gaze locks onto mine, a flash of disgust in her eyes. She knows what happened downstairs. I raise my glass in a mocking toast before heading toward the stage for tonight's main event.

Faces blur together, conversations slurring in my ears, but I don't care. I tap the microphone to test if it's on. The high-pitched squeal silences the room, and all eyes turn to me.

"Ladies and gentlemen," I begin, commanding everyone's

attention. I see heads turning, eyes on me, just as it should be. "Thank you for joining us tonight to celebrate my dear cousin and his, let's say, unexpected promotion to underboss."

Applause ripples through the crowd, and I can already feel the energy shifting in my favor. They're eating this up. I wave Antonio forward with a grand gesture. "Come on, Antonio, don't be shy," I say, grinning as I slap him on the back when he reaches the stage.

The applause fades, and I lower my voice, making sure everyone's hanging on my words. "Since we were kids, I've kept Antonio by my side because, as we all know, every leader needs a loyal sidekick." The room erupts into laughter. They love this.

Raising my hand, I signal for the crowd to quiet down. "Alright, enough joking. Let's get serious for a moment." My tone turns darker. "Antonio's been my right-hand man for years, dependable as ever. But let's be honest—he's always been second to me. Just like his father was second to mine."

There's a rush of satisfaction at the subtle jab. Antonio stiffens beside me, but what's he going to do? Nothing. The room is mine.

I smirk, savoring the moment. "He's the kind of guy who'll never step up and try to steal the spotlight. That's why he's perfect for his new role." More laughter follows. I've got them exactly where I want them.

"Antonio's been loyal. Like a dog," I add, my own laughter ringing out, loud and mocking. This is too easy. "I never have to worry with him by my side."

"I'll always have your back, cousin," Antonio says, his voice steady. I swirl my whiskey, the glass catching the light just right as I take a slow sip.

"That's what I like to hear—loyalty." I let the word linger, my smirk deepening. "It's funny, though. Where does it really stand when the stakes are high?"

The room falls into silence, all eyes on me. Perfect. They're hanging on every word.

I'm invincible.

My gaze shifts between Antonio and Alessia, who's standing off to the side and an idea forms. "And speaking of loyalty," I say, my tone turning sly. "Why don't you tell us what you really think of Alessia, cousin? What do you see when you look at my wife?"

I notice the brief shift in his expression, a hint of discomfort he can't quite hide. I love it. How far can I push him before he'll crack?

"Alessia's your wife and a respected member of our family," he answers, too calm for my liking.

"Come on," I taunt, taking a step closer. "Tell the truth. Or are you too scared?"

His jaw tightens, and I feel a surge of satisfaction. "Alessia's a beautiful woman. Intelligent. Strong-willed."

"Beautiful, yes," I sneer, leaning in. "But have you ever wondered what it would be like to fuck her? To have what's mine?"

Alessia's face flushes with humiliation, but I don't care.

"Of course not," Antonio says, still trying to play the honorable cousin. "I would never—"

"Not even back when you two were together? Before she was promised to me?" I sneer. "You never dreamed of it?"

I keep going, drunk on power and alcohol. Everyone loves this, whether they show it or not. "I'll let you in on a little secret," I murmur, my voice dripping with cruelty, half to Antonio, half into the microphone for everyone to hear. "Alessia's a terrible fuck. She's horribly boring. I'm hoping she can learn a little something about how to please a man while she's working alongside my favorite whores."

I flick my hand toward Lena, who's returned to waiting tables. She's part of the show now. "Lena here," I continue, slurring my words but still feeling in control, "begs for my cock. Her cunt drips for it every time. You should give her a go," I sneer, my grin widening as I watch Antonio's reaction. "Almost forgot—she used to let you fuck her, too."

Antonio tries to walk away, but I grab his arm, holding him in place. "Were you not able to satisfy her? Is that why she stopped letting you into her cunt?" I spit the words, watching my saliva hit his face.

Turning back to Alessia, I grin, my mind swirling with more twisted thoughts. "Maybe Alessia will spread her legs and let you try out all her holes—if you don't mind sloppy seconds." I'm inspired by the thought. "Hell, the two of you can watch me fuck Lena. Maybe you'll pick up a few new tricks."

The room goes silent. Then, the crash of shattering glass breaks through as Lena drops her tray, and I laugh. Alessia's face crumples. I don't know why. They're all acting like I said something shocking. They're pathetic.

"Enough, Vigo," Antonio says, his voice low, but he's not my boss. It's the other way around.

"Enough? We're just getting started," I say, raising my glass to take another sip of whiskey. My hand misses my mouth, and the drink spills down my shirt, but I don't care.

"The party's over, cousin," Antonio says flatly, and I glance around, not understanding why he'd want to end things so soon.

Before I can respond, Dante's already making his way over. Antonio grabs the microphone, addressing the crowd with his usual neutral expression. "Excuse me, everyone. I apologize for Valentino's behavior. He's had a little too much fun this evening, and I think it's best if we get him some fresh air."

Too much fun? They loved every minute of it.

Dante and Antonio drag me off the stage, but I'm still laughing, my steps unsteady as they take me down the back hallway. "You know I've always been meant to be the one in charge. I'm the best there is," I slur, pounding my chest with my fist for emphasis.

"Yeah, Vigo. Something like that," Antonio replies, his voice annoyingly calm.

Guido appears outside of Antonio's office. "I pulled the car out back," he says, like this is some big emergency.

"Take him home. Get him sobered up," Antonio orders. "I'll make sure Alessia gets home safely."

As they drag me toward the exit, the hallway spins, the lights blur and pulse with every unsteady step I take. "You can have her if you want," I mumble, trying to provoke him one last time. "She's useless—barely worth the effort. Maybe I should've let you have her all along."

The cool air hits me like a punch, making my head spin even more. Guido grips my arm, steadying me as he opens the door. "In you go, boss," he mutters, guiding me into the back seat.

The leather feels cold against my skin, but I barely register it. The world outside is a swirl of headlights and shadows, everything shifting in and out of focus. I blink hard, my thoughts muddled, the edges of my vision closing in.

Alessia

My drunken husband not only made a fool out of himself, he humiliated me in front of everyone in this room.

"Alessia," my father calls, his voice harsh. "Come here, now."

Keeping my head down, I walk to the table where my father sits with several men I don't recognize. "Yes, Papa?"

"Your husband expressed his disappointment in your performance as a wife."

"He was drunk," I reply, my voice tight.

"Clearly, you're lacking." He motions at my face. "If your husband feels the need to use his fists to keep you in line."

My anger flares. "How dare you—"

"Alessia," Antonio says, cutting me off as he places his hand gently on my elbow. "Can I speak to you in my office?"

"Is my daughter failing with her responsibilities at work, too?" my father sneers.

Antonio's expression remains calm. "Where I don't feel a capo's wife should be waitressing," he remarks, a hint of sharpness in his voice, "Alessia's an exemplary employee."

My father eyes him, suspicion darkening his gaze. "Valentino's methods must've had a very positive effect on her. Unfortunately, it seems she's as lacking as her mother in other ways." He leans back, crossing his legs casually. "Maybe if Val passes her around, she'll learn how to please a man."

"If you'll excuse us," Antonio interjects smoothly, gently taking my arm. "There's an important matter I need Alessia for."

I allow him to lead me away from my father and his cruelty.

"I'm glad to see you've decided to take my son-in-law up on his generous offer to fuck his wife," he calls after us, his voice dripping with mockery.

Antonio stops abruptly, his body tensing beside me. For a moment, I think he's going to snap. But then he exhales, his grip firm yet comforting as he continues to guide me away.

"I'm not to be disturbed," Antonio tells Dante, who's standing guard outside his office.

"You got it," he replies, stepping aside.

Antonio allows me to enter first, then closes the door behind us, shutting out the noise of the party. Is he planning to take Val up on his offer? My face remains stoic, though inside, my nerves are fraying.

I've survived Val. I can make it through this, too.

"Sit," Antonio says softly, gesturing to a chair.

I sit down, a mixture of anger and shame swirling inside me. Antonio pulls up a chair beside me, his eyes full of concern.

"I'm so sorry, Alessia. You didn't deserve that," he says, his voice gentle.

His kindness catches me off guard, and my resolve begins to weaken. "How can he say those things about me in front of everyone?" I whisper, my voice trembling.

Antonio reaches for my hand, his touch soft but steady. "Your father and Valentino are cruel men, blinded by their power and arrogance."

His words chip away at the wall I've built around myself. "I can't keep doing this," I admit, my voice breaking. "I can't keep pretending everything is fine."

"You've never had to pretend with me," Antonio says quietly. "You're safe here."

I hesitate, unsure if I can trust the warmth in his voice but he sounds like the Antonio I used to know.

I'm tired—so tired.

For the first time in so long, I let my guard down. Tears I've been holding back for far too long spill over. Antonio rubs soft circles on my hand, his touch soothing. A thought suddenly occurs to me. "What about Lena? Is she okay?" I ask, wiping my eyes.

He looks at me, confused. "Why would you care about Lena?"

"Even she doesn't deserve to be treated that way. No one does."

"Lena can handle herself." His voice takes on a hint of that familiar coldness again.

"Antonio," I say softly. "I'm so sorry for what Valentino did tonight. The way he humiliated you in front of everyone—"

"Don't you dare apologize for him," Antonio interrupts. "Valentino's actions are his own. You're not responsible for his behavior."

I nod, grateful for his understanding.

"I'll have Dante get your things, and I'll bring you home."

"My shift isn't over," I say, trying to steady my voice.

"I don't expect you to go back out there after that."

Sitting up straighter, I take a deep breath and square my shoulders. "I refuse to allow Valentino to make me cower," I declare, my tone braver than I feel. "If you don't mind, I'd like to finish out the evening."

"Are you sure?" Antonio asks, eyebrows raised in surprise.

"I'm sure," I reply with a nod.

He studies me for a moment. "You're too good for him, you know that? He has no idea the treasure he has right in front of him."

Pulling my hand back, I stand. "I'm going to wash my face and get back to work."

"Take all the time you need," Antonio replies, sitting back in his chair.

I walk out of the office feeling more confused than when I entered. The man sitting in that room is as deeply entrenched in this brutal world as my father and husband. Yet, I still catch glimpses of the boy who captured my heart years ago.

Antonio Luciano is a paradox that leaves me torn, unsure if I can truly trust him or if he'll betray me again.

Valentino

I'm still basking in the afterglow of last week's victory. Antonio's party was a smashing success. It was exactly what I needed to show not only my new associates but also rival families that the Comiso *Famiglia* is the most powerful family in Philadelphia. No. We're the most powerful family on the East Coast.

Everything about this house is a testament to my influence. I stop at the top of the grand staircase and glance down at the marble-floored foyer just in time to see Alessia step inside with Dante trailing behind her.

They've been going on these *walks* more often, each one longer than the last. What they don't know is I've been having them followed. My wife has been lying to me, and that ends now. I'll deal with Dante later.

"Alessia," I call out, my voice echoing.

She glances up, eyes wary. "Yes?"

"I want to speak to you in my office," I demand, my tone leaving no room for negotiation.

"I was hoping to edit the photos I took today," she replies, a slight hesitation in her voice.

"Bring your camera," I say, walking down the stairs toward

her. "I'd like to see what you've captured today as well." She exchanges a worried look with Dante. "Now, Alessia."

"Yes, Valentino," she responds quietly, before turning to walk toward my office.

Loyalty is paramount, and any hint of disloyalty must be snuffed out swiftly. My father's death was the stroke of luck I needed to seize control. After that, Marco was the next threat—one I eliminated. And I'll continue rooting out potential traitors until only the loyal and devoted remain.

"And you," I bark at Dante. "Don't go far. I'll need to speak with you after I've dealt with my wife." I turn on my heel not waiting for a response.

The door to my office is open when I arrive. Alessia stands by the window, camera in hand, her posture stiff.

This is my domain. From the dark wood panels lining the walls to the massive black walnut desk, this room oozes luxury and power. I sit down, leaning back as I observe her.

"Show me," I order.

She hesitates before walking over and placing the camera on my desk. I pick it up and begin scrolling through the images. They're good, I'll give her that. But this isn't about her talent—it's about control.

"These are impressive," I say my tone deceptively calm. "But it seems you've been busy in other ways too."

Her eyes widen slightly. "I don't know what you mean."

"I mean," I drawl. "Your little photography hobby. Taking pictures, selling them at a gallery. Did you think I wouldn't find out?"

Her face pales, but she stands her ground. "It's just a hobby, Valentino. Something to pass the time."

"A hobby?" I let out a cold, mocking laugh. "I didn't give you permission to pretend you're some kind of artist selling your pictures."

Her eyes flash with defiance, rare but intriguing. "It's something I enjoy. Something that's mine."

I rise from my chair, walking around the desk to stand over her. "You enjoy it? Did you enjoy the attention it brought? The people who saw your name? Your face?"

"It's not like that," she whispers, her voice trembling.

"It's exactly like that." I grab her chin, forcing her to look at me. "I won't have my wife making a fool out of me by sneaking around behind my back."

"I just wanted some freedom," she pleads. "Something of my own."

"Freedom?" I slam my hand down on the desk, making her flinch. "Your freedom is what I allow you. Nothing more."

Tears spill over her cheeks, but she blinks them away. "I'm sorry, Valentino."

"It's too late for sorry," I snap. "From now on, you're forbidden from going anywhere with Dante. I'll reassign you a new guard—someone I can trust. And your little photography sessions? They're over. Do you understand?"

"I'll stop going to the gallery," she begs, her voice breaking. "But please, let me keep taking pictures."

I grab her camera, raising it as if considering her request. "You misunderstood me," I say, before hurling it across the room. The camera smashes against the wall, pieces scattering on the floor.

"No," she cries, dropping to her knees, frantically trying to pick up the pieces.

I stalk across the room and grab her by the hair, yanking her head back. "You want to be on your knees?" I growl, undoing my pants. "Then make yourself useful."

Pulling out my cock, I demand, "Open."

She clamps her mouth shut, and my anger explodes. My hand connects with her face, the crack echoing through the room.

"I said, open your fucking mouth." Tears streak her cheeks as she finally obeys. I thrust into her, shoving myself so far down her throat that she gags and claws at my thighs in a pathetic attempt to breathe.

Holding her there, I relish the power I wield over her. The

way her body fights against me. "This is a picture worth taking," I sneer. "My whore on her knees, taking my cock."

I pull out, giving her just enough air to take a shallow breath before shoving back in. I don't care if I'm hurting her. She deserves it for her disobedience, for trying to deceive me. Her tears fall faster, her body trembling as I tighten my grip on her hair.

"Look at me," I growl, yanking her head up. "You need to remember who owns you."

She meets my gaze, the fear and pain in her eyes heightens my arousal. I thrust harder, my movements becoming more erratic as I near my peak. Her muffled cries and the tightness of her throat drive me to my breaking point. With her face held against my groin, I release wave after wave of cum down her throat.

When I finally let her go, she collapses on the floor, gasping for air.

I stand over her crumpled form and savor the sight of her broken and humiliated. "Who do you belong to?" I ask as I zip up my pants.

"You," she whispers through her tears.

"You'd better remember that," I growl, shoving her aside with my foot. "Disobey me again, and the price will be far worse."

She nods weakly.

"Stay on all four and get the hell out," I snap, dismissing her with a wave.

As she crawls out, broken and trembling, a wave of satisfaction washes over me. One way or another, she'll learn her place—beneath me, where she belongs.

Another problem dealt with, but there'll always be more. I've handled worse before, and I'll handle what's to come. Soon, everyone will understand the price of crossing me, and no one will dare challenge the power I command.

Antonio

Dante: I think Val found out about the gallery.

Me: What? How?

Dante: I don't know. He was waiting for us when we got back. Alessia's in his office. I'm afraid of what he's going to do to her.

Fuck. I knew something like this was going to happen. I'm about to walk into a meeting, and I can't afford to be a no-show. My hands are tied.

Me: Does he know you're involved.

Dante: Yes.

Dammit. This is a complication we don't need. I have to do damage control before this gets any worse.

Me: I'm going to try to buy us a little time. I'll wrap up here as fast as I can.

Right now, I need to remain focused on this meeting. The Carlini's have been allied with us for generations, but they're furious over Valentino's new alliances with DeLuca and Salazar. Drugs and humans were never part of either of our businesses and they want to keep it that way.

I enter the conference room where Saverio Carlini, the patriarch of his *Famiglia*, is already seated at the head of the table, his sons flanking him. The tension is thick as I sit opposite them.

"Saverio," I greet with a nod. "Thank you for inviting me."

"Antonio," he acknowledges, his voice steady but laced with displeasure. "We need to talk about your cousin's recent decisions."

"I understand your concerns. Valentino's alliances were made without consulting any of our allies. I want to assure you that this is not a direction I support." I'm walking a fine line here, hoping this doesn't backfire before I can put my plan into motion.

Saverio narrows his eyes. "Then why has it happened? We've always kept our business clean. No drugs, no humans. This alliance threatens everything we stand for."

"I agree," I say choosing my next words carefully. "Valentino initially believed these partnerships would bring us more power and wealth. But he now understands the dangerous path it's put us on. That's why I'm here—to let you know I'm fixing this."

Saverio exchanges a look with his sons, before turning his attention back to me. "What are you proposing, Antonio?"

"I'm planning to meet with DeLuca to sever all ties."

Saverio's oldest son, Danilo, leans forward. "He won't take kindly to that."

"Possibly not," I concede. "The Trombino *Famiglia* in Brooklyn is willing to allow them to move their shipments through their ports. I believe that will be an agreeable compromise for DeLuca."

Saverio steeples his fingers, his expression unreadable. "We were at your party last month. I've spoken with several of the other families since then. Valentino's instability concerns us. He's unpredictable and reckless. That's dangerous for all of us."

"I agree. What happened was unacceptable. He got carried away with the celebration." I force a relaxed smile. "I assure you it was a one-time occurrence."

Saverio's eyes narrow further, scrutinizing me. "And if it

wasn't? If he continues down this path? What are you prepared to do?"

I pause, weighing my next words carefully. This could be a test of my loyalty to Valentino—or an opportunity. If it's a test, it's one I can't afford to fail. "One night doesn't change my loyalty. I have faith in Valentino as our Capo. From today forward, we'll move in the right direction."

Danilo speaks up again. "What about Salazar? If you sever ties with him, there'll be retaliation. How do you plan to handle that?"

"We'll be ready for any backlash," I say, looking each man in the eye. "Currently they're overextended. If we strike, it'll be swift, cutting them off before they have a chance to regroup."

"You're asking us to risk a lot," Saverio says.

"I am," I reply, meeting his gaze steadily.

"I'm not convinced but I respect your commitment. We'll support you—for now. But understand, if this fails, the consequences will be severe."

"I understand," I reply, relief washing over me. "Thank you, Saverio. Together, we'll ensure the strength of both our families."

The meeting wraps up, and as I walk out, I'm already planning my next move. Valentino's downfall has to be quick, decisive.

Once I'm in my car, I call Valentino.

"How did the meeting go?" he asks.

"It went well. I convinced them to get on board."

"I knew I could count on you, cousin."

"I'll always have your back," I reply.

"There's been a development here this afternoon. I've uncovered some disloyalty," Vigo says, his tone casual, like he's talking about the weather.

My pulse quickens. "Who?"

"Dante," he replies flatly.

"What has he done?"

"Alessia's been selling her photos at a gallery downtown. And he's been helping her."

I need to shift his focus. "That sounds like an issue with Alessia, not Dante."

"Explain."

"She's challenged your authority before, right?"

"Every damn day."

"I'd bet she told him you approved of it," I pause letting the idea sink in. "You know Dante's loyal. It sounds like he was just as deceived as you"

There's silence on the other end, then a thoughtful grunt. "I don't know."

"Alessia's the problem." I push forward, hating every word, but knowing it's the only way to protect them both. "She needs to be disciplined. You can't allow her to manipulate your men."

Another pause. Then, "You're right. I've already punished her," Valentino says far too pleased with himself. "She'll think twice before crossing me again."

I release a slow breath, grateful they're both alive, even though I can't think about what he did to her. "Then we agree and consider this handled?"

"Yes, cousin," he says, finally relenting.

"Perfect," I say, shifting the conversation. "I have some news you'll want to hear."

"What is it?"

"Construction on the new room is finished. Just in time for the procession of the saints."

"That's good news indeed," he says. "Arrange for Lena to be at my disposal. I hope you had the rack I requested installed. I want her stretched out, taking it like the filthy slut she is."

"I think you'll be very pleased with what you'll find," I reply, hating him more with each passing second. "I almost forgot. I have a gift for you."

"A gift?" he asks, intrigued.

"A belated wedding present. I've been working on it for months."

"Now you have my attention," he says, laughing.

Everything's in place, the pieces perfectly aligned. Tomorrow, as the restaurant fills with patrons lost in revelry and tradition, I'll be beneath them—in the shadows. It's there that I'll carry out my plan to bury the rot that has festered among us, sealing away its darkness.

Valentino's reign ends tomorrow, and with it, the blood-stained legacy he left on our family.

Antonio

The sky is still cloaked in darkness as I unlock the backdoor of *Casa della Ombre*. I needed to arrive before the chef and the kitchen staff to have enough time to set the stage for Valentino's surprise. Procuring Prussic Acid wasn't easy, but favors are a currency in this life, and I decided to cash one in.

Mixing the chemical in water is a delicate process, each cube a lethal promise waiting to be fulfilled. It's convenient—almost too perfect—that Valentino insists on having his own personal ice cube tray. Once it's prepared, I pour the liquid into it and slide it into the freezer.

Downstairs, I handle the next part of my plan. Carefully, I pry open the wooden crate and lift out the ornate display case. Inside, encased like a sacred relic, is the rarest bottle of whiskey known to man—the 1926 Macallan, bottle number twelve of twelve, with its hand-drawn label by Valero Adami. A masterpiece of indulgence.

"It's almost a shame to waste something of such value," I murmur, admiring the bottle's pristine appearance. "But it has to be done."

After arranging the bottle in the center of the conference

table, I make my way through the tunnels to the newly built dungeon. The workmanship is impeccable. Anyone unfamiliar with the building's original layout would never suspect this room wasn't part of it.

The limestone-covered walls and heavy wooden beams create an ancient, foreboding atmosphere, like a medieval torture chamber. Six wrought-iron torches mounted on the walls provide the only light, their gas-fed flames casting restless shadows across the space. Sourced from a two-hundred-year-old barn outside the city, the stone and wood lend a sense of permanence—a space built to hold secrets.

Among the furnishings are a Saint Andrew's cross, a spanking bench, and stockades. Chains and a selection of cuffs hang along one wall, cold and unyielding, perfectly fitted for the suspension system. I was even able to find a hanging cage and a fully functional stretching rack—everything on Valentino's wish list of twisted cravings.

The dungeon waits, as silent and still as a crypt. Soon, it will be alive with the echoes of what's to come. Valentino, the self-proclaimed connoisseur of rare luxuries, will be drawn by the allure of the 1926 Macallan. His final indulgence.

He'll enter, unsuspecting, his greed blinding him to the trap laid at his feet. Just like Fortunato, lured by the promise of Amontillado, Valentino will be ensnared by his own desires. The walls, these ancient stones, will bear witness to his last breath.

Soon enough, the whispers of the past will awaken, filling this space with the echoes of retribution. And like those who've crossed the line before him, Valentino will be forever entombed —not by brick and mortar, but by the decisions he can never escape.

This room, with all its macabre grandeur, will only be used once.

After tonight, it'll be nothing more than a tomb, a monument to a life built on deceit and violence.

The Procession of Saints, a revered annual tradition, draws crowds from all over the city. Inside the restaurant, anticipation fills the air as patrons gather by the windows, eager for their glimpse of the saints as they make their way down the street. With each passing minute, the atmosphere grows more electric.

"Lena," I call as she steps out of the kitchen.

"May I have a word with you?"

She pauses, balancing a tray. "Be right there. I just need to drop this off."

"I'll be in my office."

I sit at my desk, waiting, each second stretched taut with anticipation. No one, not even Dante, knows what's about to unfold beneath their feet. I couldn't risk Vigo overhearing a conversation or intercepting a text message. If he found out, it would mean my life.

Lena enters moments later. "Sorry about that. What's up?"

"Close the door." I motion toward it with a subtle nod.

"Am I in trouble?" she asks, her voice a little strained.

"No," I say, my tone low but firm. "Have a seat."

She perches on the edge of a chair watching me intently.

"Valentino will be here soon. I'll be pulling you off the floor to take care of him."

Her knee bounces and she tenses. "I'm not feeling well today."

"You seemed fine all morning," I reply, keeping my gaze locked on hers.

"I don't want to be with him," she says quietly, almost too quietly to hear.

"Why not."

Wordlessly, Lena stands and begins unbuttoning her blouse. My horror grows with every inch of exposed skin. As the scars between her breasts come into view, I spot the crude carving of the word *whore*, and a sick churn twists in my stomach.

"What the fuck," I say, the words slipping out as my fists clench. "Valentino did this to you?"

She nods, her eyes avoiding mine.

"Close your shirt," I say, struggling to maintain my composure as I grip the back of my neck. My mind races, barely able to process what I've just seen. I assumed she'd willingly kept things going with him. After all, they've been involved for years. But this explains her strange behavior at my party.

I force a deep breath, cold calculation creeping back into my voice. "You'll be available for whatever Valentino demands," I say, the edge in my tone unmistakable. "Do I make myself clear?"

Lena stands abruptly, her face reddening with fury. "You're as sick as he is." She glares at me.

I lean back, expression cold. "About time you realized that."

Without another word, she storms out, slamming the door behind her. I drop my head into my hands. She may hate me for this, but her fear will keep Valentino unsuspecting. It's the only chance any of us have to finally be free of him.

"What's going on? Lena looks like she's about to tear someone apart," Dante says as he steps into the office, his voice startling me.

"She asked to leave early, but I told her no. Valentino insisted on having her here." I rub my temples, the tension pounding behind my eyes. "I've got no patience for this today—my head's killing me."

"Late night last night?" He smirks. "Who'd you bring home this time?"

I shrug, offering a grin. "Didn't catch her name."

He raises an eyebrow. "Speaking of Valentino, he sent me to find you. Says you've got something for him."

"I do," I reply, standing up. "We'll be downstairs. Make sure we're not disturbed."

Valentino sits at the bar, a tumbler of whiskey already in his hand, his laughter cutting through the crowded restaurant. Alessia's next to him, her posture stiff, eyes downcast. He's too absorbed in his own arrogance, drunk on power, to sense the tension simmering around him.

Lena's on the other side of the room trying to stay out of his line of sight. I catch her eye, motioning for her to come over. She hesitates, the dread on her face unmistakable but she has no choice.

"Looks like the festivities are already in full swing," he says as I approach.

"They are," I reply, keeping my tone neutral.

Valentino's gaze shifts to Lena as she walks toward us, her face pale but composed. "She doesn't look very happy," he observes with a sneer.

"Since when do you care about her happiness?" I reply, my voice cold.

Lena avoids my gaze as she comes to a halt beside me. A pang of guilt hits me, but I shove it aside. There's no room for second thoughts now.

"Make sure your tables are covered," I instruct. "We'll be a few minutes. I'll send for you when we're ready."

"Yes, Mr. Luciano," she replies, her disgust evident.

Turning to Valentino, I offer a smile. "Are you ready for your present, cousin?"

He stands, leaving both his glass and his wife behind. "I'm intrigued."

I nod to Dante, who opens the door to the hallway, stepping aside. "Follow me."

Valentino chuckles, amused by my formality. "Lead the way, cousin."

Each step is laden with the potential consequences of what I'm about to do. The seriousness of this moment isn't lost on me. But as long as Valentino lives, he'll keep tearing everything apart. The humiliation, the cruelty—it ends tonight.

We reach the end of the hallway, where the polished mahogany door awaits, concealing the dungeon beyond.

"You sure you want to see this first?" I ask, turning toward him, a hint of hesitation in my voice. "We could always head back upstairs, catch the procession. There's still time."

Valentino smirks, waving away my concern as though it means nothing. "What's gotten into you, Antonio? You're not getting cold feet, are you?"

"No, of course not. Just thinking of your wife. Alessia will wonder where you've disappeared to."

"She'll never satisfy my needs," he laughs—a deep, throaty sound that echoes down the narrow hallway. "Let her wonder who I'm fucking."

Pushing open the door, I reveal the room beyond, cloaked in dim, flickering light. Shadows play along the rough stone walls, interrupted only by heavy iron fixtures bolted securely in place. The air is thick with a lingering, oppressive stillness—a place built for secrets.

Valentino steps inside, his eyes wide as they land on the

various implements hanging from the walls, each carefully selected for both function and aesthetic appeal.

"Now this," he murmurs, running a hand over the stretching rack, "is a work of art." His fingers trace the worn wood as if appreciating every detail.

He glances back at me, curiosity gleaming in his eyes. "Is it fully functional?"

"Of course. Everything in here works exactly as intended."

Valentino chuckles, giving the rack a playful tug to see how the mechanisms move. The wooden frame groans under the pressure, the chains rattling as he tests its limits. "Oh, I can imagine the fun I'll have with this."

I remain by the door, my pulse quickening. "You think all this is really necessary?"

"Necessary?" Valentino raises an eyebrow, a hint of disappointment in his tone. "What happened to you, huh? We used to have all kinds of fun together—those wild nights, remember?"

I stiffen but keep my voice casual. "Things change."

Valentino scoffs. "Well, *I* haven't changed. I plan to use every piece of this room."

Anger simmers beneath the surface, but I swallow it down. "If you're sure," I mutter, pressing the button on the wall. The clanking of metal fills the room as the pillory descends, complete with breast clamps and heavy iron cuffs.

Valentino's eyes light up. "You got it."

"It took some doing," I say, crossing my arms, my expression cold, distant.

"You did good here, Anton. Very good."

His praise cuts deeper than I expected, a bitter reminder of just how far I've let myself get dragged into his twisted world. But then I think of Lena's scars, Alessia's bruises—the way he flaunts them both like trophies of his power. The memory of how he humiliated me at my own party resurfaces, along with the ultimate betrayal—killing my father.

"There's still the matter of my gift," Valentino says, his grin widening as if savoring the thought.

"Ah, yes, the gift," I reply, feigning nonchalance. "But there's no rush, is there? We've got all night."

Valentino's eyes gleam with impatience. "Don't keep me in suspense, Anton. You promised something special."

I nod slowly, deliberately dragging out the moment. "It is special. A rarity, just like you wanted." I pause, watching the hunger in his eyes grow. "Maybe we should head back upstairs first. The procession won't last much longer."

He frowns, waving a dismissive hand. "Forget the procession. Show me the gift."

Keeping my expression blank, I lead him down a different passageway, each step designed to build his anticipation. The air feels heavier here, thick with the scent of damp stone and aged wood—and something else, a quiet presence of death lingering just beneath the surface. I wonder if Valentino senses it too.

"You've really outdone yourself with this place," he murmurs. "But where's the real prize?"

"Patience, cousin. It's just ahead."

The tunnel narrows, forcing us closer together before we reach the door at the end. I pause, resting my hand on the knob.

"I have to warn you," I say, letting a note of intrigue slip into my voice. "What you're about to see is truly priceless."

Valentino's grin spreads wider, his greed unmistakable now. "Then let's not waste any more time."

With slow, deliberate movements, I push open the heavy door, revealing our meeting room.

"A back entrance to the meeting room?" He chuckles, his brow raised in mock disappointment. "This better not be your big surprise, Antonio. I expected more."

I suppress a smile. "You know I wouldn't disappoint you." I step aside and give him a full view of what truly awaits.

His eyes widen and he freezes in place. "Is that...?"

I nod, watching as his gaze locks onto the bottle. "Yes. The

1926 Macallan. Bottle number twelve. As rare and as priceless as they come."

Valentino steps forward, all sense of mockery gone, his focus entirely on the prize before him. He reaches out, his hand trembling slightly as he admires the craftsmanship of the bottle. "Antonio, you've outdone yourself this time."

Stepping back, I allow him to savor the moment, watching him closely. He's completely consumed by his desire, unaware of how carefully this trap has been laid.

"But," I say softly, as if offering advice, "are you sure you want to indulge right now? This bottle is something to be savored. Rushed, it loses its value."

He waves me off, his eyes never leaving the bottle. "Nonsense. There's no better time than right now."

"Of course," I murmur, my lips curling into a subtle smile as he lifts the bottle from its resting place with a reverence reserved for only the rarest of treasures. His lust for power and wealth has blinded him.

The final act of this charade is almost complete.

I force a chuckle, shaking my head. "I'm just thinking about how valuable this bottle is. Perhaps we should save this for—"

Valentino waves me off impatiently, his eyes gleaming with anticipation. "Enough with the hesitation, Antonio. I didn't come all this way for you to play coy."

He presses the call button on the wall. Lena's voice interrupts the silence, slipping into the room like a cold draft.

"How may I help you?" she asks, her tone smooth, concealing the disgust I know is festering.

"We need two glasses," Valentino says, not taking his eyes off the bottle. "And I'll take mine with ice."

"Yes, Mr. Comiso."

"You're sure you want ice?" I ask, my voice light, as if merely suggesting a refinement. "This whiskey is meant to be savored. Diluting it would be a waste."

He laughs, the sound harsh and grating, sending a chill up my spine. "You and your constant caution, Anton. A little ice won't hurt."

I nod, forcing a smile to my lips as if I agree, but inside, my thoughts are racing.

Valentino busies himself with the bottle, uncorking it with reverence, as if he's in the presence of something divine. The rich scent of whiskey fills the room, and he inhales deeply, a satisfied sigh escaping his lips.

The door opens, and Lena steps inside, moving with the grace of someone who's mastered the art of hiding her pain. She sets the tray down avoiding eye contact with either of us.

Valentino's gaze locks onto her. "Ah, Lena," he purrs, leaning back in his chair, smirking. "Just in time. After I've savored this whiskey, I intend to partake in my second favorite indulgence." His hand snakes up her inner thigh, a possessive touch that makes my skin crawl.

Lena pulls away, but not before I catch a flash of fear in her eyes.

"Do you still think you have the option to say no?" Vigo's words are venomous and filled with dark promise. "Didn't you learn your lesson last time you tried avoiding me?"

I grip my glass tightly, my knuckles whitening with the effort to stay calm. The urge to wipe that smug grin off his face claws at me, but I know I have to stay composed. This is all part of the plan. He'll get what's coming to him.

Lena doesn't respond, keeping her gaze fixed on the floor.

Valentino takes a slow sip of his whiskey, the ice clinking against the glass as he swirls it around. He turns back to me, his eyes gleaming with satisfaction. "I've got to hand it to you, Anton. I didn't think you had it in you. But this is exquisite."

"I'm glad you're enjoying yourself."

He laughs again, that cruel, hollow sound bouncing off the stone walls. "Oh, I will, cousin. Believe me, I will."

Lena steps back, her movements measured, deliberate, as if

she's trying to make herself invisible. Before she can leave, Valentino calls after her.

"Don't go too far, Lena," he warns, his eyes narrowing. "I'll be needing you very soon."

Lena pauses, her back to him. She's holding herself together by sheer force of will. For a moment, I think she might break, might turn on him, but she only nods, a barely perceptible dip of her head, before she slips out of the room.

As the door clicks shut behind her, the air grows heavier. But Valentino is too wrapped up in his own twisted fantasies, too consumed by his power, to sense the impending danger.

He takes another sip of whiskey, savoring it with a satisfied sigh. "This is the life, Anton," he says, his voice dreamlike. "Power, wealth, women—it's all mine."

I force a smile, nodding as if I'm still part of this sick game. But inside, I'm counting down the moments, knowing that with each sip, the ice is already doing its job.

With every swallow, he's sealing his fate.

Antonio

Valentino tips his head back, finishing his drink in a single, smooth motion. His eyes are dark with hunger, one that has nothing to do with the whiskey. He sets the empty glass down with a sharp clink and stands, brushing invisible dust from his expensive suit. "I think it's time for the main event," he says, his voice thick with anticipation, a cruel smirk playing on his lips.

"Of course," I reply, keeping my voice steady despite the pounding in my chest. "Right this way, cousin."

I lead him back through the narrow hall. The shadows seem to close in like the encroaching darkness of a tomb. Valentino is too lost in his own sick fantasies to notice the subtle shift in my demeanor—the way my movements become more deliberate.

The end is near, but he's too blind to see it.

His gaze sweeps over the room, lingering on the instruments of cruelty as if planning where to start his sadistic games. His twisted delight is palpable.

Closing the door behind us, I move to the far corner of the room. "There's something inside the cage I think you'll find particularly useful. A new tool to ensure Lena behaves exactly how you want." I keep my tone calm, almost indifferent.

Valentino's eyes light up with grotesque interest, his greed overshadowing any suspicion. His sickness pulls him forward like a moth to a flame. "What is it? Show me," he demands, his hands twitching with anticipation.

"See for yourself," I say, gesturing to the small compartment inside the cage. "It's custom-made. You've never seen anything like it."

Without hesitation, Valentino ducks his head and steps inside, his fingers running over the cold metal bars. His breath quickens as he fumbles with the latch. "Where is it?" he asks, impatience creeping into his voice.

I step closer, hand hovering over the door. "Just a little further inside. You're almost there."

He leans in, still oblivious to the danger, when suddenly, he pauses, blinking rapidly as his body gives the first signs of rebellion. A faint sheen of sweat forms on his brow, and he runs his hand over his mouth, as if trying to dismiss the growing discomfort. He feels it, even if he doesn't yet understand.

With a swift, brutal motion, I slam the door shut. The iron bars clang together, a finality that reverberates through the room. Before he can react, I lock the cage, the bolt sliding into place with a sharp, metallic snap.

Valentino spins around, confusion in his eyes. "What the hell are you doing?" His voice is strained, the first hints of weakness creeping into his words.

I step back, my face unreadable, watching him with cold detachment. "Did you really think you could go on like this forever?"

He grips the bars, his knuckles white as panic flashes across his face. There it is—fear. "This isn't funny, Antonio. Let me out."

But I remain still. Valentino's breath quickens, his chest heaving as the subtle signs of the poison intensify. Beads of sweat begin to drip down his temples, and his posture begins to falter.

"What's happening?" he gasps, his voice trembling. His hand

moves to his chest, rubbing at it as though trying to ease the growing discomfort there. "I... I don't feel right."

I watch him closely, knowing the cyanide is beginning to take hold. His skin pales, the sheen of sweat intensifying, and his fingers tremble as he grips the bars for support.

His body knows.

The realization dawns on him slowly as his breath hitches. Horror creeps into his features. "What have you done?"

"It's poison," I say, my voice cold and precise. "It's already making its way through your body."

"You poisoned me?" he whispers, disbelief and terror warring for control.

"I did," I reply, each word deliberate, savoring his slow unraveling.

Valentino stumbles, his legs unsteady as his hands slip from the bars. He presses his back against the cage for support, his skin turning a sickly gray. Sweat pours down his face, his breathing turning shallow and rapid.

Panic is setting in.

"Antonio, please," he begs, his voice cracking. "We're family. I'll give you anything—everything. Just stop this. Please."

I step forward, unfazed. "You think this is about money or power?" I scoff. "I couldn't care less about either. You've taken things far more important than that, Vigo."

He gasps for air, the words tumbling out desperately. "You can have her back. Alessia... she's yours. I'll give her to you—just let me live."

Valentino's eyes dart wildly, searching my face for any sign of mercy, but there is none. He's not going to escape this.

I'm unmoved by his pleas. "Did Uncle Gio beg for help when you killed him?"

"I don't know what you're talking about." He wipes the sweat trickling down his brow, his hand trembling. But his control is slipping. "My father had a heart attack. I didn't lay a finger on him."

"Semantics," I reply, my voice icy. "You may not have killed him with your own two hands, but you could've tried to help him. Instead, you watched him die."

"I was in shock. Uncle Marco told you—"

"Shut the fuck up you piece of shit," I roar, slamming my fists against the bars. "You have no right to say my father's name."

Valentino crumples to the floor, his body folding in on itself. His hands tremble as he reaches out, but I remain out of his grasp. Terror is etched into every line of his face. His skin turns ashen grey, and his body slickens with sweat as the poison continues its merciless attack.

"It was a mistake," he sputters, his voice faltering. "An awful mistake, Anton. I wasn't thinking—"

"You weren't thinking?" I echo, my voice turning as cold as ice. "You destroyed everything—my family, my life, everything that ever mattered to me. Alessia and I were happy until you went behind my back and used your father to take her away from me. You could've had anyone you wanted, but you took the one person I cared about."

"My father was your family. He stood by your side all the while you were making ridiculous deals. And how did you repay his loyalty? You put a fucking hit on him. He's dead because of you." I close the distance between us, my words laced with a fury that's long overdue. "You got everything you wanted, but that still wasn't enough--nothing's ever enough for you. Now it's your turn to face the consequences."

His breath comes in short, labored gasps as the poison ravages him. His body begins to shake, uncontrollably now.

He knows time is running out.

"For the love of God, Antonio," he sobs, his tears mingling with the sweat dripping from his brow. "I'll change, I swear. I'll leave the business and give you everything. Just don't let me die like this."

I watch the pitiful creature writhing before me knowing he deserves every second of this torture.

Reaching into my pocket, I pull out a small glass vial. Valentino's eyes lock onto it, a glimmer of hope flickering in their depths. He lunges forward, but his strength is failing, his body betraying him.

"I have the antidote," I say, holding it just out of reach. "This will make it all stop."

His shaking fingers grasp at the air between us, desperation twisting his face. "Please," he screams, his voice cracking with hysteria. "I'm begging you—please."

The sound of his groveling, his pitiful begging fills me with a dark satisfaction. Watching this man, my own flesh and blood, reduced to nothing but a sniveling coward pleading for his life.

I dangle the vial closer, then pull it back. "When Lena begged you not to cut her, did you stop?"

"What? I don't—"

"When Alessia begged you not to hit her, did you stop?"

His mouth works uselessly, searching for words. There's nothing he can say to undo the damage he's caused.

"When Uncle Gio lay dying, struggling for air, did you call for help?"

"Antonio, for God's sake," he cries, his voice thin, hoarse, and desperate.

Leaning against the cage, I hold the vial just out of reach. "Do you remember how you laughed as you signed my father's death warrant?" I ask softly. "How you smirked at his funeral, knowing all along you'd orchestrated it?"

He sobs, collapsing again, his body convulsing as the poison takes full effect. "I didn't mean it... please..."

"You want forgiveness?" I lean in, my voice low, dripping with venom. "Then beg for it. Like the dog you are."

He scratches at the floor, his body seizing, his breath barely coming now as the cyanide does its work. He's so close to death.

"For the love of God, Antonio," he breathes, his voice barely a whisper now. "You promised you'd always have my back."

I look into his wide, terrified eyes, and my voice drops to a cold whisper. "I lied."

And with that, I pour the contents of the vial onto the floor.

Valentino's scream echoes in the dungeon as I turn away, his desperate pleas fading behind me. He deserves to die in the darkness he created.

"*In pace requiescat*," I murmur, leaving him to his fate.

Antonio

I climb the steps back to the main floor of the restaurant, closing the door behind me. The party carries on, laughter and idle chatter echoing through the room. Glasses clink, voices weave together—a hollow, mocking tune over the finality I've just wrought. They revel above, oblivious to the death that lingers beneath the shadows, a secret I alone carry.

"Where's Lena?" I ask Dante, who's standing near the entrance, his sharp eyes scanning the crowd like a predator.

"I sent her to your office to wait," he replies.

Offering a brief nod, I say, "Good," before turning on my heel and making my way toward the back.

Just as I'm about to step into the corridor, Dante's voice cuts through the noise. "What did Valentino think of his gift?"

A pause settles in as the question lingers in the air. Without turning around, I reply, "He said it was to die for." My tone is flat, detached, betraying nothing.

As I approach my office, the door stands slightly ajar. My pulse quickens, but I keep my steps slow and measured, each one deliberate. Pushing the door open, I step inside.

Lena sits in the chair, legs pulled up tightly, her arms wrapped around them like a fragile shield. Her face is pale, eyes wide with uncertainty.

The door clicks shut behind me, the sound echoing through the small room. Lena flinches, her eyes snapping up to meet mine.

"It's time."

She swallows hard, her lips trembling. "Do I have to?" she whispers, her voice cracking under the weight of what she knows is coming.

Moving closer, I lean against the desk, towering over her. "Yes," my voice is firm but steady. "Valentino's waiting for you downstairs."

Her eyes widen I terror. "I can't do this," she pleads, her voice barely above a whisper. "He's going to hurt me again, Antonio."

Crouching in front of her, I force her to meet my gaze. "You're strong," I murmur, my voice low. "Just go down there and do what you need to do. It'll be over soon."

Her shoulders sag, the fight draining from her as grim acceptance settles in. With a shaky breath, Lena pushes to her feet, attempting to straighten her spine, summoning courage that's already slipping through her fingers.

"Good girl," I say, standing and stepping aside. "When you're done, come straight to me. I'll have Dante take you home."

She nods, saying nothing more as she walks out of the room. Her footsteps echo down the hall, each one a countdown to Valentino's end.

I take a minute to steady my racing heart, but my thoughts are already moving on to what comes next. Valentino's death is the key to everything I've planned—the pivot point where I take control and get the *Famiglia* back on the right track. Every step must be flawless. One wrong move and my world will come crashing down.

If anyone even suspects I'm behind this, the entire *Famiglia* could turn on me. Men have been betrayed for less. The wrong whisper, the faintest slip, and their loyalty could shift, leaving me exposed. I've seen it before.

No one survives long in this world once they've lost trust. The consequences of failure will be swift—and fatal.

Leaving the office, I walk back into the restaurant, forcing a calm smile as I rejoin the guests. I greet those around me as though nothing is amiss.

A scream cuts through the air, sharp as a blade.

Dante and I exchange a glance, and without hesitation, we move swiftly toward the stairs leading to the basement. As we do, I nod to the men positioned throughout the restaurant. They spring into action, spreading out and securing the exits. The guests murmur in confusion, their laughter dying as they begin to sense something is wrong. My men are well-trained. They maintain control, ensuring no one leaves or thinks to venture downstairs.

Dante and I descend into the lower level, the sounds from above fading into muffled whispers. Lena's sobs reach us before we even see her, growing louder with each step.

The door is open, revealing the grim scene inside. Valentino's body is slumped against the bars of the cage, his face contorted in agony, and his veins bulging grotesquely from the poison's effects. The dim light casts harsh shadows on his lifeless form, highlighting the unnatural pallor of his skin.

In the corner, Lena's huddled, rocking back and forth. Her tear-streaked face twisted in horror and disbelief. Her cries are piercing, raw. Part of me feels awful for the role I've forced her to play, but there was no other way.

Dante steps forward, his expression worried as he crouches beside her. "Lena," he says firmly. "Lena, look at me."

She doesn't respond, her eyes vacant, lost in shock. I step closer, looming over her. "Lena," I say sharply, my voice cutting through her hysteria. "You need to pull yourself together."

Her gaze finally shifts to mine, and for a moment, it's as though she's seeing me for the first time. Recognition flickers in her eyes, followed by a fresh wave of tears.

"Handle the body," I instruct Dante coldly.

"I'm on it," Dante replies, already pulling out his phone. He's quick and efficient. Two of our men who followed us down begin securing the area, making sure nothing's left to chance.

I grab Lena's arm and haul her to her feet. Her legs buckle beneath her, but I don't let her fall. "You need to get a grip," I hiss in her ear, trying to snap her out of it. "We don't have time for this."

Lena clings to me, her nails digging into my arm. She nods weakly as she tries to pull herself together. I force myself to be patient as I guide her up the stairs and straight into the office. Once inside, I sit her down in a chair, watching as she curls into herself, her body trembling uncontrollably.

The weight of what I've set into motion presses heavily on me. Valentino is dead. The plan is in motion.

Before I can fully process the next steps, the door creaks open. Alessia steps inside, her eyes wide as she surveys the room. Her gaze moves from Lena to me.

"Valentino?" she breathes, barely above a whisper.

I study her closely, watching for any trace of genuine grief—but there's none. Only a carefully crafted mask of shock. But I know better. I've seen the way she looks at Valentino, the loathing she can never quite hide.

Alessia takes a tentative step forward, her eyes narrowing as they meet mine. For a moment, we share a silent understanding.

She's not mourning him. This isn't a loss for her. It's freedom.

"I... I should..." she stammers, glancing back toward the door.

"Go ahead," I tell her gently. "After I take care of Lena, I'll find you."

She hesitates, glancing at me once more before slipping out. Alone with Lena, I lean back against the desk, crossing my arms as I observe her.

"Why haven't you killed me yet?" she asks, her voice barely above a whisper.

"If I wanted you dead, you'd already be in the ground," I

reply, my tone calm, almost indifferent. "But that's not what I want right now."

She swallows hard. "What do you want?"

"For now, I want you to keep your mouth shut." Each word is deliberate. "That's the only way I can protect you."

Lena blinks, caught off guard. "You're going to protect me? Why?"

"Someone killed Valentino, and you were the last one with him," I remind her. "For now, I'll keep you alive. But don't mistake this for kindness. Step out of line, and I won't hesitate to make you disappear."

She flinches, the reality of the situation hitting her hard. "I didn't do anything," she murmurs, her voice cracking under the weight of her innocence.

Her words hang in the air. *I didn't do anything.*

Lena doesn't know the truth—that her hands delivered the final blow.

But I can never tell her that. Her fear must remain real, her role played to perfection. Because if she falters, my carefully constructed plan will unravel. And if something happens to me, she'll be on her own.

Lena's eyes lock onto mine, a storm of fear swirling within them. "I hated him, but I would never have killed him."

That's the problem, Lena. You wouldn't have.

I push down the guilt that tries to surface, reminding myself why I'm doing this. Valentino's death wasn't just necessary. It was inevitable. And Lena, with her pretty face and broken spirit, was the perfect scapegoat.

"If you do what I say and keep quiet, I'll ensure your safety," I tell her firmly. "But make no mistake, Lena—there's no going back. You're in this now, whether you like it or not."

Lena's eyes search mine, her fear and resignation battling. Slowly, she nods. She knows there's no escape.

"Good," I reply, turning toward the door. "I'll have Silas take you to a safe house. He'll stay with you until I can get there."

"Why are you helping me?" she asks as I walk toward the door.

I freeze, my hand on the knob. "No more questions, Lena."

And with that, I walk out of the office.

I glance around the restaurant, noting the uneasy faces of the guests as they mill about, trying to make sense of the chaos. My men are still in place, controlling the scene, keeping everyone calm. I straighten my jacket, forcing a relaxed expression as I step back into the center of the room.

"Ladies and gentlemen," I begin, my voice firm yet composed, cutting cleanly through the rising murmurs. "Thank you for your patience. Unfortunately, there's been an unexpected turn of events, and we'll have to end the celebration early."

There's a beat of silence, followed by the voice of Fabrizio Ricci, an old associate with eyes as sharp as his instincts. "What's going on? Is everything alright?" His words are polite, but there's a calculated edge to them—an undertone that only someone who's lived in our world would catch.

I meet his gaze, keeping my expression carefully neutral, offering nothing but a smooth veneer. "Nothing for you to worry about, Fabrizio," I reply, sidestepping his question. "Just a minor issue downstairs." I nod to my men, signaling them to begin quietly herding the guests out. "Thank you for your cooperation, and I appreciate your understanding."

The night isn't over—far from it. As I survey the scene, watching the guests shuffle out under the watchful eyes of my men, a dark satisfaction coils deep within me.

Valentino's gone. His presence no longer taints this world.

The air has shifted, but no one truly understands the gravity of the moment. Not yet, but soon enough, they will.

Alessia

Antonio sent me home with two guards and strict orders to wait for him. I thought he'd show up sooner, but it's nearly two in the morning and I've heard nothing. The house feels stifling, as if the air itself is holding its breath. When I finally hear the sound of a car pulling into the driveway, I jump up from the steps in the foyer, my nerves on edge. Rushing to the door, I pull it open before they have a chance to knock.

The two guards step aside, and I spot Antonio walking across the driveway toward me. His shirt is rumpled, the top few buttons undone, and his tie hangs loose around his neck. His hair is disheveled like he's spent the night running his hands through it. He looks tired, but there's something about the way he holds himself—a lingering innocence beneath the ruthless exterior.

"I didn't think you'd still be up," he says, his voice low as he reaches the porch.

"My husband was found dead," I reply, the words sharper than I intend. "Do you think I'd be able to sleep without knowing what happened?"

He ignores my question, turning to the men flanking me. "Thank you for staying with her. You can go now."

They nod and disappear into the night, leaving us alone on

the porch. The silence stretches between us, thick and suffocating. Antonio sighs, his shoulders slumping as he finally meets my gaze. There's something in his eyes—something more than exhaustion. It's like he's carrying the weight of the world, and for the first time, he's allowing me to see it.

"Come inside," I murmur, stepping back to let him pass. He hesitates for a moment before walking into the house. I close the door quietly and follow him to the living room. He collapses onto the couch, rubbing his temples, looking more worn than I've ever seen him.

"How did Valentino die?" I ask, standing in the doorway, my voice quieter now.

There's something in his eyes that I can't quite place—guilt, maybe—but he hides it. "It was quick," he says, but the hollowness in his tone betrays him.

Quick. Of course. After everything Valentino put me through, all the pain, the terror, I can't help but feel cheated. Part of me wishes he'd suffered, even for a moment. That he felt a fraction of the helplessness I endured at his hands. Knowing he was spared that feels like a cruel twist of fate.

"And Lena?" I press, needing to know how she fits into this.

He hesitates, grabbing the back of his neck—an old habit of his when he's uneasy. "I'm looking into it," he says carefully, his voice steady but guarded.

I bite the inside of my cheek, frustration bubbling beneath the surface. "Antonio, you can't keep me in the dark. I know she was there. Did she kill him?"

His jaw clenches, and for a brief second, I think he might tell me the truth. But then he shakes his head, barely noticeable. "It's complicated, Alessia. Just trust me that I'm handling it."

The words sting more than they should. *Handling it.* They're a reminder of how little control I have in any of this. But I don't have the energy to fight him. "Am I in danger?"

Antonio's expression softens just a fraction before he shakes his head. "No, you're not in danger."

"How can you be so sure?" I push, hoping he'll give me more than vague assurances.

He sighs deeply, rubbing his temples, the exhaustion on his face more pronounced now. "Alessia, please. Just go to bed," he says, his voice almost pleading. "We'll talk more in the morning. I'm staying here tonight."

"Why? You just said I'm not in danger."

"It's not about that, Alessia," he snaps, the sharpness in his voice making me take a step back. "I just need to be here, alright?"

I cross my arms, frustrated, but I can tell he's barely holding himself together. "If I'm not in danger, why do you need to stay?"

He closes his eyes for a long moment, his fists clenching at his sides as if trying to keep his temper in check. When he opens them, there's a flicker of something—anger, frustration, guilt but it vanishes as quickly as it appeared. "Because I'm not leaving you alone tonight. End of discussion."

There's a finality in his tone that leaves no room for argument. I want to push him for answers, to demand the truth, but he looks so drained, so utterly spent, that I let it go—for now.

"Okay," I whisper, my voice barely audible. But as I walk to my room, a knot of suspicion tightens in my chest. There's more to this than he's telling me.

"ALESSIA," ANTONIO SAYS, SHAKING MY SHOULDER gently. "It's time to get up."

I don't remember when I fell asleep, but it feels like it's far too soon to wake up. "Go away," I mumble, trying to burrow deeper into the warmth of my blankets.

"Nice try, princess," he says, a hint of amusement in his tone. Before I can stop him, he pulls the blankets off me, leaving me exposed to the morning chill.

"Antonio," I yell, scrambling to grab the blankets. My bare legs and mid-drift are exposed in the tank top and shorts I slept in. I catch him glancing at them—a brief shadow passes over his face, but it's gone so fast I almost miss it. I yank the blankets back up, glaring at him.

"Get up," he repeats, his voice more serious now. "You need to pack some things. You're going to stay with my mom and sister for a while."

I blink at him, stunned. "What? No, I'm staying here."

"Alessia," he starts, his voice calm but firm, "this isn't up for debate."

I shake my head, anger rising. "You said I wasn't in danger."

"You'll always be a target just for who you are," he clarifies, his patience thinning. "After last night, things with the *Famiglia* are unstable. I need to keep my family in one place to make sure everyone's safe."

"I'm not your family," I snap, my words harsh.

He doesn't back down. "This is what's necessary right now. You'll be safer with my mom and sister, and I'll be able to focus on what needs to be done."

I open my mouth to protest again, but he cuts me off. "Please, Alessia. Don't fight me on this," he says, his voice softer now.

It hits me that he's not acting solely out of duty. There's something more—a genuine concern that goes beyond his role. He's trying to protect me because he wants to. But why?

"Fine," I mutter, sliding out of bed and heading for the closet. "But I'm not happy about it."

"I wouldn't expect you to be," Antonio replies, a faint smile tugging at the corners of his lips. "Just pack what you need, and I'll have someone handle the rest."

That's what they always say. They always promise to *handle* things, to take care of everything. But no one ever does. Not really.

As I gather my belongings, I sense his eyes on me, watching, but I don't turn around. There's too much I don't understand—too many emotions I'm not ready to confront.

For now, I'll play along, keeping my head down and my intentions hidden. But the moment I see an opening, I'm gone. Away from this life, from all of it.

And once I leave, I'll never look back.

Antonio

Alessia's unhappy with my decision, I knew she would be, but thankfully, she doesn't put up too much of a fight. She throws her legs over the side of the bed and stomps across the room to her closet, her movements brimming with defiance. A smirk tugs at my lips, amused by her little tantrum. My gaze trails over her—her toned legs, tiny shorts, and the curve of her breasts beneath the thin tank top, her nipples hard against the fabric.

My pulse quickens, and desire surges through me. I take a step back to the doorway, forcing myself to regain control. Alessia's beautiful, impossible to ignore, but I know she can never be mine. Not anymore. That's something I have to accept, no matter how much my body reacts when she's this close.

She throws clothes into her bag, zips it up without even looking at me, and storms past in silence. The tension between us is almost tangible, but I don't push her. My mother's house is just across the street, but I'm sure that for Alessia, it feels like another form of imprisonment.

It's the safest place for her, though. Domenica's already there. She moved in after my father's death. I already have two trusted guards stationed at the house. It only makes sense for Alessia to stay with them.

We cross the street, and I remain close, my eyes scanning our surroundings as we walk. I can't shake the feeling that something could go wrong at any moment. Until I know what the fallout from Valentino's death will be, I can't take any risks with Alessia's safety.

Once she's inside and settled, I shift my attention to the next problem—Lena. She needs to disappear. I've already set things in motion to give her a new life far from Philadelphia. I need to make sure she gets out of town as soon as possible.

Dante waits for me outside, standing by the car. His face is as unreadable as ever, but I can feel the tension radiating off him.

We drive in silence for a while, the low murmur of the radio the only sound between us. I can tell Dante's itching to say something, and it's not long before he breaks the silence.

"How did it happen?" His question isn't just about Valentino—it's about me and the role I played in his death.

I keep my gaze fixed on the road. "Vigo's death was a result of unfortunate circumstances."

"Unfortunate circumstances?"

"Yes. Sometimes things don't go as planned, and the outcome is unexpected."

"You didn't answer my question," he says flatly.

I don't look at him, but I can feel his gaze boring into the side of my face. "What do you want me to say, Dante?"

He exhales slowly, leaning back into his seat. "Nothing. You've already said enough."

I didn't confirm or deny anything, but the look that passes between us tells me he understands. Valentino's death wasn't some random accident. Dante suspects I had a hand in it, but he also knows when to stop asking questions.

As we pull up to the safe house, I feel a sense of unease. The guard that should be outside is nowhere to be seen. Dante and I exchange a steely look—our instincts screaming that something's gone terribly wrong.

"Where the hell is he?" Dante mutters, drawing his weapon as we approach the front door.

"I don't know," I reply, sliding a fresh magazine into my gun and chambering a round.

The front door's unlocked. My mind races through worst-case scenarios. Inside, the house is unsettlingly quiet, with only our footsteps breaking the silence. Every muscle in my body's on edge, scanning the shadows for any sign of movement. The stillness feels wrong—dangerous.

We round the corner and find the guard at the bottom of the stairs. His body lies twisted in a pool of blood.

Stepping over him, I take the stairs two at a time. "Lena," I shout, but the silence that follows is deafening.

I hurry down the hall with Dante on my heels. Every creak in the floorboards amplifies the tension. When we reach the door to Lena's bedroom, it's closed.

"Lena, it's me." I knock but get no response.

I turn the handle and push the door open, bracing myself for whatever's on the other side. But nothing could've prepared me for the sight of Lena's body motionless on the floor, her eyes wide, empty. The blood pooling around her is dark, almost black in the dim light.

My heart pounds furiously as I rush over and kneel beside her. My fingers tremble as I reach for her wrist, searching for any sign of life.

Her skin is cold. Lifeless.

"Lena," I whisper, my voice cracking. "Come on, don't do this."

Dante grips my shoulder firmly, pulling me away. "She's gone, Antonio. There's nothing you can do."

Rage erupts inside me, blinding, suffocating. I slam my fist into the nearest wall, the impact splitting the plaster. The pain in my knuckles is sharp, but it's nothing compared to the storm tearing through me—the crushing weight of my failure.

My breath comes in ragged gasps as I try to rein it in. "Damn it," I roar, the sound reverberating through the empty house. I came here to offer Lena a way out—a new identity, a chance to escape. I promised to protect her.

I set her up. Now she's dead because of me.

Dante's already on the phone, his voice clipped and authoritative as he arranges for a cleanup crew.

"I should've done more," I mumble, self-loathing thick in my throat. "This is my fault."

Dante watches at me, his expression one of confusion as he processes my words. "We'll find out who's responsible," he says, trying to offer some semblance of comfort.

I shake my head, the guilt gnawing at me like a sickness. "You don't understand. I set her up," I snap. "I promised to keep her safe. She's dead because I failed."

Dante's brow furrows. "Whatever happened here is something you couldn't have anticipated. We both know how unpredictable things can get."

"That's no excuse," I growl. "I should've done better. I should've anticipated the risks. She's gone because I made a mistake."

"Taking the blame won't bring her back," Dante replies, his tone calm but firm. "What we need is to find out who's behind this and make them pay."

As his words sink in, a chilling realization settles over me. Lena's death wasn't a random act of violence—it's something more calculated, a symptom of rot within our organization.

"Someone knew exactly where to find her," I say, my mind clicking into place.

"You think this was an inside job?"

"It's not a suspicion," I reply, my voice hardening. "I'm certain of it. We need to find the traitors before more people die."

"I'll get in touch with Enzo and start the investigation. We'll flush out whoever it is."

The weight of the task ahead is daunting but necessary. Securing my *Famiglia* and avenging Lena's death are two sides of the same coin. I won't stop until those who betrayed us face justice.

The road ahead will be brutal, but I've never shied away from blood. And I won't start now.

Antonio

I knew Alessia wouldn't mourn him. The thought drifts through my mind as I watch her move through the house, her steps measured, her expression a mask of grief. But it's all for show. Beneath that veil of sorrow, there's no real sadness for Valentino's death—only relief.

Alessia decided not to have a public viewing or funeral. She suggested that after all the loss our family has endured recently, a small, private gathering would be more fitting. Aunt Domenica, still drowning in her own grief, agreed without question.

Alessia plays her role with eerie precision. Her eyes remain downcast, red and puffy from crying, her voice soft and steady, as if the weight of sorrow has stolen her strength. She drapes herself in black, accepting condolences with a grace that disguises the truth.

To anyone watching, she's a grieving young wife. But I see it —the moments when her shoulders relax, the tension slipping away when she thinks no one's looking. She's not grieving Valentino. She's simply doing what she must to keep up appearances.

The power vacuum left by Valentino's death is dangerous, and Alessia, without proper protection, could quickly become a target. That's why I have to keep her close—protect her while I deal with the disaster that Vigo left behind. Once the dust settles, she can go, free to live her life however she chooses.

DANTE, ENZO, AND I ARE AT AN EMERGENCY MEETING with our allied *famiglias*, and the tension in the room is palpable. Valentino's questionable alliances and deals had already unsettled everyone while he was still Capo. Since his death, the uncertainty has only deepened. This meeting is crucial—we need to establish the next steps and ensure our allies are aligned as we move forward.

The room is filled with powerful men who've supported us for years. They exchange uneasy glances as we sit around the conference table, their respect for the tradition of this gathering evident despite the palpable tension.

Enzo, standing in as the acting *Capo*, calls the meeting to order. His voice is firm, carrying the authority that comes with his temporary role. "We're here today to address the changes brought about by Valentino's death and to establish a clear path forward."

The men nod, though some with more hesitation than others. Valentino's death has left a void, and what fills it next could shift everything. We all know the stakes are high.

After discussing the immediate state of our operations, Enzo motions to me. "Antonio has been a loyal and respected member of this family. His dedication and capabilities have been proven time and again." His eyes move around the room. "I believe the best course of action is for him to step into the role of Capo."

Murmurs of agreement ripple through the room. "With Dante as his underboss, our leadership will remain stable and all of our *Famiglias* strong."

I look around, feeling the weight of their approval settle over me. These men have known Dante and me since we were young, watched us rise through the ranks, and now trust us to lead. I'm filled with pride, but there's apprehension, too. The role of Capo is both a significant honor as well as a dangerous role—but it's one I'm prepared to assume.

I rise slowly, the room falling silent as I speak. "Thank you, Enzo. I'm honored by your confidence and by the support of everyone here." My voice is steady. "I've always done my best to serve *La Famiglia*. I'm honored and ready to continue that as Capo."

Enzo nods before turning back to the group. "Tradition would have us mark this transition with a ceremony, as we have for generations," he begins.

I raise my hand, cutting him off. "I respect tradition, Enzo, but I believe it's time to start fresh with a new legacy—one that isn't marked by ceremonies and blood." I let my gaze drift over the room, watching as they listen. "The agreement and confidence of the men here is all I need. Let that be our strength."

A moment of silence stretches before there's agreement from around the table. The tension finally begins to ease.

Enzo looks thoughtful, then speaks again. "I agree. After what's happened recently, change is exactly what we need." He turns to the room, addressing everyone present. "Antonio and Dante are the right men to lead us. Our alliances will hold strong, and our operations will continue without interruption."

A heavy silence falls over the room. One by one, the men rise, approaching me not with smiles but with somber respect, extending a hand not just in respect but in recognition of what this truly means. They call me Capo—the title falling from their lips like a vow, a binding acknowledgment of my new position.

Dante stands at my side, his expression as cold and unflinching as my own. There's no need for words between us—we both know what needs to be done. The time for action has come, and we're ready to get to work.

When everyone returns to their seats, I take charge. "We need to address the immediate problems—chief among them, the unwanted deals Valentino made with Emilio Salazar and Giancarlo DeLuca."

"We don't want drugs or humans being moved on our streets," Guiseppe Carlino speaks up.

"You have my word. Any alliances Valentino made with those organizations will not be honored by Dante or me," I explain. "They'll be dealt with accordingly, and I will return peace and safety to the streets of our city."

$$Alessia$$

Last night, Antonio made a rare appearance after dinner to inform us that, with Enzo's backing and the support of their other alliances, he's been named the new Capo. I overheard him and Dante talking—Valentino made dirty deals that have left many of the other families on edge. Antonio's going to be busy putting out fires all over Philadelphia. Which, for me, is a good thing.

Antonio still insists it's not safe for me to live alone, so I'm staying at his mother's house. He keeps two guards at the front door at all times. I hardly see him. He's up before dawn and rarely home until the middle of the night.

"You've been pacing like a caged animal for weeks," Cecilia remarks, her voice breaking through my thoughts.

I spin around, pressing a hand to my chest. "You scared me. I didn't hear you come in."

"I'm sorry. I didn't mean to startle you."

Cecilia, with her long dark blonde hair and big brown eyes, is stunning. Despite being raised in this world, she's bubbly and outgoing, her spirit unbroken. She has big dreams and her family's full support in chasing them.

"It's okay," I reply, steadying my breath. "Did you need something?"

She perches on the arm of the sofa, her eyes sparkling with impatience. "I need to get out of the house. Want to come with me?"

"We're allowed to leave?" I ask, surprised.

She laughs lightly. "Of course we are. Where do you want to go?" She dangles car keys in front of her.

I hesitate, my heart racing. I've been biding my time, waiting for the right moment to escape. With Antonio distracted by his new responsibilities, this might be my only chance. But I have to be careful.

"I'm not sure. Maybe a drive far away from here?" I suggest cautiously.

Cecilia tilts her head, studying me, her smile fading. "I know you've been through a lot with losing your husband, but I get the feeling there might be something else bothering you."

I take a deep breath and decide to take the risk. "There is," I admit, my voice barely above a whisper. "It's not something I've ever talked about."

She scoots closer. "You can tell me anything, Alessia. You know that, right?"

I've come to love this girl, like the sister I never had. "I need to get away, Cecilia. I can't stay here any longer."

Her eyes widen in shock. "Get away? Why?"

"I feel trapped. Like I'm in a cage."

"I get that." She nods slowly. "Having guards around can be suffocating, but they're not so bad once you get to know them. And they won't be here forever. Antonio will take care of everything."

"It's not just the guards. We were raised very differently," I explain. "My parents didn't love me—they only cared about appearances, deals, and alliances. I didn't get to go out with friends or go to college. I was never free to fall in love."

"Oh," she says softly.

"I was forced to marry Valentino," I continue, the words catching in my throat. "He was a cruel man. He hurt me in ways I can't even begin to describe."

Cecilia's hand reaches for mine. "I'm so sorry. I had no idea."

Tears burn at the corners of my eyes, and I let them fall, hoping they'll sway her. "You grew up in a home full of love and support. I was nothing more than a pawn. Even with Valentino gone, I'm still trapped. I need to leave. I want to be free."

Cecilia squeezes my hand, her own eyes now glistening with tears. "Where will you go? What will you do?"

"I don't know yet," I admit, feeling my voice waver. "But I have to try. I want to find out if there's more to life than this." I hold her gaze. "Will you help me?"

For a long moment, she's silent, considering my words. Then, she nods, a quiet resolve settling over her features. "Okay. I'll help."

"Really?" I whisper, hope swelling in my chest.

"Yes. But we need to be careful. Antonio will lose his mind if he finds out I helped you."

"Thank you, Cecilia. I don't know how I'll ever repay you."

She gives me a small, sad smile. "You don't have to repay me. Just promise that when you get to wherever you're going, you'll let me know you're safe."

"I promise," I reply, though I already know I can't do that.

"How long do you need to get ready?" she asks.

"Give me ten minutes to grab a few things," I say, standing quickly.

"I'll tell the guards we're going for a drive. That we need to get out of the house. Once we're far enough away, I'll ditch them. I've gotten pretty good at that," she says, smiling proudly.

"Do you think you can drop me off at the bus station?"

"Sure," she replies, then lowers her voice. "Do you need money?"

"I've been saving what I can. I'll be okay for a while," I assure her.

She nods. "I'll meet you in the car."

I hurry upstairs to my most recent cage. Grabbing my purse, I double-check that the envelope with my cash is still hidden in the lining. Pulling out my phone, I power it off, and leave it on the nightstand. I can't take anything with me that could be tracked.

At the doorway, I pause, taking one last look around the room, knowing this is the last time I'll ever see it. I'm leaving everything behind—my past, my pain, and the life that was never truly mine.

I've been trapped for so long—first by my father, then by Valentino. But now, for the first time, I can breathe knowing I'll be more than just someone else's pawn.

Today marks the start of a new chapter one in which I'll finally be free.

Antonio

The air is charged with tension as Dante and I prepare to gather the men. Word quickly spread through the ranks that I'm the new Capo. There's been no grand induction, no blood-marked ceremony, just the silent understanding that I'm now in charge. So far, I've received nothing but supportive messages. But we still have to deal with the matter of who betrayed us.

"Are you ready for this?" I ask.

"I am," Dante says, his jaw tight. "Tonight, they'll learn the true cost of betrayal."

We descend the steps, each movement carrying the gravity of what's to come. I've shut down the restaurant and summoned our men. They think it's just another routine meeting for assignments. What they don't realize is that this is far from ordinary— it's a show of strength, a warning to anyone foolish enough to consider betraying us again.

As we enter the meeting room, the men are already gathered. Some sit, others stand, their postures casual but alert. They have no reason to believe anything is different—yet. Among them are Gino and Mario, the two who sealed their fates with their betrayal. They're responsible for the deaths of our guard and

Lena. Tonight, they'll pay for it.

I catch Enzo's gaze from across the room. His expression is blank, but his slight nod confirms he's ready.

"Since Valentino's death, Dante and I have been working to ensure our long-held alliances remain secure," I say as I step forward, my voice slicing through the low murmurs. The room stills instantly. "I want to thank those who've reached out to me," I pause, scanning the faces around me.

"However," I continue, my voice colder now, "not everyone among us has been as loyal as they should've been."

The tension in the room skyrockets, and I catch the briefest flicker of panic in a few eyes. My gaze locks onto the two men standing near the entrance. "Gino. Mario," I say, my tone sharp and unforgiving.

They freeze, the color draining from their faces as they realize they've been marked. "These men thought they could play both sides. Their betrayal is the reason we're here tonight."

Mario's gaze darts around, looking for a way out, but there's none. "Loyalty," I continue, "is everything in this life. And betrayal is unforgivable."

I nod to Enzo. He and Dante draw their weapons with swift, practiced ease. Gino stammers, desperate. "Mario told me our orders were to get rid of that bitch,"

"That's a fucking lie," Mario snaps. "I had nothing to do with this."

Their protests are drowned out by the thunderous sound of two gunshots. The men slump to the floor. The room falls into a suffocating silence.

My eyes sweep over the room. "This is your only chance," I say slowly, my tone unwavering. "You will pledge your loyalty to me and *La Famiglia* now or you will take this opportunity to walk away and leave this behind. But know this—if you choose to stay, any betrayal will meet the same fate."

One by one, they pledge their allegiance to the *Famiglia*. There's no hesitation, no doubt in their voices. Now, we stand ready to face whatever comes next with renewed strength and unwavering unity.

Now I'm able to turn my attention to the next problem—Emilio Salazar and his cartel. They've been overextended in Colombia, struggling to hold onto their coca fields as rivals close in. Their grip is slipping, and I plan to exploit that.

Late last night, Dante eliminated Quito Rojas, Salazar's second-in-command. One clean shot to the skull, no witnesses. Just minutes ago, I sent the photos to Salazar. Now, I wait for the call.

When the phone rings, I don't waste time. "Consider this your only warning. Our business is finished," I say, my voice cold and flat.

"We had a deal," Salazar replies.

"You had a deal with Valentino," I say, correcting him. "But if you think you can push back, I'll make sure your enemies have everything they need to take your fields and routes. How long do you think you'll last after that?"

The silence that follows is almost satisfying. He knows he's cornered.

After what feels like an eternity, he finally speaks, his voice dripping with resignation. "You've made your point. No need for more bloodshed."

A wicked grin pulls at my lips. "Smart choice. I expect your men out of my territory by the end of the week. Stay out of my way, and we won't have any more problems."

Another pause, then a defeated, "Understood."

I hang up, the satisfaction settling in. Salazar's done. Now, all that's left is cutting ties with the DeLuca *Famiglia*, ensuring no humans will ever be trafficked through our city again.

Alessia

After a day and a half on a bus, I finally arrive in Magnolia Springs, Alabama. The sun is warm on my skin, and the small-town charm of the place should feel welcoming, but all I feel is the gnawing ache of uncertainty. Did I think this through all the way? No. I left with barely more than the cash in my pocket, a few outfits, and a cheap prepaid phone I picked up at one of the bus stops.

As I walk down the main street, the reality of my situation crashes down. I have no ID, no official documents. Getting a place to stay or finding a job is going to be almost impossible. My heart races as I scan the unfamiliar faces of the locals, wondering how long I can survive before I run out of money.

I spot a small diner and, with no better options, I pull open the door. The bells above jingle, and the aroma of fresh coffee and grilled food wraps around me. An older woman with white hair, her glasses low on her nose, glances up from behind the counter.

"Sit anywhere, sugar. I'll be right with ya," she says, her voice carrying the warmth of a grandmother, but it does little to calm my nerves.

I slide into a booth and glance over the menu tucked behind the napkin dispenser. My stomach churns with hunger, but I count the remaining bills in my pocket trying to figure out what I can afford to spend on food when I still need a place to sleep tonight.

A few minutes later, the woman appears at my table, pulling out a pencil from behind her ear and flipping open a small tablet. "What can I get for you?"

"Just a coffee, please," I say, trying to sound less desperate than I feel.

"Sure thing," she says, but as she turns to leave, another diner calls out.

"Hey Rosie. Did you forget my burger?"

She huffs, turning briefly toward the man. "Hold your horses, Pete," then looks back at me, offering a weary smile. "Sorry 'bout that. My waitress up and quit this morning, left me in a real bind."

My mind races. This could be my chance. "Does that mean you're hiring?" I ask, trying to keep my voice steady.

Her eyes narrow, studying me. "You got experience?"

"I do," I say quickly. "I've waitressed before."

Rosie's expression softens. "Well, ain't that somethin'. When can you start?"

"Right now."

She pauses, glancing over her shoulder at the man still waiting for his burger, then back at me. "We'll have to do paperwork to make it legal. Takes some time to get it all sorted."

My heart sinks. "Is there any way we could skip the paperwork?"

"You aren't running from the law or anything are you?" She looks over her glasses at me.

"Not the law. My husband," I say, my voice lowering as I brace myself for her reaction.

Rosie's eyes widen, concern etched into the lines of her face. "Your husband?"

I nod, swallowing the lump in my throat. "He was abusive,

and I left him. Is there any way you could keep it under the table. I just need a chance to start over."

Her gaze softens further, and for a moment, the diner fades around us. "You poor thing," she says quietly. She leans in, her voice dropping. "Alright. We can do that."

Relief floods through me, my shoulders sagging as I whisper, "Thank you. You have no idea how much this means to me."

"Don't thank me yet," she says with a small smile. "This place gets busy. I hope you're ready for some hard work."

"I am," I reply earnestly, then pause. "I'm Allie, by the way."

"Nice to meet you, Allie. I'm Rosie." She gives me a warm smile. "Alright, Allie. Let's get you started."

The rest of the day flies by in a blur of orders, coffee refills, and the chaotic bustle of the Bluebird Café. The work is hard. My feet ache, and exhaustion pulls at my body but for the first time in ages, I don't mind. The constant flow of customers keeps my mind off the past, and the knowledge that I'm earning my own way makes the exhaustion feel like progress.

A WEEK SLIPS BY, BUT REALITY BEGINS TO CATCH UP with me. I've been staying at the Magnolia Motor Inn, between the room and ordering all my meals, I'm running short on money. I've been trying not to eat too much at the diner, worried Rosie might start asking questions that I can't answer. But the thought of being without a permanent roof over my head keeps me up at night, panic creeping closer with each passing day.

It's late one evening just after close when Rosie takes a seat across from me, wiping her hands on her apron. "So," she starts casually. "Have you found an apartment yet?"

Her question catches me off guard. I blink, unsure of how to answer. "I... well, I've been staying at the Magnolia Motor Inn," I say, feeling my nerves tighten. "But you already knew that didn't you?"

Rosie watches me for a moment, her lips curving into a knowing smile. "It's a small town, Allie. People talk. I figured you hadn't settled in anywhere permanent yet."

"Honestly, I didn't plan this very well."

She looks me over for a moment. "Tell you what, I've got a small apartment upstairs. It's not much, but it's clean, and you're welcome to stay there until you get settled."

I blink, taken aback by her kindness. "Rosie, I can't possibly—"

She cuts me off with a wave of her hand. "Nonsense. You can pay me a little rent once you're back on your feet, but for now, consider it a roof over your head."

Tears prick at the corners of my eyes, her generosity is overwhelming. "Thank you," I whisper, my voice trembling. "I don't know how to repay you."

Rosie smiles gently, squeezing my hand. "Just promise me you'll never go back to him. That's all the thanks I need."

"I promise," I say, my voice thick with emotion.

She nods, satisfied. "Good. Now, let's get you upstairs and settled."

After showing me to the small, cozy apartment above the diner, Rosie leaves me with a set of keys and her phone number, reminding me to call if I need anything. As I close the door behind her, I lean against it for a moment, taking in the quiet, the safety.

I have a job, a place to live, and the promise of a new life.

Draco Moretti summoned me to his home. Why? I have no idea, but unease coils in my gut. I pace inside the suffocating confines of his office. Exhaustion pulls at me—I've been putting out nonstop fires, trying to right the ship since Valentino's death. The last thing I need is trouble with the Moretti family.

The door creaks open, and Draco steps in. "Antonio," he says, a serpent's smile playing on his lips and his voice smooth as silk yet edged with a sinister undertone. "I trust you've been keeping busy."

"What can I do for you, Draco?" I reply, forcing calm as I sink into the chair opposite him.

He drums his fingers lightly on his desk—a steady, almost maddening rhythm, like the ticking of a clock counting down to something inevitable. "I'm concerned, Antonio," he begins, his tone deceptively casual. "I haven't heard from my daughter in over a week. You told me she's staying with your mother?"

"She is," I say, keeping my voice steady. "She's safe."

Draco's expression remains unreadable, but his eyes are sharp —razor-like, dissecting every word. "Then why hasn't she returned my calls?" His voice drops, a threat lurking beneath it. "Alessia knows better than to ignore me."

I keep my gaze locked on his, unblinking. "I'll look into it. But I assure you, she's fine."

He leans forward, his fingers no longer drumming but resting motionless on the desk. "I'm also concerned about our alliance now that Valentino's dead."

"Our alliance is solid," I reply, feeling the tension coil tighter in my chest. "Valentino's death changes nothing."

Draco's lips curl into a smile, but it's hollow, lifeless. "I disagree," he says, his voice a whisper of malice. "Actions, Antonio, speak louder than words. If you want to ensure our families remain united, there's something you must do." His voice drops further, a shadow of intent, "It would be unfortunate if anything were to disrupt the harmony we've worked so hard to maintain."

A chill runs down my spine. "What are you suggesting?"

"You will marry Alessia," he says, the words falling like a death sentence.

"Marry Alessia?" I repeat, my disbelief barely restrained.

"Yes," he replies. "That will prove your desire to remain allied."

My pulse hammers in my chest, but I keep my expression neutral, the storm of anger held tightly in check. "This isn't necessary. Our families—"

"It is necessary," he interrupts, his tone colder than stone. "Alessia's my daughter, and I want to ensure her future is secure. If you truly want to keep this alliance intact, you will marry her."

I clench my hands in my lap, nails biting into my skin. He doesn't care about Alessia. He never has. This is about power— his power. I force a nod, my voice calm though it feels like poison on my tongue. "I understand."

"Good," Draco says, his gaze piercing. "Make it happen, Antonio."

The conversation with Draco ends abruptly, leaving a bitter taste in my mouth as I walk out of the Moretti compound. The memory of when Alessia and I were teenagers floods my mind, unbidden. Back then, I wanted nothing more than to marry her. I remember standing in front of my mirror, rehearsing how I'd ask for his blessing. I thought I could make it happen—build a life with her. But Valentino stepped in, his ambition like poison, and everything between Alessia and me was ripped apart.

Now, Draco's trying to force me into a marriage I once wanted, but I can't stand the thought of being forced into anything—especially this. I grip the steering wheel as I get into the car, my mind swirling. I'm tired, exhausted from the constant battles, and frankly, I don't want more problems with the Moretti's.

Marrying Alessia won't be out of love or desire—only to keep the peace.

The drive to my mother's house feels longer than usual, each mile stretching out as Draco's demands echo in my head. I haven't been home in weeks. I've been too consumed with managing the chaos that erupted after taking over as Capo. Most nights, exhaustion drags me down before I even reach my apartment—I end up crashing on the couch in my office at the restaurant.

But I don't want to wait on this. I need to see Alessia and tell her that this time we're both trapped.

The house glows softly in the evening light, the warmth of home almost mocking the storm inside me.

As I step through the door, Aunt Domenica greets me. "It's been too long, Anton," she says as she embraces me.

"I've been busy," I reply, the guilt settling in alongside my exhaustion. "How are you?"

"I'm well," she sighs, leading me to the living room. "It's good that you came tonight. There's something I need to discuss with you."

"That sounds serious."

Her smile is sad, the creases around her eyes deepening. "My brother in Italy sent me a ticket. He wants me to return home and live with him."

"You don't have to go," I say quickly. "Your place will always be here."

She shakes her head softly, her eyes searching mine. "It's time, Anton. Now that you're Capo, I want you to move into the house I shared with your Uncle Giovanni."

I blink, surprised by her words. "Into your house?"

"Giovanni and I made many happy memories in that home," she says, her voice catching as she blinks back tears. "You remind me so much of him, Anton. I know you'll find someone to love, someone to share your life and home with."

She reaches into her pocket, pulling out a small, worn box. Her hands tremble slightly as she opens it. "This was your grandmother's wedding ring. Giovanni gave it to me when we married, and now I want you to have it."

Silence falls between us as I take the ring from the box, its weight far heavier than the gold it's made of. This isn't just a ring—it's a legacy, a promise carried through generations. For a brief moment, I picture it on Alessia's finger, the life we could've had if everything hadn't been shattered. But now, it feels more like a chain, binding us both to a future we don't want.

I swallow hard, my throat tight. "I'll miss you, Aunt Domenica

"And I'll miss you, Anton," she replies, cupping my face with hands full of love and loss. "But you have your own path to walk now. Make your uncle proud."

I nod, barely keeping the flood of emotions at bay as she hugs me one last time. "Now, go see your mother. She's been waiting."

I find my mom in the kitchen, humming softly to herself as she prepares dinner. When she sees me, her face lights up. "Anton. I've been so worried about you."

"I'm sorry, Mom," I say, kissing her cheek.

She studies me, her eyes full of concern. "You look exhausted."

"I'm fine," I lie. "Just a lot going on."

"You won't be any good to anyone if you run yourself into the ground," she says, her voice full of motherly reprimand. "Can you stay for dinner?"

"That would be great," I reply, glancing around the room, my mind still weighed down by Draco's demands. "Where's Alessia? I need to talk to her."

My mother's smile fades slowly, confusion clouding her face. "Alessia?" she asks, her voice uncertain. "I thought you arranged for her to leave."

Her words catch me off guard. "What? No. I didn't arrange anything."

"Cecilia told me you and Alessia decided it was best for her to leave Philadelphia. She said Alessia was too emotional to say good-bye." Mom sets the spoon down carefully, turning fully toward me. "The poor girl's been through so much, I didn't think anything of it."

Out of the corner of my eye, I spot Cecilia slipping quietly out of the room. "Excuse me," I mutter as I follow her upstairs.

"Cecilia," I say sharply, pushing the door open. "What do you know about this?"

"I'm sorry, Antonio," she whispers.

"What have you done?"

Tears well up in her eyes. "I helped her get away."

"Why?"

Her voice trembles. "She felt trapped. Alessia told me how awful her life was, how Valentino abused her." Her voice cracks. "She was desperate and I just wanted to help her."

My anger surges, but I force it down, my mind replaying Draco's demand. I grab the back of my neck, trying to rein it in. "Do you know the amount of problems you created for me?"

Cecilia flinches. "I just wanted to help," she whispers.

"How long has she been gone?"

She hesitates. "Almost three weeks."

I curse under my breath. *Three weeks.* The words hit me like a punch to the gut, a wave of anger rising fast, threatening to spill over. I exhale sharply, trying to get a grip as my mind races.

Draco's already closing in, and now this—everything's unraveling faster than I can contain.

"Where did she go?" I ask, my voice tight, barely keeping the frustration in check.

"I don't know," Cecilia admits, shaking her head, her eyes pleading. "I dropped her off at the bus stop. She promised she'd call when she figured out where she was going, but she never did."

"Why didn't you come to me first?"

Cecilia's eyes fill with tears. "She felt trapped, Antonio. She told me how awful her life was growing up. How her father's demands crushed her. And then when she told me about Valentino and what he did to her." Her voice cracks, and she wipes her cheeks. "I couldn't stand to see her like that. Desperate and scared. I just wanted to help her, to give her the freedom she always dreamed of."

"I'm sorry I yelled at you," I say and take a deep breath. "Thank you for telling me, Cecilia," I say, my voice softer.

Cecilia nods, though her expression remains troubled. "I'm sorry, Antonio. I didn't mean to cause trouble."

"I know," I reply and place a kiss on top of her head. "I'll handle it."

But as I head back downstairs, I can't shake the feeling that everything is about to get much more complicated. Alessia's out there alone and if I don't find her soon, someone else will. And if they do—they won't. I can't let that happen.

"I thought you were staying for dinner?" my mother calls as I reach the front door.

"There's been a change of plans," I say, already opening the door. "Raincheck?"

"Please be safe, Anton."

"I will."

I'm barely out the door before I pull out my phone and dial Dante. He picks up on the second ring. "What's up?"

"We have a problem," I grit out, the frustration boiling over. "A huge fucking problem."

Alessia

I've quickly fallen in love with the small, enchanting town of Magnolia Springs. From its tree-lined streets to the gentle flow of the Magnolia River, this charming southern town has captivated my heart. There's a peace here, a serenity I've never known. Each day feels like another layer of my past peeling away, loosening its grip on my soul.

Every morning, the sound of birds chirping outside my bedroom window wakes me. After my shifts at the diner, I take long walks around town, letting the warm breezes wash over me. The simplicity of life here fills me with inspiration.

My new camera, bought with the money I've earned, feels like a lifeline. The click of the shutter captures moments that would otherwise be lost, slowly mending the parts of my soul that Valentino broke.

People here have started to recognize me, greeting me with smiles and nods as I pass. I return the gesture, but I keep my distance, careful not to reveal too much. Despite my guarded nature, I've grown closer to Rosie. She's a force of nature—quick-witted, full of infectious laughter, and as tough as nails. In the weeks since I started at the diner, she's taken me under her wing.

It's been easier than I expected to let my guard down with her. She's the first real friend I've ever had.

Rosie's story is one of resilience. She was widowed two years ago, her husband—her high school sweetheart, passed away after a long battle with cancer. The Bluebird Diner was their shared dream. When he died, she didn't know how she'd keep it going alone. That's when her brother, Brian, moved back to help.

Brian's kind, with chestnut-brown hair and soulful eyes. Rosie's not exactly subtle about the way her eyes light up when he's around, or the hints she drops whenever we're all together. It's obvious she hopes something might develop between us, that maybe Brian and I could end up together.

The thought makes me smile, though I can't see it happening. He's handsome, sure, and being around him is easy, but after everything I've been through, I'm not ready to let anyone in. I'm not sure I ever will be. Still, I can't bring myself to tell Rosie to stop hoping.

One Sunday afternoon, after the diner's closed, Rosie and I sit on her front porch in heavy wooden rocking chairs, sipping sweet tea. The tension in my shoulders melts away as I snap pictures of the wildflowers. They're still holding droplets of rain on their petal from a shower that moved through earlier.

"You've got a good eye, you know," Rosie says, nodding toward the camera hanging around my neck. "You take some mighty fine pictures."

"Thanks. It's something I've always loved."

"Ever thought about making it more than a hobby?" Her eyes sparkle with interest. "We get lots of tourists through here. I bet you could sell them."

I hesitate, caught off guard by her suggestion. She doesn't know I've been sending photos to the gallery in Philadelphia. "Maybe one day," I say, evading the whole truth. "Right now, I'm just enjoying the freedom to do it again."

Rosie's smile fades slightly, her expression thoughtful. "You're a tough nut to crack, you know that?"

I laugh, a sound that surprises even me. "I'm not trying to be mysterious."

She waves her hand dismissively. "I understand. You've been through hard times. I'm just glad you're here and starting to find some happiness."

Her words warm something deep inside me. When I ran, I never expected to find someone like Rosie—someone offering friendship without asking for anything in return. It's a rare gift, and I'm grateful for it.

As we sit in comfortable silence, I let myself imagine what it would be like to stay here permanently. The thought is both exhilarating and terrifying. It's been nearly six weeks, and no one's come looking for me. With Valentino dead, I'm no longer useful to my father, and Antonio doesn't have to feel responsible for me anymore.

I'm finally free. Building a future here feels like a real possibility.

Later that evening, after the sun dips below the horizon, I leave Rosie's house and take a slow walk back to my apartment. Once home, I flip through the photos I've taken, each one capturing a moment of beauty, a reminder of why I fell in love with photography in the first place.

There's one photo of a couple holding hands as they walk through the park, their fingers intertwined with quiet intimacy. The trees around them are bathed in the soft, golden light of late afternoon. Their heads are close together, sharing a secret known only to them. The world around them is blurred, softened, as if nothing else matters but this moment.

Another photo is of the river, its surface like a mirror reflecting the vibrant colors of the sunset, orange, pink, purple, melding into one another as the sun touches the horizon. The trees along the riverbank stand in sharp contrast, dark silhouettes against the glowing sky. The water is so still it gives the illusion that the river and the sky are one, a seamless expanse of calm.

And then there's the one of Rosie, caught mid-laugh, her face bright with pure joy. Her head is tilted back as if she's letting the happiness spill out. The sparkle in her eyes is infectious making it impossible not to smile while looking at it.

I linger on that last photo, a swell of emotion rising in my chest. Rosie's given me more than just a job and a place to stay—she's given me a sense of family, of belonging.

After I upload several of the photos and email them to the gallery, I close my laptop. I can't help but smile. This town, these people. It feels like I belong here. Like I'm home.

But as much as I want to embrace this new life, there's a part of me that's holding back. A voice whispers not to get too comfortable. I know the dangers of letting my guard down. My past could still creep back in when I least expect it.

Still, Magnolia Springs has given me something precious—a chance at happiness. And for now, that's enough.

Tomorrow, I'll wake up and do it all over again. I'll serve coffee and pancakes, chat with Rosie and the regulars, and continue capturing the beauty of this town that's become my sanctuary.

And maybe, just maybe, I'll start to believe that this new life is really mine to keep.

Antonio

"Cecilia took her to the bus stop and let her go?" Dante asks, disbelief lacing his tone.

"Yes." The edge in my voice betrays my frustration, and my knee bounces uncontrollably. "And I wouldn't have given a damn if Draco hadn't made that ultimatum."

"What are you going to do?" Dante presses, his eyes narrowing as he studies me.

"I can't afford to make an enemy out of Draco Moretti. I'm running on fumes here." I lean back, letting my head fall against the seat. "I don't have a choice. I have to find Alessia and marry her."

"Any clue where she might be?"

"None." I exhale sharply. "Alessia promised Cecilia she'd call once she settled somewhere, but she never did."

"You checked her phone?"

"Of course I did. There's nothing," I say, my voice flat.

"She can't have gone far."

Dante leans back, arms crossed. "So, what's the plan?"

I rub my temples, trying to ease the pounding in my skull. "I wish I had a damn clue."

The truth is, part of me wouldn't have cared if Alessia had just disappeared. If she'd started over somewhere far away where this life couldn't touch her. Hell, after everything she's been through, she deserves at least that much.

But Draco's ultimatum changes everything. It wasn't a suggestion—it was a threat. A reminder that he'd sacrifice anything, including his daughter's happiness, if it means securing more power.

If I let Alessia slip away, Draco will back out of our alliance and may become a threat to my family. I can't let that happen, not when the dust hasn't fully settled from the chaos Valentino caused.

Keeping the peace is all that matters, and if marrying Alessia is the price I have to pay, then so be it. I'll search every corner of the globe until I find her and bring her back—bring her home, to be mine. Whether either of us likes it or not.

"Do you really think she'll come back without a fight?" Dante breaks into my thoughts.

A bitter laugh escapes. "Does it matter? She doesn't have a choice. Neither of us does." The words taste like ash in my mouth. "I'll drag her back kicking and screaming if I have to."

Dante nods, but there's something in his eyes—pity, maybe? I don't need it. I don't want it.

My family and our business, they're all that matter. Following in my uncle's footsteps, keeping everyone safe, maintaining peace on the streets—that's my priority.

I'll find Alessia, and she'll become my wife. Even if it means becoming the very monster I swore I'd never become.

Antonio

I've been staring at the reports on my desk for so long that the words blur together. Dante's hacker hasn't turned up anything yet—no records, no traces. Alessia's a ghost and with each day that passes, it feels like a noose tightening around my neck.

I put a few of my closest men on the search. They're working quietly, combing through every scrap of information that might give me a lead. I have to keep it all locked down. If Draco catches wind of this, it'll get ugly fast.

While I'm focused on finding Alessia, I've put Enzo in charge of keeping the restaurant and our money-laundering operation afloat. I'm counting on him to keep business running smoothly and cover my tracks, so no one suspects how deep I'm buried in this mess.

It's all I can do to keep up appearances—make it look like business as usual while my mind races, wondering where the hell Alessia's hiding.

The worst part? Dealing with Draco. He's been calling nonstop, demanding to know why Alessia isn't answering her phone. I keep feeding him the same line—she's mourning Valentino. She needs time and asks not to be disturbed. He's calling bullshit on it. Draco knows as well as I do that she hated Valentino. But so far, I've been able to keep him away.

Until today.

"Antonio." Draco's voice crackles through the phone. "I've been patient, but my daughter has ignored me for long enough."

"She's grieving, Draco." I force calm into my tone, even though my pulse pounds in my ears. "Valentino's death hit her harder than expected. She needs more time."

"I've given her enough time," he snaps. "I'm done with excuses. Perhaps I should stop by your mother's house to see her for myself."

The idea of Draco anywhere near my mother or Cecilia makes my blood run cold. "There's no need for that, Draco," I say, trying to mask my desperation. "I'll talk to her and make sure she gets in touch."

"You have one week, Antonio," he growls. "After that, I'll deal with this personally."

The line goes dead, and I'm left staring at the phone. One week. That's all I've got before Draco blows this whole thing wide open.

I slam my fist onto the desk, frustration boiling over. "Damn it," I yell, shoving the papers aside. "Where the hell are you, Alessia?"

I can't afford to lose control. Not now. I need a plan. But every second that ticks by is a reminder I'm running out of time.

Dante's hacker is still digging through bus ticket records, but we've got nothing so far. If she had a fake ID, she could be anywhere. Hell, she could be on the other side of the world, and I wouldn't know it.

This is taking too long. I can't sit around waiting. I have to do something.

My mind races, desperate for any lead I haven't thought of yet. Then it hits me—the gallery. How did I not consider it before? Alessia's photography was always her escape, her way of expressing what she couldn't say aloud. If she left any trace behind, it might be there.

It's a long shot, but if there's even the slightest possibility it can lead me to her, I have to check it out.

The moment I step inside, the gallery feels like a different world—quiet, serene, completely removed from the chaos that surrounds me. I take a deep breath, letting the calm wash over me. Wandering around the small space, I glance at the pieces for sale.

"Good afternoon," the owner greets me as she steps out from the back room, her smile polite and practiced. "It's always a pleasure to see you."

"You as well," I reply.

"Are you interested in anything specific today?" she asks.

I glance around, keeping it casual. "Thought maybe there'd be some fresh work on display."

Her eyes brighten. "Actually, there is," she says, nodding toward a section I haven't seen yet.

Crossing the gallery, my gaze locks onto a set of photographs, each one bearing the signature *Allie* in the corner.

"These are incredible," I murmur.

"The photographer has a remarkable gift for capturing simple moments."

I scan the photos closely, hoping for some clue as to her whereabouts, but come up empty. "These aren't her usual shots of Philadelphia," I comment, frowning.

"No, they're not. These were taken in Magnolia Springs, Alabama," she replies.

"Magnolia Springs," I repeat. This is the break I've been waiting for. "It looks like a beautiful place."

"It does," she agrees with a nod. "Quiet, peaceful—a perfect escape from the city."

I nod, my pulse quickening. "I'd like to purchase this one," I say, pointing to a photograph of a couple sitting on a park bench. The woman's head rests on the man's shoulder. He gazes at her with a look of pure adoration. Something about the image strikes a chord deep inside me.

"Of course," she replies, smiling as she wraps up my purchase.

As I walk out of the gallery, the tension in my shoulders begins to ease for the first time in weeks. I have a lead—finally. Magnolia Springs. That's where she's been hiding.

Pulling out my phone, I dial Dante. He picks up almost immediately.

"I've got a location," I say without preamble. "Magnolia Springs, Alabama."

There's a brief pause before Dante speaks. "How sure are you?"

"Certain enough to bet my life on it," I reply, gripping the phone tighter.

"Magnolia Springs. Never heard of it," he says thoughtfully. "When do we leave?"

"As soon as possible. I'm not giving her another chance to disappear," I say, the determination in my voice leaving no room for argument.

"Are we flying?"

"No. We'll drive. I want to keep things low-key—nothing that will draw any unnecessary attention," I say, grateful to have him by my side.

"How long do you need?"

"Meet me at my apartment in an hour."

It doesn't matter how far Alessia's run. I'll find her and bring her back. Our lives are entwined, whether she likes it or not. That makes her mine.

And I'll do whatever it takes to protect what's mine.

273

Dante and I pull into the gravel lot of a small, run-down motel just outside Magnolia Springs. The neon sign buzzes faintly, casting a faint red glow over the parking lot. It's the kind of place that's easy to forget as soon as you leave, which makes it perfect for our needs.

Inside the motel office, the clerk barely glances up from his magazine as I check us in under fake names. I accept the keys without a word, and we head to the room at the end of the row. The door creaks as I push it open, revealing a cramped space with peeling wallpaper, a sagging bed, and the musty scent of stale air. Dante drops his bag on the floor with a grunt, and I toss mine onto the single chair by the window.

"We've stayed in worse," Dante mutters, surveying the room.

"Not by much," I reply, locking the door behind us.

Sitting on the edge of the bed with my elbows resting on my knees, I stare at the worn carpet beneath my feet. The weight of the task ahead feels like a brick pressing against my chest. How the hell am I going to find Alessia in this town without raising suspicion?

"So, what's the plan?" Dante asks, cutting straight to the point.

"I'll spend the next couple of days feeling things out," I say, pulling up a map of the area on my phone. "It's a small town. Shouldn't take long to cover the main areas."

"You sure about going in alone? We could cover more ground if we both go."

"Too risky. This place is quiet. If two strangers start poking around, people will notice. You stay here, keep an eye on the motel and surrounding area. If anything goes wrong, I'll need a quick exit."

Dante nods, but his eyes narrow slightly. "Where do you plan to start?"

"The pawn shop," I say, glancing at my phone, scanning the map. "I'll see if they have any cameras or if they've sold any recently. It's a long shot, but it's a start."

"Just be careful," Dante warns, his tone serious. "If Alessia's hiding, the locals might be protecting her."

"I know," I reply quietly. We both understand the stakes. Draco's ultimatum hangs over me like a guillotine, and time isn't on my side.

Dante straightens up, cracking his neck as he does. "I'm going to take a shower."

I lean back against the headboard, trying to slow my racing thoughts. My plan needs to be solid, but doubt keeps creeping in. Draco's threat isn't just words—it's a promise. And I can't let that bastard make good on it.

THE FOLLOWING DAY, I'M UP LONG BEFORE THE SUN, A habit ingrained by years of living in a world where every second counts. Dante's already awake, sipping on a cup of coffee from the gas station across the street.

"You ready?" he asks, motioning to a second cup sitting on the table.

I nod as I take a drink. There isn't anything left to say. We both know the plan. Now it's just a matter of execution and luck.

The out of state license plate would've drawn too much unwanted attention, so I walk the few blocks to Magnolia Springs downtown shopping area and head straight for the local pawn shop.

The store is cluttered, shelves crammed with old electronics, outdated jewelry, and dust-covered trinkets. The owner, a heavyset man, barely glances up from behind the counter when I step inside.

"Morning," I say, trying to keep things casual. "I'm looking for a camera—any come through recently?"

He lifts an eyebrow, squinting at me. "Cameras? Nah, haven't had one in here in years."

Another dead end.

The next few days drag on slowly. I spend my time walking through Magnolia Springs, blending in as much as I can. It's even smaller than I expected—quaint streets lined with mom-and-pop shops and the kind of charm that belongs on a postcard. I keep my distance, observing from the fringes, making sure no one's paying too much attention to me.

Each night, I return to the motel empty-handed, feeling the pressure mount. My window of time to find Alessia is shrinking.

On the third day, it happens. I'm walking through town, making my way past the diner when something catches my eye—a woman stepping out of a door on the side of the building. She's wearing a white T-shirt with "The Bluebird Diner" printed across the front, black leggings, and an apron tied at her waist. Her hair is pulled back into a long ponytail, and even from across the street, I know it's her.

Alessia.

She moves with an ease I haven't seen in her before, a lightness in her step. She stops, looking around as if she senses she's being watched. My pulse increases, as I stand unmoving using the building in front of me as cover. After a brief pause, she shakes her head slightly and steps into the diner.

It takes everything in me to stay rooted where I am, to not cross the street and confront her. Instead, I pull out my phone and send Dante a quick text:

Me: Found her. She's working at the diner.

Dante: What's your plan?

Me: Looks like she's living above the diner—saw her come out a side door.

Dante: Was she alone?

Me: Yeah. I'll keep watching. See if anyone else shows up. Once I'm sure she's alone, I'll let myself in.

Dante: Let me know when you're ready for me.

Me: Will do.

I pocket my phone and position myself across the street, keeping my distance while I watch her through the diner's windows. She moves between the tables, smiling and chatting with customers—she seems to fit into this place so effortlessly. It's unsettling to see her like this, so different from the Alessia I've always known. Here she seems happy.

I grab a newspaper and sit on a park bench across the street, biding my time. The hours tick by, and I wait for the right moment.

Once I'm sure there's no one else, I make my move. Slipping around the side of the building, I find a door that leads upstairs. A quick look around confirms that no one's watching, and I pull out a small set of lockpicks. The lock yields easily, and I step inside, closing the door quietly behind me.

The apartment is small, simple. The kind of place that feels lived-in but not personal. A couch, a chair, a small table—bare essentials. On the wall, a framed black and white photograph catches my eye. Two hands are intertwined, fingers gently laced together. There's an intimacy in it and, for a moment, I wonder what Alessia sees when she looks at it. Does she imagine that those hands could've been ours once. I force myself to tear my attention away from the image.

There's a strange sense of peace here, a quiet that feels foreign to me. Alessia's built a new life for herself, and I hate knowing I'm about to tear it apart. But this isn't about what either or of want. It's about survival—hers and mine.

Sitting in the armchair that faces the door, I lean back and wait.

Hours later, I hear footsteps on the stairs. Keys jingle in the lock, and the door swings open. Alessia steps inside, humming softly to herself. She doesn't see me at first, not until she turns around.

When she does, she freezes, her eyes going wide with shock. The humming stops, and for a moment, we just stare at each other.

Finally, I speak, my voice low and steady. "We need to talk."

Alessia

The bag I'm holding slips from my fingers, hitting the floor with a dull thud. Antonio's sitting in my living room, his deep blue eyes locked on mine. The hum in my throat dies instantly, replaced by a sickening twist in my stomach.

How did he find me?

The fear beneath my fury makes it hard to think. He's a part of the life I worked so hard to escape. Seeing him here, in my space, shatters that illusion.

"Alessia," he says, standing slowly, his movements calculated. "We need to talk."

"Talk?" I snap, my voice braver than I feel. "You break into my apartment to talk? Get out, Antonio. Now."

He doesn't flinch. His calm is unnerving, too steady for someone who just barged into my life. Dressed in dark jeans and a grey Henley that clings to his body, he looks out of place here, yet disturbingly at ease. "When I leave, you'll be coming with me."

My pulse races, and I step back instinctively. "I'm not going anywhere."

His gaze hardens, a silent threat lurking in those dark eyes. "You don't have a choice."

"The hell I don't." My hands tremble, but I ball them into fists, willing myself to stay calm. "You think you can just waltz in here and order me around? That's not how it works anymore."

"I can and I did." Antonio moves closer, closing the distance until I'm backed against the door. His hands come up, bracing on either side of my head, caging me in. "This isn't about what you want, Alessia. Hell, it's not even about what I want." His voice is low and controlled yet edged with an unspoken threat that makes my skin prickle.

I shove at his arms, but he doesn't budge. "You can't just drag me back like I'm some possession. I'm not yours to control."

"You're not a possession," he says, but there's no warmth in his words, no reassurance.

"No," I say, my voice trembling. "I have a new life here. You can't take that from me."

"This isn't up for discussion." His words are final, an iron door slamming shut between me and freedom. "Go pack your things."

A bitter laugh escapes. "And what am I supposed to tell my boss and the people I've come to know here?"

His jaw tightens. "You'll figure it out."

I want to scream, to claw at him. Anything that will make him understand that I've built a life here, one without him or the twisted world I escaped. But his eyes bore into mine, unyielding. I step away, trying to put some distance between us. "No," I whisper. "I'm not going back. I won't."

"I'm not asking," he says, reaching into his pocket. "I don't want to hurt you, but you're leaving me with no choice."

Before I can react, his arm flashes forward. The sting in my neck is quick, sharp.

"What... what did you..." I stumble back, my hand flying to the spot where he jabbed me. A slow, sinking feeling overtakes me as my vision begins to blur. "Antonio—"

He catches me as my legs give out, lowering me gently to the sofa. The last thing I see is the regret clouding his eyes.

"I'm sorry, Alessia," he whispers as the darkness swallows me whole.

When I come to, my head is heavy, and my mouth is dry. I'm in a car, the low vibration of the engine thrumming beneath me. I blink, trying to focus, but the world tilts around me.

"Finally awake?" Antonio's voice cuts through the fog.

I try to sit up, but my body feels like lead, and when I turn my head, I realize I'm in the back seat of an SUV. Dante's driving, his expression as cold and unreadable as ever. Antonio sits beside me, watching, waiting.

"What did you do?" My voice is hoarse, barely more than a rasp.

Antonio holds out a bottle of water, unscrewing the cap before handing it to me. "Drink slow," he says, his tone softer now but still firm. "I couldn't let you stay, Alessia. Not with everything happening."

I hesitate, but my throat is too dry to resist. The cool liquid grounds me as I bring it to my lips. The water is a small relief. I want to scream, to hit him, but my limbs won't cooperate.

"I hate you," I whisper, the words tasting bitter on my tongue.

"I know," he says quietly, his gaze fixed on the road ahead. "But you're safe with me."

Safe. The word twists like a knife in my chest. Safe isn't what I want. What I want is my freedom, the life I built. But with every mile we drive it slips further and further away.

Silent tears blur the world outside, and I know that, like my life here in Alabama, it's fading away.

Antonio

The SUV glides along the highway, the steady rhythm of the tires on asphalt filling the silence in the car. Alessia's out cold beside me, her body slumped against the door. The drug I gave her hasn't worn off yet, but I know the peace won't last much longer. When she wakes up, there'll be hell to pay.

Dante casts a sidelong glance at me from the driver's seat, his jaw set, tension radiating from him even though he stays silent. He hasn't said a word since we left her apartment, but I don't need him to. The tight grip on the steering wheel says it all—he's not happy about how I handled this.

I didn't have a choice.

Now, hours later, she stirs beside me, a low groan slipping from her lips. Her eyelids flutter open, and the instant Alessia realizes where she is, a fierce spark ignites, her anger unmistakable.

"Finally awake?" I ask, my voice steady.

She straightens, her breath coming faster as her eyes lock onto mine. "What did you do?" she demands.

I twist open a bottle of water and hold it out to her. "Drink slow," I say, keeping my tone calm. "I couldn't let you stay, Alessia. Not with everything happening."

She hesitates, her eyes flicking between the bottle and my face. But I know she needs it, the drugs will have made her throat dry. After a beat, she snatches it from my hand.

"I hate you," she whispers, the venom in her voice unmistakable.

Her words cut deeper than I'd like to admit, but I don't flinch. "I know but you're safe with me," I reply quietly.

"Safe? You drugged me," she whispers the accusation.

There's nothing I can say that'll make this situation better. Nothing that'll take away the betrayal she feels. She wants her freedom, but she can't have it. Not in the way she wants. What she doesn't know is that I'm the only thing standing between her and an even worse fate.

As we drive, the tension between us thickens. I need to tell her. I have to explain what this is really about—why I had no choice but to bring her back. But how do I tell her that this isn't just about going back to the life she tried so hard to leave behind? How do I explain that I'm taking her into a new kind of prison, one where I'll be holding the keys?

But I'm not Valentino. I'll never be him. He took pleasure in control—in breaking her.

Yet, no matter how much I try to convince myself that I'm different, it doesn't change the fact that I'm about to take away her freedom. The thought makes my stomach turn, but I push it down. This is the only way to ensure everyone's safety.

Out of the corner of my eye I watch her. Alessia's beautiful, even now, with tension etched into every line of her body. But that beauty is nothing compared to the storm brewing in her eyes. A storm she'll undoubtably unleash on me when I tell her the truth.

A few hours later, Dante exits the highway and steers into the lot of a roadside convenience store. The sun is higher in the sky now, casting harsh light across the pavement. He parks the SUV, cutting the engine. The sudden silence is almost deafening.

"We should stretch our legs," Dante says, his voice low as he glances at me. "Take a break."

Before Alessia can move, I reach across her, gripping her wrist just enough to get her attention. "Listen carefully," I say, my voice dark, low. "You're going to behave, or I won't hesitate to drug you again. Do you understand?"

Her eyes burn with anger, that same fire still blazing inside her, untamed. She presses her lips together, defiant as ever. "Fine," she spits out, the bitterness dripping from every word.

I release her wrist, but inside, I can't help the surge of pride. Alessia's her beautiful, defiant self. Still whole. Still unbroken. A part of me wishes I didn't have to be the one to drag her back, but it's that fire I need to protect.

"Good. Now let's get out."

She doesn't argue, just throws the door open and steps out, slamming it behind her. I watch her walk toward the restroom, her shoulders rigid with barely contained fury. I don't take my eyes off her until she disappears inside.

Dante steps out of the car and joins me as I lean against the wall outside the restrooms. He studies me for a moment, the weight of what's happening hanging between us.

"You gonna tell her about her upcoming wedding?" he asks, his voice cautious but direct. He knows the score, knows the stakes. We've been in this life long enough to understand how complicated the next steps will be.

I shake my head, keeping my gaze fixed on the ground. "Not yet. I'm not saying anything until I have to."

Dante crosses his arms, his posture relaxed but his eyes sharp. "And when will that be?"

"As soon as we get home," I reply, my voice flat. "I've already arranged everything. The ceremony will be private. It's all lined up."

We both know what this is really about. Draco's orders to marry Alessia are a power play, his way of asserting control over me and keeping her tied to the *Famiglia*.

But what Draco doesn't realize is that I'm shifting the game. I might be following his command, but I'm doing it on my terms, in my time. By handling this my way, I'm ensuring I still hold the upper hand, not him.

"She's not going to take this well, you know."

"She doesn't have a choice," I say, my voice harsher than I intend betraying my nerves.

We both know this is a disaster waiting to happen, but there's no way to stop it—no way out.

A few minutes later, Alessia reappears. She glances at me, then looks away, like she can't stand the sight of me.

"Are you hungry?"

"No," she snaps, the anger in her voice barely contained.

"When's the last time you ate?" I press, not willing to let this go.

"What's it to you?" she shoots back, glaring at me.

I'm trying to keep my frustration in check, but she's not making it easy. "You're with me. And as long as you are, I'll make sure you're taken care of."

She scoffs, crossing her arms tighter over her chest. "I don't need you to take care of me."

Dante gives a quick jerk of his chin toward the store. "I'll leave you two to figure this out." He walks off, leaving me alone with her.

"I know you don't want to hear this, but I'm not your enemy, Alessia."

She turns her head slowly, her eyes filled with pure loathing. "You really think that?"

"Whether you believe it or not, it doesn't matter. I'm responsible for you now."

"Responsible? Is that what you call dragging me back to a life I don't want?"

"I don't expect you to understand," I reply, keeping my tone even. "But I have my reasons."

"Your reasons?" she says quietly, but the anger in every word is undeniable. "What reasons could possibly justify dragging me back to hell? You're no better than—"

"Stop right there," I cut her off. "I'm not him, Alessia. I'm not doing this to hurt you. I'm doing this to protect you."

She glares at me with barely restrained fury. "Protect me? By kidnapping me and dragging me back to Philadelphia? That's not protection, Antonio. That's imprisonment."

"I know it feels that way," I say quietly, trying to reach her through the wall she's put up. "I'm asking you to trust me."

"At one time, I thought you might be different." She lets out a hollow laugh, shaking her head. "What a fool I was. You're no different than Val and my father. I hate you for this." She turns on her heel and gets back into the car, slamming the door.

I watch her go, my chest tight with the weight of her words. She'll never see it from my perspective—not now, at least. She hates me for taking away the freedom she fought so hard to claim. And she's right to feel that way. But what she doesn't understand, what I don't know if she'll ever see, is that I'm nothing like Valentino or Draco.

To them, Alessia's nothing more than a pawn, a tool to broker power. But to me, she's always been so much more. I'm not doing this to control her. I'm doing it to protect her from the dangers lurking in the shadows—dangers she doesn't see.

I don't give a damn if the Moretti's remain our allies. My *famiglia* wields enough control in Philadelphia to ensure Draco and his organization are nothing if he isn't aligned with us. However, if I don't go along with Draco's demands, I fear he'll take Alessia and give her to someone who won't care about her passions. Someone who'll use her and hurt her—who'll break her spirit. I'd never forgive myself if that happened.

Dante returns, carrying a bag in one hand. He gives me a pointed look. "Get yourself something to eat. I'll stay with her."

Inside the store, I grab a box of granola bars—something I've seen Alessia snacking on before. I don't know if she'll actually eat them or throw them back in my face, but it's a small gesture I hope she'll accept. As I make my way through the aisles, I try to shake the image of her storming away, the words she hurled at me echoing in my mind. The way she looked at me like I was no better than the men who've hurt her.

At the self-serve coffee station, I fill three cups, the aroma a brief distraction from the ache tightening in my chest. Alessia will never see this marriage as anything but a betrayal. I'll prove that I'm different. Somehow, I'll make her see this isn't about power or domination—this is about keeping her safe and giving her the life she deserves.

Even if she hates me for it.

After paying, I step outside to find Alessia leaning against the SUV, her arms crossed. My eyes fall to the curve of her chest, the way her T-shirt clings to her body. To the swell of her breasts, the way they rise and fall with each angry breath she takes. For a brief moment, I'm drawn in by something I have no right to be focusing on. I quickly correct myself.

Dante stands next to her, his posture relaxed, as if he's completely unaffected by the tension radiating from her. I can tell from his expression that he thinks I should tell her everything now.

I hand Dante his coffee without a word, then offer one to Alessia. She doesn't even look at me, just stares straight ahead, ignoring the cup like it's poison.

"Alessia," I say softly, trying to get her to look at me. "Don't be so stubborn. I'm not your enemy."

When she turns, her gaze is icy. "You sure about that?"

"It's only coffee," I reply, holding the cup out to her again.

Her eyes flicker to the cup, then back to me, suspicion still clouding her expression. "And what? I'm supposed to believe this makes everything okay?"

I shrug, keeping my tone light. "For now, yeah."

She hesitates for a moment, then sighs, taking the cup from my hand. "Fine," she mutters, her voice barely above a whisper. "But this doesn't change anything."

"I know," I say, relieved she's at least willing to accept this small gesture. "But it's a start."

She doesn't respond, just turns away again, but this time, she takes a sip of the coffee. It's a small victory, but I'll take it.

"We should get back on the road," Dante says.

Alessia climbs into the backseat without a word, her movements stiff. I slide in beside her as Dante starts the engine, and we merge back onto the highway. Silence fills the car, thick with the weight of unspoken words. I know the truth I need to reveal will shatter whatever fragile peace remains.

But the truth is, I can't hold it off forever.

Alessia

We've been driving for so long that I've lost track of time. The highway stretches ahead, endless, swallowing the last pieces of my freedom. I rest my head against the window, but no matter how hard I try to blink them back, the tears come, silently slipping down my cheeks.

There's no winning this, no escaping it. I'm trapped, just like I've always been.

"What's wrong?" Antonio's voice breaks through the silence.

I don't respond. I can't. The walls I've built are cracking, and if I say anything, they'll shatter completely. But I need this—one small piece of closure before everything is ripped away from me. Slowly, I turn my head, wiping my eyes on the back of my hand.

"Did you bring my phone?"

"Why?"

I'd rather not ask for anything or be in his debt, but I have no choice. "I need to call Rosie," I say, my voice rough. "I left without telling her anything. She deserves to hear from me that I'm gone."

Antonio doesn't respond right away. His face is set in that controlled, unreadable mask he wears so well.

"I can't let you do that without conditions," he finally says.

"You can call, but it stays on speaker. I need to hear everything that's said. And after you're done, I'm destroying the phone."

I want to tell him to go to hell, to shove his terms back in his face. But if I push too hard, he'll take the only chance I have to say goodbye.

"Of course. Can't trust me to make a simple phone call without an audience, can you?" My words are sharp, meant to cut, but it's a pathetic defense, and we both know it.

His eyes lock on mine, but his expression doesn't change. "It's not about trust, Alessia. It's about making sure you don't do something reckless."

"Reckless," I echo, shaking my head. "Right." I hesitate, staring down at the phone in my lap. "Fine. I won't be saying anything that puts you in danger. You're too paranoid."

"Don't push me," he warns.

I nod, biting back the urge to say something in reply. Instead, I take a deep breath, and he hands me my phone from the center console, its weight suddenly heavier in my hands.

Without looking at him again, I dial Rosie's number, my fingers trembling. I put the call on speaker and wait. It rings once, then twice, before her familiar voice fills the silence.

"Hello, sugar." Rosie's voice is bright and cheerful. "What's up, honey?"

I take a shaky breath, trying to steady myself. "Rosie," I start, but my voice cracks despite my efforts to keep it steady. "I... I had to leave."

There's a pause on the other end. When she speaks again, her tone is laced with concern. "Leave? What do you mean? Is everything okay?"

I swallow hard, fighting back the tears threatening to spill over again. "I got a call. My mother's gravely ill. I'm on my way back home."

"Oh no." Her concern deepens, and I picture the worry etched on her face. "Are you sure it's safe? I mean, with your husband and everything."

I squeeze my eyes shut, willing myself to stay strong. "It'll be fine. I had to go."

"When will you be back?" Her voice is small, hesitant, as though she already knows what I'm about to say.

I glance at Antonio. He's looking straight ahead but I know he's listening closely. My chest aches, and I swallow over the lump in my throat. "I won't be coming back. I'm so sorry."

The silence that follows is deafening. For a moment, I think she's hung up, but then I hear her take a shaky breath. "I don't know what to say."

"I want to thank you," I manage, my voice catching on a sob. "For everything. You made it feel like home."

"Are you sure there's nothing I can do?" she asks, her voice filled with desperation.

"No," I whisper. "There's nothing you can do. But I'll never forget you, Rosie. I promise."

We say our goodbyes, and when the line finally goes dead, the weight of it crushes me. My heart aches with the finality of it all. Everything I've built, every friendship, every piece of happiness—it's all slipping through my fingers.

Silence stretches as I sit there, staring at the phone in my lap. Beside me, Antonio shifts slightly, but he says nothing. His presence is a constant reminder of the life I'm being dragged back into, a life I've tried so hard to escape.

"Thank you," I say quietly, not looking at him.

He nods, his voice low. "You did what you needed to do."

The passing landscape blurs as tears burn the back of my eyes. Speaking to Rosie did nothing to ease the ache inside me. If anything, it's only made it worse.

My life in Magnolia Springs is over. It slipped through my fingers like it was never mine to keep. With each passing mile, I'm being dragged back into a world I hate.

A world with no escape.

Alessia

The familiar skyline of Philadelphia comes into view, its towering buildings reaching up to greet the fading light of the day. The sun hangs low, casting a warm, golden hue across the city, making the glass and steel of the skyscrapers shimmer with the last rays of sunlight. But instead of feeling like I'm going home, dread coils in my stomach. My heart rate spikes, and nausea churns in my stomach.

Antonio sits beside me, silent. He's hiding something. I can feel it in the way his body grows more tense with each passing minute. Part of me wants to ask him, but the other part of me doesn't want to know.

He pulls out his phone, his voice low but firm as he speaks. "Meet me at the house within the hour. We don't have time to waste." He ends the call without waiting for a response, sliding the phone back into his pocket like he hasn't just made some life-altering decision. I have no idea who he was talking to, but the tone in his voice only intensifies the sense of dread creeping through me.

"Where are you taking me?" I ask, trying and failing to keep the tremor out of my voice.

Silence. Antonio doesn't even glance my way. His lack of

response stokes my fury and fear, each feeding off the other. I look at Dante, catching the brief exchange of looks between him and Antonio. Something unspoken passes between them. Whatever's happening, they're both in on it.

Dante drives through the city with a calmness that's at odds with the tension in the car. The bustling streets of downtown give way to quieter, more residential neighborhoods. My heart pounds harder with every familiar block, a sickening realization setting in as Dante finally pulls the car into the driveway of Giovanni and Domenica's house.

"What are we doing here?" I demand, my eyes narrowing as I look around.

Antonio opens his door, stepping out casually. "This is where we live," he says flatly, like it's the most natural thing in the world.

I scramble out of the car, following close behind him. "What do you mean, this is where *we* live?"

He doesn't break stride as he responds, his tone clipped. "My aunt gifted me the house before she returned to Italy."

"Domenica went back to Italy?" The words tumble out in shock. "When?"

Antonio finally stops, turning to face me with thinly veiled impatience. "We'll talk about it later. Let's get inside."

Taking a step back, I say, "I'm not going in there."

"You'll go on your own, or I'll put you over my shoulder and carry you inside. Your choice, Alessia."

My fists clench at my sides, ready for a fight, but I know deep down it's futile. If I try to run, Antonio will catch me, and he'll drag me in without a second thought. There's no one who'll stop him from doing whatever the hell he wants with me.

"Fine," I spit out, pushing past him. Every step feels like I'm walking toward my own execution.

The dark walnut door opens, and I step inside. The familiar scent of the house wraps around me, but instead of comfort, it's suffocating. "Now tell me what the hell is going on," I demand, my voice shaking with anger.

His eyes meet mine, calm but unyielding. "The judge is on his way," he says, his tone as casual as if he's discussing the weather. "We're getting married."

The words leave me momentarily breathless. "What?" I regain just enough composure to speak, though disbelief and horror linger. "No. Just...no."

"This isn't a negotiation. It's happening, whether you agree or not."

"You're insane if you think I'm going to marry you."

"Your agreement isn't necessary," he replies. "The judge is on my payroll. He doesn't care if you're willing."

Antonio's gaze sharpens. "You can make this difficult and drag it out, or you can put on a smile and get it over with. Either way, it's happening."

He's right. I'm trapped, and no amount of fighting will change that. But the thought of surrendering to him, of being bound to another man who wants to control me, makes me sick.

"You're a monster," I whisper, my voice trembling. "I'll never forgive you for this."

"You'll adjust," he says. "Go take a shower and change your clothes before the judge arrives," he says like he's offering me a choice when we both know I have none.

I look down at my Bluebird Diner T-shirt and black leggings, both of which I've been wearing for two days straight. "No," I say, digging my heels in.

He shrugs. "Suit yourself." Motioning to Dante he says, "Keep an eye on her. I'll be quick."

ANTONIO RETURNS, FRESH FROM HIS SHOWER AND dressed in a charcoal suit perfectly tailored to every chiseled angle of his body. His presence fills the room, drawing my eyes to him despite myself.

His damp hair falls slightly over his forehead, giving him a casual, effortless look. My eyes trace the sharp line of his jaw. The way the collar of his crisp white shirt sits perfectly against his neck. He's put together, composed, and undeniably attractive.

But I force myself to stop looking. It doesn't change who he is —a man who's about to force me into both a life and a marriage, I don't want. My attraction quickly morphs back into disgust as I remind myself that beneath the polished exterior is the monster who's taken everything from me.

The doorbell rings, echoing through the house. Antonio strides to the door, and a stern, gray-haired man carrying a worn leather briefcase enters. The judge, I assume.

They exchange a few quiet words. The man doesn't even spare me a glance as he steps further into the room, his gaze only shifting when Dante joins them. Antonio turns to me, his expression hard as stone.

"Let's get this over with," Antonio says, his voice low, commanding.

I force myself to stand, following them into the office. The judge doesn't waste any time, launching into the ceremony with a practiced monotone that strips the words of any emotion. It's all formality.

This isn't a wedding. It's a prison sentence.

The judge looks to Antonio. "Do you have the rings?"

A bitter laugh almost escapes me. Of course, there are no rings. This isn't a real marriage. But then Antonio reaches into his pocket, producing a small velvet box. When he opens it, my breath catches.

Inside rests an antique gold ring, its band thin but sturdy, intricately engraved with delicate filigree that spirals around the entire circumference. At the center sits an oval-cut sapphire, deep blue like the ocean at night, framed by smaller diamonds that catch the light with a subtle glimmer.

Antonio slides it onto my finger. It's undeniably beautiful, but there's something more—it's old, steeped in history, as though it's been passed through generations. It feels out of place on my finger. It's too personal, too precious for something as cold and calculated as this marriage.

"It looks stunning on you," he says his hand lingering on mine. "We'll shop for wedding bands together," he whispers, his voice low and intimate, as if this is something we're doing out of love, not force.

"By the power vested in me by the Commonwealth of Pennsylvania, I now pronounce you husband and wife," the judge says, his voice cutting through the thick tension in the room. "You may kiss the bride."

Antonio turns to me, his eyes dark and unreadable. I flinch as he leans in to kiss me—brief and cold, a show of possession more than affection.

Antonio and I stand side by side as the judge places the marriage papers on the table in front of us. He reaches for a pen, his movements deliberate as he signs his name with a steady hand. There's no hesitation, no second thoughts—just the cold finality of his decision.

He holds the pen out to me. My fingers tremble as I stare at the dotted line where my name's supposed to go. Part of me screams to stop this madness. But there's no escape, no way out of this nightmare. With a shaky breath, I force myself to sign Alessia Luciano.

The judge watches impassively, waiting until I've finished before taking the papers and adding his own signature with a flourish. He tucks the documents into his briefcase. "Congratulations," he says, though there's no genuine sentiment behind the word.

"I'll see you out," Dante offers. The men turn and head for the door, leaving me standing there, numb and defeated.

As the door clicks shut, the reality of what's just happened crashes down on me. I'm married to Antonio. The words feel foreign, impossible, like I've stepped into a nightmare I can't wake up from. My heart pounds in my chest, and a wave of rage washes over me, sharp and all-consuming.

"I'll never forgive you for this," I whisper, my voice trembling with the force of my emotions. "I'll never call you my husband."

Antonio's blue eyes, cold as a winter sky, meet mine. "Hate me all you want, Alessia. It won't change a thing. You're mine now."

I tear my gaze from his. "Where did this ring come from?" I ask, trying to keep my voice steady, though the words come out tight, strained.

He hesitates, and for a moment, something flickers in his eyes —something almost vulnerable. "It was my grandmother's," he begins, his tone different now, less controlled. "She gave it to my uncle Giovanni, who gave it to Domenica. Before she left for Italy, she passed it on to me."

The history of the ring tugs at something deep inside me. It's as if, despite everything, a thread of connection and love are woven into it. I don't know much about Antonio's grandmother, but I loved his Aunt Domenica. Knowing that I'm wearing something that's a tangible representation of the love she shared with Giovanni stirs emotions I don't want to face.

Antonio continues, his voice tinged with uncertainty. "I hope you like it. If not, I'll take you to pick something you'd prefer."

The sincerity in his tone is disarming, and for a moment, I'm caught off guard by the thoughtfulness behind the gesture. But just as quickly, my anger resurfaces.

"What happens now? Are you going to spend our wedding night with one of your whores? Or will you rape me, like Valentino was so fond of doing?"

His face pales. "Alessia," he murmurs. "I'm sorry for everything Vigo did to you. I'll never be able to undo the damage he caused. But I'm not him. I'm not anything like Valentino, and I swear to you, I will never hurt you like that."

His words hit me harder than I expect.

"I know you were forced to say those vows." His eyes lock

with mine. "But I meant every word. I'll be faithful to you," he says, his voice low. "And I won't force you into my bed. I'll wait patiently for you to come to me on your own. I'm confident you will, eventually," he breathes. "I'll take care of you and protect you with everything I have."

His words hang in the air, and for a moment, I'm caught in his spell. The sincerity in his words is undeniable, but it doesn't stop the bitterness and rage I feel. I can't let myself believe it. I won't.

"The guest room has been made up for you," he adds, his voice quieting again. "I hope you'll find it suitable."

With that, he turns and walks out of the office, leaving me standing there, alone.

When the door clicks shut behind him, my knees buckle beneath me. I grip the edge of the desk for support, the cold wood grounding me. I can't allow myself to break down.

But the truth is, I'm exhausted.

I glance down at the ring on my finger—a family heirloom, passed down through generations. My thumb traces the intricate designs, the cold metal a constant reminder of the vows I was forced to say.

Years ago, when we were young and in love, I dreamt of this moment—Antonio's ring on my finger, a promise made between us. But this ring isn't a symbol of love, it's ownership. And that boy is gone, replaced by a man—a Capo who now holds my life in his hands.

So why are Antonio's words, the promises he made, lingering in the back of my mind. A part of me, the girl who once loved him, longs to believe him. To hope that maybe he'll keep his word to not hurt me. But then I remember Valentino. The way he manipulated me. Used me. Hurt me

"Don't be naïve, Alessia," I whisper aloud. "Men like Antonio don't know how to love without causing pain."

With that thought swirling in my mind, I leave the office. My footsteps echo in the empty hallway as I make my way to the guest room. When I push open the door, I'm greeted by a beautifully furnished space.

The pale pink linens on the bed are soft and inviting, with an array of plush pillows propped against the headboard. The room is luxurious, almost too much so. Like it's a carefully crafted illusion meant to make me forget it's nothing more than a cage.

I move to the dresser, opening one of the drawers to find my clothes neatly folded inside. I see more of them hanging in the walk-in closet. Antonio's control over every detail of my life is evident in each corner of this room.

It's too much to think about tonight.

After a long, hot shower, I slip into a pair of shorts and a tank top, crawling into the large bed. The soft sheets do little to comfort me. Closing my eyes, the tears finally break free, sliding silently down my cheeks.

I don't know what my future holds, but one thing is certain—I'll never allow Antonio to get close enough to hurt me again.

Antonio

After Dante leaves, I lock up, securing what I intend to be a home—our home. Alessia's free to come and go as she pleases. But the life we lead, my job as Capo, means neither of us can escape the necessity of having guards. They're always there, lingering just beyond sight.

Exhaustion pulls at me as I make my way upstairs, the steps creaking as I go. Passing by her room I notice the door slightly ajar. I pause when I hear the soft sound of her tears.

The urge to go to her, to hold her, is overwhelming, but I promised her I wouldn't touch her. I force myself to keep moving, my feet heavy as I retreat to my own room. The ache in my chest is no longer from exhaustion, but from knowing she's hurting. And I can't do a damn thing about it.

Kicking off my shoes, I shrug out of my suit jacket, draping it over the arm of the chair. My body wants nothing more than to collapse into bed, but the shrill ring of my phone stops me. Draco. His name flashes across the screen like an omen.

I swipe to answer, pressing the phone to my ear. "It seems you've found my daughter," his voice slithers through the line.

"Good evening to you too," I reply, keeping my tone measured, though my grip on the phone tightens.

"How did Alessia respond when she found out you drugged her and hauled her back from Magnolia Springs?" Draco's says, his voice dripping with sick amusement.

There's only one way he'd know that. "You had her followed?"

"Someone had to keep tabs on her, Antonio. Clearly, it wasn't going to be you," he replies without hesitation.

"What do you want, Draco?"

"Don't be so touchy." His laugh is like nails on a chalkboard. "I'm just letting you know I'll be there first thing tomorrow to take my daughter off your hands."

His arrogance sends a surge of rage through me. "Excuse me?"

"I changed my mind about our little arrangement. You're too soft—too weak. Alessia needs a man who will crush her defiance, someone who won't hesitate to break her. I've promised her to someone far more capable of doing just that."

The fury inside me snaps like a taut wire. My tone is icy, lethal. "You're too late. We were married tonight."

Draco explodes. "You went behind my back?" His rage is tangible with the promise of violence in every syllable. "A rushed farce of a wedding doesn't change anything, Antonio. It can just as easily go away."

"Alessia's mine," I growl. "You won't come anywhere near her."

Draco's fury seethes. "You've just made the biggest mistake of your life, Antonio."

The call disconnects.

A message comes through almost immediately.

Draco: I'm coming for her. Tell Alessia to be ready.

My fingers curl around the phone, knuckles white as I read his threat. The darkness inside me stirs, hungry, ready to come out to play. I'll burn this world to the ground before I let him take her.

My response is swift, precise.

Me: If you try, you'll regret it for the rest of your short, miserable life.

I hit send, imagining Draco's reaction. He believes he has the upper hand. Thinks he can play me like he did Valentino. He has no idea what he's unleashed.

If Draco Moretti wants a war, that's exactly what he'll get.

"Double the number of men," I bark the order into the phone. "And make sure they remain out of sight."

"Will do," Dante replies, his voice steady on the other end.

"I also want men watching the Moretti Estate. If Draco makes a move, I need to know about it. I won't let anything—" My sentence dies in my throat as Alessia steps into the kitchen. Pink shorts hug her toned legs, and a tiny black tank top leaves little to the imagination. Her dark hair is a mess of waves, and her hazel eyes blaze with fury.

"My wife's awake. I have to go." I disconnect the call and slide my phone into my pocket, trying to gauge how much she overheard.

Alessia crosses her arms over her chest, her gaze cutting through me like a blade. Fury radiates off her in waves.

I force a smile, attempting to soften the tension. "What can I make you for breakfast?"

"I can cook for myself."

"I'm aware. But this is our honeymoon. Let me—"

"I don't give a damn about *your* honeymoon," she snaps. "And I don't need you pretending like this is normal. It's not."

I move to the fridge, opening it to scan what's inside. I asked Cecilia to order some staples, but I have no clue what she got. "We'll need some groceries, but I can make you an omelet or French toast. What do you prefer?"

"Why are you doing this?" she demands, her voice still harsh but with an edge of suspicion.

"Because you deserve to be treated well, Alessia."

"I don't want to play house with you. I need my life back."

I take a slow breath, trying to steady the conversation before it spirals. "I'm not pretending. I just want you to feel comfortable here."

Her eyes narrow further. "Comfortable? With guards hovering just out of sight? I'm not blind, Antonio. You say I'm not a prisoner, but I know they're watching me. So yeah, I sure as hell feel like one."

I let the words hang in the air, not rushing to defend myself. She's angry—rightfully so. No amount of soothing will make her see this differently right now. "You're not a prisoner. You're free to come and go whenever you want."

"Free?" She lets out a harsh laugh. "You drugged me and forced me to marry you. And you want me to believe I'm free?"

"Yes," I reply, my voice firm but low, unwavering under her accusation.

Her expression falters, just for a moment. "What's the catch?"

"No catch," I say, moving back to the counter. "Just coffee?"

"Fine, I'll have coffee," she mutters, her voice clipped.

I grab the French press and begin preparing her half-caff blend, the silence between us growing heavier. She watches my every move as though she's waiting for me to make a mistake, to reveal the trap she thinks I'm setting.

While the coffee brews, I make her an omelet anyway. She might hate me, but I'm not about to let her starve. When the food's ready, I set the plate down in front of her, a small smile tugging at my lips.

"You expect me to eat that?" She pushes the plate away from her.

"It's not poisoned, if that's what you think."

"Prove it."

Without hesitation, I stab a forkful of the omelet and take a bite. She watches me intently as I chew and swallow. After a moment, she cautiously picks up her fork and starts to eat. I don't make a big deal out of it, but inwardly, I feel a sense of relief. It's progress, no matter how small.

I sit across from her with my own plate of food, the silence still tense. "You don't have to waitress anymore."

Her head snaps up. "Really?"

"Unless you want to," I add quickly, gauging her reaction.

She raises an eyebrow, her voice sharp again. "Am I allowed to go for a walk? Or do I need to ask your permission for that, too?"

I meet her challenging gaze without flinching. "Of course you can go for a walk. You don't need to disguise your trips to the gallery either. All I ask is that you're honest about where you're going so I can make sure you're safe."

Her expression shifts, confusion creeping in. "I don't have to ask permission?"

"No, Alessia." I shake my head. "You're not my prisoner."

"What about guards? Do I have to have them?"

"They'll always be there, but they'll remain out of sight. You won't even know they're around unless you need them. I want you to have your privacy." I pause, a thought coming to me. "Unless you want me to go with you. I'll always make that a priority."

Her hostility softens, but only slightly. "Why are you *really* doing this? Why are you letting me have this freedom?"

I meet her gaze, choosing my words carefully. "Because it's your right, Alessia. It's your life." An idea hits me, something that might chip away at the walls she's built. "You should open a bank account for the money you make from selling your photographs."

Her fork stills. "How do you know about that?"

"I have my ways," I reply with a shrug.

"And you'd let me do that?"

"It's your money."

Her defenses waver for the first time. "I've never had my own bank account. My father wouldn't allow it. After we got married, Valentino took my ID. I don't even know where it is."

The mention of Valentino sends a surge of anger through me, but I keep it in check. "I'll search the house."

Alessia's silent for a moment, absorbing my words. I stand and begin clearing her plate, giving her space to think. While I load the dishwasher, I add, "As soon as I find it, we'll open that account. Then, you can decide what you want to do next."

I want to show Alessia that this marriage doesn't have to be something she fears—that it can be different, *we* can be different. But I know earning her trust will take time. Time to remind her of what we used to feel for each other, before all the lies, before the darkness swallowed everything.

She watches me, her expression still guarded, the distance between us as far as ever. But there's something in her eyes—fragile but real. Curiosity, maybe even the faintest glimmer of hope.

A spark of the connection we once had. It's barely there, but it's enough to give me hope that somewhere deep down, she remembers.

Alessia

Antonio's offering me freedom, but why? There's no way he'd give me any sort of independence without wanting something in return. I know better than to trust that easily. Still, I'm not stupid. I'll take what I can get while I figure out his angle.

But first, I need answers.

I watch him as he loads the dishwasher, my mind racing. "Why are you watching my father's house?" I ask, keeping my voice steady.

Antonio's shoulders sag slightly, and for a moment, I expect him to lash out or avoid the question. But he doesn't. He takes his time drying his hands, then turns to face me, leaning against the counter. "Draco's the reason I went to find you," he starts carefully, each word measured. "He was trying to reach you, but you weren't answering his calls or texts. He said he was worried about your safety."

A bitter laugh escapes before I can stop it. "That would be a first." My father has never cared about my well-being. His *concern* has always been about control.

Antonio's expression hardens, but he presses on. "He was also concerned about the alliance between our families after Valentino's death."

I narrow my eyes, the pieces falling into place. "That's why you married me?" My fists clench at my sides.

"Yes," he confesses, meeting my glare head-on. "But there's more." He pauses, choosing his words carefully. "Last night, after you went to bed, Draco called again."

Rising to my feet, I begin to pace as I wait for him to continue.

"He knew where you were the whole time, Alessia. He had you followed, and he used me to bring you back." His voice drops, but I catch a flash of something on his face—fear, maybe, though he tries to hide it. "And then he told me he's promised you to someone else."

My heart stumbles, and I freeze, the blood draining from my face. The words hang in the air like a death sentence. My father's always been ruthless, but hearing Antonio confirm that he was planning to hand me over to someone else is too much, even for him.

"When Draco found out we were married, he lost it," Antonio continues, his gaze never leaving mine. "He threatened to take you by force."

Nausea twists in my stomach, mixing with deep-seated fear. I swallow hard, trying to find my voice. "So, what happens now?"

"It changes nothing about what I promised you," Antonio says, his tone unwavering. "You're still free to live your life, Alessia."

"That's incredibly generous of you," I snap, my anger flaring up again. "You say I'm free, but you're still forcing me to stay married to you? You won't let me go?"

"No, I'll never let you go," he says without hesitation. His eyes lock onto mine, filled with a determination that makes my heart pound for reasons I don't fully understand. "But I'll do everything in my power to keep you safe and to make sure you're happy."

"Happy?" I scoff, shaking my head in disbelief. "I'll never be happy as long as you're forcing me to stay here."

He flinches, just barely, but I catch it. And for a split second, I think I see pain in his eyes, but he quickly hides it behind that wall of control. "Maybe not," he concedes quietly. "But I'll make damn sure you're safe. Draco won't touch you. I won't allow anyone to harm you."

The air feels too thick, the room suddenly too small. Fear creeps in at the edges of my mind—fear of my father, of what he might do, and the fear of being trapped in this marriage forever. Antonio's words echo in my head, *I'll never let you go.*

"Why should I trust you? You left me. You said I wasn't worth fighting for."

"There's no reason you should," Antonio replies lifting his hand and tucking a strand of hair behind my ear, his fingers lingering on my cheek. "But I'll do whatever it takes to earn it back. This time, you have my word—and I'll prove it, every single day, as long as it takes."

I want to scream and push him away, to accuse him of being no different than my father or Valentino.

But I can't.

His voice carries so much sincerity that it rattles me. My mind scrambles for a reason to dismiss his words. A reason to not believe him.

"You say that now. But what happens when you decide I'm just another pawn in your game? What happens when you realize I'm not worth the trouble?"

His expression softens, his gaze deepening with something almost tender. "You're not a pawn, *tesoro.* You never were."

Tesoro. The word hangs between us, unfamiliar and unexpected, a term of endearment he's never used before. It catches me off guard, and I hate the way hope blooms in my chest, unbidden and unwelcome.

"Then what am I, Antonio?" I snap, stepping back to create

distance between us. "A prize? A responsibility? Something to conquer?"

"You're my wife," he says, his voice quiet but firm. "I'll say it again. I'll say it as many times as I need to until you believe me. I won't let anyone hurt you. Not even me."

Not even me. His words reach into a place I'd locked away long ago, stirring feelings I thought I'd buried.

"You don't get it, do you?" I whisper, more to myself than to him. "It's not just about my father, or Valentino. It's about you, Antonio. I don't know how to trust you."

He steps closer, and I instinctively tense but he stops just short of touching me again. "I know you don't trust me. I haven't earned that yet. I'm asking you to give me a chance. Just one chance to prove I'm not like them."

"And what if you betray me?" My voice wavers. "What if I let my guard down, and you hurt me like they did?"

"If I betray your trust, if you're hurt because of me, then, I'll let you go," he says, his voice filled with conviction. "But I promise you, Alessia, I'm not here to win you over with empty words. I'll earn your trust, one damn day at a time."

His promise weaves its way through my defenses, no matter how much I fight it. I want to tell him I'll never believe him, never trust him. But the truth is, a small part of me already does—and that terrifies me more than anything.

Behind the hardened man standing in front of me, I catch glimpses of the boy I once loved—the boy who made me feel safe, who felt like home. But if I were to believe him, to open my heart to him, and he hurt me again... I don't know if I'd survive it. Some breaks can't be mended, and I'm not sure the pieces of me could ever be put back together.

"I can't," I whisper.

He nods, as though he expected that answer. "I understand. I don't expect it to happen today or tomorrow. That won't stop me from working to earn your trust. And when you're ready, I'll be here."

"Don't make promises you can't keep," I warn, my voice sharp as I rebuild the walls around my heart, shutting down the part of me that almost dared to hope.

"I never do," he replies, then turns and walks away.

The room feels empty without him. I sink into the chair, my mind a whirlwind of emotions. My gaze falls on the ring on my finger, a reminder of Domenica and Giovanni's love. I hate that it makes me think about what could be—what might have been if things were different.

But more than that, I hate myself for even wanting to believe Antonio's telling the truth. Because if I do, I'm terrified I'll fall for him all over again—and this time, it will consume me completely.

Loving him would be like surrendering to the darkness, letting it wrap around me until I can't tell where I end, and he begins.

If I lost him—that's something I wouldn't survive.

Antonio

What the hell was I thinking? Why did I beg Alessia to trust me—to give me a chance? I tell myself this marriage isn't about love. It's nothing more than a business deal. If that's true, then why did it sting when Alessia said she'd never trust me? Why did it burn when she asked me to let her go?

Because it's a lie, and I know it.

There was a time when I loved her—when we were younger, before everything went to hell. Alessia was the girl I couldn't stop thinking about, the girl I loved. But life has a way of messing shit up.

I thought I buried those feelings, shoved them deep inside where they couldn't reach me. Yet now, being close to her, hearing her voice, those feelings are clawing their way back to the surface. I had to leave, had to get away from her before I made more promises I'm not sure I can keep.

There's too much to do, too much to fix. First on my list is finding Alessia's identification cards. I step outside, hoping the fresh air will clear my head.

"Anton," my mother calls from next door.

"Good morning," I reply, walking over, even though I feel anything but good.

"You look exhausted. You really need to take better care of yourself."

"It's been a long few days," I admit. "Dante and I had an unexpected trip to Alabama."

"Alabama?" she asks. "Does this have to do with Alessia?"

I hesitate, uncertain how to explain the last twenty-four hours. "It does," I say, my throat tightening as I admit the truth. "We were married last night."

Her reaction isn't immediate. She blinks, her expression unreadable. The seconds drag on, each one more tense than the last. "I didn't realize you still had feelings for her." Her voice is quiet and cautious.

I shake my head, trying to untangle the mess in my mind. "It's not like that," I manage, stumbling over my words. "It wasn't supposed to be like this."

"Then what is it like?" she asks, sitting beside me. "Explain it to me."

How do I tell her I forced Alessia to marry me? The truth lodges in my throat.

My mother's always been strong willed. When her father tried to arrange a marriage for her, she refused. She stood up to him, insisting she be allowed to marry for love. And here I am, bound to Alessia in an arrangement that feels like a betrayal of everything my parents taught me.

"This wasn't something I planned. Hell, I didn't want to marry her," I admit, rubbing the back of my neck, a nervous habit I've had since I was a kid.

Mom's eyes search mine, her expression a mix of concern and curiosity. "Then why did you do it, Anton? You've never been the type to act on impulse, especially not with something this important."

"It was necessary," I say, the words tasting bitter. "Draco insisted on it. I didn't have a choice."

Her lips press into a tight line. "Draco Moretti insisted, and you just went along with it?"

My frustration flares, but I keep my voice steady. "I didn't have an option."

"There's always an option, Anton," she says, disappointment lacing her words.

"What's done is done. We're staying married."

"And what about you?" she asks softly. "How do you feel about it?"

How do I feel? Conflicted doesn't even begin to describe it. "I don't know," I admit, staring at the ground. "I didn't expect to feel…"

"To feel what?" she presses gently.

"I shouldn't be feeling anything for her, but I do," I admit. "And it's confusing as hell."

Her expression softens. "This is your heart we're talking about. If you feel something for her, no matter how complicated, you owe it to yourself to figure out what it is."

"You and Dad made it look easy."

"I loved your father with all my heart, but it wasn't always easy," Mom says, her eyes filling with tears. "There were times when our desires clashed, and I struggled with insecurity and jealousy. But your father never let me carry those burdens alone. He was patient when I faltered, strong when I needed him. Love isn't only about the easy days, Anton. It's about standing by each other through the darkest nights."

She takes my hand, her touch warm and comforting. "We learned to compromise, respect each other's differences, and never let life's challenges make us forget why we fell in love in the first place. That's the secret. It's not about perfection, but perseverance and trust."

Mom wipes a tear from her cheek. "Don't let fear of loss hold you back from love. If you care for Alessia, give yourself a chance to see where it might lead. The journey, though difficult, may be more beautiful than you ever imagined."

"I've done terrible things," I say quietly. "I don't deserve someone like Alessia."

Her grip tightens on my hand. "You deserve happiness, Antonio. Don't let anyone, not even yourself, convince you otherwise."

"Alessia hates me. She'll never trust me, no matter what I do."

"She has every right to be angry and afraid. I saw the bruises. I know what Valentino did to her," she replies, her tone gentle. "You're going to have to earn her trust."

"What if she never loves me back?" I ask before I can stop myself.

Her smile is faint, but there's a knowing look in her eyes. "Do you want her to love you?"

"I don't know," I admit, running a hand through my hair.

"Give yourself time to figure it out. Allow Alessia time, too. Love isn't something that happens overnight, especially not when she was forced into this marriage. Be patient and kind—the man I know you are in here." She points to my heart.

I nod, though the knot in my chest doesn't ease. "I'll try. But I'm not going to lie, I don't know if I can be that man."

"You're stronger than you know, Antonio," she says softly. "Don't let this slip away before you give it a chance."

Her words stay with me as I leave, echoing in my head like a distant warning. *Don't let it slip away.*

Talking to my mom always brings a sense of clarity. As I walk across the street, hope takes root—just enough to make me believe that, despite everything, I might find a way to make this work.

THE HOUSE ACROSS THE STREET, THE ONE ALESSIA shared with Valentino, is a reminder of the nightmares that still haunt her. Stepping inside, the walls seem to press in, as if they've absorbed every moment of darkness that unfolded here. I make a mental note to have it torn down—erase every trace of what happened within these walls.

I sit behind Vigo's desk, rifling through drawers, searching for her identification cards. The papers are scattered, meaningless. My mind is a battlefield, torn between wanting to protect Alessia and the inevitable truth that I'm too dark, too damaged—someone like me has no place making promises to someone like her.

I'll never raise a hand to her like he did, but that doesn't mean I won't hurt her. I'm no saint. There will come a day when, despite my best intentions, she'll get hurt. It might be a harsh word spoken in anger or a decision made in haste.

My life is unpredictable and dangerous—that's the scariest part. I pick up my phone and text Dante.

Me: I need more guards on my house and Alessia.

Dante: I doubled the number last night.

I grit my teeth. Why is he choosing now to argue? I hit his contact and wait for him to pick up.

"I gave you an order. Why the fuck do you think you can question it?" I bark as soon as the call connects.

"Woah, calm down," Dante replies. "If you need more men, I'll make it happen."

"I'm sorry," I mutter and drop my head into my free hand. "Draco's threats have me on edge."

"I get it. I'll put more men on it."

"Alessia cannot be harmed. She's been through enough."

"We'll keep her safe, Antonio. You have my word."

We finish the call, and I set the phone down on the desk.

I was raised in this world, the one where getting my hands dirty wasn't just expected, it was required. I've faced danger more times than I can count, stared down the barrel of a gun, but never felt true fear—until now.

Because this is different. I'm not afraid of bullets or blood. I'm afraid that no matter how hard I try, I won't be able to keep my darkness from seeping into Alessia's life. That I'll fail her in ways I can't take back. I'll see the pain in her eyes and know it was me who put it there.

But despite everything, I'm a selfish bastard. I want Alessia more than I've wanted anything in my life. I want to protect her, yes—but I also want to keep her. No matter the cost.

And that, more than anything, is the real danger.

Alessia

O nce I gather my composure, I go back up to my bedroom and take a hot shower. The water scalds my skin burning away the fog left behind from everything that's happened.

After I'm dressed and my hair's dry, I decide to take Antonio up on his offer to leave the house. He encouraged me to visit the gallery so that's what I intend to do.

I unzip the suitcase, expecting to find the camera tucked between my things. But as I pull out the clothes, hastily thrown in without a second thought, unease crawls up my spine. My hands move faster, tossing aside the tangled mess of fabric. Where is it?

No camera.

Antonio or Dante must've packed the bag, and there's no way they would've known to look for it. Of course they didn't grab it. My pulse races as the realization sinks in. It's gone.

The loss hits me hard, leaving me dizzy and breathless. That camera was everything—my refuge, my tether to the dreams I barely let myself hold on to. Rosie gave it to me when she found out how much I loved photography. It belonged to her late husband. I've treasured it ever since, knowing how much it meant to her.

And now, it's gone.

I check my wallet, but there's only fifty dollars inside. Nowhere near enough to replace it. My only hope is that Ophelia has sold some of the photos I sent her a couple of weeks ago and that she hasn't sent the money to Alabama yet.

Just as I'm about to lose it completely, the doorbell rings. The sudden sound jolts me out of my spiraling thoughts, and I head downstairs to see who's here.

When I open the door, I'm surprised to see Antonio's mother standing there with a warm smile.

"I hope you don't mind me showing up unannounced," she says kindly.

"Antonio isn't home right now."

"I didn't come for him. I came to see you," she says, her smile genuine. "I wanted to welcome you to the family."

I stare at her, stunned. "Antonio told you?"

"He did, and despite the circumstances, we're glad to have you."

My emotions, already on edge, tip over, and the tears I've been holding back flow freely. "I'm sorry," I murmur, wiping at my face, embarrassed.

Nicki steps forward, enveloping me in a warm embrace. "Oh, sweetheart, there's no need to apologize. It's okay to not be okay, especially after everything you've been through."

"Would you like to come in?" I ask, stepping aside and gesturing toward the living room.

We move to the couch and sit down. I shift uncomfortably, my hands fidgeting in my lap as silence stretches between us. Nicki sits beside me, her posture relaxed, though her eyes remain perceptive and observant.

"I'm not usually this emotional," I start, my voice shaky. "It's just... I thought I was finally free, away from all of this madness. Alabama was supposed to be my fresh start. I had a job and a place to live. It wasn't much, but it was mine."

Nicki listens intently, not judging, just letting me talk.

"Then, two days ago, I walked into my apartment and Antonio was sitting there." The memory still feels raw, like an open wound. "He didn't give me a choice. He forced me to come back here."

I pause, my throat tight, the truth pressing against my lips. I could tell her about how Antonio drugged me—took away my ability to fight, my chance to decide. But what would that accomplish? Nicki's kindness might not stretch that far. Some things are better left unsaid.

"I'm sure that was quite an unwelcome surprise."

"I thought I was free, but it was just an illusion."

Fear of trusting anyone in this family takes hold. I can't tell if this is a trap, if I've already said too much. Will she tell Antonio? Will he punish me when he gets home?

Nicki watches me closely. "You're worried because you opened up to me?"

I nod slowly.

"We don't know each other well," she continues, her voice gentle, "but I hope that can change. If there's one thing you should know about me, it's that I don't support arranged or forced marriages. My father wanted to saddle me with one," she chuckles. "But I dug my heels in and refused. Marco and I raised Antonio and Cecilia with our values."

Her expression tightens. "I'm not pleased with how my son handled things," she admits. "Our world isn't easy, but that doesn't excuse his actions."

I'm surprised by her honesty. "I understand that my father put him in a difficult position, but it doesn't change how I feel. Trusting someone who forced me back into this life seems impossible." I try to compose myself.

"Antonio said some things before he left, things that reminded me of who he was when we were young. But that was a long time ago. So much has happened since then—I'm not sure trusting him is even possible."

"Trust takes time, especially when it's been broken. What Antonio did was wrong, and it's okay to be angry, to be hurt."

"I don't know what to think. My father and Val only ever saw me as a bargaining chip to be given to the highest bidder. No one's ever cared about me

"It's okay to take your time. No one expects you to just forgive and forget," she pauses. "If Antonio wants your trust back, he'll have to work to earn it."

I bite my lip. "I don't know if I'm strong enough to get through this."

"You're stronger than you think, Alessia," she says with a reassuring smile. "Allow yourself the space to figure things out, at your own pace."

"Thank you, Nicki. I'll try."

"Just remember, you're not alone in this. You have family now, even if it's complicated," she says with a warm smile. "I'm right next door and will always be there for you."

As she leaves, I'm left with a swirl of emotions—uncertainty and a faint spark of something I haven't felt in a long time.

AFTER THE INCIDENT WITH THE CAMERA, THE DAYS blurred together in a haze of frustration and helplessness. It took a full week for me to gather the courage to finally step outside.

As soon as my foot hits the pavement, I pause, scanning the empty street. For a moment, I half-expect someone to leap out and drag me back inside—to remind me that my freedom is still just an illusion. But no one comes.

The air is still, and the street is quiet, almost eerily so. It hits me like a punch to the gut—I'm almost twenty-two, and I've never been completely alone. There's always been someone watching—guards hovering close by, shadowing my every move, ensuring I never forget how controlled my life is.

It seems that Antonio kept his promise. His guards are nowhere to be seen. The realization surprises me. I hadn't expected him to follow through, but for now, he's allowing me this sliver of freedom.

The longer I walk, the more uneasy I become. My father's threats lurk in the corners of my mind, and I glance around, but there's no one I recognize, no shadowy figure lurking nearby. Still, I can't shake the feeling of being watched.

I focus on the steady rhythm of my footsteps, the warm breeze brushing against my skin. By the time I reach the gallery, my anxiety has eased.

Ophelia looks up when I step inside. Her surprise is evident. "Allie. I didn't realize you were back in town."

"I just got back," I say, managing a small smile. "I was wondering if any of my photos sold."

"Oh yes, quite a few, actually. But I sent the money order to your address in Alabama."

I force a nod, pushing down the disappointment. "That's okay. I'll wait until the envelope gets returned here."

"I'm sorry for the mix-up."

"There's no need to apologize," I reply, trying to make it sound casual. "I came back much sooner than I anticipated."

"I hope everything's okay?"

I'm momentarily at a loss, but I recover quickly. "It will be."

"Do you have any new photos? I'd love to see what you've been working on."

"Not yet. It's going to take a little while before I'm settled enough to take new ones. But I'll bring some by when I do."

"Take your time," she says gently. "I'm glad you're back."

The walk home feels longer. The streets blur as I replay the disappointment over and over in my mind. I needed that money. It was supposed to be the start of saving for a new camera. But that envelope will never find its way back to me because Allie Morgan doesn't exist—she never did.

When I finally reach the house, Antonio's just walking up the porch steps. His expression softens when he sees me. Despite everything, I find comfort in his presence—a security I can't quite explain.

$$Antonio$$

It's taken a week of searching the house, but I finally found Alessia's things. Valentino had hidden them in a place I never suspected—a secret room concealed behind a false wall.

I'd been in Valentino's office countless times. He trusted me enough to allow me access, but I never imagined there was more to it than met the eye. After days of fruitless searching, frustration got the better of me. I was angry—angry at Valentino for his secrets, angry at myself for the entire mess.

I started yanking books off the shelves, throwing them to the floor. One of them—a large, leather-bound volume—hit the ground harder than the rest. The sound it made was wrong—off. I stopped, staring at the space on the shelf where it had been. Something clicked.

That's when I found it.

Behind the empty space on the shelf, a hidden lever. I pulled it without hesitation, and the wall beside the shelf slid open, revealing a narrow, windowless room I'd never known existed. The air inside was stale, untouched. The kind of place meant to stay hidden forever.

In the center of the room was a steel safe. It didn't take long to crack it open. Inside were Alessia's passport and photo ID, along with a stack of forged passports—Valentino's way of controlling her, or worse. I destroyed the forgeries and pocketed Alessia's actual belongings. She would've never found this room. Valentino made sure of that.

As I step onto the front porch, I spot her coming around the corner. She's finally ventured out of the house after days of hesitation. She's been growing more distant with each passing day. I've tried to get her to open up to me, but with everything that's happened, everything I've done, she's barely speaking to me.

It's driven a wedge between us that I'm not sure how to fix. I was hoping the fresh air might help, that maybe it would clear her head. But as she draws near, it's clear nothing has changed. There's something wrong. Her face is tense, her expression guarded, and the smile she forces doesn't reach her eyes.

"How was your walk?"

"It was nice."

I study her for a moment trying to find any hint of what's bothering her, but she avoids my eyes.

"I found something," I say, reaching into my pocket, feeling the cold edges of the items I retrieved.

Alessia's eyes widen when she sees what I'm holding. Her hands tremble slightly as she takes them from me. "Thank you," she murmurs, her voice soft, distant, like she's somewhere else entirely.

There's a pause, a lingering silence between us. . "Are you sure everything's okay?" I ask gently, not wanting to push too hard but needing to know what's going on.

Her fingers trace the edge of the ID, her lips parting as if to speak, but the words seem trapped. Finally, she exhales. "My camera got left in Alabama."

I don't respond right away, hoping she'll ask me to replace it, to let me do something—anything. But she doesn't. She just stares down at the ID, as if it holds the answer to something far beyond either of us.

And with that, an idea forms. Her birthday is in three weeks —an opportunity to maybe make things right, to give her something that might bring a little light back into her life. But I don't say a word. Not yet.

"We'll figure it out," I say, though the sadness still lingers in her eyes.

As we walk into the kitchen, something outside catches my eye. Through the French doors, I spot a dark shape on the patio table. A shiver of cold dread crawls down my spine.

"What's wrong?" Alessia asks, her voice laced with concern.

"Stay here," I order. Hurrying out, every nerve is on edge. A bloody knife glints under the afternoon light. Next to it is a small, folded piece of paper, stained red at the edges. The note feels heavy in my hand, like the weight of something dark creeping closer.

I unfold it slowly. The words inside are brief but chilling:

"Deep into that darkness peering, long I stood there wondering, fearing. Your every step is watched, Alessia. Beware the shadows, for they may not let you escape next time—nor your keeper."

"Oh my God," Alessia whispers from behind me.

I whirl around, my pulse roaring. "I told you to stay—" The reprimand dies in my throat when I see her face. She's gone pale, her eyes locked on the blood-stained knife.

Anger surges inside me, but I push it down, forcing it to stay buried. There will be plenty of time for anger. Right now, I have to be calm, for her. "It's okay," I say softly, pulling her close.

She trembles against me, but she doesn't pull away. Instead, she leans into me, fragile, as if she's about to break. "I'll take care of this. You're safe," I promise, pressing my lips to the top of her head.

Alessia nods, but she says nothing.

I need to find out who did this, and how they got this close to my home.

"Let's get you inside," I say, guiding her back into the house. Her eyes stay on the knife as if it's still calling to her.

"Whose blood..." Her voice trails off.

"I don't know, but I'll find out," I reassure her. "I won't let anything happen to you."

After settling her on the couch, I head to the kitchen to make a cup of the tea she's always liked. *Christmas Eve*, a blend of cinnamon, vanilla, and orange. As soon as I open the tin, the familiar scent takes me back to another time.

On cold days after school, we'd sit under the bleachers, and she'd always have a cup of that fragrant tea. She once told me how her nanny, the only person who made her feel special and cared for, used to make it for her when she was little. Those smells, cinnamon, vanilla, orange, are forever tied to her.

When I was going to Alabama to bring her back, I made sure to order it online. I wanted something familiar in the house. Something to remind her of the times when she could still smile, when she felt warmth and comfort—even if just for a little while.

As I move through the kitchen, memories of her flood my mind. I remember so much about her, the way she used to smile, the light in her eyes when she talked about her dreams. And now, I'm trying to piece together what's left of those days, hoping something as simple as this tea might help bring a little of that back.

While it steeps, I text Dante.

Me: Drop whatever you're doing and get to my house.

Dante: What's going on?

Me: I'll explain when you're here.

I bring the tea to Alessia. "Careful, it's hot."

"Thank you," she murmurs, her voice barely audible. She looks down at the tea, then back up at me, her eyes softening just a little. "You remembered."

"I remember everything," I reply, my voice low.

And I do. Every detail, every memory of who she was before all of this. It's all still with me, no matter how much has changed.

"Dante's on his way. We'll figure this out." But even as I say the words, a familiar darkness coils deep within me—a shadowy presence, reminding me that whoever did this won't stop. They've made that hauntingly clear.

Minutes later, the doorbell rings. I stand to answer it, but Alessia's hand shoots out, gripping my arm.

"Don't leave me," she pleads.

My heart clenches at the vulnerability in her voice. She's openly reaching for me—seeking comfort from me. I wish it didn't have to happen under these circumstances. I want her to feel safe with me because she wants to, not because she feels she has no other choice.

"I have to let Dante in," I say softly, covering her hand with mine. "I'm not going far."

She hesitates but slowly releases me. The warmth of her touch lingers on my skin as I walk to the door.

Dante steps inside, his expression dark. "What happened?" he asks, keeping his voice quiet.

"Someone left a message. It's on the patio," I say, my voice low, almost growling. "Take care of it." I look over my shoulder to where Alessia sits, her legs pulled up to her chest and her arms wrapped around them. "I need to make sure she's okay and then I'll meet you in the office."

He gives a curt nod, heading out to deal with the knife.

I crouch in front of her. "*Tesoro*," I murmur. "I'm going to talk to Dante. I need you to stay right here, okay?"

Her gaze lingers on me, searching for reassurance I can't fully give. "Okay," she whispers.

"I'll leave the door open. If you need me, just come in."

I hate leaving her alone, but we need to get right on this. The sooner the better.

"When did this happen?" Dante asks, holding up the plastic bag containing the bloody knife.

"Sometime while we were out," I say, sinking into my uncle's old chair. "We got home about twenty minutes ago. The knife was already there."

"Draco?"

"It has to be," I say, my jaw clenched. "No one else has the nerve to come this close."

"You need more security," Dante says, his tone firm. "Guards outside and an alarm system."

"I won't turn this house into another cage to keep her locked in," I snap, the words slicing the air between us.

"It doesn't have to be forever," he counters. "But until this threat is dealt with, we can't leave either of you exposed."

The floor outside creaks, and I know Alessia's in the hall listening. I close my eyes for a moment, trying to steady myself. As much as I want to shield her from all this, there's no escaping the world we live in.

I just hope I can protect her—without losing her in the process.

Alessia

The sight of the blood-soaked knife on the patio sears itself into my mind, a grotesque reminder of the world I've tried so hard to leave behind. My heart hammers in my chest, but beneath the fear, there's a cold certainty. There's only one person capable of sending such a twisted message.

My father.

Draco Moretti never does anything without a purpose. This was a message he knew I couldn't ignore—a warning that he's done waiting. My hands tremble as I grab my phone, dialing the number I know by heart. It rings once before he picks up, his voice slithering through the receiver, smug and full of venom.

"I thought that might get your attention," my father says, his tone dripping with satisfaction.

My grip tightens on the phone. "What the hell do you think you're doing?" I spit, my words laced with fury.

"Is that any way to greet your father?" he replies smoothly.

"What do you want?"

"I'm merely reminding you of the promise you've broken."

"*I* haven't made any promises," I snap, my voice trembling despite my efforts to stay calm. "You're trying to scare me, but it's not going to work."

"Scare you?" he laughs, sharp and cruel. "No, darling. I'm simply ensuring you understand where your true obligations lie. I've already arranged your future—my gift was just a reminder of your place."

"I know my *place*, father. It's with my husband," I force out, my voice filled with as much conviction as I can muster.

There's a pause, a chilling silence that stretches out before he speaks again. "We both know your marriage is a charade," he says, his voice darkening. "But don't worry—I can take care of that."

I have to make him believe this marriage is real. "It's not a charade. I'm in love with Antonio," I lie, desperation creeping in. "And I'm pregnant with his child."

THE SILENCE THAT FOLLOWS IS SUFFOCATING. I HOLD my breath, hoping it will be enough to stop him. But when he speaks again, his voice is colder than ever. "Pregnant?" he spits, disgust saturating the word. "You think that will stop me? That I'll abandon my plans because you're carrying his bastard? You're even more foolish than I thought."

Fear surges through me. "Papa, please—"

"I promised you to another," he snaps, cutting me off. "And I intend to keep that promise. I was willing to let Antonio remain alive, even though he took you without my blessing. Now, you've left me with no choice but to kill him."

"Don't you dare," I hiss, a mix of anger and fear twisting inside me. "If you touch him, I swear—"

"Watch your mouth, little girl," he sneers. "Tell your husband his days are numbered. I'm coming for him, and when I'm done, there won't be anything left of the man you claim to love."

The words hit like a slap. Before I can respond, the line goes dead. I'm left sitting on the couch, the phone still clutched in my hand.

What have I done?

Cold dread settles over me as my father's words echo in my

mind. What was I thinking, telling him I'm pregnant? I thought I could protect Antonio, make my father back off. Instead, I've only made things worse.

Somehow, I have to find the courage to tell Antonio. The thought of his reaction terrifies me. Will he see this as a betrayal? Will there be consequences?

My legs feel like lead as I make my way to his office, the door open just like he promised. I pause outside, my heart racing as I overhear Antonio and Dante in conversation, their voices low and serious.

"You need more security," Dante insists. "Guards at the house and a security alarm system."

"I won't turn this house into another cage to keep her locked in," Antonio replies firm, but weary.

"It doesn't have to be forever. But until this threat is dealt with, we can't leave her or you exposed."

"I don't need a security system," Antonio argues. "I'm perfectly capable of protecting my wife."

"I'm not saying you aren't," Dante counters. "But men like Draco don't play by the same rules. We need to be prepared."

"I've already increased the number of guards."

"You need an actual security system and guards at the doors," Dante presses. "Think about it, Anton. It's not just about us anymore it's about protecting Alessia."

Antonio's trying so hard to keep his word, to make me feel safe, and I've gone and made everything worse. Swallowing hard, I step forward.

He looks up, his gaze locking onto mine. The moment he sees the tears in my eyes, his expression shifts from concern to something deeper, something that cuts through the tension between us. He rises from his chair, closing the distance between us in a few long strides.

"Alessia," he says gently, his hand cupping my cheek. "What's wrong?"

"Can I talk to you alone?" I ask, glancing at Dante.

Antonio nods at Dante. "Give us a minute."

Without a word, Dante steps out, leaving a tense quiet in his wake. I feel as though I'm standing on the edge of a cliff, ready to plunge into the unknown.

"I called my father," I say, my voice unsteady. "He's the one who left the knife and the note."

"I guessed as much," Antonio says.

"There's more."

"Go on."

"I told him I was pregnant," I say, my words barely above a whisper. "With your child."

Antonio's eyes widen slightly, but he remains silent, waiting for me to continue.

"It was a lie obviously," I confess, the words rushing out. "I thought if he believed I was carrying a baby that's half Moretti, he might back off. But it didn't work. It only made him more furious. He said he was going to kill you."

Antonio turns away, grabbing the back of his neck. I brace myself for his reaction, terrified of what comes next.

"I'm so sorry," I whisper.

Slowly, Antonio turns back to me. "This isn't your fault," he says, his voice low and controlled.

Tears spill down my cheeks, a mix of relief and fear swirling inside me. "I'm so scared," I admit. "I don't want him to hurt you."

Antonio's gaze softens as he steps closer, gently wiping away my tears. "You don't have to worry about me," he says, his voice filled with quiet resolve. "And I won't let him hurt you, either."

"I thought I could handle him on my own and make him back off."

Antonio shakes his head, tilting my chin up so I'm forced to meet his eyes. "You're not alone anymore," he murmurs, his thumb brushing over my lower lip. "From now on, you don't contact him without me. Promise me, Alessia."

His eyes hold me captive. "I promise," I whisper, breathless.

His hand slides to the back of my neck, pulling me closer. My heart pounds as the warmth of his presence surrounds me. He's so close, but it's a closeness that makes me feel safe and protected.

"Good," he whispers, his voice husky. "Because I won't let him take you from me."

The sincerity in his words tugs at something deep inside me. Without thinking, I lean in, pressing my lips to his. Antonio responds instantly, his lips soft against mine, the kiss tender, filled with unspoken promises. My hands find their way to his chest, feeling the steady rhythm of his heart beneath my fingers.

Antonio rests his forehead against mine. "Don't be scared," he whispers. "Let me in, *tesoro.* I'll protect not only your body but your heart as well."

"I don't know how," I admit.

"You don't have to have all the answers. We'll figure it out together."

Tears well up again, but this time, they're tears of hope. "I want to trust you," I whisper. "I want to try."

He smiles, a small, reassuring smile that makes my heart ache in a way that's both painful and beautiful. "That's all I ask," he murmurs, pressing another kiss to my lips.

Antonio holds me close as if he's afraid to let go.

"As long as I'm breathing no one will ever hurt you again," he breathes

As I look into the endless blue depth in his eyes, a new feeling takes root—faith. Faith in him, in us, and in the fragile hope that we could become something more.

T he past few weeks have been tense, filled with arguments with Dante about installing a security system. He pushed hard, but I stood my ground—this house isn't going to feel like a cage. I'm fully capable of protecting my wife without making her feel trapped.

Today, though, my focus is entirely on Alessia. It's her birthday, though she doesn't realize I remember, which will make the surprise even more meaningful. I set a sleek black box with a silver bow on the side table in the living room. Inside is a new camera. She misses her photography, and I miss the light in her eyes when she's behind the lens, fully absorbed in capturing the world as she sees it.

The smell of garlic and tomatoes fills the air as I stir the sauce, glancing at the clock. Alessia left early this morning with Cecilia. She'd been hesitant to reach out, worried that Cecilia might be angry at being left in the dark. Cecilia, on the other hand, was certain Alessia would hate her as an extension of her anger toward me. Thankfully, they were able to reconnect and have grown close, something that's brought them both a sense of peace.

Their outing worked in my favor today, giving me the chance to prepare. I don't mind cooking, but baking—that's another story. I followed the recipe to the letter. It's nothing fancy, just a simple vanilla cake with frosting, but I hope it'll make her smile. *Happy Birthday Alessia* is scrawled in shaky gel writing. I stare at it, wondering if it's enough.

I want tonight to be perfect.

Stepping back, I glance at the table set for two, thoughts drifting to how far we've come. Just a few weeks ago, she was all anger and distance. Something I don't blame her for. She thought she'd escaped this life, and I dragged her back. Worse, I forced her into a marriage she didn't want.

It was a necessary evil, but evil nonetheless.

Since the knife incident, she's lowered her defenses—just enough to let me slip through. It's a subtle shift, barely noticeable, but it's there in the quiet moments we share. The way she looks at me now, with an expression other than fear or distrust. There's more—something warmer yet fragile. I've made it a point to be here more often, leaving the restaurant in Enzo's capable hands.

Alessia needs to see that I'm here for her, that I'm invested in this. In us.

We've even started doing simple things together, like watching those old eighties romance movies she loves, Say Anything and Pretty in Pink, films I'd never choose on my own. But now, I watch her, captivated by the way her eyes light up during those moments when the characters confess their love. I want to be the man who makes Alessia look like that.

Sometimes we cook together. Alessia taught me how to bake cookies like her Nonna used to—just soft enough in the middle. She laughs when I mess up, when flour ends up on my face or sauce splashes on my shirt. Her laugh—it's like music, something I could lose myself in. There's something intimate about sharing these everyday moments with her.

She's hesitant, still guarded, but she's letting me in. Slowly. She's allowing me to see the real Alessia, the one she's kept hidden for so long. And damn it, I'm falling for her.

I'm falling hard.

It's not only about my need to protect her, though that instinct is stronger than ever. It's about her trusting me, leaning on me, needing me. I want to be the man she turns to when things get hard, the man who makes her feel safe. I want her love, even if I don't deserve it.

But I can't let my guard down. Draco's threats hang over us like a storm cloud, and every day the danger grows. I haven't told Alessia that the messages keep coming. Ominous notes have been left at the restaurant and another outside our house.

I'm trying to shield her from as much as possible, but I see the fear in her eyes every time my phone rings. How her body tenses as if expecting the worst.

Each night before we go to our separate rooms to sleep, I double-check the locks. But it isn't enough. She's still scared, and I hate that I can't take that fear away.

Draco needs to be dealt with. But how? I can't just kill him and be done with it—he's her father, and that complicates everything. Starting an all-out war would mean losing everything, including her.

The front door creaks open, pulling me from my thoughts. I glance at the time—she's right on schedule. A smile pulls at my lips.

"Antonio?" Her voice is soft, uncertain.

"In the kitchen," I call, setting the glasses of wine on the table. I turn as she steps in, her eyes going wide at the sight of the table, the dinner I've prepared, and her cake.

"What's all this?" she asks, her voice thin, as though she can't quite believe what she's seeing.

I MOVE CLOSER, MY HEART POUNDING HARDER THAN I care to admit. "Happy Birthday, *tesoro*."

She blinks, clearly taken aback. "How did you know?"

"Back in high school, you tried to keep it quiet, but I never forgot."

Her eyes well up with tears, and for a moment, I think I've done something wrong. I step closer, worry settling in the pit of my stomach. "If you don't like it, I can make something else, or we can order out—"

"It's not that," she whispers, her voice thick with emotion as she looks between the dinner and the cake sitting on the counter. "No one's ever done anything like this for me before."

"You've never had a birthday party?"

"No," she says, shaking her head slowly.

I stare at her, at this woman who's been through more than I can imagine, and all I want to do is erase the years of pain and neglect. When we were younger, I thought I'd be her first for everything—her first love, her first kiss, her first in every way that mattered. That was stolen from me. Stolen from us.

But tonight, I get to be her first for this. Something pure.

I swallow the bitterness that rises in my throat. "Then I'm glad I get to be the first," I say softly, brushing my thumb over her cheek. I hold her gaze, my voice lowering. "And even though I missed so many of your firsts, I promise I'll be your last."

Her eyes widen slightly at my words, but she doesn't pull away. Instead, she watches me, something unreadable stirring in her expression. I pull out her chair, motioning for her to sit. When she does, there's a soft, genuine smile on her lips.

"Thank you," she whispers, her voice barely audible. She glances at the table and then back at me. "For all this. It's perfect."

I brush my thumb over her cheek again, letting the moment hang between us. "I plan on making you feel special every chance I get."

She laughs, the sound light, and I can't help but grin in response. "You're going to spoil me."

"That's my plan."

Dinner isn't extravagant—just pasta, bread, a salad. By the way she savors every bite, you'd think I prepared a five-star meal. When I bring over the cake, her eyes light up, and I'm certain I want to spend the rest of my life trying to make her smile like that.

After we finish our cake, I lead her to the living room.

"I have one more surprise," I say, handing it to her.

"You didn't have to get me a present."

"I wanted to. Open it," I encourage.

She unwraps it eagerly. The moment she lifts the lid and sees the camera inside, her face lights up, and she lets out a soft gasp.

"Antonio." She looks up at me, tears welling again.

"I know how much you've missed it."

She sets the camera down carefully and walks over to where I'm standing. "Thank you. This means more to me than you'll ever know."

"You mean more to me than you know," I murmur, cupping her face in my hands.

For the briefest moment, I see it—hope.

I brush my lips against hers. The kiss is tentative at first, a gentle connection that feels fragile, as if any sudden movement might shatter the moment. I expect her to push me away, but she doesn't.

She leans into me, and the world narrows to just this moment. The feel of her lips on mine, the warmth of her body against me. The danger and threats all fade into the background.

I don't deserve her trust, but I'll spend every day proving I'm worthy of it.

"I want you to know," Alessia says quietly. "I've never had sex of my own free will."

Her confession hits me harder than I expected. I know she's been through hell, but hearing it said so plainly, so vulnerably, stirs a mix of anger and grief I can't ignore. It's a reminder of everything we've lost and everything we're still fighting for.

"We can wait," I say, my voice low. "We don't have to do anything you're not ready for."

She looks up at me, her eyes searching mine. "I don't want to wait," she whispers, her voice trembling. "I've already waited too long. I want to be with you, Antonio."

I hold her gaze, every protective instinct firing in my blood.

"I'll be gentle," I promise, my lips brushing against her skin. "If you want to stop, just tell me, and I will."

She runs her fingers through my hair before rising onto her toes, pressing her mouth to mine. The kiss is soft, as though we're both learning how to do this—how to be together again. I lift her easily, her legs wrapping around my waist. Her warmth seeps into me like a slow burn, igniting every nerve.

Carrying her upstairs, our lips stay connected, the kiss growing more urgent with each step as if we're trying to make up for all the time that's been stolen from us. When I lay her down on the bed, her eyes lock onto mine, filled with a mix of trust and something more profound—something that makes my pulse race.

Slowly, reverently, I undress her, taking my time, savoring each moment as more of her is revealed to me. For so many years, I imagined this—dreamt of her like this, bare beneath me, trusting me completely. Each touch feels like the fulfillment of something that was always meant to be.

I trail my lips along her collarbone, down the curve of her neck, across her shoulders, tasting her skin and memorizing the way her breath hitches with each touch. She's everything I've ever wanted and so much more.

"You're so beautiful," I murmur as I slide her leggings off. My hands trace the smoothness of her thighs, and I can't help but marvel at how perfect she is.

Alessia pushes up on her elbows, watching as I pull my shirt off. Her eyes linger on my tattoos before her teeth catch her lower lip.

"Spread your legs," I say, my voice dropping an octave.

"I'm scared."

"I won't hurt you." I lower myself over her and brush a kiss against her lips.

Her gaze holds mine, seeking more reassurance. I kiss her again, letting my touch say what my words can't, showing her the depth of my promise. Slowly, her body softens beneath me as her hands slide over my shoulders, pulling me closer.

My touch is light against her skin as I trail kisses down her neck to her breasts. I tease one nipple, taking it gently into my mouth while my fingers trace the other. Her breath quickens, each soft sound a quiet invitation. "Do you like that?" I ask, looking up at her.

Alessia responds by arching her back into my touch, silently communicating her pleasure. My lips trail down her stomach. As my hand slides across her hip, she lets out a small sigh.

I part her legs and run my finger through her arousal. "You're so responsive."

"It feels so good," she whispers, her voice barely audible.

"Do you want more?" I ask, my finger teasing her entrance

"Yes," she breathes.

"Tell me what you want." I urge as I feather kisses along her inner thigh.

"Kiss me," she whispers.

"Where?"

"There," she says so quietly I can barely hear her.

"Where's *there?*"

"Antonio," she says my name, frustration in her voice.

I glance up at her with a grin. "You'll have to be more specific, *tesoro.*"

"My pussy," she says softly. "I want you to kiss me there."

Desire courses through me, going straight to my cock. "As you wish." Without hesitation, I part her folds, my tongue sweeping over her clit with a slow, deliberate stroke, savoring the softness of her. Her taste, warm and intoxicating, fills my senses as I circle her clit again, flicking my tongue over the sensitive bud. Gradually, I pick up the pace, each soft moan from her lips driving me closer to the edge.

Tracing slow, deliberate circles with my tongue, I savor every response as her body reacts beneath mine. I slip one finger inside her, easing into a gentle rhythm before adding another, pressing deeper. Her moans grow louder, her body arching as I find her G-spot and massage it, while my tongue moves in soft, rhythmic strokes over her clit, coaxing her pleasure with every touch.

Her body writhes, and I steady her with a firm grip on her hip. "Antonio," she breathes my name, and I push her closer to the edge.

"It's okay," I murmur. "Just relax and let it happen."

"I don't know how," she whimpers.

She fists the sheets, her legs tensing as her climax builds. Her walls tighten around my fingers, and with one final thrust of my tongue, she shatters, crying out my name as her orgasm takes over.

Her body trembles, lost in ecstasy as I continue drawing out every wave of pleasure. A warm rush flows over my fingers as I push her even higher. I don't stop until the final tremors fade, her body gradually surrendering to the soft aftermath of release.

I've dreamed of this moment, imagined her taste for years. Alessia watches as I bring my fingers to my mouth, licking them clean. She tastes even better than I'd imagined. "Delicious," I say, savoring the word.

She covers her face with her hands. "Don't," I say gently. "There's nothing to be ashamed of."

"I've never had a man's mouth on me," she whispers, her voice soft and almost shy. "And I've never felt anything like that."

"It's only the beginning," I say, popping the button on my pants and sliding them down. "Because now that I've tasted you, I'll never get enough."

Seeing me naked for the first time, her eyes roam my body, stopping on my hard cock. "What's that?"

"Piercings," I reply, climbing over her and capturing her lips in another kiss. "They won't hurt," I promise, my voice dark and full of need. "I need to be inside you, *tesoro*."

I wait, watching for any sign that she's ready. Her fingers trail softly down my back, her touch light yet sure. She shifts beneath me, her body opening, a quiet, unspoken invitation.

Guiding myself to her entrance, I ease in slowly, savoring the tight warmth that envelops me. A low groan escapes me. "Look at how perfectly we fit," I murmur, pulling back slightly before thrusting deep within her.

I move in a slow, steady rhythm, our bodies merging. Her breath catches, and I press my lips to hers, filled with desperate need. Every inch of her is like home—the piece I've been missing

"I can feel your piercings," she breathes, her voice thick with pleasure.

"Do you like them, *tesoro*?" My hips move faster, pulling a moan from her.

Her nails dig into my back as our pace quickens. "Yes," she gasps.

"I want to take my time," I say, my voice strained. "But I don't think I can hold back much longer."

"Then don't," she whispers.

I let go, driving into her over and over, her body pulling me to the edge. "You were made for me."

"Antonio." My name falls from her lips like a prayer as she clutches my shoulders, her body coming apart beneath mine.

The sensation of her squeezing around me pushes me over the edge. I know I should pull out, but I can't bring myself to do it. I thrust one last time and surrender to my own release, groaning as my cock pulses, filling her with my cum.

I collapse onto her, my lips finding hers again, claiming her as I come down from the high. Gently, I pull out and settle by her side, wrapping her in my arms. Her body feels warm, soft, perfect against mine. But after a moment, she whispers, "You came inside me."

"I did," I admit. "But I'm clean. I haven't been with anyone in almost a year."

"I'm not on birth control," she says, her voice soft but unsure. "After Val died I didn't need it so I stopped taking it."

A slow smile spreads across my face. "Good," I say, brushing my thumb over her lips. "Maybe you'll end up pregnant with my child for real."

Alessia's breath catches, uncertainty washing over her face.

She blinks up at me. "A baby?" she whispers, almost as though she's thinking out loud.

"I want you to be mine in every way possible." The thought fills me—her carrying my child, bound to me forever. "But only if you're ready for it," I add, letting the words linger, hopeful, yet patient.

"I didn't expect this," she admits. "I didn't think you'd actually want a baby." Her eyes search mine as if trying to make sense of what I'm saying.

I hold her gaze, steady and sure, wanting her to see the truth in my eyes. There's no doubt, no hesitation. I know this might be overwhelming for her, and I hadn't allowed myself to imagine it before. But now that we're here—now that I'm here with her—it feels undeniable, like it's exactly where we're meant to be. A part of me wants this more than I ever expected, more than I thought possible. I brush my hand over her stomach, the idea settling into place.

"I didn't have a good example of what it means to be a mother. I'm not sure I'd be any good at it," she says softly, her hand resting on mine. The warmth of her touch stirs something deep inside me, something primal. "But the idea of being yours like that..." Her voice trails off, vulnerable, unsure.

"You have so much love to give." I tighten my grip on her hand. I want to tell her everything. How she's the only one who's ever mattered to me, how I've dreamed of a future where she's mine, but before I can speak, the sound of shattering glass echoes through the room. Tires screech outside as a car speeds away.

"What was that?" Alessia cries.

I push myself up, heart hammering in my chest. "I'm going to find out. Stay here," I say sharply, pulling my pants on in a rush. There's no time for hesitation. Grabbing my gun from the nightstand, I check the chamber to make sure it's loaded. "Lock the door and don't leave this room until I come back."

Her eyes are filled with fear, but there's no time to reassure her right now. I move quickly, making my way down the darkened hallway, every nerve in my body on high alert. The adrenaline surges through my veins as I descend the stairs.

When I reach the living room, my worst fear is confirmed. The front window is shattered, shards of glass scattered across the floor, and among the debris lies a brick with a piece of paper wrapped around it.

Unfolding the note, my blood runs cold as I read the words scrawled in jagged handwriting:

The walls are closing in, stone by stone, inch by inch. There will be no escape, Alessia. Your fate is sealed.

Draco.

He's getting bolder, no longer content to lurk in the shadows. I crush the note in my fist. He's playing with fire, awakening a monster he won't be able to control.

A soft creak behind me pulls me from my thoughts. I turn to find Alessia standing at the bottom of the stairs, worry etched on her face. She's wearing one of my T-shirts, the fabric hanging loosely around her.

"I told you to stay in the room," I say, my tone harsher than I intend. The hurt in her eyes softens my resolve. Reaching out, I pull her into my arms. "I'm sorry. I didn't mean to yell."

"I was scared something would happen to you."

Her arms wrap around me, her body warm against mine, calming my fears. But it doesn't last. I pull back, needing her to understand the gravity of the situation. "That's why you need to stay where I tell you. I can't do what I need to if I'm worrying about you."

She nods, but her eyes drift toward the shattered glass. "What does it say this time?"

"It's not important," I lie, keeping my voice steady despite the weight of the situation. My gaze drops to her feet, noticing the shards of glass scattered around her. "I don't want you getting cut."

Without another word, I lift her into my arms, cradling her close as I carry her back upstairs. "I want you to sleep in my bed tonight," I say, more firmly than before. "In our bed," I correct myself, my voice softening as I realize what I'm asking.

She rests her head against my shoulder, her trust in me clear despite her fear. "I'd like that, too," she whispers.

I settle her gently into the bed, watching as she curls into the blankets. Her eyes are wide, still full of worry, and I can feel the tension radiating off her.

"Antonio," she whispers. "I'm scared."

I slip out of my pants and ease in beside her, pulling her close. "I won't let anything happen to you," I murmur against her hair.

She presses closer, but her body remains tense. "Do you think we should have a security system installed? Maybe put some guards at the door?"

I pull back slightly to look at her. "Are you sure that's what you want?"

"I think so. I can't keep living like this, always waiting for something bad to happen."

A slow exhale escapes as my hand brushes through her hair. "If that's what you want, I'll do it. Anything to make you feel safe."

Her breathing slows as she processes my words, and the tension in her body starts to ease. "Thank you," she murmurs softly before drifting off to sleep in my arms. I hold her close, my mind still racing. As her breathing slows and evens out, I'm left wondering if I've been too complacent—too stubborn to protect her the way I should. I can't let my pride get in the way anymore.

Quietly, I slip out of bed and grab my phone, stepping into the hallway as I dial Dante's number. It rings several times before he finally picks up, his voice groggy and low.

"We've got a problem."

"What's wrong?"

"Draco sent another message. Through my front window."

"I'm on my way," he replies without hesitation.

"I want you to move forward with the security system. And I need men stationed at the door—tonight."

There's a brief pause before Dante speaks. "You're sure?"

"I am," I say firmly, glancing back at the bedroom where Alessia is finally resting. "It's what she needs."

"I'll handle it," Dante replies before hanging up.

Back in the bedroom, I stand at the edge of the bed, watching Alessia sleep peacefully, unaware of the true extent of the danger just beyond our walls. After a deep breath, I pull on my clothes.

"I'll be back soon," I whisper as I brush a soft kiss across her forehead. She stirs slightly, but her breathing remains steady.

With one last, lingering look, I slip out of the room. The emotions I'd buried, smothered under years of silence, have clawed their way back to life, fierce and unrelenting. Alessia has always been the one, the pulse in my darkened heart.

Now that she's mine, nothing in this world or the next will take her from me again.

Alessia

The soft light of morning filters through the curtains, casting a warm glow over the room. I stretch out, reaching for Antonio, but find nothing. His side of the bed is untouched, cool against my fingertips. Disappointment tugs at me, but I push it aside and slip out of bed. After last night, I'm sure he's already busy with work.

I'm still wearing his T-shirt. Knowing it was on his body yesterday is comforting—I may never give it back. The fabric brushes against my bare legs as I head downstairs. When I reach the kitchen, the sight surprises me. Dante's sitting at the table, a cup of coffee in his hand, his posture as composed as ever. His eyes dart away from me with practiced subtlety.

"Good morning," Antonio says, crossing the room. He presses a gentle kiss to my lips.

"I was looking for you," I say quietly.

"I'm sorry you had to wake up alone."

"Did you sleep at all?"

He shakes his head, dark shadows beneath his eyes betraying the sleepless night. "No. We're still dealing with the fallout from last night."

I glance at Dante, who keeps his gaze averted, focused on

making another cup of coffee. "What's going on?" I press, worry rising.

"There've been some unexpected complications, but nothing we can't handle." Antonio's thumb brushes my cheek, his touch a quiet reassurance. "You should go upstairs and get dressed. More of my men are on their way, and I wouldn't want to have to kill anyone for looking at you."

"Antonio." I give his arm a playful shove. "You wouldn't."

"Oh, I would, *tesoro*," he murmurs, his breath warm against my ear. "You're mine, and I don't share." The intensity in his voice sends a shiver down my spine—a mix of possessiveness and protectiveness that's both comforting and unnerving.

I meet his gaze, recognizing the seriousness despite his playful tone. "You're impossible," I say, though I can't hide the smile tugging at my lips.

ANTONIO GRINS, THE CARING MAN BENEATH THE ruthless Capo breaking through. "Go on, get dressed," he says, pressing a kiss to my forehead. "I'll have breakfast ready when you come back down."

"Thank you."

As soon as I leave the room, I hear Dante ask, "She's wearing your shirt?"

I pause, lingering in the hallway, listening.

"Things are changing between us," Antonio replies, his voice low but clear. "We're growing closer."

"Are you sure it's not just jealousy because Draco wants her back?" Dante questions.

"I'm falling in love with her," Antonio replies, without hesitation. "And it terrifies me."

My breath catches. He's falling in love with me?

Moving quietly up the stairs, my thoughts race. I sit on the edge of the guest bed, Antonio's words echoing in my mind. He's falling in love with me. It's something I never believed possible.

I've always kept people at arm's length, guarded with my heart. But these past few weeks with Antonio have been different. There's a bond between us that feels deeper than attraction, a connection that's raw, unguarded—real.

After everything he's put me through, could we really have a future together? Is a man like him even capable of love?

ANTONIO'S MEN HAVE BEEN IN AND OUT OF THE HOUSE all day—some faces familiar, others not. Unlike Valentino and my father, Antonio doesn't shoo me away while he gives orders. In fact, I think he prefers keeping me close. His men don't seem bothered by my presence either. Although they don't directly interact with me, each has been polite.

Still, I feel the tension in the air, and I can't ignore how tired Antonio looks. He hasn't slept, and it shows. The sharpness in his eyes is dull, the lines on his face more pronounced. I've seen him like this before—so focused on everything except himself. I know he's focused on protecting me, but I worry about him, too.

"Antonio, you need to rest," I say softly, standing beside him while he pours another cup of coffee.

He glances at me, a tired smile tugging at his lips. "I'll rest later, *tesoro*."

I know there's no point in arguing, so I let it go for now. As I turn to leave, he takes my hand. "How about you grab your camera, and we'll go for a walk?"

"That sounds perfect," I reply, hoping fresh air will help clear both our minds.

As we prepare to leave, I glance around at the room full of men. I never thought I'd feel comforted by the presence of so many armed guards, but with Antonio, it's different. Instead of feeling trapped or suffocated like I always did around my father and Valentino, I find myself wanting to help, to lighten the burden he's carrying. I don't want him to face this alone. For the first time, I don't want to run—I want to stand by his side. But I still have no idea how to shoulder any of this.

Outside, the warmth of the sun melts some of my tension. Antonio keeps a watchful eye as we walk, his hand tightly holding mine. I don't think my father is reckless enough to make a move in broad daylight, especially in such a populated area, but Antonio's protective instincts never waver.

"Can we stop by the gallery?" I ask after a while. "I want to let Ophelia know I'll have new photos soon."

Antonio raises an eyebrow, a hint of amusement in his gaze. "Sure," he says. "Wherever you want to go."

Snapping photos along the way, I capture moments of the bustling city. As we come upon Love Park, an idea hits me. "We don't have any pictures of us," I say, tugging him toward the iconic Love sign.

"I'm not much for pictures," he grumbles, trying to resist.

"Please." I bat my eyelashes playfully. "For me?"

He rolls his eyes but can't hide his smile. "Fine. But I'll take that," he says, snatching the camera from my hands.

"Give that back," I laugh, reaching for it.

"You're always behind the camera," Antonio teases, snapping several pictures. "I want some photos of my beautiful wife for my office."

"Really?" No one's ever wanted photos of me. My father didn't have any personal pictures in his office and there were no family portraits on our walls.

"Yes, really," he says, his voice low and sexy. He steps closer, pulling me into a kiss, capturing a few selfies with the camera. "Hopefully I didn't cut our heads off," he chuckles.

In moments like these, when it's just us, I almost forget the darkness that surrounds us. I cling to these peaceful moments, hoping they'll carry me through the inevitable trials ahead.

We reach the gallery, still laughing. "I'll wait out here," Antonio says.

"No way. I want to introduce you to Ophelia. Please," I say, giving him a playful pout. "It won't take long."

He hesitates, then smirks. "Alright, *tesoro*. Let's go."

"Allie, what a wonderful surprise," Ophelia greets us as we step into the gallery. She glances at my camera with a smile. "I hope this means you'll have more photos soon. I've had some many customers asking for them."

"It does," I reply, unable to keep the grin off my face. "I wanted to introduce you to my husband, Antonio."

Ophelia's expression shifts slightly, but she quickly composes herself. "It's a pleasure to meet you," she says, though I can sense her wariness.

Antonio nods politely. "Likewise."

Ophelia continues to eye him warily. I'm sure she recognizes him from his involvement in the mafia, but she doesn't say anything.

"Your wife has such talent," she continues smoothly. "I've been trying to convince her to have a gallery show. Maybe you can help me talk her into it?"

Antonio turns to me, his gaze steady. "Is this what you want, Alessia?"

A smile tugs at my lips as I nod. "I'd love it."

Without hesitation, he replies, "Then it's yours, *tesoro*. Whatever makes you happy."

His words fill me with a sense of joy I didn't expect.

Ophelia claps her hands, her excitement contagious. "Wonderful! How soon would you like to get started?"

"I'm not sure," I admit, glancing at Antonio.

"This is all you," he says, gracing me with a sexy smile that makes my insides melt.

"Can we discuss it, and I'll call you?" I ask.

"That works," she replies, her eyes sparkling. "It's going to be perfect."

As we leave the gallery, I turn to Antonio, still stunned. "You really think I should do this?"

He looks down at me, his eyes sincere. "Absolutely. I've always known how talented you are, Alessia. It's time the whole world knows."

His words fill me with warmth, but something in his expression shifts. "What's wrong?" I ask, suddenly uneasy. "Is it my father?"

"No, nothing like that," he says, leading me to a quieter spot in the park. "There's something I need to tell you."

"You're making me nervous."

He takes a deep breath. "I've been buying your photos for the past few years," he admits. "At first, I didn't know they were yours. But when I found out, it only made me love them more."

I stare at him, unsure how to feel. "Why?" I ask after a moment.

"At first, I was drawn to them because they captured something raw and real, something I rarely see. Something about them spoke to me," he says, his voice low, thoughtful. "When I found out they were yours, it deepened the connection. Knowing they were a part of you, the only part I could have. It made me love them even more."

I swallow hard, his words settling deep inside me, leaving me unsure of what to say. "What did you do with them?"

"They're still in my apartment," he admits, a slight smirk tugging at his lips. "I hadn't exactly planned on moving, but, then I went to Alabama to get you and things changed rather quickly."

A sense of curiosity blooms inside me. I want to see this part of him—his world before everything changed. The place where he kept pieces of me. "Will you take me there?"

Antonio's eyes darken slightly. "Of course, *tesoro*." He pulls me close, his lips brushing my temple. "I'd love to show you."

We walk in silence through downtown toward South 9th Street. I've been to the restaurant countless times and knew Antonio lived above it, but I've never been inside his apartment. My mind races with questions—what will it reveal about him? Will it feel like the person I know, or something entirely different? As we step through the door, I'm caught off guard by how personal the space feels.

The sophistication of the apartment surprises me. It's open, bathed in natural light that reflects off the rich, dark wood floors, creating a striking contrast with the soft, neutral tones of the walls. The sleek, modern furniture exudes masculine elegance, yet the plush pillows and cozy area rugs add a warmth that makes it feel like a home. Everything is in its place, neat and orderly, but lived in.

"I'm surprised," I admit, glancing around. "It's nothing like I pictured."

Antonio chuckles, his eyes softening. "I have to give all the credit to Cecilia. She refused to let me live in a place that looked like a college dorm room." He laughs, a rare sound, filled with warmth as he speaks of his sister. "When she puts her mind to something, she's unstoppable. Kind of like someone else I know," he adds with a smirk.

He leads me to the end of a hallway, his hand resting on the doorknob. There's a momentary pause as he looks back at me with a small smile before opening the door and stepping inside. This room is starkly different from the rest of the apartment—minimalist and bare. A simple dresser, a small bedside table, and a bed. The walls are a deep, somber gray.

Antonio moves to the closet, reaching up to pull down a box from the top shelf. It's labeled *Alessia's Photography* in thick, black marker. He sets it down on the bed and opens it, revealing neatly stacked photos. My breath catches as I lean in to look. These are the images I've taken over the years, but now, seeing them here, they feel different—more personal.

"This is more than just a collection," I whisper, running my fingers over the edges of the photos. "It's like you've kept a part of me with you all this time."

He steps behind me, wrapping his arms around my waist, his breath warm against my neck. "Even before I knew they were yours, I felt a connection to these photos," he murmurs. "One I couldn't ignore."

This isn't simply about the photos—it's about the connection that kept us tethered even when we were forced to be apart.

"Back in high school, when you stopped speaking to me, I thought you got bored," I say, my throat tightening with emotion. "I assumed you were like all the other men in this world."

Antonio's expression deepens, his gaze never leaving mine. "It was never like that. Things were complicated, beyond either of our control. As much as it killed me, I had no choice but to stay away." He brushes a strand of hair behind my ear, his touch tender. "But I could never be bored with you. You're all I ever wanted."

"Show me," I whisper, my voice trembling with anticipation.

He captures my lips in a searing kiss, pulling me closer as everything else fades away. His hands move over my body, each touch igniting something deep inside me. I cling to him, feeling the urgency in his movements, the raw desire between us impossible to deny.

My hands slide down his chest, savoring the hard planes of muscle beneath my fingers. As I reach the waistband of his pants, I slowly sink to my knees, looking up at him as I undo them.

"Alessia," he breathes, his voice thick with need.

"I've never done this before," I confess. "But I want to try."

Desire flares in his eyes, dark and intense. "I should be the one worshipping you," he growls, his voice low and strained. "But fuck, I want to see your pretty lips wrapped around me."

Tentatively, I take him in my hand, stroking gently before pressing my lips to the velvety tip of his cock. The way his breath hitches sends a thrill through me.

"You look so fucking beautiful with my cock in your mouth," Antonio rasps, his voice thick with arousal.

Antonio's reaction is immediate, a deep groan escaping him as his fingers thread through my hair, guiding me with a gentle pressure as I take more of him into my mouth. Tears spill from my eyes.

He pulls back quickly. "Shit, I'm sorry. I should never have—"

My hands snake around his ass pulling him toward me as I swallow his length again. This time controlling my breathing as I work his length in and out of my mouth. The salty taste of his arousal intensifies my desire. His sharp intake of breath each time I explore a little further reassures me that that I'm doing the right thing. Knowing I'm the one bringing him pleasure is a powerful feeling.

His whispered encouragements, laced with deep, husky notes, become my guide. I'm attuned to every shift, every shudder. As my confidence grows, I cup his balls while I take him deeper sucking before I slowly release him letting my tongue swirl around his piercings.

"Fuck Alessia, I can't help it," he rasps as he threads his fingers through my hair wrapping it around his hand.

Looking up, I nod given him permission. His hips begin to buck as I squeeze his sac with my palm before releasing it and allowing my fingers to explore the space between his balls and ass.

"Not going to last," he grits through clenched teeth. He tries to pull away, but I shake my head and continue to suck him deep working my lips and tongue over ever hard inch.

I pull back slightly, teasing him with my tongue before taking him deeper, my hands exploring every part of him. His breathing grows ragged, his control slipping.

His eyes, dark with arousal, never leave mine, holding a silent conversation and deepening our connection.

Antonio's grip on my hair tightens. "Alessia," he breathes my name on an exhale, followed by a low, guttural moan as he spills into my mouth. "I don't deserve you, *tesoro*," he says, his voice filled with awe.

"That was incredible," he says, a smirk playing on his lips. "But now it's my turn."

Before I can respond, he guides me over him. His hands grip my hips as he urges me to straddle his face. "I want to taste you," he says, his voice thick with desire.

"Antonio, I—"

His hands grip my hips, guiding me up until I'm straddling him, my core hovering just above his mouth. With his arms hooked under my thighs, he holds me firmly in place, his tongue plunging into me, making my body jolt with surprise.

"Oh my god," I murmur.

His mouth clamps around my clit sucking it into his mouth causing my head to fall back on an exhale.

Antonio continues teasing me, licking and probing, devouring me with kisses. His hands roam over my body. One follows the curve of my hip while the other works its way to my breast.

I arch my back, pressing myself against his tongue, biting my lip to stifle my whimpers.

He stops momentarily. "Don't hold back, *tesoro*. I want to

hear every fucking sound." His voice holds an edge of dominance which only adds fuel to the fire burning inside me.

"Please don't stop," I beg.

The words are barely out of my mouth when he thrusts his tongue inside me, drawing a scream from my lips. His thumb finds my clit rubbing it in small circles.

His touch drives me to the edge, and when I finally come, a cry escapes. The release is overwhelming, but Antonio's arms are around me, steadying me as I collapse against him.

The warmth of his embrace cocoons me, allowing the tears to flow freely. They're tears of release, of fear and pent-up feelings that had no outlet until now, mingling with the profound relief that comes from being cared for so deeply.

As I settle against him, my breathing slows into a steady, peaceful rhythm. Antonio's hand strokes my back, each touch gentle and reassuring.

In this quiet space, a profound connection deepens between us, binding us in ways that feel more powerful than I'd ever thought possible. It's a union not only of bodies but of hearts, of souls.

I lift my head and brush my lips softly against his. With careful, tender movements, he rolls me onto my back and positions himself over me. Slowly, he slides inside me, making love to me with unhurried, intimate strokes.

He moves with a deliberateness that tells me he's as consumed by this moment as I am. Antonio's eyes never leave mine, conveying love and a fierce protectiveness that makes my heart swell. Beneath him, I feel worshipped and adored

When we finally climax, each pulse feels like an unspoken vow, our bodies speaking truths our voices never could.

We lie entwined, lost in the quiet aftermath. In this moment, I feel the depth of our bond. It's not just physical it's a connection rooted in something far deeper, something neither of us can deny.

Antonio

Alessia lies beside me, her leg draped over mine as her fingers trace lazy patterns across my chest. Her touch is soft, almost hesitant, as if she's still testing the waters after everything we've shared. I tighten my arm around her, pulling her closer, savoring the warmth of her bare skin against mine.

She shifts slightly, breaking the comfortable silence. "What are you planning to do with all those pictures?"

I can't help but smile, already anticipating her reaction. "I'm thinking about remodeling the restaurant. Using your photos as the inspiration for the new design."

She props herself up on her elbow, eyes widening. "Are you serious?"

"Completely," I reply, her excitement contagious. "The place needs an update, and your work deserves to be seen."

Her gaze softens, disbelief flickering in her eyes. "And the gallery show?" she asks, voice quieter now. "You're really okay with me having it? Even with everything going on?"

I know no one's ever supported her dreams before, not like this. I brush a strand of hair away from her face, letting my thumb graze her cheek. "I'm more than okay with it, *tesoro*. It's time the world sees how talented you are."

The way she looks at me makes my chest tighten. It's not just appreciation—it's deeper than that. And it terrifies me.

Before I can say more, her phone buzzes on the nightstand, shattering the moment. Her body tenses as her hand reaches for it.

The color drains from her face as she reads the message. "He knows where we are," she whispers. "We're being watched."

She passes me her phone, and I read the message.

The pendulum swings, inching closer with each breath you take. No matter where you go, Alessia, you remain under its relentless gaze.

The number from the message is already disconnected when I dial—not that I'm surprised.

"Get dressed," I say, trying to keep my voice steady for her sake. "We can't stay here."

Her hands shake as she reaches for her clothes. I hate that she's seeing just how bad things have gotten, but there's no way to keep her in the dark anymore.

The sun's beginning to set, casting long shadows across the room. Walking home now isn't an option. I grab my phone and call Dante.

"We're at the restaurant. I need you to bring the car."

"No problem," he replies.

I glance at Alessia as she finishes getting dressed. Lowering my voice, I add, "A text message came through to her phone. We're being followed."

There's a brief pause. "How long ago?"

"Just now."

Another silence follows. I can almost hear Dante calculating the situation. "I'll be there in ten. I'm bringing extra men. We'll sweep the area before you move."

"Thanks. See you soon." I hang up and turn to Alessia,

catching her gaze. I try to keep my tone calm. "Dante's on his way. We'll be home soon."

She walks over and wraps her arms around my waist, resting her head on my chest. "Why is he doing this?"

I hold her tighter, the tension in her body feeding the storm building inside me. I've been more patient than I should have. I've been more patient than I should've been. I gave Draco a warning —told him to stay away from her.

I never wanted this to escalate, never aimed to start a war, but he ignored my warning. Now, Draco Moretti is about to learn the cost of pushing me too far.

"I don't know," I say, running my fingers through her hair. "Let's head downstairs. We can have the chef prepare something for dinner, and we'll take it home."

We slip downstairs to the back of the restaurant and find Enzo going over the books. He looks up as we approach.

"I didn't expect to see you two here this evening," he says, raising an eyebrow.

"It was an impromptu visit," I reply, taking a seat and motioning for Alessia to sit beside me.

"Mrs. Luciano," Enzo greets with a smooth tone, but his sharp eyes look between us. "Always a pleasure."

Alessia nods slightly. "Thank you."

"I'm glad you're here. We received another message."

Before he can respond, Dante walks in. "We've got a problem," he says but stops short when he notices Alessia.

"What is it?" I ask, my pulse quickening.

"There was a 911 call from the Moretti estate," he continues, his tone clipped. "There was a situation."

"What kind of situation?"

He looks to Alessia and then back to me. "Mrs. Moretti was found dead."

Alessia's hand grips mine tightly, her breath catching. "What?" she whispers.

"It's an apparent suicide," Dante adds, his eyes narrowing.

"Like hell it is," I snap, struggling to keep my temper in check. "This has Draco written all over it."

"According to the police, Moretti wasn't there," Dante continues. "He's supposedly out of the country on business."

"How's that possible? We've had eyes on the house the whole time."

Dante's gaze shifts to Alessia. "I was hoping she could help us answer that."

My senses go on high alert. "What are you implying?"

"Just that she grew up there," Dante says, his voice measured. "Do you know if there are any secret exits or places where your father could slip away unnoticed?"

"I don't... I... Um..." Alessia stumbles over her words.

Gently, I tilt her chin up. "*Tesoro*, look at me. I know this is hard, but we need your help. Were there any rooms your father kept locked? Any places you weren't allowed to go?"

"There was one time, when I was a little girl and my parents were fighting," she says blinking back tears. "I was trying to find some place to hide. Someplace I thought my father wouldn't find me. I found a door that led to a cellar. I wasn't able to hide for long. He found me," she recounts, with horror reflected in her eyes. "He forbade me from ever going down there again. Then, he took his belt to me to make sure I didn't forget."

Dante and I exchange a quick glance. "A cellar could have a hidden way out."

I turn back to Alessia, my voice soft. "You did good, *tesoro*."

She nods, though her lips tremble slightly.

Enzo clears his throat, his expression unusually tense. "This is getting out of control. Nicoletta and Cecilia need to be sent to Italy—it's the safest option." His gaze shifts to Alessia. "She should go with them."

Before I can respond, Alessia straightens beside me. "No," she says firmly. "I'm not leaving. I refuse to run."

Enzo raises an eyebrow in disapproval. I'm sure he thinks I should force her to go. And maybe I should. But I can't.

"Alessia stays with me. But my mother and sister will go. The fewer people I have to worry about, the better."

Enzo sighs. "Fine. But don't say I didn't warn you."

Without a word, I draw Alessia closer. Right now, she's all that matters, and there's nothing, and no one, that will take her from me.

Alessia

The grief over losing my mother has taken me by surprise. It's not that we were close. She spent most of her life drowning herself in alcohol, trying to stay numb against my father's infidelity. But she was still my mother. And now that she's gone, there's an emptiness—not for what we had, but for what could've been.

Without a doubt, I know my father killed her. That's the hardest part—living with the certainty that he saw her as nothing more than a liability, a loose end. The man who gave me life is the same man who took hers. It leaves me wondering what kind of poison might be running through my blood.

I'd like to believe his sudden disappearance means he's done with this twisted game. That maybe whoever I was promised to accepts I'm married to Antonio and no longer wants me. That my father's done haunting me. But I know better. I'd be a fool to believe that.

I'm a *loose end* now, and my father doesn't leave loose ends. He killed my mother, and I know I'm next.

Antonio sent Nicki and Cecilia to Italy a little over two weeks ago. They weren't thrilled about leaving, but they didn't argue either. They're as used to this life as I am, but in a much different way. They've always known the love of their family, so instead of putting up a fight, they accepted it with a quiet understanding.

Cecilia begged me to go with her. Although she doesn't know the full extent of the threats, she knows that they somehow involve a danger to me. When a tear slipped down her cheek, I nearly cracked. But when I looked at Antonio, I knew I couldn't leave.

Still, a part of me wonders if I should've gone. Maybe disappearing across the ocean, far from my father's eyes, would've been the smart choice. But another part of me refuses to give him that satisfaction. He hasn't left. He's watching, lurking in the shadows —I can feel him. Running would only prove what he's always believed—that I'm weak, afraid.

That might've been true once. But not now.

Not anymore.

Alessia

My gallery show is tonight. It feels surreal, like a dream I never fully allowed myself to believe was possible and it's coming true right in front of me.

I stare at the black dress draped over the edge of the bed. It's stunning—long, elegant, with just a hint of sparkle that catches the light. Antonio's taste is impeccable, as always. He told me he wanted me to feel special tonight, and this dress is everything I never knew I needed.

I'm about to slip into the dress when there's a knock at the door. Antonio steps inside, his eyes sweeping over me before revealing a small, delicate box in his hand.

"What's that?" I ask, smiling at the sight of him in his tuxedo.

"I wanted to give you something before we head out," he says, crossing the room to stand in front of me. "Close your eyes."

I do as he asks, the anticipation making my chest flutter. There's the soft click of a box opening, followed by the cool metal of a necklace being fastened around my neck.

"You can open them now."

"Antonio," I whisper. Dangling from a delicate gold chain is a small camera with a diamond embedded in the lens. "It's beautiful."

He gently tucks a strand of hair behind my ear, his touch lingering. "Not as beautiful as you, *tesoro*."

He stands behind me, pressing a gentle kiss to my bare shoulder, his lips leaving a trail of soft, lingering touches down my skin. His hands glide along my sides, tracing the curve of my hips and sending a shiver of anticipation through me.

My breath catches, every nerve igniting under his touch. He's learned my body so well, discovering each sensitive spot, knowing just where to touch to make me crave more.

His fingers dip lower, exploring the wetness between my thighs. "You're so responsive," he murmurs, his lips ghosting my neck, sending a shiver through me. "I love the way your body reacts to me."

A soft mewl escapes my lips. He chuckles, his breath warm against my skin. I glance up at the mirror and catch his heated gaze. Our eyes lock as he slides a finger deep inside me.

My head falls back as he slides in a second finger, his thumb finding my clit and rubbing slow circles until I'm breathless. Just as I'm about to fall over the edge, he pulls away, and I can't help but groan at the loss.

He turns me to face him, capturing my mouth in a heated kiss. We devour each other, his hands exploring every inch of my body. Pulling down the cups of my bra, he lets my breasts spill free, his fingers twisting and tugging at my nipples. I arch into his touch, a soft moan slipping from my lips. "Bend over the bed," he says, his voice rough and commanding.

I shift into position as he drags my panties down my legs. The sound of his zipper fills the air, and I part my legs, inviting him in. He teases me, sliding the tip of his cock through my slick folds before pressing deep inside me from behind.

His movements are agonizingly slow. "Please, Antonio," I beg.

"What do you need, *tesoro*?" His voice is dark, teasing.

"More," I gasp.

With those words, he thrusts deep, and every thought fades away. There's only sensation—Antonio moving inside me, pushing me higher until a wave of pure ecstasy crashes over me. My body trembles beneath him as he grips my hips, pulling me closer while he chases his own release.

"I want everyone in that room tonight to know you're mine," he whispers against my skin, placing kisses along my spine.

His possessiveness stirs something deep inside me. Something more powerful than the pleasure we've just shared.

"Yes, Antonio," I breathe. "I am yours."

He holds my hips tightly, our bodies still connected. I think he's going to say more, instead he slowly pulls out. I move to stand, but Antonio presses a hand to my lower back "Stay here."

He disappears into the bathroom, and I hear the water running. A moment later, he returns with a warm washcloth, gently cleaning between my legs before helping me to my feet.

"You should get dressed before I change my mind, and we miss your show," he says, a playful glint in his eyes.

THE CRISP EVENING AIR WRAPS AROUND US AS ANTONIO and I step out of the car in front of the gallery. There's already a line that stretches around the block. My stomach flutters with a mix of nerves and excitement at seeing the crowd waiting to enter.

Antonio walks around the car to open my door, offering me his hand as I step onto the smooth pavement. His sharp gaze sweeps over the crowd with a subtle intensity. "I would've preferred a more visible security presence," he says, standing close.

Dante discreetly positioned several men in suits who blend seamlessly with the attendees. I'm able to pick them out easily. Their sharp, watchful eyes tell me they're here for our protection.

I lean in, keeping my voice low. "I don't want my father overshadowing tonight. This is our moment."

Despite his concern, his expression softens, and he kisses my temple. "Are you ready to wow your fans?"

"Let's do this," I respond, a smile breaking through my nerves.

As we walk toward the gallery entrance, his hand rests at the small of my back, guiding me with steady reassurance. The murmurs of the crowd grow louder as we approach, and I take a moment to absorb it all before we step inside.

Ophelia greets us at the door, her face alight with excitement. "Alessia, you look stunning!" she gushes, stepping aside to let us in. "The crowd outside is buzzing. They've been waiting for hours."

We enter the gallery, which hasn't yet opened to the public. The pristine white walls are adorned with my framed photographs, each one carefully lit to highlight its details. The space is serene, the calm before the inevitable storm of guests.

Antonio looks around, his face lighting up with genuine admiration. "*Tesoro,* it looks even more incredible than I imagined." He pulls out his phone and snaps a few photos of the displays. "I'll send these to my mom and Cecilia."

"I wish they could be here."

"They'll be here for the next one," he assures me.

As we walk through the gallery, Ophelia explains where she placed each series, her enthusiasm palpable. "Your Magnolia Springs series is right at the entrance to draw people in," she says, pointing to the large prints of tree-lined streets and the peaceful Magnolia River. "And over there are your urban shots of Philadelphia. The contrast between the city and nature is breathtaking."

"Thank you for everything," I say, my heart full of gratitude.

Ophelia beams, clearly pleased with our reactions. "There are only a few minutes until we open. I'll leave you two alone."

The tranquility of the gallery is soothing, a calm before the storm of guests. I bask in the momentary peace as we reach the final display—a series of black and white portraits that are particularly close to my heart. I pause, taking in the expressions of the faces I'd captured, each one unique, yet universally human.

As we finish our walk around, Antonio takes one last photo, a selfie of him and I, before he puts away his phone, takes my hand, and smiles. "Let's go make some memories."

Ophelia swings the doors wide open as she extends her arms, her voice ringing out warmly. "Welcome, everyone, to Alessia Luciano's showcase."

The crowd begins to flow in, their eyes bright with curiosity and appreciation. The energy shifts as people move through the space, pausing to admire each photograph, discussing the depth and beauty of the images.

I stand slightly to the side with Antonio, observing the initial reactions. It's a surreal feeling watching strangers connect with the moments I've captured. Each person is drawn to different elements of the imagery. Some pause longer at the urban landscapes, discussing the vivid contrasts and textures, while others are captivated by the emotional depth of the black and white portraits.

Antonio squeezes my hand, a silent gesture of support and shared joy. We make our way deeper into the crowd, ready to engage with our guests. As I meet the eyes of several attendees, their faces light up with recognition and they offer their congratulations.

A woman approaches me with a bright smile. "Your work is incredible. This piece," she gestures to a shot of a vintage boat on the lake, "it's so evocative. It feels like I'm right there."

"Thank you," I say, my heart swelling with pride. "I'm glad it resonates with you."

As the night progresses, the gallery buzzes with excitement. The air is filled with the scent of champagne and the sound of murmured appreciation. I continue to make my way through the crowd. My heart swells with each compliment

Tonight is beyond anything I'd ever dared to dream.

In the midst of the evening, Ophelia approaches me with an

apologetic smile. "I hate to interrupt, but I need to steal you away for a moment. One of your pieces sold before the doors even opened. The buyer specifically requested your signature. I meant to tell you earlier but it slipped my mind."

"Of course," I say.

She smiles gratefully. "I left it on my workbench in the back."

Turning to the group of guests I've been speaking with I offer a warm smile. "Please excuse me for a moment." My heels click softly against the floor as I head toward the back room.

Once inside, I glance around, expecting to see the piece laid out for me, but the workbench is empty. Confused, I search the room, check the shelves, and bend down to sift through the framed pictures stacked beneath the table.

While I'm still crouched, a soft rustling sound catches my attention from the corner of the room. Assuming it's Ophelia, I straighten up and call out, "I'm glad you came back. I can't seem to find the picture anywhere." I stand and look toward the sound, waiting for her to answer.

But before I can process anything else, a sharp sting pierces my neck. My hand flies up instinctively, but it's too late. Dizziness washes over me, and the room tilts violently. Panic surges through me as I try to scream, but my voice won't come. My legs buckle beneath me. The last thing I feel are strong arms catching me as everything fades into darkness.

Antonio

The evening hums with the soft buzz of conversation and laughter, punctuated occasionally by the clinking of glasses. I stand amid a small group of new fans of Alessia's work, but my attention's divided. My gaze often drifting across the room, searching for her in the crowd. She moves among the guests with a quiet grace that makes her appear as if she's floating. The pride swelling in my chest is almost unbearable. This is her night—her dream come to life.

"I'd love for your wife to do a commissioned piece," one of the men says. "Would she be willing to do that?"

"You'll have to ask her," I reply with a smile, scanning the room again. "Though, I seem to have lost track of her." Concern nudges at the edges of my thoughts. "Excuse me," I say, stepping away from the group.

"When you find her, send her my way," he calls after me, but I barely hear him as I push through the crowd, eyes scanning for Alessia.

I move from one cluster of guests to the next, searching every corner of the gallery, but there's no sign of her. Reaching Ophelia, I try to keep my voice level. "Have you seen Alessia recently?"

"She went to the back to sign a piece for a collector," Ophelia says, her tone light. "It shouldn't take long."

"Thank you. I'll go check on her."

"Before you do, could you help me with this frame?" she asks, motioning toward a crooked display.

I pause, torn. I glance at the back room and then to the frame. Reluctantly, I make a quick adjustment, then another, and another until Ophelia's finally satisfied. But as I'm about to step away again, she asks, "Could I trouble you with one more thing? The light on the—"

"I need to check on Alessia first," I cut in, unable to shake the feeling that something's wrong. Without waiting for her reply, I hurry to the back room.

"Alessia?" I call out, pushing the door open, but silence greets me. I step further inside and notice the door to the alley slightly ajar. A cool breeze slips through the crack, sending a chill through me. I move swiftly, my steps almost noiseless as I approach the door.

That's when I see it—a knife pinning a note with an unmistakably ominous message to the workbench.

Like the rarest of vintages, Alessia's been locked away.
Hidden deep where no one can find, in shadows cold and gray.

Panic tightens its grip as I whip out my phone to call Dante. Knowing every second counts, I curse myself for letting her out of my sight, even for a moment.

"How's the show?" he answers, his tone casual.

"Alessia's gone," I growl, my voice tight with fury. "He took her."

"Dammit," Dante snaps. "How long ago?"

"Maybe twenty minutes. I need every available man on this. Now."

"I'm already on it," he replies, his voice turning hard and businesslike. "I just sent a message to our men. I'm on my way."

"There's another one of those damn notes," I clench my jaw, fury rising. "He's taunting me."

"Don't touch the paper. Eric's on his way," Dante instructs. "He'll have our tech team enhance it. Hopefully they can pull some fingerprints. Anything that'll give us a lead." Dante's voice crackles through the phone. "We'll find her, Antonio."

My hands are trembling as I shove the phone into my pocket, trying not to let the panic spiral. How the hell did I let this happen? I should've been watching her, should've been more vigilant. Dammit. Why didn't I see this coming. How could I have been so blind, so careless?

Instead, I was too busy soaking up the pride of her success, letting myself feel some small sense of victory in her happiness, like an arrogant fool.

I promised to protect her. Now she's gone. He took her and I'm standing here like an idiot, scrambling to play catch-up as every precious second slips through my fingers.

A surge of anger rises, hot and fierce. I want to lash out, to destroy something, anything but I know that won't help Alessia. It won't bring her back any faster. Right now, I need to remain focused and channel my anger into finding her.

Racing back to the gallery, I pull aside the men Dante stationed at the party. My voice is a low hiss as I explain, "Alessia's been taken. Keep your eyes open and cover the exits while I clear the gallery."

Understanding the gravity of the situation, they immediately disperse through the crowd and get into position. I take a deep breath, steeling myself for what comes next. Stepping to the front of the gallery, I address the guests, my voice cutting through the noise.

"Ladies and gentlemen," I say, and the room falls silent, confused faces turning toward me. "Unfortunately, we need to end tonight's event early due to a building emergency. Please exit the gallery calmly and quickly. Thank you for your understanding and cooperation."

The crowd stirs, muttering in confusion, but they begin to file out. As the room empties, I try calling Draco, ready to demand Alessia's return. The call doesn't go through—his number's been disconnected. I try Alessia's phone next, but it goes straight to voicemail.

"Dammit."

"Boss," Luis calls. I spin around to find him gripping Ophelia by the arm. "We caught her trying to leave with the guests," he says, his tone grim.

My blood turns cold. "Why were you running?" I demand, my voice sharp. "What do you know about my wife's disappearance?"

Her face crumbles, her voice trembling with fear. "Alessia's brother came by the gallery earlier this week. He told me you were holding her against her will and that he was desperate to save her."

"He offered me a substantial amount of money to help him," she cries. "My gallery's on the brink of bankruptcy. I thought I was helping her."

I step closer, my fists clenched. "Alessia doesn't have a brother."

Tears well in her eyes as she stammers, "I swear, I thought I was helping her."

My patience snaps. "Because of you, Alessia's in real danger. Do you even realize what you've done?"

Ophelia sobs, pleading for forgiveness. "I didn't know— please, I didn't know."

"Take her to the holding room beneath the restaurant," I order, my voice icy. "I'll deal with her later."

As they drag her away, her frantic pleas echo through the now-empty gallery. "Please, Antonio. Don't kill me. I didn't know. I swear."

"Wait," I command, striding across the room with purpose. I stop inches from her face, my eyes cold, my voice low and venomous. "You better pray I find Alessia unharmed. Because if I don't, you'll be begging me for death."

The weight of my fury is suffocating. I close my eyes, forcing myself to breathe.

"I'm coming for you, *tesoro*," I whisper into the silent room, praying to whoever will listen—just let me get to her in time.

Alessia

I struggle to blink open my eyes, my mind grappling with the haze of disorientation. My mouth is painfully dry, each swallow feels like sandpaper is dragging down my throat. The room around me is shrouded in darkness, unfamiliar and foreboding. I'm lying on a single dirty mattress, the only thing between me and the cold, hard floor.

Panic begins to seep into my bones. I'm no longer in the black gown I wore to the gallery. Instead, I'm dressed in an oversized man's button-down shirt, the rough fabric scraping against my skin. My heart slams in my chest. Who undressed me? How did I get here?

Desperation claws at my throat as I stumble to the door, pounding it with both fists.

"Hello?" My voice cracks, echoing in the small space. "Can anyone hear me? My husband will come for me. If you want to live, you'll open this door."

I scream for what feels like hours, but in reality, is probably mere minutes. My voice is ragged and I'm exhausted and trembling. Defeated, I drag myself to the opposite corner of the room, and slide down the wall, drawing my knees tightly to my chest.

My breaths come fast and shallow. The room feels like it's shrinking, pressing in on me from all sides.

The metallic click of the lock shatters the silence, and my heart leaps to my throat. The door creaks open, revealing the silhouette of a man, his form shadowed but unmistakable.

It's my father.

His face is twisted in fury, eyes gleaming with contempt.

"Papa," I whisper. "What's going on?"

"Don't play dumb, Alessia," he replies, his voice too calm, too steady. "I told you I had plans for you."

"I'm not a commodity to be traded or used," I manage, my voice gaining strength.

"You ungrateful bitch," he snaps, venom lacing his words. "You've ruined everything."

"Just let me go and I'll tell Antonio I don't know who took me," I beg, trying to bargain with him. "You can disappear, and we can pretend this never happened."

He throws his head back, laughing, the chilling sound echoes in the small room. "Do you think I'm stupid enough to fall for that?"

"I'm not asking you to trust me. I'm asking you to save yourself. If Antonio finds me here, he'll kill you."

His voice drops, icy and sharp. "Luciano doesn't give a damn about you. You're just a warm body for him to stick his dick in."

Each demeaning word feels like a lash, stripping away at my composure, leaving me raw.

He paces in front of me, gesturing wildly. "I have plans for you, little girl. A promise I need to fulfill." His movements are erratic, each step punctuated with bitterness.

"I thought I made it clear that I'm married," I say forcing my voice to remain steady.

He stops, turning to face me with a twisted grin. "I've already taken care of your marriage."

"What did you do?" I whisper as fear tightens its grip on me.

"I haven't hurt your precious Antonio—yet," he laughs, the sound sharp and cruel. "But I did make your marriage license disappear. Congratulations, you're a single woman again."

He stops pacing, reaching into his pocket before tossing something toward me. It flutters across the floor.

"This," he sneers, "will take some effort to erase."

I scramble to pick up the paper. When I turn it over, I gasp. An ultrasound picture. My hands tremble violently as the reality crashes over me. I'm pregnant.

Before I can even process the shock, my father grabs a fistful of my hair, yanking my head back. Pain shoots through my scalp.

"You're a whore, just like your mother," he spits, disgust twisting his features. "So desperate to keep a man that you let yourself get knocked up."

His fist connects with my face, the impact sending a searing jolt of pain through my cheek. I scream, clutching my cheek. "What are you doing?" I sob.

"Your future husband doesn't want you carrying that bastard's spawn," he growls, striking me again. "But don't worry, Daddy will make this little mistake go away."

"No, Papa, please," I cry, curling into a ball, desperately trying to protect my stomach, to shield the tiny life inside me. "Please, stop."

His kicks come relentless, each one an explosion of agony. My ribs, my back, my head—his blows rain down, leaving me gasping for breath. The room spins. My vision swimming as my body crumples under his assault.

I try to scream, but the sound is trapped in my throat. His foot connects with my head, sending a burst of white-hot pain blinding me. Over and over, fists and feet tear into my body until everything fades to a dull roar of agony, and I begin to lose the battle to stay conscious.

With the darkness closing in, the only thing I can hold on to is the fragile life inside me and the desperate hope that this isn't the end.

Antonio

I'm going to burn this fucking city to the ground. Draco has her—I know he does. There won't be a damn stone left standing by the time I'm done. My men are scattered across the city, searching every dark corner and crevice.

But it's quiet. Too quiet. No trace of Draco or Alessia. It's like they've disappeared.

The sun's beginning to peak over the horizon, dragging another day with it, and still nothing. Each hour that slips by feels like a countdown to losing her forever. I have to force myself not to think about what he's doing to her—what condition she'll be in when I find her. Because I will find her.

Dante walks beside me as we step into the restaurant. Inside, she's waiting—Ophelia, the one responsible for Alessia's disappearance. I've questioned her already, but there's something she's holding back. I'll get the truth out of her if it's the last thing I do.

"Tell me again," I demand, my voice like stone.

Her hands tremble, and her face turns pale. "I—I've told you everything," she stammers.

"I'll decide when you've told me everything. Now, talk," I roar.

She glances at Dante, looking for some kind of reprieve, but finds none. "A man came to the gallery last week," she says, her voice gaining strength. "He said he saw signs for Allie's—I mean, Alessia's—show. He told me he was her brother. Said you were holding her against her will. I thought—"

I cut her off with a sharp laugh. "You thought you were saving her? Because you know who I am. You automatically assumed I was some monster she needed rescuing from? You didn't even bother to ask Alessia if she needed help." I lean in closer, my voice turning to a growl. "You handed her over to a man you didn't even know—like you were doing her a favor. What kind of fucking idiot are you?"

She flinches, wringing her hands. "He was so convincing. He told me she ran to Alabama to get away from you, but you hunted her down and dragged her back." She swallows hard. "He... he showed me pictures. Of her bruises. Said it was you. I didn't know—"

"Bullshit." My fist slams onto the table, and she jumps. "You didn't know because you didn't ask. You let some stranger walk in and take Alessia without even confirming who the hell he was."

"I thought—"

"I don't give a fuck what you thought," I snarl, my rage boiling over. "You handed her over to him like she meant nothing. Now, she's in the hands of a monster who wants her dead."

Her face goes ashen. "I swear, I didn't know. I thought I was helping."

"I'm done listening to this same bullshit story," I snap, my patience unraveling. "You thought you were helping? You thought wrong."

Her breath hitches, and I see the fear in her eyes. She should be scared. I reach for my gun, my fingers brushing against the cold steel.

"Antonio, no." Dante steps in front of me, putting his hand on my chest. "Killing her won't get us any closer to finding Alessia."

"She handed her over to Draco."

"And she'll pay for that," Dante says. "But not now. Not like this."

"She's lying," I growl, eyes locked on the woman. "She's leaving something out. She knows more."

"Maybe," Dante admits, casting a glance at her. "But if you kill her, we'll never know. Keep her alive—for now."

I take a step back, still seething but aware that Dante's right. My eyes don't leave her. "You'd better hope you remember something else," I hiss. "Because next time, no one will stop me."

She's shaking now, tears streaming down her face.

"Let's go. She's useless."

Her sobs echo behind us as Dante closes the door and locks the room.

My phone vibrates in my pocket. I yank it out, expecting an update from my men, but it's an unknown number. I glance at Dante before answering.

"It's him," I say, connecting the call. "Where is she?"

Silence. Then, a distorted, almost playful voice whispers through the line.

"The beating of her heart grows faint. Come alone, or it will never beat again. No weapons, no tricks. The pit awaits you."

The line goes dead, but a text follows seconds later with an address. I know the place—an abandoned building on the outskirts of the city.

It's a trap. It reeks of one. But I don't have a choice.

"What did he say?" Dante asks, watching me closely.

"The call dropped. It was a bad connection," I lie, pocketing the phone before he presses for more.

His eyes narrow. "That didn't sound like nothing."

I turn my back to him, forcing myself to think, to plan. If I tell him where I'm going, he'll insist on coming. And if he does, Alessia will be dead before I can get to her. I need to shake him off, make him think it's something else—anything else.

"Antonio, what the hell did he say?" Dante steps closer.

"I told you. It was a bad connection. There's some old business I need to check on. I'll call you later."

Dante crosses his arms. "You expect me to believe you're running off to handle *old business* while Alessia's missing?"

I meet his gaze, my voice steady. "We've got men all over the city. I can't sit here and do nothing. I have to follow up on some things."

"Then we'll go together."

"No," I say, shutting him down. "I need someone I trust keeping an eye on things here while I check this out. If we're both gone, we might miss something important."

Dante studies me, eyes narrowed, but he knows me too well. He knows I'm lying. The clock's monstrous ticking gnaws at me, as though time itself is conspiring against me. Every second wasted here is another Alessia might not have.

I step closer, locking eyes with him. "Listen to me. No matter what happens, getting Alessia back alive must be your top priority. You understand?"

He blinks, startled by the urgency in my voice. "What are you talking about? Of course, it's the priority."

"Promise me, Dante. If something goes wrong, if I don't come back." The words slip out. "I'm counting on you to make sure she's safe. You get her out of this mess. Whatever it takes."

"Don't talk like that. You're coming back."

"Promise me," I demand, gripping his shoulder. "Say it."

After a long pause, he exhales sharply. "I promise. I'll keep her safe."

I release him, a strange sense of finality settling over me. "Good."

Dante studies me, suspicion still lingering. "Where are you really going?"

"You trust me, right?" I ask, holding his gaze. He nods, albeit reluctantly. "Then trust me to handle this. I'll call you the second I know anything."

He exhales, though the tension in his shoulders doesn't ease.

"Fine. But if I don't hear from you in an hour, I'm coming after you."

I nod and head for the door before he changes his mind. "Deal."

Outside, I break into a sprint, heading for my car. I can only hope I get to that address before it's too late.

Antonio

My car skids to a stop in the gravel lot outside the decaying building. Cracked windows leer down at me, weeds strangle the walls, and the stench of rot hits me the second I step out of the car. My pulse thrums violently as I wrench the rusty metal door open and step into the darkness.

Inside, it's pitch-black—no light, no sound, just oppressive silence. I pull out my phone and turn on the flashlight. The weak light casts eerie shapes on the walls, distorting the room into something grotesque.

My breath catches as the beam lands on a piece of parchment lying at the center of the room.

Proceed into the depths, where the light flickers and the shadows cling.
If you dare descend, there, you will find what you seek.

"Where the hell do I go?" My voice echoes in the large, empty space.

I scan the room. Every inch of this god forsaken place feels alive. Like it's watching me, waiting for my next move. Hoping I fail.

Then, something catches my eye.

At the far end of the room, tucked in the shadows, a stack of broken crates lies in disarray. The edges are jagged, splintered, as though they'd been thrown there in haste. My steps are slow, deliberate, each one pressing the tension further into my muscles. I instinctively reach for my gun, only to be reminded it's not there.

I shove the crates aside, dust swirling up in a choking cloud. Coughing, I wave my hand to clear the air and spot what the crates were disguising—a small, hidden entrance leading underground.

There's no turning back now.

A set of narrow, brittle stairs descends into the darkness. The wood groans under my weight, each step creaking ominously, a dying echo as if the tunnel itself protests my presence. The damp air is thick with mildew and decay, clinging to my skin. My heart constricts with every step as I picture Alessia trapped down here in this dark and desolate place. Terrified and alone.

As I descend deeper, I hold the flashlight steady, the beam bouncing off the damp, crumbling walls. The silence stretches, broken only by the echo of my footsteps and the distant drip of water. Up ahead, I spot a faint glow spilling into the tunnel.

Rounding the bend, I find a room with the door wide open. I hurry toward it and step inside the dimly lit space. At the center, two figures stand, waiting.

Draco. Emilio Salazar.

And Alessia.

She's slumped in the corner, her wrists bound behind her back, head hanging to one side. Even in the dim light, I can see the bruises marring her skin. The rise and fall of her chest barely visible. Fear like I've never experienced threatens to consume me.

My vision narrows, a red-hot roar pounding in my skull, but before I can take a step toward her, Draco's voice slices through the air like a knife.

"Well, well, look who finally showed up," he drawls, a sneer twisting his lips. "It's almost poetic, isn't it? After all the death, all the suffering, you come here thinking you can save her—only to meet your own end in the very darkness you tried to pull her from."

I don't respond. My focus is locked on Alessia, on the fragile movement of her breath. Every fiber of my being screams to rush to her, but I force myself to stay still. If I make a wrong move, she'll die before I can even reach her.

Draco steps closer, his footsteps slow and mocking. "I always knew it would come to this," he continues, savoring each word. "You and me. But I didn't think I'd have the pleasure of watching you lose everything first." His eyes flick to Alessia, her limp body. "She put up a fight. I'll give her that. Not that it did her any good."

My fists clench at my sides. "You're her father."

Draco laughs a sharp, bitter sound that grates against my nerves. "Her father?" He spits the words like a curse. "She's nothing to me. Never was. Did you really think because we share blood, I'd feel some kind of obligation? A sentimental pull?" He sneers. "She's a pawn, Antonio. Just like everyone else."

Rage coils tighter, twisting into something feral. "Any man who would do this is nothing more than a coward," I growl, my voice deadly.

Draco's eyes flash with something dark before his smirk returns. "Coward? No, Antonio. I'm practical," he sneers. "She was never more than a cunt to be used as leverage, nothing else. Power is the only thing that matters, and she was useful for that. Love and family are lies weak men tell themselves. In the end, it's all about survival, and I'll do whatever it takes to win."

I can barely contain the disgust roiling through me. "You think torturing your daughter makes you powerful?"

He shrugs, almost bored. "She's just another weak link in a chain I'm about to break. But what I can't understand is why so many men are willing to throw everything away for a chance to fuck her. Maybe I should get my dick wet and see what all the fuss is about before I pass her off.”

Salazar laughs, and my control slips. My vision narrows on Draco as he continues, his voice dripping with mockery.

“You could’ve had everything—power, wealth, control. But here you are, another idiot chasing after a piece of ass. You should’ve fucked her and let her go. Instead, you’re about to die.”

“You’ll never win, Draco. No matter what you think you’ve accomplished here, you’re already finished.”

“Oh, I’ve already won, Antonio. Both of your fates were sealed the second you cared.”

My heart pounds, my body coiled, ready to strike. But I can’t. Not yet. Instead, I grit my teeth, my eyes darting between Draco and Salazar. He hasn’t spoken yet. He’s watching, a predator in the shadows, waiting for the right moment. If I make a move too soon, if I slip even once, they’ll kill her before I can do a damn thing about it.

“You’re wrong,” I say, the words low and dangerous. “About everything. You’ll never touch her again.”

“Oh, I already have, Antonio. What’s it like to see the person you claim to *love* suffer because of your mistakes? You could’ve stopped all this if you’d given her back to me like I asked. But you didn’t. And now look what you made me do.” He moves his foot toward Alessia, nudging her limp body with casual cruelty. “She’s already broken. There’s nothing left to save.”

Draco’s words hang in the air like a death sentence, but I don’t take his bait. I refuse to let him see the fire raging inside me. I need to survive long enough to rip these bastards apart and get Alessia out of here alive.

“Any last words?” Draco taunts, his smile widening.

Salazar shifts slightly, eyes narrowing. Draco’s poise falters just for a moment. And then I hear it—the sharp crack of gunfire, echoing through the tunnels like a death knell.

Draco flinches, his bravado vanishing as he turns to the kingpin, frantic. "I delivered her, just like we agreed. She's yours. But I'm done here."

Without another word, Draco bolts, a coward to the very last second.

Salazar's eyes lock with mine. There's no more time. It's him or me.

I lunge.

A savage growl rips from my throat as we collide. The force sends both of us crashing to the ground in a brutal tangle of fists and fury. He's bigger and stronger, but rage fuels me. I slam my fists into his face, each punch connecting with sickening cracks of bone and flesh. Blood sprays from his mouth enraging him.

His fist smashes into my ribs, a blow so hard it drives the air from my lungs. I grunt, pain radiating through my chest, but I don't stop. I can't. He swings again, catching me across the jaw. Stars dance at the edge of my vision, but I force myself to stay conscious. His next punch splits my lip, the coppery taste of blood filling my mouth.

He's a brute, but I'm faster. My rage doesn't care about the pain. I spit blood and launch myself at him, my fists hammering into his gut. Every hit lands with a brutal thud, driving him back.

Salazar knows the stakes as well as I do. Only one of us is leaving here alive. He throws a wild punch, catching me on the side of the head. The world tilts, my balance slipping. He seizes the opportunity, slamming his elbow into my back and forcing me to the ground. My head spins. The taste of blood is thick on my tongue.

Before he can finish me, I roll to the side just in time to avoid his boot slamming down where my head had been. I kick his leg out from under him, sending him stumbling, giving me the opening I need. My fists fly again, crashing into his ribs. The sharp crack of bone echoes in the small room.

He swings wildly, landing a blow to my cheek. Pain flares through my skull, but it only fuels me on. I roar and slam my knuckles into his face. This time, his nose shatters under the force. Blood gushes down his face as he staggers.

Grabbing him by the throat, I slam his head against the crude stone wall. The wet, sickening crunch of his skull against the jagged rock is like music. Over and over, I drive his head into the stones, relishing the sound of breaking bone, the feel of his body growing weaker with every blow.

His groans turn to gurgles as blood fills his throat, but I don't stop. His fists flail weakly, desperate slaps that have no power left behind them. His legs give out, and still, I keep going.

Finally, his body slumps, limp and broken, blood pooling around the unrecognizable mess. I kneel over what's left of his body and raise my fist one last time, bringing it down to end his worthless life.

Without another thought, I'm at Alessia's side, my hands trembling as I press my fingers to her neck searching for a pulse. It's faint, but it's there.

"Alessia," I whisper, my voice cracking as I brush her blood-matted hair away from her bruised face. She doesn't stir. My hands shake as I work frantically at the knots, freeing her hands. "You have to keep fighting. Don't you dare leave me, *tesoro*."

I pull out my cell to call for help, but there's no service. Panic claws at the edges of my mind, but I shove it down. There's no time for fear. I have to get her out of here.

Scooping her fragile body into my arms, I cradle her against me as if she might shatter with a single wrong move. Her head lolls against my chest. For a moment, I close my eyes, focusing on the sound of her breath. She's still alive. Barely.

As I step back into the labyrinth of tunnels, the beam from my flashlight sweeps over the stone walls, casting twisted shadows that seem to warp and close in with every step. I pause, blinking as my eyes try to adjust, but the walls seem to shift. Everything feels disorienting, distorted.

Gunshots. Distant, echoing through the maze of tunnels, but impossible to pinpoint. Left, right—somewhere between.

Clutching Alessia against me, I move quickly. My boots slam against the wet stone, each step reverberating through the narrow passageways. Every second is stolen, a race against time.

Each tunnel looks the same, every corner a potential dead end. My breathing grows ragged, not just from the effort of carrying her, but from the dread crawling up my spine. I'm making too many mistakes.

"Stay with me, Alessia," I murmur. "I'm getting you out of here. Just hold on."

She doesn't stir, doesn't respond. Panic fuels my steps, driving me faster. I have to keep moving.

The gunshots grow louder, bouncing off the walls, leading me like a cruel beacon. I turn another corner, praying this one doesn't lead to a dead end.

Please, let this be the way out.

I need to get us above ground so I can call an ambulance. The questions, the mess—all of it can wait. I'll deal with the aftermath, clean it up, pay the right people to make sure it disappears. The only thing that matters is getting Alessia to a hospital and keeping her alive.

I can't lose her. Not now. Not ever.

Up ahead, I finally spot what I've been searching for—the familiar steps leading back up. The way out. My legs burn with every step as I climb, her limp body growing heavier in my arms as my own strength begins to fade. But I push through it. I have no choice.

When I reach the surface, gasping for air, I glance down at my phone—still no signal in this damn building. I clutch Alessia tighter and push through the door, finally bursting into the open air. The second I'm outside, the signal bar flickers to life. I quickly dial for help, my breath coming in ragged gasps.

The phone rings once, twice, before a calm voice answers, "911, what's your emergency?"

"My wife," I gasp, barely able to force the words out. "She's hurt—bad. I need an ambulance. Now."

"Stay calm, sir," the dispatcher replies. "Where are you located?"

I rattle off the address, my voice trembling as I glance down at Alessia's pale face, her breath so shallow it's nearly undetectable. "She's not... she's barely breathing. You need to hurry."

"Help is on the way," the dispatcher reassures, but it's not fast enough. Time is slipping through my fingers like sand.

I disconnect the call, the sound of the dispatcher's voice lingering in my mind like a hollow echo. My legs buckle beneath me, and I drop to my knees, cradling Alessia's limp body in my arms. The cold ground presses against me as I rock her gently, willing her to keep breathing.

My phone buzzes again. It's Dante.

"Where are you?" he asks.

"I'm outside. In the parking lot," I choke out, my throat tight, every word a struggle. "I'm waiting for an ambulance. She's barely breathing." My voice cracks, raw with fear. "I can't even see her chest move. She's slipping away and I can't do a god damn thing to stop it."

"You will not fucking lose her," Dante growls, his voice harsh but laced with an urgency that mirrors my own panic. "She's strong, Antonio. You hear me? You hold on to her. Don't let her go. The ambulance is coming, and they'll do everything they can." His voice softens, just a fraction. "You're not losing her, Anton. Not like this."

I press a trembling hand to her cold cheek. "I never should've let her out of my sight. This is all my fault."

"You did everything you could. The only thing that matters right now is getting her through this. Focus on that."

I close my eyes, sucking in a deep breath, trying to push back the suffocating panic. "Where are you?"

"I've got Draco," he says, his voice tight with barely restrained fury. "I shot him, but the bastard's still breathing. What do you want me to do?"

I glance down at Alessia, her skin pale as death. A surge of fury burns through me, white-hot. "Make him suffer, Dante," I growl, my voice low and lethal. "Make sure he suffers and then burns in hell."

"He will."

The line goes dead.

I hold Alessia closer, my voice barely a whisper as I lean in. "Help is on the way. Stay with me. Please, *Tesoro*, stay with me."

Dante

I've known Antonio long enough to recognize when he's lying. *Old business.* He got a message from Draco, but he's not going to tell me what it was. Instead of arguing with him and wasting time, I let him walk away. But the second his back is turned I grab my gear and follow. If he thinks I'm going to let my best friend, my brother, handle this alone, he's dead wrong.

I tail him, keeping my distance as he heads toward the docks to an abandoned warehouse. The place reeks of a trap, but I hold back and watch him disappear inside. My instincts scream at me to follow, but I know Antonio. He's got his own game to play, and if I storm in too early, I'll ruin it.

Once he's disappeared, I slip in behind him and find a yellowed paper on the floor, the hand-scrawled note barely legible. With my gun drawn, I move deeper, down the narrow steps that lead into twisting tunnels beneath the city.

Voices drift up ahead. I slink through the damp passageways, trying to stay hidden in the shadows. Every step is a calculated risk, and the deeper I go, the more distinct the voices become. I'm close.

Suddenly, behind me, the unmistakable sound of footsteps. My pulse spikes. Someone else is here and they're close. Ducking around a corner, I press my back against the cold, slick stone wall, hoping to vanish into the darkness.

Crack!

The gunshot is deafening in the tight space, the bullet whizzing past my head and slamming into the wall behind me.

"Shit," I hiss, diving behind an old support beam, squeezing off a shot of my own. There's a grunt, followed by the dull thud of a body hitting the floor. One of Draco's men.

I have no time to breathe as more footsteps echo through the tunnel. Another figure sprints toward me, gun raised. He fires, missing me by only inches. I charge after him, blood pumping, adrenaline taking over. Shots ring out, bouncing off the walls as I chase him down.

Another round—closer this time. I duck, firing off two more shots. One finds its mark. The man stumbles, clutching his side before collapsing onto the stone. His body twitches once, then goes still.

Not knowing how many more men are down here, I don't slow down. As I round the next corner, that's when I see him.

Draco Moretti.

He's slinking through the catacomb-like tunnels like the rat he is, trying to escape. My body reacts before my mind can. I fire. The shot is precise, hitting him in the leg. He crumples to the ground with a pained groan, clutching his bleeding thigh.

With my gun raised, I stalk toward him. He reaches for his weapon, but I kick it away, sending it skittering across the stone. Grabbing him by the collar, I drag him to the nearest wall and slam him against it. His breath comes out in sharp, wheezing gasps, pain and rage battling in his eyes. But still—arrogance. He thinks he's in control.

"I figured you'd show up," he spits, his voice strained but smug.

I press my gun to his temple, leaning in close. "By the time I'm done with you, you'll wish I hadn't."

"Make him suffer, Dante," Antonio's voice is venom, pure and raw. "Make sure he suffers and then burns in hell."

"He will," I promise, and then disconnect the call.

Draco's bloodshot eyes narrow, even as blood trickles down his temple. "You talk big, but we're the same. You kill, just like I do," he rasps, the words laced with bitterness.

I tighten my grip on his throat, cutting off his breath, my voice low and seething. "The difference is," I growl, yanking my knife from its sheath, the cold steel gleaming in the dim light, "I protect my family. You betrayed yours." I press the blade to his side, dragging it across his skin, slow and deliberate.

"You think that makes you better than me?" His eyes gleam with twisted satisfaction as he winces through the pain.

"Better than you?" I repeat, my voice low, dangerous. "Killing you isn't about being better. It's about making sure you never hurt anyone again."

His smirk falters, just for a second, but it's enough. I squeeze his throat harder, savoring the way his bloodshot eyes widen in panic.

Draco's breath rasps as blood trickles from the corner of his mouth, but that sickening grin never falters. "Tell me, Dante? Are you fucking her too? Is that why you're here? Two men fighting over a whore who's only good for spreading her legs." He chuckles, dark and cruel. "I do have one regret," he leans in, his breath hot and rancid. "I should've fucked her myself. Now I'll never know what the fuss is about."

Before I even realize it, my fist crashes into his face, the sickening crack of bone echoing through the tunnel. Draco grunts, blood spurting from his broken nose, but the bastard still grins through the pain.

"You filthy piece of shit," I snarl, grabbing him by the throat and slamming him harder against the wall. "Your only regret is not raping your daughter." Draco gasps, his breath coming in ragged bursts as I squeeze tighter, watching the life drain from his bloodshot eyes.

"You want to talk about regrets, Draco?" I growl, pressing the cold steel of the knife to his cheek, my voice low and venomous.

Without waiting for a response, I drag the blade across his face in one swift motion. Blood wells from the cut, spilling down his skin as his body flinches in pain, but he stays silent, refusing to give me the satisfaction of his screams. I keep him pinned, watching the blood trickle down his face.

"You're not going to die quick," I whisper, leaning in close. "You'll suffer for everything you did to her."

Draco's laugh is a sick, guttural sound, a mix of blood and cruelty. "Did she tell you her little secret? Hmm? Did she tell you she was carrying my grandchild?"

The words hit like a punch to the gut, and for a second, the air is sucked from my lungs. He's lying. He has to be. But the way his eyes light up tells me there's some truth in his twisted words.

"But I took care of it. With any luck, they're both dead by now."

"You sick bastard," I roar, as I slam the knife into his shoulder, the blade driving deep. This time, Draco screams, the sound sharp and guttural as I twist the knife, savoring the agony etched on his face.

"You killed your own grandchild?" I snarl, my breath ragged with anger. "You tortured your daughter, left her to die, and now you've got the nerve to laugh about it?"

"I never wanted Alessia. You think I care about some bastard grandchild?" His laughter turns to a wheeze, mocking and breathless. "Whose baby is it? Antonio's? Yours? Or some other bastards?"

I can barely see through the red haze clouding my vision. Without thinking, I yank the knife from his shoulder and slam it into his leg, twisting it viciously. His scream tears through the air, raw and ragged.

"You sick, twisted fuck," I snarl. "You have no right to even speak her name."

Draco's face contorts with pain, but that sneer still clings to his lips. I tighten my grip on the knife. "You think your poison can change who she is? You'll never touch what's good in her. That's something you'll never understand."

I rip the knife out, blood spilling onto the cold stone floor. Draco barely has time to gasp before I grab his hand, yanking it forward and forcing his trembling fingers to splay out on the ground.

"Antonio should be here for this," I snarl, pinning his hand under my boot. "He should be the one to tear you apart for what you did to his wife and child, but since he can't, I'll make sure you suffer for both of them."

Draco's sneer falters as I raise the knife again and slam the blade down into his hand, severing two fingers.

"Let's see how much leverage you have without these." I kick the severed digits aside, watching them roll into the growing pool of blood at his feet.

Without hesitation, I drive the blade deep into his chest, grinding it against the bone. Draco's body convulses, agony contorting his features. His breath comes in ragged, shallow gasps. I twist the blade harder until it catches against bone. "You're nothing but a monster," I growl through clenched teeth. "And monsters don't deserve to live."

The blade sticks, lodged against his ribs. I pull hard, feeling the sickening crack of bone breaking beneath the pressure. Draco lets out a choked scream, his body jerking violently as I wrench the blade free. The wet, sickening sound of metal leaving flesh fills the space. I sit back on my heels and watch the blood flow faster now soaking through his clothes.

The crimson liquid puddles at his feet, a macabre painting of Draco's undoing. His body trembles as his life slowly slips away.

His unfocused gaze meets mine and for a moment I see fear creeping in. The realization that death is not far off.

Around us, the shadows close in as if even the darkness itself knows death is near.

I lean in, my voice barely above a whisper. "The pit waits for you, Draco. There's no escaping it. You'll fall, just like the rest of us. But you'll fall alone."

He tries to speak, but all that comes out is a gurgle of blood. I grab him by the hair, yanking his head back, exposing his throat. "This is for Alessia," I whisper, before dragging the blade across his neck in one swift, brutal motion.

Blood gushes from the wound. Draco's breaths come in ragged gasps

And I know he knows.

In those final moments I see it. The desperate need. The fear.

He's lost. Not just his life—everything. Alessia, the power he craved, even his own legacy.

With my grip steady on the knife, I watch him die.

There's no satisfaction in it. Only cold, final justice.

Antonio

The ambulance ride is a blur of flashing red lights and wailing sirens. Blood drips into my eye from the gash above my brow, and my ribs scream every time the ambulance hits a bump, causing the entire compartment to lurch, but I don't care.

I deserve this agony for letting it happen to her. If she's broken, then I should be, too.

My beautiful wife, the woman I swore to protect, lies strapped to a gurney. I grip her hand like a lifeline, as if my touch alone is keeping her tethered to this world. I whisper her name, begging her to stay with me.

The paramedics work around me, their movements quick and mechanical as they fight to stabilize her. One threads a needle into her arm with practiced precision, hooking her up to an IV while the other attaches sensors to her chest. The steady beeping of the heart monitor fills the cramped space, but it does nothing to calm my terror.

An oxygen mask is placed over her mouth and nose. I watch in helpless agony as they adjust the flow. Her breaths are so shallow, I fear any one might be her last.

"Sir, you're in the way," one paramedic says, his tone firm. "You need to let go of her hand. We need the space."

Let go? The thought is absurd. Her hand is the only thing anchoring me to reality, the only proof that she's still alive. If I release her, she'll slip away. I can't let that happen.

"No."

"Sir—"

"Work around me," I snap.

"Your wife is in critical condition," he says, his patience fraying. "We need to be able to move freely to help her."

"You don't understand. If I let go, I'll lose her." My words tumbling out in a frantic rush. "She can't leave me. So, you'll have to figure it out."

Tears blur my vision, but I barely notice. I cling to her hand desperately. She's everything I am—everything I love. I can't let go. Not now. Not ever.

"*Tesoro*," I murmur, my voice breaking. "Please. I need you. I can't do this without you."

When we finally pull up to the hospital, the back doors burst open and chaos erupts. A team of doctors and nurses rush toward us, barking orders and spouting medical jargon. I stumble after them, my legs weak, barely carrying my weight, the pain in my ribs screaming with every step.

Alessia's hand is ripped from mine as they rush her toward the trauma unit. My heart lurches as I watch her disappear behind a set of double doors. I try to follow, but hands press against my chest, firm and unrelenting.

"You can't go back there."

"Move," I shout, trying to push past. "I need to be with my wife."

"Sir, you need to stay out here," he insists. "Let the doctors do their work."

"I'm not leaving her." My voice is hoarse, desperation choking me.

"Sir, please," he says, his tone soothing, as though talking to a caged animal.

I don't give a damn about rules, I need to be with her. My ribs throb as I argue, the pain finally breaking through my panic. Instinctively, I press a hand to my side.

"You're injured too," the nurse says, his voice firm but kind.

"I don't care about me," I snap, trying to shake off his hold. "I'm fine."

But he doesn't let go. His hands remain steady as he guides me to a chair, not taking no for an answer. "My name's Liam. I'm a physician's assistant, he says. "Dr. Hill's with your wife. He's one of the best trauma doctors we have. He'll doing everything he can for her."

"Her name is Alessia," I mutter.

Liam's expression softens. "Alessia's in good hands, I promise." He crouches down, examining the cut above my eye. "Let's get you patched up so you can be there for her when she wakes up, alright?"

The fight drains out of me, leaving only exhaustion and fear in its wake. My shoulders sag in defeat. "Fine. Just make it quick."

Liam gives me a reassuring nod before gathering supplies. "Looks like you're having trouble breathing," he observes, pulling on gloves.

I sit back in the chair, my hands gripping the armrests. "I've had worse," I mumble.

He drags a metal tray over, a faint smile tugging at the corner of his mouth. "I'm sure. But right now, I'm responsible for you, and I'm not cutting corners," he says, his eyes meeting mine. And I'm pretty sure Alessia would want me to make sure you're in one piece. Don't want to get on her bad side." He smiles.

A weak chuckle escapes me. "She's tough," I whisper. "A fighter."

"She is," Liam agrees as he cleans the cut. "And tough women need their stubborn husbands in one piece. So let me take care of you for her, okay?"

I stay silent this time, the sting of the needle barely registering. My focus already drifting back to the doors, waiting for any news.

"Just a few stitches," Liam continues, his voice almost soothing as he works. "Then we'll get those ribs x-rayed."

Minutes drag by and I close my eyes, my thoughts are miles away—with Alessia and the promise that they're doing everything they can to save her.

"Alright, that should do it. You'll have a bit of a scar, though." Liam says, pulling off his gloves. "I'm going to put in the orders for your x-rays. I'll be back shortly to take you over."

He walks away, leaving me alone in the sterile silence of the treatment room. The moment the door shuts, I pull out my phone to text Enzo.

Me: I found her.

Enzo: Where are you?

Me: The hospital. That fucker beat her.

Enzo: How bad?

Me: She was unconscious and barely breathing when I found her. They won't let me see her.

Enzo: What about Draco?

Me: Dante has him. I gave the order.

Enzo: What do you need?

Me: A cleanup crew at the warehouse.

My mind sharpens as I assume the role I know best. Capo. Business. Order.

Enzo: Done.

Me: And a lawyer. Someone's going to start asking questions soon.

Enzo: Already on it. Guards are en route. Focus on Alessia. I'll handle the rest.

Me: Thank you.

The door swings open again. Liam returns with a wheelchair. "Ready to get those ribs checked?" he asks with a wry smile.

I look at the wheelchair, then back at him. "No," I say flatly, shaking my head. "I'm not using that."

Liam raises an eyebrow, clearly used to stubborn patients. "You're telling me you'd rather limp across the hospital in pain instead of sitting for a few minutes? I gotta admit, I'm impressed by your commitment to making life difficult."

"I'm walking," I reply, standing up slowly. The sharp ache in my ribs makes me wince, but I push through it.

Liam chuckles, holding his hands up in mock surrender. "Alright, your call. Just don't tell my boss I didn't offer the luxury option."

As we head to radiology, Liam lowers his voice. "They're still running tests on Alessia, but right now, she's stable."

Stable. The word sticks in my mind, offering a sliver of hope. "Thank you."

The X-rays are agony, each breath a knife twisting in my chest. After what feels like an eternity, I'm returned to my room. Liam pulls up my scans.

"Good news," he says, almost surprised. "Your ribs aren't broken. Just bruised."

"Lucky me," I mutter as my phone buzzes again.

"I need a few minutes," I say, already connecting the call.

He nods, not saying anything, but I catch the knowing look in his eyes. He recognizes me. "Take your time," he says, as he steps out of the room.

I bring the phone to my ear. "Dante," I say, my voice low.

"Draco's dead."

"Did he suffer?"

"Yes. His end wasn't painless."

"Good," I reply, my voice cold. "Where's the body?"

"It's in a deep, dark place where he'll never be found."

Twisted satisfaction curls through me knowing Draco's remains have been left in some cold, forgotten place. Gone. Forever erased from this world—except the hell he left behind for Alessia.

But it's not enough. His death doesn't undo the damage he caused.

"How's Alessia?" Dante asks, his tone gentler now.

"They're still running tests," I say, the knot in my stomach tightening.

"I'm on my way to meet with Moretti's second-in-command now," he continues. "I need to be sure they don't retaliate for this. I'll let him know what Draco did to Alessia and the—" Dante's voice falters, but he quickly corrects himself. "To Alessia. I'm hoping when he hears the full extent, he'll see reason."

A doctor enters, his face grim. "I have to go," I say, ending the call.

I move to stand, but the doctor raises a hand. "No need, Mr. Luciano. You can stay seated." I ignore him, pushing to my feet as every muscle in my body tenses. Standing makes the pain in my ribs flare, but it grounds me. "I'm Dr. Hill, I've been overseeing your wife's care."

"How is she?"

"Mrs. Luciano's injuries are quite extensive." He pauses. "Two broken ribs, a concussion, and multiple contusions all over her body."

My heart slams against my chest. The air in my lungs becomes harder to find.

"We're monitoring both her and the baby closely."

"The baby?" I ask, unable to comprehend his words.

The doctor hesitates, his tone gentler now. "Alessia's eight weeks pregnant. The baby has a strong heartbeat, but given her injuries, we need to keep them both under observation for the next few days to ensure they remain stable."

The room spins. I stumble back, gripping the bed's edge to keep myself upright.

Pregnant. Alessia is pregnant.

The doctor continues, but his voice sounds distant, muffled. Something about the ICU, monitoring her, keeping her stable. His words blur together, drowned out by the single fact echoing in my mind—Alessia's pregnant. She and our baby were nearly beaten to death.

"I need to see her."

The doctor looks wary, hesitant. "The police are on their way. It would be best if you spoke to them first."

Rage flares hot and fast, but I rein it in. Barely. "I'm not answering a damn thing until I see my wife. The police can wait."

The doctor tenses. Then, an unspoken understanding passes between us. He knows who I am, knows there's no use arguing. After a long pause, he exhales. "Alright," he says quietly, resignation in his voice. "Follow me."

I'M LED DOWN THE HALL TO HER ROOM. THE MOMENT I see her, my legs falter, forcing me to grab the doorframe for support. I can't move. Can't breathe. All I can do is stand there, frozen, unable to process reality.

"I know it's difficult to see someone you care about like this. But for now, she's stable," Dr. Hill says. "What she needs most is to rest and heal."

His words barely register. My gaze is locked on Alessia, lying so still, surrounded by wires and machines that beep in the background. Her face is battered and swollen. She looks so tiny and fragile.

"Come in and sit with her." The nurse who's adjusting her IV says.

My legs feel heavy as I move toward the bed.

"I'm Alora, one of the nurses taking care of your wife," she says softly, offering a kind smile. "I'll be just outside. If you need anything, don't hesitate to call me."

Unable to find my voice, I nod and stumble to the chair beside Alessia's bed. My hand reaches for hers instinctively. It's so cold. I swallow hard, trying to push down the storm of emotions threatening to consume me.

When Alora finishes, she hesitates for a moment, then reaches into her pocket and hands me something—a small piece of paper. "This is for you," she whispers.

My hands tremble as I take it. I look down at the grainy, black-and-white image. It takes me a moment to process what I'm looking at. When I realize what it is, my heart skips a beat.

"Congratulations," Alora says quietly.

Congratulations. The word feels foreign. Out of place in this environment. I stare at the ultrasound, the proof of the tiny life nestled inside Alessia's body. For a fleeting second, the chaos in my mind stills.

"She's strong," Alora adds. "And so is your baby. We'll take good care of them both."

The joy I should feel at this moment is overshadowed by the fear that plagues me. "Thank you," I manage, my throat tight.

She nods and slips out of the room, leaving me alone in the suffocating quiet staring at the faint outline of our baby. Does Alessia even know she's pregnant?

My eyes drift back to my wife. The fear, the guilt—it's too much. My strength crumbles, and I break. Silent sobs wrack my body as I hold the ultrasound, terrified of losing her. Terrified of losing them both.

I never imagined loving something this much—someone I haven't even met yet. The thought of a future without them—I wouldn't survive it.

I can't lose them. Not like this.

I don't know how long I sit there, drowning in my grief and fear, but then I feel it—a faint movement. Alessia's fingers twitch.

I look up just in time to see her eyes flutter open. "You found me," she whispers, her voice barely audible.

I nod, choking back tears. "I'll always find you, *tesoro.*"

Her eyes slip closed again, but not before her hand squeezes mine, a weak but undeniable connection.

A sense of peace settles over me. But it's fleeting, because I know what still needs to be done.

Alessia

I wake slowly, my body aches with the slightest movement. The steady beeping of machines fills the quiet room. It takes a moment to remember where I am. When I do, the memories come flooding back. Panic begins to overwhelm me until I reach down and feel his warmth.

Antonio's slumped in the chair beside my bed, his head resting on the mattress. His breathing is deep and steady, lost in sleep. Gently, I run my fingers through his hair. He stirs and his eyes blink open. He appears disoriented for a second, until his gaze locks onto mine.

"*Tesoro*," he breathes and sits up straighter

"Good morning," I whisper.

He swallows hard, his thumb brushing over my knuckles in a tender, almost desperate rhythm. "I was so scared," he admits, his voice breaking. "I thought I'd lost you."

"I'm right here," I assure him, though seeing the fear still etched on his face makes my heart ache. "You found me."

But instead of relief, his eyes remain clouded with guilt.

"Antonio," I murmur, my voice trembling. "Is our baby okay?"

"You know about the baby?" His expression shifts, surprised.

"My father told me," I say, closing my eyes briefly to block out the memory. "That's why he beat me. He was trying to kill the baby."

Antonio's expression darkens —his rage so palpable it seems to charge the very air between us. My breath catches at the intensity of his emotions. Slowly, he closes his eyes. His chest rises and falls as he draws in a deep, shaky breath, fighting to rein in the storm swirling inside him. His hands unclench, and the tension in his body eases, though the fire in his eyes still simmers.

With deliberate care, he reaches into his pocket and pulls out a small piece of paper, handing it to me. "He didn't succeed."

I take the ultrasound photo from his hands. Tears blur my vision as I stare at the tiny image.

"The baby's really okay?" I whisper, needing to hear him say it again to make it real.

Antonio nods, his gaze softening as he leans closer. "The baby's okay, *tesoro*." He pauses, his voice raw with emotion. "I'm so proud of you. You fought like hell, and because of that, you saved both of you." His thumb gently traces my cheek, his eyes filled with admiration.

A weight lifts from my chest. But something still feels off. "What aren't you telling me?"

His eyes close for a moment, his face filled with conflict. When he opens them again, there's a vulnerability there that I've rarely seen. "I'm so sorry, *tesoro*. I failed you."

I shake my head quickly. "No, Antonio, you didn't—"

"I broke my promise," he cuts me off, pulling his hand back.

"What are you talking about?"

"I promised that if I ever hurt you, I'd let you go." He looks away, pain twisting his features. "And I broke that promise. You almost died because of me."

I try to protest, but he continues. "As much as it's killing me, I have to keep my word. I'll make sure you and the baby are safe, always. Neither of you will ever want for anything. But I have to let you go."

I can't believe what I'm hearing. "Stop," I say, shaking my head.

Tears brim in his eyes, but he says nothing.

"You didn't hurt me," I begin softly. "You did everything you could to protect me. You came for me. You saved me."

His lips part to respond, but I press my fingers gently against them again. "You're nothing like Val. You're nothing like my father. They abandoned me. Hurt me. But you?" My voice softens as I lower my hand, resting it over his. "You've fought for me. Every single time."

His breath shudders, and I squeeze his hand, willing him to believe my words. "I love you, Antonio."

"You love me?" he breathes.

"I've never stopped loving you, and I'm not going anywhere. I need you. We need you."

For a moment, the world stills. Antonio's eyes search mine, and then his expression softens. His hand cups my cheek. "I love you, Alessia," he murmurs, his voice rough with emotion.

His lips find mine in a tender kiss, the weight of everything we've been through melts into that one moment. I pour all my love into it, hoping he can feel how much I mean every word.

But just as our lips part, there's a knock at the door. The spell is broken as one of the guards steps inside, his expression tense. "Mr. Luciano, the police are here. We've held them off as long as we could. They're demanding to speak with you both."

Panic surges through me at the mention of the police. "Antonio," I whisper, reaching for his hand.

"Shh," he soothes, brushing his thumb over my knuckles. "You don't have to say anything. I'll handle it." He turns to the guard. "Is Baldini here?"

"He is," the guard confirms.

Antonio's voice hardens with authority. "Send them in, make sure he's with them."

Moments later, the door swings open, and two police officers enter, followed by Antonio's lawyer, Lorenzo Baldini. The tension in the room thickens as they approach the bed, their expressions unreadable.

One of the officers clears his throat, eyes flicking between Antonio and Baldini before he speaks. "We have some questions for Ms. Moretti," he says, his tone polite but firm. "We'd prefer to speak with her alone."

Antonio's jaw tightens instantly. "Absolutely not," he snaps, his voice sharp. "I'm not leaving her."

Baldini steps forward, his voice low but firm. "Officers, my client has the right to have legal counsel present during any questioning."

Before tensions rise further, I speak up, squeezing Antonio's hand again. "I'm willing to answer your questions," I say, my voice steady despite the nerves fluttering in my chest. "But both Antonio and our attorney will remain in the room."

The officers exchange a glance, clearly weighing their options. After a tense moment, the one holding the clipboard nods. "Very well," he says, conceding. He flips through his notes, then looks back at me. "Can you tell us what happened? Who did this to you?"

Antonio's fingers are intertwined with mine, a silent promise that he's with me through this. I straighten my shoulders and lift my chin, finding the poise I was raised to embody. I know exactly what I need to say, and more importantly, what I can't. In our world, truth is layered, and I've learned how to navigate it carefully.

"My father had me abducted from my photography exhibit," I begin. "I don't know where they took me. The place was unfamiliar, some kind of warehouse, but my father was there. He... he beat me." I take a shaky breath. "He was trying to kill me—and my unborn child."

The officers exchange a glance, scribbling furiously on their notepads. Every word I say is measured, balancing between the truth and the pieces I must leave unsaid. I can't involve Antonio in this—not more than he already is.

One of the officers looks up, his tone professional but probing. "Do you know where your father is now?"

I pause, my heart pounding in my chest. I know exactly where my father is. He's dead. Antonio made sure of that, but that's not something I can admit to them.

Antonio squeezes my hand gently in silent support.

"No," I say, shaking my head. "He left me there to die."

The words are true, but they don't tell the whole story

The officers jot down more notes, their faces impassive. "You're certain you have no idea where he might be now?" the other officer presses.

I shake my head again, keeping my voice as steady. "No. As I said, when my husband found me, my father had already left. He's been hiding for months, I'm sure he's crawled back into whatever hole he came from." I keep my gaze fixed on them, hoping they don't see the cracks in my story.

A pause hangs in the air before the office continues, his tone more pointed. "Your husband passed away over a year ago, Ms. Moretti. Are you sure your memory is intact? It's possible the concussion could be affecting it."

The use of my maiden name makes me pause. I hadn't noticed until now, but it stirs a memory of what my father said—his final threat about erasing any trace of my marriage.

"My name is Mrs. Luciano," I correct him, my voice firm but controlled. "And my memory is just fine. My husband is right here," I say, glancing over at Antonio, feeling the steadying presence of his hand in mine.

"There's no record of a marriage between you and Mr. Luciano," one of them says cautiously, watching for my reaction.

Before I can respond, Lorenzo steps forward. "Mrs. Luciano has been through a traumatic ordeal. She needs rest," he states, his eyes steady on the officers. "If you have any further questions, please direct them to my office."

Reluctantly, they gather their notes and leave the room without further protest.

The moment they're gone, I turn to Antonio, my heart racing. "They said we aren't married," I whisper, the weight of my father's manipulation crashing down on me. "This is his doing."

Antonio's expression darkens, but his voice remains calm. "What do you mean?"

I take a shaky breath. "My father told me he had any record of our marriage destroyed. It was part of his plan to give me to that man."

Antonio looks at Lorenzo, who nods. "I'll look into it," he says before excusing himself, leaving us alone.

For a moment, there's silence between us, the tension from everything that's just been said lingering in the air.

I take a deep breath. "What happens next? With us?"

Antonio's gaze softens as he moves to sit on the edge of the bed. He reaches out to cup my cheek. "You're my wife in every way that matters. I don't care about papers or licenses. I love you."

Tears begin to fall. "I love you so much, Antonio."

His thumb wipes my cheek. "We'll get through this, *tesoro*. I swear it. You, me, and our baby. Together."

Alessia

I've been in the hospital for nearly a week—an eternity, if you ask me. With the constant poking and prodding, I've felt more like a science experiment than a patient. The bruises on my body are beginning to fade, shifting from deep purple to mottled yellow-green, though the ache in my ribs remains.

It took threatening both the doctor and Antonio that I'd walk out on my own before they finally agreed. Thankfully, I'm going home today.

Antonio sits beside me, his hand resting lightly on mine as we wait for my discharge papers. There's something weighing on me —something I can't leave unsaid.

I shift slightly, gathering the courage to speak. "Antonio," I begin softly, turning to face him. "What happened to Ophelia? You haven't mentioned her other than to tell me she was somehow involved."

He stiffens beside me, and I brace myself for the truth. "Ophelia set you up and allowed you to be taken."

My heart sinks. "That can't be true. Ophelia wouldn't do that to me."

"She said a man came to the gallery, claimed he was your

brother. He told her I was holding you against your will, that I beat you. He offered her money to get you alone so he could *rescue* you."

"I'm sure she thought she was helping," I whisper as the pieces begin to fall into place. "She didn't know the truth about my father or Valentino."

Antonio shakes his head clearly frustrated. "She didn't even bother to ask you. She just let him take you."

Tears well up in my eyes as I grasp the reality of the situation. "I should've told her everything—about Valentino, about my father, about you. Maybe if she knew the truth—"

"It doesn't matter," Antonio says firmly. "She believed a lie instead of coming to us. She played right into Draco's hands."

"Where is she? Is she okay?" I ask, my voice steady but laced with tension.

He looks away for a moment before meeting my gaze again. "She's fine, *tesoro*. She's in the basement at the restaurant."

My chest tightens at his response, and I sit up straighter, my voice firmer. "You're holding her in that room, aren't you? The torture room? I know why you did it, but my father's gone. You need to let her go."

"I can't just let her walk away. She knows too much."

I shake my head, refusing to back down. "Ophelia's not a threat, Antonio. She was unknowingly caught in the middle of this mess." I wave my hand. "You don't need to punish her."

His jaw tightens, his gaze narrowing. "This isn't about punishment. It's about making sure nothing comes back to hurt us. I refuse to take any more chances."

I take a deep breath, trying to calm myself. "I understand that, but keeping her there? Against her will? You're better than this," I say, lowering my voice. "You're not like them."

He flinches at the comparison, and I see the conflict in his eyes. I reach for his hand, squeezing it gently. "Please, Antonio. Let her go."

His hand tightens around mine, his brow furrowing as he

considers my words. There's a long pause, and I hold my breath, waiting for his response.

Finally, he exhales, the tension in his shoulders easing. "I'll let her go," he says quietly, but his voice remains firm. "But she'll leave with a warning—a courtesy I'll only extend this one time."

"I understand," I say and rest my head on his shoulder.

Antonio presses a kiss to my forehead.

There's a knock on the door a moment before it swings open. I expect to see someone with my discharge papers. Instead, the doctor steps in, followed by a nurse pushing a machine. "I'd like to do one more ultrasound before we let you go," he says.

This time, I'll be awake for it. I glance over at Antonio, and he gives my hand a reassuring squeeze, though the concern in his eyes is unmistakable. Even though everything has been fine so far, there's still a lingering fear—what if something goes wrong?

The doctor prepares the machine while the nurse spreads cold gel across my stomach. I flinch at the chill, but Antonio's hand remains warm and steady in mine, anchoring me.

The room is silent. I hold my breath as the doctor moves the transducer across my belly, searching. Antonio shifts beside me, leaning in closer, his eyes fixed on the monitor.

Then, without warning, a sound fills the room—a rapid, rhythmic thumping.

The baby's heartbeat.

It's strong and steady, and the moment I hear it, I release the breath I didn't even realize I was holding. The relief is so overwhelming that tears fill my eyes.

Awe and emotion soften Antonio's face. "Our baby," he breathes.

"Everything looks perfect. The baby's healthy and growing just as expected."

Antonio lets out a shaky breath, his eyes glistening with unshed tears. His lips brush against my forehead in a tender kiss. "You've given me everything I never knew I needed," he whispers, his voice thick with emotion. "You've made my life whole, *tesoro.*"

I nod, unable to speak through the lump in my throat. How could I respond to words like that? Before Antonio, I'd never truly known what love felt like. It's overwhelming and terrifying all at once. Inside his embrace is the safest place I've ever been. He's my protector, my partner, and now, the father of my child.

For the first time in my life, I'm not just surviving—I'm living, and I never want to let this go.

Antonio

It's been several weeks since Alessia was discharged from the hospital. Things should have settled down by now, but they haven't. I'm pacing in my office, the phone pressed against my ear. Frustration boils over and I can no longer control my anger as I shout into the phone.

"What do you mean it's gone? How the hell did Draco get to the judge?" My voice shakes with fury. "I pay you more than enough to handle this. Fix it. Now."

Lorenzo tries to calm me down, but I'm too far gone to listen. "I don't care what it takes. Draw up new papers. I want this sorted immediately."

The words are barely out of my mouth when I hear movement behind me. I turn and see Alessia standing in the doorway. Although her face is calm, her eyes tell me she's heard everything. She shakes her head, silently asking me to stop.

"I'll call you back," I mutter into the phone before hanging up. Turning to her, I ask, "What's going on? Why don't you want this fixed?"

Alessia walks over, her fingers brushing against my arm. "I don't want your attorney to fix anything with the papers. I want to marry you. For real."

Her words catch me off guard. "We're already married."

"Not a forced ceremony with a judge who's been paid off," she says, her voice soft but firm. "I want a real wedding. Just us, in front of our family, promising forever."

Our love story didn't begin yesterday—it's been years in the making. I think back to the first time I saw her, how she lit up the room. Even at our young ages, I saw my forever with her. Then, I lost her to Vigo's schemes. But somehow, through all the chaos, we found our way back to each other. A real wedding—something we choose, not forced by circumstances, is exactly what we deserve.

I pull her into my arms. "You really want to marry me?"

"Yes."

"I'll make arrangements for my mom and Cecilia to come back from Italy."

"They don't need to come back," Alessia says, her fingers tracing my hand. "We can go to them."

"You want to get married in Italy?" I ask, even though I already know the answer.

"It's what I've always dreamt of," she smiles, her eyes lighting up. "The waves crashing and the sun setting while we say our vows."

I remember how she used to talk about this back when we were younger—how she pictured having a wedding by the sea in Italy. I see that same look of wonder in her eyes now.

"I need to be sure this is what you really want."

"Antonio, I'm not marrying you because I have to. I'm marrying you because I want to." She looks up at me, her eyes shining with so much love it nearly takes my breath away. "I'll never stop choosing you. Not in this life. Not in any."

Her words stir something primal in me. Before I can respond, I pull her in for a searing kiss, pouring every ounce of my love and desire into it.

Her fingers grip my shirt, and the heat between us intensifies as our bodies press together. I pull back just enough to look into her eyes, my thumb brushing over her lips, already swollen from our kiss.

Without a word, I take her hand and guide her toward the door. The warmth of her touch ignites a fire inside me. My heart races with every step, each one more urgent than the last. The air between us thickens with unspoken desire, the tension so palpable it tugs us closer with every breath.

Before we make it much farther, Alessia slips out of my grasp, teasing me with her hands trailing down my chest. My pulse quickens, and I pull her in for another kiss, rougher this time. My hands slide under her shirt, feeling the warmth of her skin.

As I push the fabric higher, my hands cup her bare breasts. My thumbs graze over her sensitive nipples before I lean down and take one into my mouth. The way her body responds as she arches into my touch drives me wild.

Her fingers work quickly, fumbling with the buttons of my shirt, pushing it off my shoulders. The second it's gone, I pull her closer, kissing down her neck as I continue to palm her breasts. We move together, the urgency building as we strip off clothes in a trail leading to the bedroom.

We break apart for a second, barely making it another few steps before I press her back against the wall, my lips on hers again. Her hands move to my jeans, fingers brushing against me. I let out a low growl of approval as her hands tug at my belt. Her fingers quick and desperate.

By the time we stumble into the bedroom, we've left a trail of clothes behind us. At this moment, all that exists is her, me, and our intense desire, drawing us closer with every breath.

I lower her gently onto the bed, my touch reverent, worshipping her every curve. With her being pregnant, her body's more responsive, more sensitive. The way she shivers when my lips brush her skin. The way her breath catches at even the slightest touch—it's like her entire body is alive with sensation, attuned to my every move.

My hands slide over her thighs, and her legs part instinctively.

"Antonio, please," she breathes. "I need more."

"As you wish." I spread her wide as my mouth explores her, teasing her soft folds. Her arousal coats my tongue as I slowly lick, savoring every moment.

Sliding a finger inside her, I move slowly at first, letting her adjust before picking up the pace. She lifts her hips, but I hold her in place, circling her clit with my tongue until her moans fill the room. I add a second finger and pick up the pace, bringing her closer and closer to her release.

"Come for me, *tesoro,*" I whisper, hooking my finger to stroke that sensitive spot inside her.

Her release builds, her moans turning into cries as her orgasm hits, and I feel the flood of her pleasure. I slip two fingers inside her ass, pushing her even higher, making her cry out with raw intensity. Her arousal coats my face as I continue to lap and suck every last drop of her pleasure from her.

I kiss my way back up her body. When I reach her lips, I pause, resting my forehead against hers. Our breathing is ragged, hearts pounding.

"You're incredible," I whisper, my voice rough with desire.

She pulls me in for a kiss, tasting herself on me as her body arches into mine. Rolling us over, I guide her to straddle me. "Do you feel how hard I am for you?" I ask, lifting my hips up to press against her. "How badly I need to be inside you."

Slowly, tantalizingly, she rubs her wetness against my cock, making me ache to be buried inside her. My piercings graze her sensitive skin and she shudders from the sensation. Her eyes stay locked on mine as she slowly lowers herself down, taking me in. We both groan as the sensation consumes us.

Her movements are slow at first, each sensual roll of her hips driving me deeper inside her. I watch her, mesmerized by the way she moves, her breath coming in soft, uneven gasps as she picks up her pace.

"Alessia," I murmur, my voice hoarse with desire. "You feel so fucking good."

Her eyes meet mine, and in that moment, time stops, and I forget to breathe. The feel of her, the warmth, the way her body molds to mine. It's overwhelming, and I'm lost in it. Drowning in her.

Each thrust drives us closer to the edge. Her hands move to her breasts, massaging them and rolling her pert nipples between her thumb and forefinger. The way she touches herself, the pleasure etched on her face, drives me crazy.

I can't hold back anymore. My hips move faster as I take control of the rhythm, searching for the perfect angle, that spot where I know I can take her over the edge. This is more than simple desire—it's something much more profound. Every touch, every movement is a reaffirmation of everything we've been through, everything we've survived.

Her body tightens around me, trembling with the intensity of what's building between us. I reach up, capturing her lips with mine, swallowing her cries as I give in to the all-consuming need to be as close to her as possible.

"Come for me," I whisper against her lips, my voice raw, every muscle in my body tensing as I push us both closer to that edge. "Let go, *tesoro*."

Together, we come undone. A perfect storm.

Afterward, I hold her close, her head resting against my chest as our breathing slows. My hand drifts down to her stomach, where our baby is growing. A smile tugs at my lips, and I press a kiss to her hair.

"*Tesoro*," I murmur, my voice full of emotion. "I love you so much."

"I love you, too, Antonio. Always."

Alessia

We surprise Antonio's family—my family by showing up in Italy. Domenica's brother, Francisco, was the only one who knew we were coming. When we step into his home, their faces light up with joy. The hugs that follow feel like home.

Somehow we succeeded in keeping everything a secret until we could tell them in person.

Over dinner, Antonio and I share our biggest news. "We're having a baby," I announce, my voice filled with happiness. As soon as the words leave my lips, the room erupts in excitement.

Cecilia gasps, her hand flying to her mouth. "I'm going to be an aunt," she exclaims.

Nicki's eyes filled with tears. I know she must be thinking about Marco. Antonio reaches out, gently squeezing her hand. "I wish he was here, too," he says, his voice thick with emotion.

She smiles through her tears, brushing them away with the back of her hand. "He'd be so happy for you, Anton," she whispers, her voice carrying a bittersweet edge that makes my heart ache.

I watch the tender moment between Antonio and his mother. The love they share is pure and unbreakable, a bond so deep it makes me ache inside. I never had that with my own mother. There's a finality to that loss, one I'll never shake.

I blink back tears, my heart swelling with gratitude. Antonio's given me something I never thought possible—a place to belong and a family that loves me without question or pretense.

He's given me a home.

Of course, we didn't tell them everything. Some things are better left unsaid. I didn't want to burden them with the truth about my father and what he tried to do. They know he's no longer a threat. That's enough.

What matters now is the future and the life Antonio and I are building together.

THE WARM AFTERNOON AIR IN SICILY IS FILLED WITH laughter, and the scent of fresh herbs drifting in from the kitchen where Domenica and Antea are bustling around. They insisted on doing all the cooking, including baking dozens of delicious wedding cookies. I've been sneaking into the kitchen eating them all day.

Sunlight streams through the open windows, casting a soft glow over the room. Nicki's curling my hair while Cecilia applies my makeup. Their voices blend in a comforting rhythm as they chat and tease me, filling the space with love and laughter.

Surrounded by the love of family, I'm overwhelmed by a joy I've never known. My heart feels lighter than it has in years, and a giddy kind of happiness bubbles up inside me. I allow myself to fully embrace it, without fear knowing I belong here.

Nicki finishes the last curl and steps back, scanning my reflection with a satisfied smile. "We'll give you a few minutes to get dressed," she says.

I nod, watching them quietly slip out, the door clicking shut behind them.

The room falls silent, and I exhale, letting the peace of the moment wash over me. As I smooth my hand over the slight curve of my belly, a smile tugs at my lips. I pause, allowing myself to settle into this moment.

"Are you ready for this, little one?" I whisper, my fingers gently caressing my abdomen. "Your papa and I are about to be married."

A soft flutter, like the tiniest brush of wings, makes my breath catch. I close my eyes, overwhelmed by the connection I feel. "I hope you know how much you're already loved." I press my hand a little firmer, treasuring this moment. "We'll make sure you feel this kind of love every day. I promise."

I linger in the stillness before turning to the ivory dress hanging nearby. It's simple yet breathtaking in its elegance.

The bodice is fitted, with intricate lace detailing along the neckline and sleeves, while the skirt flows gracefully, leaving room for my growing belly. The back dips slightly, revealing just enough to feel timelessly romantic.

I carefully slip it on, the lace brushing against my skin as I fasten the tiny buttons along the side. The fabric drapes perfectly, floating around me with each movement. I can't help but smile as I catch my reflection in the mirror.

A soft knock on the door pulls me from my thoughts. "Come in," I call.

Nicki steps inside, her eyes sweeping over me. "What do you think?" I ask, smoothing the lace on my dress.

She takes a moment before answering, her voice warm. "You look absolutely breathtaking, Alessia. I want you to know how proud I am of you and how grateful we are to have you in our lives. You've brought a light to Antonio that was missing for so long."

Her words hit me straight in the heart, and I blink back tears.

I reach out to hug her, feeling the bond between us deepen. "Thank you. For everything."

"Oh, Alessia," Cecilia gushes as she steps back into the room. "You're absolutely glowing."

"It's perfect, isn't it?"

"Antonio's going to lose it when he sees you. We'll be lucky if he doesn't cart you away before the ceremony," Cecilia says with a giggle.

I laugh, feeling my nerves ease just a little. "I'll make sure to keep my running shoes hidden, just in case. Though I don't think I'd mind if he did." I give a playful shrug.

"I'd pay good money to see that."

I laugh again. Cecilia's right. Antonio hasn't seen me since yesterday. Domenica and Nicki insisted on us following the tradition of not seeing the bride before the ceremony. We agreed, but we've also allowed for one modern twist.

I can't wait to see him—well, almost see him.

After Cecilia puts the finishing touches on my makeup, we walk to the small room where Antonio's waiting on the other side of the door. My heart races knowing he's just feet away.

Cecilia carefully positions me to the side. "Okay, stay right here," she says. Then, she opens the door just enough for my hand to slip through.

My fingers tremble slightly as I touch the wood, knowing Antonio is right there on the other side. A moment later, I feel his hand brush against mine.

"There," Cecilia says softly, her grin fading into a tender smile as she steps back.

"Antonio," I whisper, my throat tight with emotion.

"*Tesoro*," he replies, his voice sending warmth rushing through me. "I feel like I've been waiting for this moment my entire life."

Tears prick my eyes, but I blink them away.

He's quiet for a moment, and I imagine him on the other side, just as overwhelmed as I am. When he speaks again, his voice is softer, filled with a depth that makes my chest ache.

"You've changed my life, *tesoro*. You took all my broken pieces and put them back together—you've made me whole. I can't wait to start forever with you."

My tears fall freely now. "I love you, Antonio. More than words can ever say," I whisper. "You've given me a life and love I never dreamed possible."

I grip his hand tightly, knowing that the next time I see him, it will be as I walk down the aisle to become his wife.

There's a click from Cecilia's camera as she snaps a few pictures, capturing this perfect moment. The connection we share, even through the door, is so powerful it takes my breath away.

"Okay, you two. Time's up," Cecilia announces.

I let out a shaky laugh, squeezing Antonio's hand one last time, not quite ready to sever our connection, before reluctantly letting go.

"See you soon, *tesoro*," Antonio murmurs, his voice full of promise.

"Soon," I whisper back.

Alessia

Our wedding ceremony is being held on Francisco's property, a breathtaking stretch of land perched on a cliff overlooking the sea. The crisp air of early fall wraps around me as I step outside. It's a perfect evening, with just a hint of a breeze carrying the scent of saltwater and fresh earth.

The light has softened, more intimate now as daytime gives way to evening. As the sun begins its slow descent, it paints the horizon in rich shades of orange and violet, streaked with pink and gold. The waves below shimmer like liquid gold as they crash against the rocks.

A handful of our closest family and friends are gathered, seated in rustic wooden chairs facing the sea. The intimacy of the group makes the moment feel even more special. It's peaceful, serene—the kind of beauty that feels almost surreal. The backdrop couldn't be more perfect.

I couldn't have imagined any of this—the love, the freedom I feel now. For so long, I lived in a cage, trapped by fear, my life dictated by others. But then Antonio came into my life and unlocked the door. With him, everything changed. He didn't just free me from my past—he showed me what it means to be loved without limits. To feel safe in a way I never thought possible.

As I stand here, about to marry the man who transformed my world, I realize I'm not just free—I'm whole. His love is my anchor, my compass, and my wings all at once. He's given me the life I never believed I deserved.

Today, as I prepare to walk toward him, I feel his love wrapping around me, steady and unshakable.

The soft, melodic sound of music drifts on the breeze. In the distance, the breathtaking arch comes into view. Francisco handcrafted it from driftwood, adorning it with wildflowers, olive branches, and vibrant autumn leaves. The deep oranges, reds, and creams glow in the last rays of the setting sun. It feels timeless, as if nature itself is blessing our union.

Cecilia gives me a quick, reassuring hug before walking gracefully down the aisle, a simple path lined with candles swaying gently in the breeze. Her radiant smile lights the way as she takes her place beside Antonio and Dante, who stand beneath the arch alongside Father Bill. Everything about this moment feels perfect.

And then it's my turn.

Each step is slow, deliberate, as though time itself has paused, allowing me to fully embrace this moment. My dress brushes lightly against the ground, the lace flowing with each movement.

My eyes find Antonio and everything else fades away. The way he looks at me—like I'm the only thing in the world that matters, makes my heart skip a beat. The distance between us feels both infinite and yet too short all at once.

As I get closer, the faintest smile tugs at his lips, his eyes brimming with emotion that matches mine. My breath catches, and I have to remind myself to keep walking. Every step brings me closer to the man who has shown me a love so deep it feels like it's always been a part of me.

When I finally reach him, my hand trembles as he takes it in his, his grip steady and sure. For a moment, time seems to stop. The world falls away, leaving just the two of us standing here, connected by something more profound than words. I know with absolute certainty—this is where I belong. Where I've always been meant to be.

Father Bill clears his throat, drawing everyone's attention. "We gather here this evening," he begins, "to witness and celebrate the union of Antonio and Alessia, who have chosen to walk life's path together. In this sacred place, surrounded by the beauty of nature and the love of those closest to them, they will pledge their love and support for each other, not just for today, but for all the days to follow."

The waves below create a soothing rhythm, a backdrop to Father Bill's words. "Antonio and Alessia have chosen to write their own vows," he continues, a soft smile on his lips. "These are their personal promises to one another, spoken from the heart. Antonio, would you like to begin?"

Antonio squeezes my hand gently, his eyes never leaving mine. His gaze is filled with so much love and emotion that for a moment, I forget to breathe.

"Alessia," he begins, his words tender. "I never knew love like this existed until you came into my life. You changed everything. You brought light into all my dark places, healing wounds I didn't even know I had. With every moment, you've shown me what it means to be truly seen. But I also never knew real fear until I faced the possibility of losing you. In those moments, I realized just how much of my heart belongs to you."

Tears slip down my cheeks. Antonio reaches up, gently wiping them away with his thumbs, his touch tender and full of love.

"You've taught me that true strength isn't about fighting battles. It's about opening yourself up completely and being vulnerable. You are my heart, my soul," he continues. "Today, I vow to stand by you, to protect you, and to cherish you. I will honor the family we're building, and I promise to love you with everything I am for all the days we have ahead."

I take a deep breath, trying to steady my voice as I begin my vows. "Antonio, you've shown me a love I never thought I deserved. A love I didn't even know could exist." My voice wavers, but I press on. "You've been my strength when I had none, my anchor in the storm. But more than anything, you've been my freedom. With you, I've found a life I never dared to dream of and a love that fills every part of me."

My grip on his hand tightens as the words flow from my heart. "I promise to stand by you through everything—every joy, every challenge, every moment we'll share. I love you with all that I am and without hesitation. I promise to build a life with you that's full of joy, hope, and the kind of love that grows deeper with each new day."

A tear slips down my cheek. "I will forever be grateful for you, for us, and for the family we're about to become. I vow to love you, honor you, and cherish you for all the days we have ahead."

Antonio's eyes glisten with unshed tears, and the connection between us hums with unspoken words— more powerful than anything I could ever say.

We exchange rings—simple platinum bands engraved with the words *Nel tuo amore, sono libero*. In your love, I am free.

Father Bill offers a gentle smile, his expression serene as he speaks the words that seal our union. "I now pronounce you husband and wife."

Before I can fully absorb the moment, Antonio pulls me into his arms, his lips meeting mine in a kiss that's soft yet powerful, infused with everything we've been through and all the promises of what's to come.

The cheers of our family swirl around us, distant yet comforting, but in this moment, it's just us—completely lost in the world we've built together, standing at the threshold of our future.

In his arms, with our love enveloping us, I feel a peace so deep it anchors my soul to his. I know, with unwavering certainty, that this is where I'm meant to be—today, tomorrow, and forever.

Epilogue

ANTONIO: THREE YEARS LATER

The soft sound of Marco's laughter fills the room, echoing through the quiet space like the sweetest melody. He's on his knees, his chubby little hands busy with toy cars, blissfully unaware of anything other than his play.

I watch him—this boy, my son who's so full of life and light. Marco Giovanni. His name carries a piece of the past, a legacy I vowed to honor. Yet his presence feels like a gift from a world beyond, something I don't deserve but can't bear to lose.

I lean back, letting the years and memories settle over me like a shroud. My eyes drift to Alessia, resting on the couch, her hand lovingly cradling her belly, where our second child grows in the quiet warmth. We chose not to learn the baby's gender, savoring life's last mystery. Her beauty, even now as she drifts between sleep and waking, is effortless.

Alessia's touched my heart in ways no one else ever could. She's the light that pulls me from the darkness that once consumed me. Without her, I'd still be lost, adrift in that endless night I once knew too well. She speaks of the freedom I gave her, but she doesn't understand—she's the one who unlocked the chains and opened the cage that imprisoned me.

I wasn't always a man capable of love. Darkness was my only companion for so long. My world was one of chaos, blood, and violence. Of endless nights filled with uncertainty and fear I could not escape. *"All that we see or seem is but a dream within a dream."* That was my existence. I was adrift, caught in an endless spiral of nightmares I wasn't sure I'd ever wake from—survive.

Alessia's my beacon in this world of shadows. The thought pulls at something deep inside me—a truth I've come to learn. *"Her love had given me a new sense of life, a new sense of being. The world was no longer dark and dreary."* I've learned this truth well —my life, my soul, is wrapped in shadows, in secrets. But Alessia, and now our children, are the beauty that balances it all.

As I look at Marco, so full of life, and then at Alessia I understand something with a certainty that chills and comforts me at once. *"The boundaries which divide life from death are at best shadowy and vague."* I've walked that line and seen what lies on the other side. I know death as an old companion. I've walked in its shadowy silence, but each day, I choose life.

I choose them.

Marco's laughter rises, filling the room. His toy cars rumble over my feet.

"Broom. Broom. You're a big mountain, Daddy," he squeals, and I smile at his innocence and joy.

As if she can sense the depth of my thoughts, Alessia stirs. Her eyes meet mine, so soft and full of love. Her smile—God, it still takes my breath away. *"My life, my soul, my bride."* She's the reason behind every decision I make, the guiding star that leads me through the darkest night.

"The truest and most beautiful love that ever warmed a human heart." That's how I feel when I look at her. Her love doesn't just warm my heart—it saves me, day after day, in ways I'll never fully deserve.

In a world that seeks to tear me apart, she makes me whole.

And as long as I have my *tesoro*, as long as I hear my son's laughter, the darkness will never swallow me again.

And so, I sit here, in the quiet peace of our home, watching my son play and feeling the unconditional love of my wife, I understand. I'll always feel the pull of the abyss whispering to me like a forgotten memory. I'll always carry shadows within me. That darkness is a part of who I am, a part of the world we navigate. The world we rule together. When I need, I embrace it—welcome it.

But I no longer fear it.

Together, we've forged something beautiful from the darkness that once threatened to consume us.

To love her is to love life itself.

And so it is for me.

THE END

Also by Tara Conrad

Find Tara's Books Here

About Tara

Tara Conrad is the author behind the sizzling and passionate romance stories that ignite the senses. Her novels celebrate the fiery intensity of desire. They're known for having a blend of deep emotional connections, relatable characters, and captivating plots that ensnare readers from the very first page to the last.

Tara is the mother of four incredible, kind, and talented adult children. She also has one son-in-love who will always be her favorite.

Tara is Nana to the most perfect baby boy. He owns her heart and soul.

Tara is married to her soulmate and Dominant, George. They recently celebrated their 30th anniversary and are more in love today than yesterday. George encouraged Tara to begin writing, and with each passing day, she's more thankful for his insistence that she tell her stores and for his partnership on this journey. There is no one else in the world she'd ever want by her side. He is her happily ever after.

www.ingramcontent.com/pod-product-compliance
Lightning Source LLC
Chambersburg PA
CBHW070402310726
48977CB00003B/523